CLANDESTINE

BOOKS BY ISAAC HOOKE

Thrillers

Clandestine

Military Science Fiction

ATLAS
ATLAS 2
ATLAS 3 (June 2015)

Science Fiction

The Forever Gate Compendium

CLANDESTINE

A THRILLER

Isaac Hooke

This is a work of fiction. All characters, names, organizations, places, events and incidents are the product of the author's imagination or used fictitiously.

www.IsaacHooke.com

ISBN-13: 978-0-9947427-0-4
ISBN-10: 0-9947427-0-3

Cover design by Isaac Hooke

contents

To my mother, father, brothers, and
most devoted fans.

Fight where you are needed.

prologue

The rifle cracked and Suleman felt the blood spray his face as the kneeling individual beside him toppled like a discarded sandbag. Sanguine fluid trickled down the flagstones toward the river, joining the blood of those who had fallen before.

Suleman was next in line.

The Sunni militants had captured the lot of them an hour earlier. Waving the black standard of the Islamic State, they had stormed the village and caught the Iraqi army members stationed there at unawares. The militants had proceeded to divide the survivors into two groups by sect, Sunni and Shia. The Sunni were allowed to repent.

The Shia were not.

Suleman heard the balaclava-clad executioner shift behind him.

"I'm Sunni!" he lied. "I repent!"

But it was too late to switch sides.

Allah help me.

There came a moment of absolute stillness. He looked out at the wide river before him, at the reeds, at the blue sky. So peaceful. So beautiful. He would miss it. All of it.

The report of the assault rifle thundered through the air, and Suleman experienced a sharp pain within his right ear. He let himself fall. The paving stones struck his face like a baseball bat but he gave no outward sign that he'd felt the impact. He didn't even flinch. Didn't dare.

The executioner moved on to the next victim and fired. Suleman heard a thud beside him. It was a muffled sound, as his left ear was to the ground, and his right ear seemed deaf entirely. He opened his eyelids a sliver: the lifeless eyes of his friend stared into his own.

Somehow, Suleman had survived. The rifle had missed. Or misfired. Whatever the case, Suleman was alive.

Alive.

Slowly receding in volume as the executioner moved down the line, the relentless crack of the assault rifle continued over the next half hour, with the occasional pause thrown in while the rifleman reloaded. Blood flowed down the flagstones by the truckload.

Suleman didn't move the entire time. He lay there motionless. Waiting. Hoping.

And then the rifle reports ceased.

Suleman dared not get up. Not yet. He remained in place, lying beside his dead companions, baking beneath the hot Iraqi sun, ignoring the flies that dined upon him and the bodies of the dead in macabre swarms. He focused on the pain in his right ear, clung to that agony with all his being. The throbbing reminded him he was still alive.

When darkness finally hid the massacre from watching eyes, Suleman weakly lifted his head. There was no movement around him. Hearing had returned to his right ear, though sound was still muffled through the organ, which pulsed with faint pain.

Suleman scrambled to his knees, hardly able to believe he had survived the day. Why had Allah spared him and no one else?

He turned around to observe the village in the distance and froze.

In the moonlight he saw a man seated cross-legged on the flagstones behind him. An assault rifle rested over his legs. An American-made M16A4.

"Salaam," the man said. "I am Abdullah. Your executioner."

Suleman stared at him in horror.

Abdullah's mouth peeled back in a fierce smile, teeth gleaming in the moonlight. "Is it true what you said earlier? You repent?" The man spoke Arabic with a strange accent, making him difficult to understand.

Feeling a shred of hope, Suleman moved his cracked lips to answer but no sound came. He couldn't even grunt, his throat too parched from lying in the sun all day.

"Nod your head. Yes or no."

Suleman bobbed his chin up and down.

"You are the sniper trained by the Americans?"

Confused as to how the man knew this, again Suleman nodded in assent.

A hard edge came to Abdullah's voice. "If you are lying, you understand what I will do to you, don't you?" His fingers caressed the rifle.

Suleman bobbed his head a third time.

Abdullah handed Suleman a water bottle and he drank greedily. The cool liquid burned his throat. He choked, coughing.

When Suleman had recovered, he tried to speak. "I—" It hurt to talk. He cleared his throat and took another sip. "Repent."

"Good," Abdullah said. "I knew you would. You have risen from the ashes and are reborn. From this moment forth you are no longer a Shia rejector. You no longer believe the successor to the prophet was his own son-in-law. You no longer believe the direct descendants of Muhammad were infallible manifestations of God. Do you understand?"

Suleman nodded fervently. He would agree to anything in that moment.

"Let it not be said that the Caliphate is unmerciful." Abdullah offered him a towel. "Clean yourself up, sniper."

As he took the towel, Suleman suddenly understood the reason Allah had spared him.

To serve that man.

* * *

The unexpected banging at the door startled Habib awake. He rubbed his eyes in the dark and rose from the soft bed.

So far his hegira to the land of the great Caliphate was going very well. He had traversed passport control at Atatürk airport in Istanbul with ease, and had flown to Gaziantep unimpeded. Allah was with him.

All that remained was to meet the smuggler who would take him across the border to Syria. Perhaps that was him at the door?

As Habib reached the entrance, masked gunmen burst inside his hotel room.

Everything happened so fast: before he knew what was happening they had dragged him to the main room and thrown him face down onto the table. While the others held him down, one of the gunmen proceeded to violate him.

"No!" Habib shouted, but it was too late. "No no no."

The pain was manageable, but the indignation, the humiliation...

"You like it, don't you," his torturer said in Gulf Arabic. "You're a homosexual!"

"I'm not!" Habib sobbed.

Cellphone cameras flashed.

"We know what you're planning, boy! We know!"

He glanced at the large, decorative plate at the center of the table, hardly able to see through the tears. He blinked a few times until the image came into focus. The plate was held vertically by a wooden frame. Burnished to a shine, it acted like a mirror. Habib saw the reflection of the masked man who thrust against him repeatedly from behind. An awful sight.

He was about to look away when something else caught his eye. Beyond the violator he saw another gunman dressed in black, standing apart from the others in the hallway.

"I'm not going to be a part of this," the lone man declared in English.

Everything suddenly became clear to Habib.

Americans.

The man in the hallway turned to go, but then made a mistake. Perhaps he didn't know he was standing in just the right location for Habib to see his reflection, or perhaps in his hubris he didn't think it mattered, because he pulled off his balaclava.

In that instant those exposed features were forever seared into Habib's memory. Bronzed skin. Gaunt cheeks. Disjointed nose. Tightly-cropped beard. The American could have almost passed for a Gulf Arab.

And then the man stormed from view and was gone.

The terrible violation ended and Habib was thrown into a corner of the room, where he huddled on the floor. Blood trickled down his bare leg.

"Sodomites go to hell, Habib," one of the masked infidels said in Arabic. "What do you think of that?"

Habib could only weep. He was vaguely aware of a strange noise in the background. It sounded like... a printer of some kind?

In a few moments the infidel threw photos on the floor in front of him. "We're going to send these to your family, post them online to the most popular jihad forums, and put them on your Facebook page for all to see. Everyone is going to know you're a sodomite. *Everyone*. You know what the crime for homosexuality is where you're going? Or where you're *from*? You're screwed, boy. In more ways than one."

Habib buried his face in his hands. Allah had abandoned him.

"Of course, none of that has to happen," his masked torturer continued. "If you agree to do certain things for us once you reach Syria."

As Habib listened to what the infidel expected of him, he felt a growing sense of repulsion. He wanted to die. How could Habib betray his beliefs? His brothers? There was no point in living, not if he had to do these things. But like the man had said, Habib would only go to hell when he died.

He decided to do what the torturer asked, if only to defer those eternal fires a while longer. Perhaps someday Allah would grant him vengeance. And maybe, just maybe, Habib might even find a way to reopen the path to paradise.

He thought of the face he had seen in the mirror and smiled. When the Americans least expected it, he would strike.

one

Ethan fingered the Kalashnikov slung over his shoulder. The rifle was a PK-10, an AK-47/AKM clone manufactured by the cottage gunsmiths of the region. Not as good as a factory-produced rifle but it served its purpose.

Roughly two of every ten male passersby carried a gun. PK-10s. Chinese machine guns. Austrian Glock pistols. There was one weapon, however, that almost every man wore without fail, and that was a *jambiyah:* a large, curved ceremonial dagger tucked into the belt in front of the navel. The hilt was a sign of status. The more expensive hilts were made of ibex or rhino ivory, and depending on craftsmanship, could cost upwards of ten thousand US dollars. Most of the hilts Ethan saw today were of cheap plastic or cow horn.

The men sported white shirts and wraparound sarongs, with black Western-style blazers on top to complete the look. They wore shawls around their heads or shoulders, wrapped and colored in a manner that varied by tribe. Mustaches were prevalent, though the more devout wore beards styled in the mustachless Abe Lincoln fashion.

Men who traveled together frequently held hands in friendship. Almost everyone had golf-ball sized lumps of *qat* in their cheeks—it was past 3 PM, the end of the workday for many Yemenis, and time to start chewing the amphetamine-rich leaf.

The women wore full veils, with a small slit for the eyes. That, combined with the long black robes draping them from head to foot made them seem like shadowy, roaming ghosts. Some of the older women draped colorful sheets around their existing clothing so that they appeared as strange parodies of the ringwraiths from Lord of the Rings.

Ethan sported a light-green *thawb*—an ankle-length robe favored by the devout—and wrapped his shawl in the southern fashion. He fit right in with his tanned olive skin and Abe Lincoln beard: for all intents and purposes he was simply another villager who had moved to Sana'a to make a living. He drew the line at qat, however. Ethan had dipped tobacco back in the day, but that was a far more benign habit in his view, considering the dependency effects induced by cathinone, the amphetamine-like compound in qat. Ethan had quit dip cold turkey, and he wasn't about to get himself addicted to something nastier. He padded the inside of his cheek with a substitute made from paper instead.

Even though the city of Sana'a was cloistered in a mountainous valley at an altitude of twenty-two hundred meters, the temperature proved a dry, scorching hundred degrees. Ethan kept to the shade, using the dilapidated stone wall of the Old City as a sunshade. Hawkers who sold wares beneath canopied booths accosted him in harsh, guttural Arabic.

A grubby beggar sat against the wall near a pile of trash and held out a beseeching palm. Ethan placed a crisp pink and green banknote in the man's hand. It was a one thousand rials bill, worth five bucks.

While the beggar thanked him profusely, Ethan pivoted slightly to look back the way he had come. Satisfied that no one was following, he moved on.

He traveled beneath the thousand year old Yemen Gate. Only one vehicle at a time could fit the close-quartered streets, though most of the traffic was pedestrian. The blocky buildings rose as high as nine stories, with outer facades decorated in geometric patterns via strategically placed fired bricks; white gypsum outlined the arched doorways and windows. The upper windows had decorative wooden shutters that allowed unveiled women to look down upon the street without passers-by seeing them. Minarets poked up beyond the rooftops, overlapping the yellow-brown mountains that provided backdrop.

Political graffiti was scribbled in Arabic on a few buildings, with such cheerful slogans as "America is the mother of all terrorists" and "Death to Israel," alongside sketches of the Statue of Liberty with a fleet of—presumably hijacked—jumbo jetliners pointed at it.

Ah Sana'a. A place where old and new abutted. Where one could find a bazaar with canopied booths and stalls standing incongruously beside a modern supermarket. Or pass street vendors selling goat kabobs a few doors down from the KFC.

On cue, the call to afternoon prayer filled the air.

"Allahhhhhahhhhhhhahhhhhhhhhoo akbar." The haunting voice of a muezzin drifted through the streets. "Allahu akbar."

There were more than a hundred mosques in the Old City, and they all announced at the same time, using loudspeakers in their minarets to compete for attention, giving the call a strange echo.

The dome of a white mosque, two streets away, poked above the sand-colored buildings. His destination. It was one of the more radical mosques in Sana'a, and its Friday sermons were legendary for their anti-Western rhetoric. Thankfully it wasn't Friday: he wasn't in the mood.

Ethan reached the mosque. Several shoes formed a neat row outside the entrance, with the occasional rifle leaning against the marble wall beside the owner's footwear.

Ethan removed his sandals and set his PK-10 against the wall. There was a tall vase near the entrance, where visitors spat their discarded qat. Ethan scooped the bolus of paper from his mouth with a curved finger and tossed it into the chewed detritus.

He entered, taking his place among the rows of men in the carpeted prayer hall. Women prayed in a separate balcony—they were mildly encouraged to stay home.

When prayers were done, Ethan retrieved his shoes and rifle, and then loitered outside as groups of men gathered for quick chats. He recognized some of the regulars.

A black Land Cruiser abruptly pulled up and three masked gunmen rushed out. They closed on Ethan.

"The rifle!" one of them shouted. "Give it to me!"

Ethan complied.

The others rudely shoved him into the SUV. Someone slid a black hood over his head.

He was jerked back in his seat as the vehicle sped away, tires squealing.

two

The unseen man beside Ethan patted him down and discovered the Android smartphone. The window opened and closed. Ethan guessed the man had tossed out the device.

A short while later the vehicle slowed and Ethan felt the barrel of a nine-millimeter press into his ribcage.

"Say nothing," the gunman said.

The hood was lifted and Ethan blinked several times whiles his eyes adjusted. The kidnappers had removed their balaclavas and hidden their weapons. They were tribal men. Tanned, weathered features. Abe Lincoln beards. Mid-twenties.

The Land Cruiser was queued behind several other vehicles at a military checkpoint. The SUV reached the front. Two Yemeni soldiers stood on either side of the Cruiser, while a third kept watch from beside an old-style Soviet BTR-50 armored personnel carrier that blocked the other lane.

"Visiting relatives," the driver told the guard.

M60 machine gun looped over one shoulder, the soldier glanced in the backseat at Ethan and the others, then waved the vehicle forward. When the Land Cruiser was on its way, the kidnappers replaced Ethan's hood.

Half an hour and two checkpoints later the SUV came to a final stop and Ethan was forcibly hauled from the vehicle. As the men escorted him up unseen steps, Ethan couldn't get the image of the recent journalist beheadings from his mind, and he wondered if a similar fate awaited him. He tripped, but the kidnappers caught him and led him onward.

The stairs leveled out and his footsteps soon became muffled—he had passed indoors. The hood was removed.

He stood in a large foyer, relatively austere for its size. Shelves lined the walls, overflowing with Islamic texts. There was a white, immaculate leather sofa near the door.

The kidnappers brought Ethan to a spartan reception room. At the center, twelve young militants, most seeming no older than twenty-five, were gathered on the wooden floor around two individuals in their forties: one of the men was rather portly, while the other was gaunt, his face all bony angles. Seated cross-legged, both of them dressed nearly identically in long white thawbs and headgear, with devout beards. The hilt of the heavier man's jambiyah was crafted from ibex horn, while the lean one had a dagger with an intricate grip of black rhino ivory. Ethan recognized the latter man as Sheik Jasir Al-Khayr, though the big one was unknown to him—likely the owner of the house.

In front of the sheik was a large bowl filled with chicken and saffron rice; a wide plastic sheet protected the floor underneath.

Al-Khayr raised a hand, beckoning him forward.

Ethan complied, passing several AK-47s and PK-10s placed in an orderly line against the wall. He did his best to portray a confidence he didn't feel. Most of the young men regarded him with suspicion, a few, outright contempt.

"*As salaamu alaykum.*" The sheik spoke the traditional welcome in the dialect of the Hadhrami, an eastern tribe. Despite his slight build, his eyes were crafty, intense.

"*Wa alaykuma salaam,*" Ethan answered. The uvular fricative in the word "alaykuma" came easily to him these days, though when he was first learning to speak the glottal sounds he often pretended to gargle water in the back of his throat.

Al-Khayr gestured toward the rice bowl. "Partake, please. We eat early today."

The young militants made room for Ethan. He joined them, grabbing a plate and shoveling rice and chicken into the dish with a cupped palm. Then he sat down and began to eat.

There was a certain way to consume rice with the fingers in polite company. The right hand was used. Since the rice was cooked to a sticky consistency, one could readily grab clumps of it with the fingers. After doing so, one simply raised the hand and used the thumb to slide the grains into the mouth.

"That is an interesting dagger," the sheik said, nodding at the weapon attached to Ethan's belt. "Where did you get it?"

"My father gave it to me," Ethan said between bites.

"May I see it?"

The man was trying to get a feel for him, Ethan knew. Giving the dagger to Al-Khayr would be a tremendous show of trust, as most men never let anyone save immediate family members handle their jambiyah.

Ethan thoroughly wiped his fingers on the provided paper towel and unsheathed the blade, handing it over.

The sheik held the weapon up to the light and reverently studied the pure white ivory handle, which was hewn into the shape of a kneeling man at prayer. The blade scintillated in the light, obviously of high quality, too.

"I will give you four million rials for it." That was roughly equivalent to twenty thousand US dollars.

Ethan smiled inwardly. So Sam had been correct about his zeal for the daggers. Too bad the plan had changed.

"It is not for sale."

Al-Khayr regarded Ethan uncertainly. "Everything is for sale." Obviously he was a man who was used to getting what he wanted.

"Not everything," Ethan said.

The tension in the room increased a notch.

Abruptly Al-Khayr broke into a smile.

"You are right," the sheik agreed. "Some things cannot be bought.

Loyalty, for example."

Al-Khayr handed back the dagger and the tension dissipated. That he had returned the blade showed he trusted Ethan to a degree, especially since he must have realized the weapon was slightly more than ceremonial, with a blade like that.

When they finished eating, the group members lounged Yemeni-style on their sides, elbows propped on cushions. They took care not to point the soles of their feet at anyone else.

The sheik placed some *bukhoor*—incense made from woodchips soaked in scented oil—inside a vase-shaped burner. As the hot stone heated the woodchips, the fumes filled the air with the sweet, smoky smell of frankincense.

"What do you think of what we do here?" Al-Khayr said into the silence.

Every eye in the room turned toward Ethan.

"Death to the Americans," he said.

"Death to the Americans," the sheik agreed. He paused, then added: "Usama here tells me you have a way to defeat their drones." He nodded toward the young man Ethan had met at the mosque the Friday before.

"I know a way, yes," Ethan said warily. He had expected more pleasantries.

"Please tell us how you came by this knowledge."

Ethan had rehearsed his story several times. If he made a mistake, and the sheik didn't believe him, he was dead. "I studied electronics in Britain. I built quadcopters and fixed-wings as a hobbyist, and also during an internship at a commercial drone company in London. I know precisely how they work."

"Commercial drones are far different than military drones," the sheik said.

"Not so different. The concepts are the same."

Al-Khayr switched to English. "You say you studied in Britain? Which school?" His accent was distinctly British.

"Sheffield." Ethan answered in English, himself laying on the British accent thickly.

"Ah. I know of this university. It is famous. Though this begs the question: How could the family of a Taiz tribesman afford the fee?"

"There was an academic scholarship: The Science International. I applied. I won. Barmy, isn't it?" Ethan purposely used the British slang for crazy.

The sheik stroked his beard. "Interesting." He switched back to Arabic. "I would love to dissect your entire academic background someday, but for now, tell me, how do we defeat the drones? The short, layman version, please."

Ethan glanced at those young faces. Some were still suspicious, but most seemed eager. Of course they would be. American drones were the biggest threat to their existence.

"It's all about GPS," Ethan said. "When you jam the communications frequency of the drone by introducing signal noise, you cut it off from its remote operations center, activating its 'return to home' feature, which relies on GPS satellites to automatically fly the drone back to its home point. Military drones use an encrypted GPS receiver, so you have to jam that too, forcing it to use the unencrypted civilian signals. Now here's where things gets interesting. GPS is spoofable. The signals from the satellites are weak, and can easily be outpunched by transmissions from a television tower, or even a laptop, MP3 player or phone with the right equipment. So when the drone switches over to the unencrypted band, you outpunch the satellites, perfectly replicating and aligning their signals, then you send false data: report the drone's true position to start with, and gradually walk it to the location you desire."

"You can make these jammers and GPS spoofers for us?" Al-Khayr said.

Ethan nodded. "With the proper equipment, yes."

The sheik pursed his lips. He glanced at the owner of the house, who shrugged noncommittally.

"Welcome to Al Qaeda in the Arabian Peninsula," Al-Khayr said.

Smiling widely, he clambered to his feet and embraced Ethan.

It seemed too easy. Though outwardly the man appeared pleased, Ethan had a feeling the sheik didn't entirely buy his story.

What Al-Khayr said after sitting down only confirmed Ethan's suspicion.

"We are planning a martyrdom operation tomorrow in Tahrir Square, during the Houthi rally. I would like you to be involved."

Ethan didn't know what to say. He had come to the man offering a way to defeat the US drones, and now he wanted Ethan to be a suicide bomber?

Sensing his shock, the sheik grinned derisively. "You will drive the martyr to the square and remotely detonate his vest. You will escape unharmed. Think of it as a rite of passage."

Ethan shifted uneasily.

"You oppose this attack?" Al-Khayr said. The others were passing around a bowl of qat, and it reached the sheik in that moment. He grabbed a small branch, breaking off several leaves and stuffing them into his mouth, and then handed the bowl to Ethan.

"Not at all." Ethan stared at the leaves uncertainly, well aware that everyone was watching him. A true Yemeni would never refuse qat.

Not Qat. Anything but Qat.

Hell with it. He separated a couple of leaves and shoved them between his lips.

"The attack is good," Ethan said. It was difficult not to grimace as the leafy, tannin flavor permeated his tongue. "Many Houthi will die." Al Qaeda in the Arabian Peninsula particularly hated the Houthi, who were Shia.

"If you are not comfortable with martyrdom operations, and the death of civilians, you should not have come."

"I'm comfortable," Ethan said, but he was distracted, and not because of the qat or any qualms he might have had about the attack.

The red dot of a laser sight had appeared on the sheik's reclining chest.

three

Sheik!" Ethan hurled himself forward, pummeling the man. He used his momentum to drag Al-Khayr to the floor.

A glass window shattered behind Ethan, and one of the young men who had been seated beside the sheik collapsed. Blood oozed from a quarter-sized hole in the youth's temple. The back of his head had exploded, and loose brain matter splattered the floor in clumps.

Ethan spat out the bolus of qat. "We have to get out of here!" He told the sheik.

Al-Khayr was apparently no stranger to violence—he quickly recovered his wits and rose easily in Ethan's arms.

Usama hurried forward to screen the sheik from the shattered window, while another youth did the same for the homeowner beside them. The remainder of the group mobilized, grabbing the weapons leaning against the wall and racing toward the front of the house, where the intermittent, firecracker-like sound of gunfire echoed from outside.

Ethan scooped up an AK-47, as did Usama and the sheik. The three of them started toward the back hall, but Al-Khayr paused when he realized the homeowner wasn't coming.

"Muhammad, what are you doing?" the sheik said.

The plump man shook his head. "I will not be forced from my home. Nor will I allow an esteemed guest to be taken captive or killed. It is an insult beyond comprehension. Go. May Allah protect you."

Al-Khayr nodded sadly. "May Allah protect you as well my friend."

Usama led the way toward the back hall, followed by the sheik, while Ethan brought up the rear.

The trio reached a kitchen. There was a door on the far side that apparently led outside. Wide windows flanked the walls.

Usama advanced at a crouch. Ethan and the sheik followed, warily making their way across the room.

The far door slammed open. Two men wearing helmets and combat fatigues burst inside. They carried ballistic shields; from the notch in the upper left of each shield protruded the barrel of a Heckler and Koch G36C assault rifle. They looked like Yemeni soldiers with their tanned faces and scraggy beards.

"Drop your weapons!" one of the men shouted, speaking Arabic with a Houthi accent.

Usama and the sheik opened fire with their AKs.

Knowing what was coming next, Ethan wrapped an arm around the sheik's chest and, wary of the spray from the man's AK, yanked him down behind the kitchen counter.

"What are you doing?" Al-Khayr said.

"Saving your life!"

The loud report from a Heckler and Koch filled the air.

Usama dropped, the back of his head cored in much the same manner as the earlier man.

"We have to surrender!" Ethan said.

The sheik ignored him and leaned past the counter, letting off a rifle burst.

Idiot, Ethan thought.

He spun his own rifle around so that he could use the butt as a weapon.

"Sheik, behind you!" Ethan said. Before Al-Khayr could react, Ethan rammed the stock of the AK into the back of his head, knocking the sheik to the floor.

"We surrender!" Ethan shouted. "We surrender!"

"Drop your weapons and kick them where we can see them!" one of the soldiers answered.

Ethan lowered his Kalashnikov to the floor and kicked it past the counter. He did the same with the sheik's. Al-Khayr was already starting to stir.

The two figures rounded the corner. One watched Ethan and the sheik, while the other covered the rear. Another pair of soldiers came forward shortly, wielding G36Cs without the shields.

The nearest man pointed the barrel of his HK at Ethan's face. "On the ground. Now! Hands behind your back!"

Ethan did as he was told.

The man flexicuffed him and rudely hoisted Ethan to his feet. Beside him, the other soldier cuffed the dazed sheik.

Ethan was loaded into one of two black Toyota Fortuners that had pulled up behind the house. Al-Khayr was placed in the second SUV.

Ethan sat against his bound hands, the flexicuffs digging into his wrists. Someone lowered a black hood over his head.

Not again.

He heard sporadic gunfire, and the fierce clatter as bullets raked the chassis. The vehicle rocked to and fro. The engine whirred as the Fortuner abruptly accelerated, and he heard what sounded like a gate breaking open.

Ethan knew there would be no pursuit. Any other vehicles parked at the house would have had their tires shot out. These were professionals.

About a minute later momentum Ethan yanked to the left as the vehicle navigated a tight bend; then he was dragged forward as the Fortuner came to an abrupt halt. From the sounds and movements around him, Ethan had the impression the men were removing their helmets and shoving them under the seats. He felt silk momentarily brush his face, and he thought the men were throwing robes over their clothing.

"I think we're good," someone said from the front seat. English. American accent. "Will?"

The hood slid from Ethan's face. He blinked a few times, letting his eyes accommodate to the light. He recognized the war-torn Al Hasaba district outside, which still bore signs of the clashes between the presidential guard and the opposition tribal forces from the Battle of Sana'a three years ago. Several of the residences lay in ruins, with the former occupants forced to live inside makeshift lean-tos.

Rough fingers pulled his arms to the side and the cuffs binding Ethan's hands fell away. He brought his wrists forward, flexing the fingers to restore circulation.

He glanced at the man who had cut his binds. Above that thick Abe Lincoln beard and tilted Roman nose, ironic eyes gazed from an olive face. He could have easily passed for a devout Yemeni, especially with the white thawb he wore then.

The man was, in fact, American. A former SEAL named William Hest. A military contractor, he currently worked for JSOC, Task Force 78, one of the top hunter-killer teams in the region.

"Damn it," William said with a thick Texan drawl, examining one of his fingers. "Think I broke a nail back there." The actual words came out "Thank I brack a nya-al."

Ethan forced a smile. "Funny." His own accent was more West Coast. He unsheathed the ceremonial dagger and dropped it in William's lap.

"Hey, I don't want that," William said. He tossed the tracking device into the cup holder.

"What took you guys so long back there anyway?" Ethan asked.

"The drone operator was having technical difficulties," William said.

Doug, another member of Task Force 78 and also the spitting image of your typical Gulf Arab, was the driver. He glanced in the rearview mirror. "I should have brought along my custom QAV 400. Sometimes I wonder about the stuff the DIA gives us."

"Glad to know I was in good hands," Ethan said sarcastically.

"The best." Doug grinned. "Oh, and here's your money." He reached back, offering the one thousand rials bill Ethan had given him on the way to the mosque.

"Keep it."

"What did you think of my performance?" Doug said. "Wasn't I the best beggar you've ever seen?"

"Definitely. Must feel good, knowing you have a job lined up for yourself when you're finished here."

William patted Ethan on the shoulder. "Thank you for flying JSOC airlines. We hope you enjoyed your stay in beautiful, friendly Sana'a. Come fly with us again real soon now."

four

Ethan reclined on a couch inside a house on the outskirts of the Old City. He was in a small guest room, seated before a coffee table. His handler, Sam, sat across from him. She wore a black abaya robe, and the full veil of her hijab was currently lifted so that her face was exposed. On the table in front of her lay the long black gloves that completed her outfit.

She was a senior non-official cover case officer, or NOC, in the Defense Clandestine Service, clandestine arm of the Defense Intelligence Agency, or DIA. She'd originally been part of the Strategic Support Branch before it was absorbed into the DCS. Like the CIA, her agency had case officers, linguists, analysts, and so forth, but it was hampered by far fewer congressional reporting requirements. Sam had hinted that she answered directly to the Secretary of Defense and the President.

Ethan's job description wasn't as clean cut. Officially, he didn't exist. Unofficially, he worked directly for Sam as an independent contractor. His work usually involved multiple roles, and blurred the lines between case officer, private investigator, kidnapper and assassin. The latter seemed to be the work he was involved with the most these days, though he was never actually allowed to use the word assassination in official reports—the DIA preferred the term "High Value Targeting."

"Sheik Al-Khayr cracked yesterday," Sam said.

The sheik would be at The Weave, an old textile factory just north of Sana'a. A DIA black site, it was used for discreet detentions and interrogations. To avoid any irksome congressional inquiries, the interrogators would likely be from the Political Security Organization, Yemen's foreign intelligence service.

"Anything you can share?" Ethan said, only mildly curious. She wouldn't reveal anything that might affect operational security.

He heard the subtle vibration of a cellphone; Sam reached into an inner pocket of her abaya and retrieved an Android model phone. She read a message and began texting a response.

"Well, first off," she said while typing on the touchscreen. "We prevented the martyrdom operation in Tahrir Square during the Houthi rally. Secondly, the sheik spilled the PIN for his cellphone, and from it we've recovered the numbers and email addresses of Al Qaeda members throughout the region. Arms dealers, oil smugglers, kidnappers, you name it. Even better, the sheik gave us the 'onion' addresses of two private dark web forums run by the militants, along with his username and password. The man is an intelligence gold mine. It's a good thing we moved when we did. He was literally the catch of the year. He could be the key to unraveling Al Qaeda in the region. You should get a medal for your involvement. But, you know how it is."

"Yes," Ethan said. "Cue the unsung heroes theme."

Sam had to move fast on the remaining targets, Ethan knew. That was another reason she had hired her own team. As news of the sheik's capture spread, emails and phone numbers would change, and the dark forums would die.

Even so, Ethan doubted he would be involved in the next leg of operations in Yemen. "So what's next for me?"

She finished texting, locked her phone, and looked up. "You."

"Me. My cover is blown."

She nodded slowly. Sam had been forced to launch the operation early. The sheik was only in town for those two days and any delay risked losing him. The original plan had been to sell or give Al-Khayr the bugged dagger and then capture him at a later date, but Sam had moved up the time frame when she caught wind of the suicide attack in Tahrir Square; also influencing her decision in the matter was the fact that the sheik was notorious for detecting and evading bugs.

Although the DIA team had made an effort to downplay Ethan's involvement—making it look like he had saved the sheik's life, for example—it was inevitable the blame would fall upon him. His visit coincided with the kidnapping, after all; it would be fairly obvious to surviving Al Qaeda members that Ethan had played a part.

"I'm reassigning you," Sam said simply. Her ambiguous response told him she didn't entirely believe his cover was blown, but she wanted him to stay under Al Qaeda's radar for a while anyway.

"Reassigning me."

She laughed. "Don't be so dour. You make it sound like I'm relegating you to a desk."

Ethan felt a sudden dread in the pit of his stomach. "Are you?"

"Hardly. An operative as valuable as yourself would be utterly wasted at a desk. Besides, if I did that, I think I'd be seeing your resignation. If I don't put you to use in one war or another, someone else will."

Ethan shrugged. He couldn't disagree there.

"Instead," Sam continued. "I'm reassigning you to one of the most target-rich environments in the Middle East. A place where we currently have a serious dearth of assets and intel. I've already got the legends made up."

She tossed a passport and birth certificate onto the coffee table.

"Are you going to tell me where this mystical target-rich land resides?" Ethan said, leaning forward to grab the legends. "Or are you going to leave me in suspense?"

She smiled obligingly. "I believe it's time you made your hegira to the great Caliphate in Syria."

"The great Caliphate." Ethan wasn't all that shocked. "Islamic State?" Ethan opened up the passport. His new identity was apparently that of a Saudi Arabian national.

"The very same. Ever heard of the 'Selous Scouts?' A spec-ops regiment of the Rhodesia Army. They operated from 1973 to 1980."

"Rhodesia."

"It was a British colony, or at least a successor state, until the reconstitution of the country as Zimbabwe in 1980."

Ethan raised an eyebrow. "Selous Scouts..."

"Yes. Their mission was to infiltrate the terrorist cells of the guerrilla factions in the country. These guerrillas sought to end the white majority rule in Rhodesia through insurgency and terrorism, but the Selous Scouts applied asymmetric warfare tactics to destroy them from the inside out. Essentially, British soldiers learned to act and talk like terrorists, then infiltrated the cells, gathered intelligence from behind enemy lines, and acted upon it directly. They obeyed the five D's: detect, deceive, disrupt, delay, destroy.

"I want you to be one of my Selous Scouts. Go undercover as a foreign jihadi. Recruit local assets. Use insurgent tactics to attack Islamic State targets from within, and lay the blame at the feet of rival militant groups such as Al Qaeda." She paused. "If you think about it, everything you've done up until this moment has been part of your training, preparing you for this mission."

"An operation of this scale, this complexity..." Ethan scratched his beard doubtfully. "I could be out there for years."

"Foreign jihadists can leave whenever they want. It's an unwritten rule. The usual tenure seems to be about six months to a year."

"Basically until they're injured or die. Am I right?"

Sam pressed her lips together. "Look, if you don't want to do this, I'll understand."

Ethan smiled grimly. He noticed she hadn't brought up compensation. Smart. Because it wasn't about the money. Doing something that no one else could do—going undercover, infiltrating enemy camps, and wreaking havoc in the name of freedom and justice—well, that was what Ethan lived for. The potential long term of the operation was what bothered him, but he smothered that concern. The thought of having to work behind a desk...

"No, I'll do it. I'm your man. Like you said, this is what I've trained for my entire life. I'm a weapon. Use me."

Sam folded her arms, seeming suddenly defensive. "I've also purchased William's contract. He's no longer a member of Task Force 78, and is now under my direct command. I'm sending him with you. You'll meet another operative in Turkey who'll join the two of you and arrange for transport into Syria. He'll brief you on the details."

Ethan frowned. He understood why she had become defensive. "William and I are good friends, and we go way back, but I'm more of a lone wolf, you know that. And who's this third operative? Do I know him?"

"You do. Aaron Berkley."

Aaron was a former Army Ranger he'd fought with in Iraq. One of the few people who could do what Ethan and William did. Last time Ethan had seen him, Aaron had been working on some operation for Sam in the southern highlands of Yemen.

"Sam, look—-" Ethan began.

"The three of you will be working independently," Sam interrupted quickly. "You still get to be lone wolfs, but you'll support each other as necessary. Trust me, when you're surrounded by brainwashed fanatics whose sole purpose in life is death by glorious jihad, it's good to have normal people to ground you."

"Are you speaking from experience?" He knew she had done deep cover work of her own, but he wasn't familiar with the extent of it. He'd heard her speak two dialects of Arabic to contacts over the phone, but that was about it.

Sam didn't blink. "You know I am."

Against his better judgment, Ethan capitulated. "All right. Fine. They can come."

"Good. You're our test group. If this operation is successful, we're going to expand, repurposing more units into Selous teams to infiltrate terrorists cells throughout the region."

"Where are you going to find the people?" Ethan said doubtfully. "You know what I do is a very specialized job."

"Oh I know," she said. "But we'll find them."

Ethan frowned.

"The goal is to eventually spread like a virus," Sam continued. "Ravaging the enemy from the inside."

"Until they develop antibodies," Ethan said. "And stop accepting recruits so readily."

"The openness of most terrorist groups to foreign fighters is their downfall. If our actions cause the Islamic State and other groups to stop accepting recruits, or require all newcomers to go through some complicated vetting process, then we slowly choke them of badly needed combatants. We win either way."

Ethan set the passport down on the coffee table. "So I was thinking of spending a week in the Mediterranean."

Sam smiled sadly. "No rest for the weary. Your flight leaves tomorrow. Better start brushing up on the Saudi accent you'll need for your new identity. Your mujahadeen brothers await."

five

Ethan stood in line at the passport control of Atatürk airport, Istanbul. He was in the "other nationalities" queue, a line that was a good hundred people long. There were eight service desks at the front of the queue, but only one of them was manned. The bored-looking official thumbed through the passports at what seemed a glacial pace.

Ethan glanced over his shoulder and spotted William a few spots behind. He made eye contact with the other operative, but neither of them offered any further signs of recognition.

Ethan took in the cornucopia of cultures around him. The Iranians in their dark blazers and white dress shirts with the collars open to the chests. The Omanis in their violet thawbs and cap-like *mussah* head-dresses whose designs could have belonged on elaborate curtains. The southern Gulf Arabs with the pure white *keffiyeh* shawls held in place by tasseled black agal loops. And of course the Western-dressed Turks.

Ethan was looking forward to infiltrating the Islamic State. He was given a tabula rasa: it was up to him to create his own leads and missions. Actually getting there, however, was the first big hurdle. As there were no international flights to Syria due to the fighting and sanctions, Ethan and William had to fly to Istanbul first, then board a domestic flight to Gaziantep near the Turkish border. From there they would make their way to Syria, following the conventional foreign jihadi route.

As he neared the front of the queue Ethan retrieved his passport. He thumbed to the photo page and glanced at his details. His name was "Emad Al Zahrani," a Saudi Arabian national born in Riyadh.

His turn came. Ethan stepped forward and presented his passport and the printout of the e-visa he'd purchased online to the man at the desk. The official took both items and said in bored, broken Arabic. "How long are you stay in Turkey?"

"I am staying for seven days," Ethan answered in formal Arabic, using an accent appropriate to a speaker of the Urban Najdi dialect of Saudi Arabia. During the flight, he'd practiced the nuances of the language via the Arabic MP3s he'd downloaded into his phone. He had mastered the tongue in a previous op and only needed a quick refresher; it helped that he'd spent most of his time in Riyadh's King Khalid airport lounge chatting with the locals.

"Where are you stay?" The mustached man flipped through the passport.

"The Princess Hotel, Gaziantep." Ethan offered a printout of his hotel reservation.

The official looked up and his eyes narrowed slightly. He didn't accept the printout. "Gaziantep? Near Syrian border?"

"Yes. Here is my reservation."

The official ignored the paper and waved over a nearby airport officer. He spoke to the man in hushed Turkish. Ethan caught the word "Gaziantep."

The airport officer seized the passport and told Ethan, "Come."

Exactly what he was hoping to avoid. Secondary screening.

Ethan was strip-searched in a windowless, steel room that was much like a prison cell—it even had a toilet and sink. The experience was unpleasant, but at least the obese officer didn't take his fingerprints. Some countries, like Singapore, did that automatically when someone was transferred to secondary. It was only a matter of time before other countries started adopting similar biometric security measures. That would make traveling under aliases very difficult in the future. Airport entry would have to be avoided entirely. Ah, the ever-changing world of espionage.

After the search he was led to a small questioning room. Ethan sat on one side of a steel desk, an airport official the other. The man possessed a handlebar mustache that made him look strikingly similar to Saddam Hussein. A laptop and landline phone rested on the desk in front of him, beside Ethan's travel documents and hotel reservation. Ethan's backpack lay on another table nearby, its contents rudely strewn across the surface.

Another official, this one clean-shaven, leaned against the back wall, overseeing. Both of them wore white dress shirts with dark ties.

"What is your reason for traveling to Turkey?" the seated official began in accented Arabic.

"I am here for my cousin's wedding."

"What is your cousin's name and where does he live?"

"Aadil Al Zahrani. He lives in the city of Gaziantep."

The official made Ethan supply an exact address.

"Where is this wedding to take place?" the man asked.

"Boyaci Mosque, Gaziantep."

"Are you going to meet anyone else other than this cousin?"

"No."

"Is anyone picking you up at the airport?"

"No. I'm taking a taxi."

"Where was your passport issued?"

"Saudi Arabia, of course."

"When was your last visit to Turkey?" The official flipped through the blank pages of the passport.

"This is my first time," Ethan said.

"What kind of work do you do?"

"Consulting. Information Technology."

"Are you an employee, or do you own this business?"

"It is my business."

"Give me the website."

"I don't have one."

The official frowned. "You work in Information Technology and do not have a website?"

Ethan shrugged. "Most of my business is word of mouth."

"Where is the wedding taking place?" The official repeated the earlier question, trying to catch Ethan off guard.

Ethan held back a smile. "Boyaci Mosque," he said.

The man asked many of the previous questions again, and Ethan gave the same answers.

"Are you going to Syria?" the official finally asked.

"No."

"Are you a terrorist? Are you affiliated with Al Qaeda or Islamic State? The PKK?"

"No to all."

He glanced at Ethan's meager rucksack on the table. "Do you always pack this light?"

Ethan shrugged. "Is it illegal to bring a small bag?"

"You pack like you don't expect to return."

Ethan glanced at the printouts in front of the man, which included his flight information. "I have a return ticket."

A flicker of a smile formed on the official's lips. "A return ticket." He shoved the landline phone toward Ethan. "Call your cousin."

Ethan entered the number he had memorized.

The official pressed the speakerphone button and Ethan set down the handset.

"Allo?" came the voice over the line.

"Salaam, Aadil, it is Emad," Ethan said in Arabic.

"Ah, Emad, it is good to hear from you!"

"Yes, well, I'm stuck in secondary screening at Atatürk. They wanted me to call you."

The official lifted the handset, canceling speakerphone mode, and proceeded to grill "Aadil," asking the same questions. Ethan had complete confidence in his contact. Even so, because he was unable to hear the responses, he couldn't help the nervous sweat that trickled down his ribs. When the official switched to Turkish, which Ethan didn't understand, his discomfort only increased.

The man abruptly hung up and shook his head. He looked angry, disgusted.

Ethan held his breath. Had his contact contradicted any of his answers?

"You guys are getting good," the official said in Arabic. "Too good." He folded his arms.

"What do you mean?"

"He corroborated your story perfectly."

Ethan found it difficult to hide his sense of relief.

"But let's cut the bullshit," the official continued. "The man is obviously your Islamic State contact. Someone you met over an online forum. If I try to call that number back tomorrow, I'll get a dead connection. It's a Burner number, isn't it?"

Burner was a cellphone app anyone could install to get disposable phone numbers for texting and calling purposes. Ethan shook his head. "I don't know what you're talking about."

"On the jihadist forum, your contact promised you that everything you were searching for, you would find in Syria. That the so-called Islamic State was a chance to be part of something new. Something big. A chance to find God. That Raqqa, the capital, was a city of pure Islamic Law, a place of prayers, peace, and hope."

Ethan crossed his arms. "As I said, I don't know what you're talking about."

"The jihadist is lying to you," the official said. "If you go to Syria, you will not find peace. Or hope. Or even God. You will find war and death. And do you know what you'll be fighting for? A repressive regime whose interpretation of sharia law is... brutal, to say the least. There are at least two beheadings a day in Raqqa, the capital. Stonings are a weekly occurrence—for the local populace, it's like going to the cinema. Women are whipped for dressing the wrong way. There's no music. No smiling. No laughter. It is a place of repression and sorrow. Is that really something you're looking forward to?"

Ethan remained silent.

The official sat back. "You seek purpose in your life. You think jihad will help you find it. You want to be a martyr, fighting to defend your fellow Muslims. But as you murder the so-called infidels in the villages you conquer, and watch your companions brutally rape their widows, eventually you'll realize that every word I spoke is true. That this so-called state is perverting everything you believe in, and that you have made a very grave mistake. But by then it will be too late to get out."

Ethan stared at the official calmly. *You're preaching to the choir, dude*, he thought. Still, he had to give the man credit for trying. He likely gave the same speech to every suspected jihadi. Too bad it probably always fell on deaf ears.

Ethan forced a smile. "I am here for a wedding."

The official glanced at the man behind him with an exasperated expression that Ethan interpreted as, "Why do we bother?" He returned his attention to Ethan. "You're not even Saudi, are you?" He held up the passport. "This is a forgery. A good one, I admit, but you would have been wiser to use your real passport. We are going to arrest you."

Ethan said nothing. He knew the travel document was perfect. Not some passport made in a seedy backroom somewhere, but issued by the Saudi government itself. The official was merely trying to rattle him in some last ditch attempt at extracting a confession. Either that or he was looking for a bribe.

On cue the official snapped his fingers and the second man reached for the wallet that was laid out with the rest of Ethan's belongings on the side table. He handed it to the first official, who counted the money and removed a crisp purple bill: two hundred Turkish lire. "This is your jihad entry fee."

A female aide entered the room, placing a shoebox on the table. Inside was Ethan's phone. He knew they hadn't found anything incriminating on the device—he'd issued a hard reset before landing and wiped all the data. Even so, they had probably imaged its contents anyway.

The official exchanged a few words with the aide in Turkish, and then he sighed, switching to Arabic once more. "You are free to go."

* * *

Ethan took the shuttle to the domestic terminal and passed through security control. He picked up a chicken wrap from the Tadında Anadolu restaurant in the food court and met up with William, who was engaged in an animated discussion with a man who appeared to be Jordanian.

There was no reason for him and William to pretend they were on individual journeys anymore—the Turkish officials didn't have the manpower to tail Ethan throughout the airport, and even if someone did confront him, he would simply claim he'd met William for the first time in the departures lounge of Riyadh's King Khalid airport.

He took a seat and let William introduce him to the Jordanian, who apparently worked as an importer of ripoff goods from China. The newcomer excused himself a moment later, saying he had a flight to catch. William expressed interest in distributing the bogus goods, and he wouldn't let the Jordanian go until he'd obtained his contact details. When the man was gone William continued tapping at his cellphone screen, likely making notes about his new asset.

Ethan retrieved his own Android while he ate the wrap. He issued a hard reset and wiped the data again, in case the airport officers had installed some trackerware app while he was in custody.

"Well that was fun," Ethan said, putting the smartphone away.

William looked up from his cell. "What?"

"My little adventure in passport control."

"Oh." William returned his attention to the smart device. "How much did they take?"

Ethan shrugged. "Two hundred lire. You weren't detained?"

"Nope. I slipped the deskman ten lire when I saw what happened to you. He didn't even glance at my passport."

"Bastard."

William arose. "I'm getting a snack."

He returned a few minutes later with a kebab. "Ah, goat meat." William bit into a chunk. "I developed a taste for the stuff back in Iraq. Remember that game we used to play with the locals? What the hell was it called again? The game with the dead goat."

"Buzkashi," Ethan said. "And that was Afghanistan, not Iraq."

"That's right," William said. "It's all a blur these days. Anyway, who but Afghans could come up with a game that involves dragging around a dead goat from horseback and trying to get it between two goal posts? I mean come on. They must have been standing around playing soccer when someone unleashed their AK-47 at the ball in a fit of rage after a bad goal. And then they thought, well shit, how the hell are we going to play now? Then a goat bleated nearby, and all their heads turned toward the animal at the same time. 'Are you thinking what I'm thinking?' Joe Afghan said to his friends. Then they all leaped onto their horses and ran the goat down, cut the fucker's head off, and then started playing Buzkashi with its decapitated body. Brings new meaning to the phrase 'playing with your food.' Imagine what the game would be like with announcers. He goats, he scores!"

Ethan finished his wrap. "It was certainly an... interesting game."

William grinned; goat juices trickled down his chin. "You can't tell me you didn't enjoy bashing those Afghans from their horses while dragging that damn goat around. You were a badass out there."

"Yeah, it was a real joyride," Ethan said sarcastically, though in truth he liked the game. It was surprisingly fun, mostly because of the novelty factor.

William finished the last chunk of meat. "What the hell did they call the dead goats used in the game again? Cock something."

"*Kokpar*," Ethan said.

"That's right! Cock part. Gonna drag my cock part around the field and score myself a goal! Ahh, I miss the good old days. Still, you have to wonder about a society whose favorite pastime is dragging around dead goats."

"You do indeed." Ethan stood, and the two of them proceeded toward the boarding gate for the next flight.

six

The domestic Pegasus Air flight landed in Gaziantep a few hours later. Ethan and William shoved their way past the pitchmen in the arrivals area and boarded a taxi. It smelled of vomit and sweat, but at least the air conditioning worked.

Gaziantep was the center of pistachio production in Turkey, and in fact the latter syllables of the city's name were derived from the Turkish word for pistachio, *antep fıstığı*. With a population of over a million people, Gaziantep was a modern, clean city with well-maintained streets. The twin minarets of the Grand Mosque were the tallest structures in the city and jutted above the skyline like two gleaming swords ready to fight for the faith.

As the foul-smelling vehicle moved into the town center, the buildings became crowded. The two-level structures were made of the more traditional calcareous stone, and their close proximity to one another reminded Ethan of the Old City in Sana'a, though the bland white-walled structures lacked the quaintness of the latter city.

The call to prayer issued as the vehicle passed a mosque. The driver didn't react at all, nor did the other vehicles, or the pedestrians on the sidewalk. Perhaps their behavior wasn't all that surprising, considering how secular Turkey was. So much for fighting for the faith.

The taxi arrived at the Princess Hotel in the downtown core. Ethan paid the fare and emerged into the steppe climate. After the air-conditioned car, it felt like an oven out there.

Ethan checked them in. By the time he climbed the stairs and dropped off his backpack in the generously decorated suite, both he and William were covered in sweat. An air conditioner furnished the room—but when Ethan set the fan level to full, all the device did was recirculate the air at the same temperature. He opened the window but the heat from outside was worse so he closed it and pulled the shades shut.

Fighting the weariness wrought of sixteen hours of traveling, he wedged a rubber doorstop from his backpack beneath the entrance. Then he grabbed the versatile radio-frequency detecting SK199 ink pen from his gear and proceeded to go over the place with William. As he worked, Ethan thought vaguely about Sheik Jasir Al-Khayr, who had likely used similar off-the-shelf equipment to find trackers.

It took almost half an hour—and all his remaining energy—to search the room from top to bottom with William, and when they were both satisfied that there were no bugs, they flopped down on their respective beds for some well-deserved shut-eye.

A knock at the door awakened Ethan a few hours later.

"Open up you sons of camels!" someone shouted in Arabic from the hall outside. The accent was Yemeni.

Ethan recognized the voice immediately. It belonged to the same man who had vouched for him over the phone during secondary screening at Atatürk airport. He groggily hauled himself upright and kicked aside the rubber wedge.

A tanned, bearded individual stood in the entryway. He looked like a younger version of Al-Khayr. He was dressed in traditional Yemeni garb, with a lavender thawb matching his tribal headgear. He wore an ornate jambiyah dagger in front of his navel. On his back was a small rucksack, and tucked under one arm was a silvery MacBook Pro.

Aaron.

Ethan warmly clasped the hand of his friend and teammate, then led him inside.

The smell of fried dough permeated the air, and the stains at the bottom of the brown paper bag Aaron carried beneath the MacBook promised greasy delights. Aaron dropped the bag on a nearby table. "Baklava?"

Ethan grabbed an odd-looking bun from the bag and examined it. The top was sprinkled with the region's famous pistachios. "Baklava? Looks like a samosa gone bad." He bit into the honey-soaked, layered pastry. "Pretty good," he admitted.

"Clean?" Aaron asked, gesturing at the walls. He was referring to eavesdropping devices.

"It's clean," William answered, snatching a baklava from the bag.

The three of them took seats around the table.

"Last time I saw you," Ethan said between mouthfuls. "You were headed down to the Yemen highlands to team up with the Houthis."

Aaron frowned. "I had a helluva time convincing them I wasn't an Al Qaeda spy. They never really brought me into their inner circle. Too bad, because they're going to be running the country soon. Long story short, Sam pulled me and sent me here."

"You've filled out a bit since the last time I saw you," William said.

Aaron shamelessly grabbed a baklava from the bag. "I figure I might as well stock up on the fat stores now while the getting's good. Once we cross the border, it's going to be lean times, baby."

Ethan nodded at the jambiyah dagger at Aaron's waist. "Tracking device?"

Aaron shook his head. "We're going in black. No trackers. Sam doesn't want to give the Islamic State a reason to chop off our heads."

"Myself, I'm kind of glad we're going in black," William said. "I'd prefer not to have the DIA breathing down my throat."

"That's not Sam's style," Ethan said. "Too bad about the trackers, though. If we could find a way to smuggle them in undetected, they could prove useful during an emergency extract scenario."

"Yeah, except there will be no emergency extracts," Aaron said. "If you get in shit, you're looking at the quick reaction force."

A buzz came from Aaron's robe. He fetched an Android phone

from his pocket and read the on-screen message.

That reminded Ethan of something.

"Sam mentioned the cellular coverage in Syria might be nonexistent," he said.

"You got that right," Aaron said, replacing his smartphone. "According to my contacts, there's no coverage at all these days. At least not in the areas we'll be operating in. But we do have this." He retrieved a small black object from his backpack. It had a thick, foldout antenna and a digital display.

"Satellite Internet?" Ethan said.

Aaron nodded. "Ground Control's Iridium Go model. It'll probably be confiscated at some point, though. Might be better to leave it behind."

"What's the plan on maintaining contact with Sam, then?" William said.

"The same way every other muj keeps in touch with his family: Internet cafes, which use their own satellite hotspots. We have reports that the Islamic State has seized hotspots from private owners to install in their own compounds, so we might not even have to leave home."

"That's good, because I don't think there will be many Internet cafes where we're headed," Ethan said.

"There are actually quite a few in the capital. Raqqa."

"You're assuming we'll even be assigned to Raqqa," William interjected.

"We will," Aaron said. "For a short time anyway. That seems to be the path most foreign jihadists take. After training, the militants bring the new recruits to the capital to show off what the Caliphate is capable of. Kind of a dog and pony show to make them feel good about their decision to join before the emirs ship them off to the war zones to serve as cannon fodder."

"I'm really looking forward to *that*," William said sarcastically.

"What about your MacBook?" Ethan nodded at the laptop. "Will they confiscate it?"

"They might, but I doubt it. They usually let the foreign fighters keep their laptops and phones, though I'd be careful to delete any music, movies or photos. The muj sometimes get special treatment in regards to what sorts of media they're allowed on their devices, but best not to risk it."

"So, when we use the local Internet services to keep in touch with Sam," Ethan said. "I'm assuming we'll have a way to encrypt our traffic?"

"Of course." Aaron retrieved an envelope from his backpack and dumped three USB sticks on the table.

"*Amn al-Mujahid*?" Ethan said, guessing at the contents of the USBs. That stood for "The Mujahid's Security."

"Yup. Latest windows revision."

The Al-Fajr Technical Committee was established by jihadis in September 2012. Affiliated with Al Qaeda, the group produced encryption software to help mujahadeen communicate "safely and effectively." The latest incarnations of the software could be installed on Windows desktops or Android phones and used to send and receive encrypted emails, texts, videos, and so forth. The nice thing about running the same software other jihadis did was that if the sticks were confiscated, no one would think twice about the contents—he loved the irony of using their own tools against them.

"There's also software included on the USB to remove any stealth key loggers or screen recorders," Aaron continued. "And any other tracking malware the Islamic State or cafe owners may have installed on their computers. Plus, there's a little goodie called readme.txt.exe you may be familiar with."

"Regin?"

Aaron nodded.

Ethan had used that specific malware before. All Windows computers were set to hide file extensions by default, so that particular executable would appear as readme.txt, a text file. Most people clicked on text files named readme without thinking, and once that nasty file was clicked, it would infect the target computer with a modular cyberespionage tool known as Regin, developed and maintained by two full-time teams working for the NSA and MI6.

Remote operators could tailor the software to specific targets in real-time, as long as the target system had a working Internet connection. It could capture screenshots, take control of the mouse and keyboard, log keystrokes and passwords, monitor web activity, retrieve deleted files, and so forth. Regin made use of several state-of-the-art stealth techniques to stay under the radar, such as encrypted virtual file system containers and payloads, and it had the ability to infect and store parts of itself on other machines in the same network. It could even embed itself in the firmware of certain commercial hard drive brands. It also had an auto-update feature, facilitating long-term intelligence gathering—it's ever-evolving footprint allowed it to continually evade virus scanners.

"Check it out." Aaron indicated a collapsible button on the topside of the USB that blended seamlessly with the black surface. "A hidden button that saves your current GPS location to a custom folder on the stick for later retrieval. Also includes a mini Laser Target Locater Module. Hold down the button and after a second it emits a visible spectrum laser. Use it like a laser pointer to identify any nearby target you want to acquire—hold it steady, and the built-in laser range finder will compute the GPS coordinates of the target and record them."

"And who says we never get James Bond stuff?" William said.

Ethan shrugged. "Repurposed cellphone technology."

"Well, there's more," Aaron said.

"Don't keep me in suspense," Ethan mocked.

Aaron winked. "Squeeze the middle like this." He pinched the center portion. "And yank the top." He pulled the tip: the end telescoped outward. "And it becomes an RF antenna. When we connect it to our Androids with the built-in adapter, we can use it to send encrypted texts and voice messages among ourselves, or any other agency embeds within typical RF radii—around one mile in cities, or up to fifty miles if we're standing on top of a mountain. Very useful for the areas of little to no cellular coverage we'll be working in."

"That's great and everything," Ethan said. "But tell me how this is better than a two-way radio?"

"Well, it's a lot less obvious, for one. Very under the radar. We come in carrying something like a military-grade PRC-153, that's going to scream 'spy' to the muj. Anyway, here, give me your phone and I'll install the app for the antenna. I'll also pop in the mobile version of Amn al-Mujahid and the other stuff we'll need to stay in touch with Sam, since I'm assuming you wiped your cell before landing."

Aaron opened up his laptop and Ethan handed him his smartphone.

While the other operative worked, Ethan examined the USB. He held it to eye level and depressed the laser. Sure enough, a small red dot appeared on the far wall. "This is great and all that, but you know it's useless for long range targets, right?"

"That's why we have these," Aaron said, producing a small, binocular-like object from the backpack.

Ethan regarded the item dubiously. "Looks like a hobbyist-grade range finder. Something a golfer might use."

"More like a surveyor. It's the TruPulse 360 R laser range finder, except we've replaced the laser with a Class 4 to boost the range, and added in an anti-reflective coating to the lenses for glint reduction. Basically a GVS-5 in a consumer shell. It sends its data to the phone via Blueteeth and—"

"Bluetooth," William corrected. "Really grates on the nerves when people mispronounce common words." He spoke it *mis-prah-nance* with his Texan drawl.

Aaron cleared his throat. "As I was saying, it sends the data to an Android app I'm installing on your smartphone that determines the altitude, latitude and longitude of the target via GPS."

"Well if we're going to carry these, why not just go with a LLDR 2H?" William said. That stood for the Lightweight Laser Designator Rangefinder, the compact 2H model, also known as AN/PED-1A.

"You shitting me?" Aaron said. "That's just as bad as bringing military radios. Worse. We carry US Army target designators into the Islamic State, you can bet they'll take them away, then schedule our heads for the chopping block."

"Point taken," William said. "But what's stopping them from taking away this surveyor crap, too?"

"Nothing. But other foreign jihadis have successfully brought in golf and sports range finders, so we should be fine. Oh." Aaron grabbed a small leather case from the pack. "Also got this for you."

Aaron handed the item to Ethan and returned his attention to the laptop.

Inside the leather holder was the lockpick set Ethan had requested from Sam. He perused the selection of picks and bump keys. It would suit his purposes, and was low tech enough that the Islamic State definitely wouldn't bother him about it.

"Sam told me you'd brief us on the plan to get into Syria," Ethan said. "So what's the deal? We simply drive across the border and swear allegiance to the Islamic State?"

"Pretty much. I've been in touch with a people smuggler. He'll get us into Syria and drop us off at an IS checkpoint."

"Where'd you find him?"

"IS is very active on social media. I sent a text to a public Kik Messenger account, saying we were three men on hegira to *Shaam*." Syria.

"You're sure the account wasn't an NSA honeypot?" Ethan interrupted. The NSA and other intelligence agencies often created fake Islamic State accounts and posted contact information in an effort to catch foreign jihadists.

Aaron shrugged. "I passed the account Sam's way first, and she confirmed it wasn't NSA. But as I was saying, I messaged the dude and asked how we could join our brothers, and he returned the phone numbers of three local smugglers. So I called one and set us up. By the way, we're not supposed to dress too traditionally during the crossing. We draw less attention that way."

"What about weapons?" Ethan said, glancing at Aaron's backpack.

"Not allowed."

"What do you mean? Not even pistols?"

"We won't get through if we bring weapons of any kind," Aaron said. "According to the recruiter, IS will provide assault rifles anyway."

"Assault rifles?" William asked suspiciously. "What kind of assault rifles?"

"AK-47s."

William threw up his hands. "I'm so sick of those damn things. I've never fired a more inaccurate rifle in my life. I'll take an M16 any day of the week over an AK."

Aaron shrugged. "Hey, we're clandestine operatives now, not the pampered spec-ops soldiers we once were." He returned Ethan's Android.

"You never know how good you have it until you give it up," William bemoaned.

Ethan unlocked the phone, navigated to Apps, and swiped to the last screen. He saw the green, flamelike icon for Amn al-Mujahid but nothing else. The icons for the other new apps would be hidden, he knew.

Aaron showed him how to use the hidden apps.

"That leaves only one more question," Ethan said when they were done. He snatched the greasy bag from the table but it proved empty. "When do we get more baklavas?"

seven

Aaron called the people smuggler shortly thereafter and arranged for transport early the next morning. Ethan spent the rest of that day exploring Gaziantep and eating the baklavas and pistachios the city was famous for. He slept well that night, the last good rest he would have for quite a while, and at five a.m. checked out.

Like him, the other operatives were dressed in a T-shirt and jeans, with their keffiyehs stowed away. For Ethan, it was odd removing the headgear after all that time, and he felt almost naked without it. But the goal was to look like an ordinary Syrian or Turk at the border crossing, so the keffiyeh had to go.

It was still dark out when a brand new supermini Renault Clio pulled into the loading area.

"That's our ride," Aaron said.

"Apparently smuggling pays off," William said.

"If you knew how much I paid the man," Aaron grinned. "You'd quickly realize we were in the wrong business."

A Turk got out, introducing himself as Maaz. He opened the Renault's trunk and the three of them stowed their backpacks inside.

"Take these." Maaz distributed three travel documents.

Ethan accepted his. It was a Syrian passport. He opened to the photo page. The same picture he had on his Saudi passport was on it, though the keffiyeh had been edited out.

"Come here." Ethan angrily led Aaron away from the others. When he was out of earshot, he said, "You gave this man my photo?"

Aaron shrugged. "He needed it to make the passports."

"I don't want my picture in some terrorist computer network."

Aaron shook his head. "These smugglers are disorganized as hell. Your picture won't be showing up on any terrorist networks anytime soon, trust me."

Ethan was about to argue his point, but he let it go. Aaron was probably right.

"Besides, he's just a people smuggler," Aaron continued. "Only loosely related to the Islamic State."

"Yeah? Bet he's on the White House kill list somewhere."

"Probably."

Ethan returned to the vehicle and sat in the cramped passenger seat, nearly banging his head on the upper frame of the door in the process. William and Aaron took the backseats and the journey south began.

"Where are you from?" Maaz said in a colloquial, difficult to understand Arabic.

"Saudi Arabia," Ethan answered.

Maaz nodded. "You will love it in Shaam."

"You live there?" Ethan said.

The smuggler chuckled. "No. My calling is here, in Turkey. To help men like you make their hegira. I am too old for the Caliphate."

"You can't be more than forty," Ethan said.

"My point exactly. They need young men. Men who can fight. All the administrative positions are already filled." He glanced at Ethan askance. "You are twenty-nine? Thirty?"

"Twenty-eight," Ethan lied.

"A good age." Maaz drove on in silence. A moment later: "You have brought weapons?"

Ethan shook his head. "We were told not too."

"Good. You will be given weapons in the Caliphate. Along with room and board. And a salary, of course."

"What about wives?" Aaron said hopefully. From his tone, Ethan thought he was only half joking.

"Oh yes, if that is what you want, you will all get wives." Features brightening, Maaz glanced at Aaron in the rearview mirror. "Beautiful wives. There are plenty of women to be had. *Dawlah* will provide." That mean the State.

"Foreign wives?" Aaron said.

Maaz pressed his lips together. "Perhaps. There are many foreign women in the Caliphate. I have smuggled women from Pakistan. Afghanistan. France and Britain even."

The sun rose, and soon the streets of Gaziantep were behind them, replaced by pistachio farms. The verdure gave way to the dry steppe where only the occasional bushes clung to life amid the bedrock. Once in a while a decrepit village passed into view: rusting machinery, concrete houses clustered around a small mosque, grubby, half-naked children.

A Turkish checkpoint blocked the highway shortly, but the police officer waved them through. According to Maaz the police were stopping only pickup trucks and semis that day. Looking for oil smugglers who fed the Islamic State war machine.

In forty-five minutes they reached the city of Kilis, close to the Turkey-Syria border. In another ten minutes they were at the Oncupinar border gate, a steel trellis supporting an arched metal canopy over the highway. Flanking it, barbed wire fencing spanned the border from horizon to horizon.

Maaz bribed the Turkish gendarmerie border guard with the equivalent of ten US dollars and they were on their way. On the Syrian side they were stopped almost immediately by armed men standing in front of an old eight-wheeled Soviet BTR-60 armored personnel carrier.

"Free Syrian Army checkpoint," Maaz said underbreath.

One of the guards approached the driver-side door. He carried an RPD light machine gun slung over one shoulder.

Maaz rolled down the window.

"Passports?" the guard said.

Maaz collected the Syrian passports and handed them to the guard, who opened the documents to the photo pages in turn, checking that the faces matched.

"Do you have any weapons?" the guard said.

Maaz shook his head.

The guarded leaned forward, as if scanning the area between seats for hidden arms, then he surveyed the occupants once more. "Where are you going?"

"Family," Maaz said. "Aleppo."

The guard handed the passports back to the driver, then furrowed his brow. "Haven't I seen you before?"

Maaz shrugged. "It's possible. I have a big family."

The guard hesitated and then finally waved them on.

Maaz drove through. Glancing in the rear-view mirror, he laughed softly. "Idiots," he said smugly. "I've seen that one at least five times. Others even more often. They always let me pass."

Maaz drove for about ten minutes and then veered onto an unmarked dirt road, heading east. Fifteen minutes later he turned south onto another paved highway and floored the accelerator.

"Must be quick here," Maaz said. "In case they're following!"

Ethan glanced in the passenger side mirror but didn't see any pursuers.

The highway there, unlike the Turkish side, had plenty of potholes, and the Clio hit several of them along the way, jolting Ethan. He banged his head on the low ceiling every time.

"Can we slow down, *please*," Wiliam said from the backseat.

Finally Maaz eased off the accelerator. There were still a lot of potholes, but at least the Turk had a better chance of avoiding them.

Ten minutes later Maaz reached another checkpoint: a mangled iron fence had been strewn across the road, with a Hyundai pickup parked in the lane beside it. The vehicle was a technical—a double-barreled ZU-2 was bolted to the truck bed. The black standard of the Islamic State waved beside the anti-aircraft gun.

Two AK-47-totting mujahadeen in balaclavas manned the check-point; the closest militant approached the driver side.

Maaz lowered the window.

"Salaam, my brothers," the mujahid said, ignoring the driver to address Ethan. "You have come to join Dawlah?"

Ethan leaned forward. "We have."

The militant removed his mask. He was a teenager, maybe eighteen or nineteen years old, with a downy, cropped jihadist beard. "Welcome, my brothers. Welcome! You have made it!"

eight

About an hour later Ethan found himself sitting beside Aaron and William in the bed of a different pickup truck, headed southeast along the dry steppe. The highway proved just as poorly maintained as the area near the border, and Ethan was jolted by a pothole every ten seconds or so.

He had retrieved the red and white-patterned keffiyeh from his gear and was wearing it, though he was still dressed in a casual T-shirt and jeans. Twice he checked his phone for a cellular network during the ride, but never found a signal.

The pickup stopped on the outskirts of a Syrian village. Two twenty-year-olds with AKM rifles greeted the teenaged driver. Ethan hopped down from the truck bed only to find himself the prompt recipient of a hug.

"Salaam!" the militant who embraced him said. "I am so glad you have made your hegira! Come, I will take you to the emir. I am Abdul. What are your names?"

"I am Emad Al'Saudi," Ethan said. Translated, that literally meant Emad the Saudi. It wasn't uncommon for foreign fighters to use an alias for their last names, especially one related to their country of origin.

William introduced himself as Wafeeq Al'Saudi and Aaron as Aadil Al'Yemeni.

"Most of our trainers are Saudis and Yemenis!" Abdul said excitedly. "You will fit right in."

Ethan wasn't sure whether that was good or bad.

Abdul threaded through the white-walled, flat-roofed houses, leading the way into the Islamic State border camp. Untilled wheat fields surrounded the concrete buildings of the former village; various structures had been erected in the withered pastures to support the training exercises. Large canvases patterned in digital desert camouflage had been raised over the more obvious constructions—when viewed from the air, those patterns would readily blend in with the dry yellow grass.

In a field nearby, recruits of all ages shot at plastic bottles filled with dyed water. Everyone wore fatigues: there was desert digital, desert plain, and forest digital. Probably American-made.

Abdul skirted the center of town, where some kind of urban combat exercise was taking place. Ethan spotted several armed recruits in fatigues and balaclavas, hunched outside a doorway. Two recruits ducked inside the concrete house at the same time, one going high, the other low. Another militant filmed the whole sequence on his cellphone, while two civilian children watched quietly from the second-floor balcony across the street.

Abdul led them to an obstacle course, where a group of recruits surmounted hurdles such as barbed wire, wooden logs, and climbing nets. It looked like a playground compared to the obstacle course Ethan had experienced in his own SEAL training. Patterned tarps camouflaged much of the course.

An instructor in a black turban was shouting encouragement at the recruits. Beside him a man maybe ten years older than Ethan watched with folded arms. He wore fatigues patterned in desert-digital, and his head was wrapped in the same red and white-checkered keffiyeh that Ethan wore. Acne scars pocked his lined face. He had an aura of command about him.

"Emir Haadi," Abdul said in respectful tones.

The pockmarked man looked over his shoulder questioningly.

"New recruits." Abdul nodded at Ethan and the other operatives.

Haadi broke into a fatherly grin. "Welcome home, brothers." His

Rural Saudi accent was the Arabic equivalent of Appalachian English, so thick that Ethan barely understood it. "Come, let's get you processed."

The emir led them inside one of the low-slung concrete houses and sat behind a steel desk. He offered each of them bottled water.

"Your hegira went well?" Haadi said.

"As well as could be expected," Ethan answered, sipping his water.

"You are from Riyadh?"

Ethan nodded.

"I recognize the accent," Haadi said. "Tell me, how is the Euphrates River this time of year?"

Ethan frowned. "There is no Euphrates in Riyadh."

Haadi smiled. "No, there isn't."

"There is a lake, though," Ethan continued. "In Al Sallam Park."

Haadi's eyes became distant. "Ah, Al Sallam Park. It is beautiful this time of year." He abruptly pointed at their rucksacks. "Place your packs on the table, please."

The emir rummaged through their belongings: Qurans, duct tape, flashlights, batteries, matches. He paid no attention whatsoever to the USB sticks, instead homing in on their passports, which he set down on the table in front of him.

Haadi discovered the satellite hotspot and frowned. Ethan had elected to bring it along after all, in case the Islamic State was stupid enough to let them keep it.

"What is this?" Haadi said.

Ethan kept his cool. "Personal wifi."

"Laptop, okay. Phone, okay. This, not okay." The man set it aside.

Ethan glanced at Aaron, who shrugged in an I-told-you-so manner.

Next Haadi had them spread their legs, palms on the wall, and patted them down.

Haadi discovered their phones, which he didn't care about because there was no cellular network coverage. When he found the TruPulse 360s, he activated each device in turn and confirmed they were indeed range finders and nothing more. He also came across the lockpick kit Ethan had, and after a quick search through the picks and bump keys, he placed it alongside the other "allowed" items.

Finished his search, Haadi returned to his desk, flipped open a laptop, and typed up the information from the passports. With the built-in webcam, he snapped a photo of each of their faces. Ethan had gotten angry with Aaron earlier for sharing his photo with Maaz, but that was nothing: now Ethan's picture was stored in a terrorist database for real.

"Do you have a Dawlah *tazkiyah*?" Haadi asked. That meant a character reference from someone already part of the Islamic State.

Ethan shook his head. "We know no one here." Sam had hinted other embedded assets were already in play, but she was loath to reveal their identities, as was only right.

Haadi furrowed his brow. "As Saudis and Yemenis, I would have expected otherwise. There are many radical mosques that could have vouched for you. How did you get here?"

Aaron repeated the story about how he'd gotten in touch with a public Kik Messenger account associated with the Islamic State.

Haadi pressed his lips together. "So you didn't actually know your recruiter personally?"

"No."

"The route you took for hegira is more typical of Western holy warriors. And if you *were* Western fighters, I would be forced to run a security background check. We've caught their intelligence agents in our midst before. It won't happen again, not on my watch."

Ethan thought about what Sam had told him about choking off recruits by forcing the Islamic State to perform more thorough vetting. So it was already starting. Good.

Haadi tapped his lips. "But you're not Western fighters. So I will allow you to recite the pledge of *bay'ah*"—allegiance—"to the Islamic State. Raise your index fingers."

Ethan clenched his right hand and lifted his index finger, forming that oft-mimicked gesture posted online by Islamic State supporters.

Most Westerners had no idea of the symbolism behind the act, but it alluded to the belief that Allah was the only God, one of the five pillars of Islam and a component of the daily prayers. *There is no God but Allah, Muhammad is the messenger of God.* Those words, known as the *Shahada*, were written on the black standard of the Islamic State itself.

The gesture also symbolized the wielder's willingness to die for Islam, the one true faith, and reaffirmed the group's dedication to wiping out all other inferior ideologies. They wanted one God, one religion, one state. Worldwide.

"In the name of Allah the merciful we hereby swear allegiance," the emir said.

"*In the name of Allah the merciful we hereby swear allegiance*," Ethan and his companions repeated.

"To the Prince of the Faithful."

"*To the Prince of the Faithful*."

"And the Caliph of the Muslims."

"*And the Caliph of the Muslims*."

"Abu Bakr al-Qurashi." That was a name the leader of the Islamic State, Abu Bakr al-Baghdadi, used to claim descendance from the Prophet.

"*Abu Bakr al-Qurashi*."

"Allahu akbar!"

"*Allahu akbar!*"

Haadi returned their rucksacks and brought them to a supply house, where they picked out fatigues in their sizes, but did not put them on. Then he led them back toward the obstacle course.

On the way, he said, "I am the emir of the camp, but I also personally run the orientation brigade, which you are now a part of. All new recruits start with me until the class-up to war training. You are at a bit of a disadvantage, because you have arrived near the end of orientation, and after this Sunday, day of rest, you will be assigned to the war brigade. But, Allah willing, you will quickly adapt."

At the obstacle course, Haadi walked straight to a youth who had finished early and was waiting on the sidelines for the next round to begin.

"Ibrahim," the emir said.

A village boy just out of puberty, Ibrahim snapped to attention. He had the features of a Syrian. Probably conscripted from the locals.

"Assign them to quarters and get them changed," Haadi said. "Then bring them back."

"Any chance of breakfast?" Aaron asked hopefully.

"The life of the mujahid is austere," the emir said.

Ibrahim led them to a concrete house on the northern outskirts of the village. Inside, the blankets of other mujahadeen were strewn across the floor, with backpacks serving as pillows. Ibrahim found an open area near a crumbling wall and instructed the three of them to set down their rucksacks.

"You will notice there are no locks," Ibrahim said with a wide smile. "You do not have to worry about thieves. No one will steal from you here."

Ethan and the others changed into the fatigues Haadi had given them.

"You are from Yemen?" Ibrahim said on the way back to the obstacle course.

"Saudi Arabia," Ethan corrected him.

"We have people from all nationalities here. Omani. Afghani. British. French. And you know, it is amazing. Without Islam to bind us all, we would probably be at each other's throats. But instead we love one another. We don't all speak the same language, but we don't have to. There is always someone to translate. We are all brothers."

It sounded similar to the propaganda Ethan had heard spouted by recruits online.

He was distracted by a faint buzzing in the sky, nearly identical to the sound of a small Cessna. He glanced skyward, squinting. Though he couldn't see it, he knew a drone, probably an MQ-1 Predator, was up there somewhere.

"They don't bother us," Ibrahim said.

"Not yet," Ethan countered.

"They won't attack," Ibrahim insisted. "The mighty West is afraid of us."

Ethan chuckled softly. "Which is exactly why they will attack, eventually."

After a day of physical training, with pauses for prayers, they returned to their quarters and a cook prepared a supper of chicken and rice, which they ate with their hands in the dining room under candlelight.

The atmosphere was almost festive. Without a doubt, everyone was overjoyed to be there. The fifteen other recruits introduced themselves, but Ethan forgot most of the names the instant he heard them, though he noted there were a proportionately high number of Osamas and Muhammads in the lot. If he ever needed to call someone by name, by guessing one or the other he had a good chance of getting it right.

"I still can't believe I'm here," an Osama said in Arabic. A young militant beside him translated the words into English for some of the others. "We are achieving the dreams of our beaten down brothers, brothers who have been stepped on and humiliated for the last century, simply for what they believed in. We fight for a Caliphate, for what we believe in, defending our fellow Muslims.

"Already the West has pledged resources and training to our enemy. And they promise airstrikes will come, soon. Let them do their worst, I say, because even if we lose, we win. We will drain the West of its resources, sending their economy into collapse. It costs them a trillion dollars to wage war against us. It costs us almost nothing. Only our lives. And that is no cost at all, but a gift. We end this war in paradise, but the infidel, he ends it in hell."

"Takbir!" someone shouted. That literally meant, "the term for god is great." In the Islamic world, instead of applause, someone would shout "takbir" and the audience would respond with "Allahu akbar."

"Allahu akbar," the group replied on cue.

"Takbir," someone repeated.

"Allahu akbar."

"Takbir."

"Allahu akbar."

And so the evening went.

Later, they dispersed throughout the house to relax in their assigned berthing areas. Most of the recruits studied the Quran in groups by candlelight or flashlight. Heated arguments erupted about the various *hadiths*, or traditions, therein. The name of Allah was bandied about in nearly every sentence.

Splashing and scrubbing sounds came from the adjacent room. Ethan peered past the door and observed some of the recruits washing clothes in a basin. The water would be from the communal well, as there were no working sinks or taps.

What sounded like a diesel motor abruptly started up outside.

"Power's back," an Omani said. He was a Muhammad. He had a laptop plugged into the wall and the blue charging light on its side had activated.

He produced a power bar, and those with phones plugged them into the available outlets. Ethan's own cellphone was almost fully charged, so he didn't bother charging it. However he did check to see if there was a carrier signal. Nope.

Laptop in hand, Muhammad sidled over to Ethan. "Do you have FireChat?"

Ethan shook his head. "What's that?"

"Off-the-grid instant messaging. It uses wireless mesh networking to allow us to connect our phones without any cellphone coverage. We can use it to exchange messages in battle, or to plan operations. Here, I'll hook you up." Muhammad produced a cord and plugged it into his laptop. He looked at Ethan expectantly. "Your phone?"

Ethan reluctantly handed his smartphone over, and watched very carefully as Muhammad launched an application called MobieGenie on the laptop.

"It is okay, I'm not going to hack your phone," Muhammad joked.

Ethan smiled politely.

When the youth was finished, he disconnected the Android and showed Ethan how FireChat worked. Watching the scrolling messages, Ethan was underwhelmed to discover that the exact same debates occurring in the adjacent rooms regarding the Quran were taking place camp-wide via the texting app.

Muhammad proceeded to install FireChat on the phones of Aaron and William. The two operatives scrutinized the installation process just as closely as Ethan had, and seemed similarly disappointed when they finally ran the app.

The generator shut down half an hour later and the call for lights out came.

As Ethan lay there in the dark, he heard the distant buzz of a Predator drone. The unmanned aerial vehicle was only performing surveillance. Still, when the approval for airstrikes came, the training camps would probably be among the first targets.

Sam would lobby for a delay until she was certain where her operatives were. Even so, she was only a small player in a political board game whose participants spanned multiple countries, agencies and militaries. She had no guarantee of getting what she asked for.

Selous Scouts, Ethan thought. *Why the hell did I ever agree to this?*

He smiled grimly.

Because it's my job.

nine

The following days were a blur of PT (physical training), which included several four-mile jogs and obstacle course runs. Ethan had intended to act like the exercises were harder than they were, but he didn't have to do much pretending: the program *was* difficult. He was definitely feeling his age.

The brotherhood and camaraderie among the young men was incredible, and helped him get through each day. Indeed, the esprit de corps was so infectious that Ethan had to constantly remind himself not to become attached to the youngsters. They were jihadis, he reminded himself. Single-minded fanatics willing to die for a cause they didn't truly understand.

On the second day, during a rotation on the obstacle course, while climbing the rope net, Ethan closed on a militant named Hatam, a dark-skinned British-Pakistani whose eyes blazed with zeal. As Ethan approached, the man kicked him in the ribs; Ethan slipped and would have plunged the five meters to the ground had he not managed to grip a lower rung in time.

Hatam continued over the top with a triumphant smile, and as he passed Ethan on the way down he called him a "pig fucker" through the net. So much for the camaraderie. It seemed even jihadist training camps had their share of dirtbags.

Ethan confronted Hatam behind a house later, during a break. "You have a problem with me. Let's work it out."

Fear flashed in Hatam's eyes for a moment, though the zealous flames quickly overwhelmed it. "There is no problem."

"Good." Ethan slammed his fist into Hatam's abdominal region. The man doubled over, retching.

Hatam didn't bother Ethan after that.

There were classroom sessions, too. Some involved a few biased geopolitical topics, such as the "petrodollar system" that guided US foreign policy in the Middle East for the past several decades, and the Sykes-Picot agreement that drew the artificial borders of Iraq and Syria after World War I. However, the majority of the topics were religious in nature, such as the benefits of martyrdom and the requirement of jihad. The students recited phrases such as "dying in jihad is the greatest glory" and "killing infidels pleases Allah."

A lot of class time was devoted to the Islamic State's rendition of sharia law. Insulting Allah, the Prophet, or Islam was punishable by death by beheading. As was spying, renouncing Islam, or engaging in homosexuality—though homosexuals were sometimes tossed off tall buildings for variety. Adultery: death by stoning. Thievery: amputation of the left hand. Armed robbery: amputation of the left hand and right foot. Masturbation: eighty lashes. Drawing graffiti, spreading slander, smoking cigarettes or drinking alcohol: eighty lashes plus a three-day jail sentence for the first offense, and one month for the second. Failure to obey the dress code: fifty lashes.

Throughout everything, the students dropped whatever it was they were doing to pray at the required intervals, five times a day. A certain loud, pompous instructor gave the sermon after Friday prayer; he exhorted the youths to keep fighting, and to never give up in the face of the infidel. He reminded them that if they died in the service of Allah during their sacred jihad, they would wake up in *jannah* surrounded by nubile women. Sadly, judging from the gleaming eyes around Ethan, most of the recruits believed it.

As the week wound down, an Islamic State minibus arrived, and those in the later phases of training boarded. After the bus left, Ethan and the others immediately classed-up to War Training I. All that meant was in addition to daily PT and obstacle course runs, they also low-crawled beneath live fire, engaged in hand-to-hand combat, and practiced target shooting. For the latter, the weapon of choice was an AK-47 assault rifle, though they also trained on Soviet-made Makarov pistols—Aaron sarcastically referred to them as macaroni pistols, and sometimes during practice, when he was out of earshot of other jihadists, he quietly sung, "he stuck a feather in his hat and called it macaroni."

Their training was rounded out with a few sessions on PKM machine guns, M-37 mortars, and RPG-7 grenade launchers, though only a few students got to fire those because of supply limits.

Ethan and the other two operatives pretended to have zero military training in the beginning, and purposely shifted their aim when practicing target shooting. As the days passed, they allowed themselves to "improve," so that soon they were near the top of the class in terms of marksmanship.

The classroom sessions morphed during that time, covering practical topics such as the different ways to subdue and kill a man, interrogation resistance techniques, passport and ID forgery, and how to navigate by the stars and sun.

The days were fairly regimented, and Ethan and the rest of the brigade fell into a regular pattern. Dawn prayer. Quran study. PT. Breakfast. Obstacle course or jogging. Target practice or classroom session. Mid-day prayer. Lunch. Target practice. Afternoon prayer. PT. Hand to hand combat training. Evening prayer. Dinner. Personal time. Sleep. Night prayer.

The hand-to-hand combat drills were probably the least helpful. Ethan almost laughed when he saw the instructor flaunting his martial arts skills. It seemed to be some kind of Wushu, the most showy, useless martial art out there. Sure it had lots of flashy moves, but in hand-to-hand those moves were useless, as most close-up combat eventually degenerated into a wrestling free-for-all. Brazilian jujitsu was Ethan's martial art of choice, and *that* was something to be respected. Even so, he was a bit rusty, and the combat sessions helped him get his groove back.

New men arrived at random hours every day, and were assigned to the orientation brigade. Sometimes existing recruits would stop what they were doing to greet the newcomers, at least until an instructor yelled at them.

The Islamic State minibus arrived a couple of weeks later to pick up the latest graduates. Ethan and the others immediately classed-up to War Training II. They spent the next few weeks learning the intricacies of close-quarters battles. They performed drills on how to sweep buildings and secure a perimeter while under fire. They learned various patrolling techniques, and methods and tactics for engaging the enemy.

There was limited sniper training for those who had demonstrated good marksmanship, and it involved Soviet Dragunov SVD sniper rifles. An instructor with a thick Saddam Hussein-like mustache who had served as a sniper in either the Syrian or Iraqi army led the course. While the urban sniping he taught was relatively straightforward—choose a hide and support other infantry—the rural sniping was the typical torture. The instructor took sadistic pleasure in making the recruits set up hides over cowpies or anthills. Ethan would wait for hours perched in the field, smelling like shit, having ants attempt to crawl up his nose, while he waited for another student to lift a paper target in a random window of a house.

The last two weeks were a blur, as Ethan suffered from terrible dysentery. Hatam was uncharacteristically buoyant during that time. Ethan ignored the dirtbag and forced himself through each day; by the end of the War Training II he was almost back to himself.

Part two wound down and the recruits sat through a graduation ceremony. At the conclusion of Haadi's speech, the emir said, with a yawn, "You are the best group mujahadeen I have ever had the privilege of training."

That night after midnight Ethan slipped away from the barracks and, avoiding the patrol, made his way to Emir Haadi's house. The front door was unlocked.

Ethan searched the main office in the dark, using the dim light of his cellphone screen—he didn't dare use the flash, which he considered too bright. He found nothing useful, intel-wise, and the emir's laptop—his target—was nowhere in sight.

He heard restful breathing in the next room but, deciding not to tempt fate, he turned back. The potential intelligence he could glean from the laptop was of limited value: he would probably find nothing more than the recruits' travel documentation. True, the data would help foreign governments arrest them when and if they returned home, but the DIA had plenty of operatives working on fighter identification already: a favorite tactic was to pose as Muslim women online and get into Skype conversations with Islamic State militants. The operatives would claim to be looking for husbands, and once they determined whether the victim was on a laptop or a phone, they'd send a photo with the appropriate viral payload—a variant of Regin, incidentally—that gave complete access to the device. They'd keep the militant talking while sifting through their storage for identifying documents and pictures. On the rare occasion they even found battle plans.

The Islamic State minibus arrived a few days later, dropping off camp supplies and picking up Ethan and the other graduates of part two. On the side was written, in Arabic, *Dawlah Islamiyah al Iraq wa Shaam*. The Islamic State of Iraq and Syria.

Three women cloistered together in the back of the bus. Wearing *niqabs*, or full black veils, none of the black ghosts said anything, nor would they during the whole trip. That was the first time Ethan had seen any women since leaving Syria, and he suspected they were foreigners on their own hegira. Ethan had heard rumors that women were billeted on the north side of the village, in an all-sisters house. The minibus must have made a stop there beforehand, giving the women a chance to board secretly.

The minibus drove to the Islamic State stronghold of Al-Ra'i, where the passengers transferred onto a bigger bus, joining graduates from other border camps. There wasn't enough room for everyone, so the group was split. Ethan bid farewell to Ibrahim and those other graduates who were separated.

Ethan, William and Aaron overnighted with the remaining recruits in a mosque guesthouse, then set out again in the morning. They headed southeast across land that alternated between dry steppe and desert, passing other Islamic State-controlled cities on their journey, including Al Bab and Manbij. The bus stopped several times to traverse mujahadeen checkpoints. At least the roads were decent, with only the occasional pothole. Highway traffic was minimal.

At one point during the ride, a recruit excitedly announced that he'd connected with the phone network. Ethan turned on his Android and sure enough obtained a signal, albeit a very weak one. After dismissing the MTNSyria welcome message, which encouraged him to "feel at home while he roamed on the MTN network," Ethan emailed Sam an encrypted update. The weak signal faded shortly thereafter.

The dry grassland became more prominent as they neared the Euphrates, and the scenery soon turned green, at least for a while. The bus crossed the river via the Tishrin Dam, passing another checkpoint, and then the desert consumed the countryside once more.

The sandy landscape eventually gave way to bedrock, and bedrock to farmland as they approached the Euphrates again. The occasional abandoned village came into view—white-washed homes with blast-damaged walls and bullet-riddled windows. Burnt out pickup trucks and other vehicles sometimes strewed the roads. The small mosques Ethan saw weren't immune to the damage, and many were partially collapsed.

Roughly four hours from Al-Ra'i the bus approached a city whose stooping buildings covered the landscape from horizon to horizon. Road traffic had picked up, though Ethan thought it was less than what it should have been, that close to a major city.

When the bus reached the outskirts it slowed down, coming to a rolling stop as it neared another checkpoint.

The two young mujahadeen on duty immediately waved them through.

"Salaam my brothers!" one of them shouted. "Welcome to Al Raqqah! Welcome home!" He fired his AK-47 into the air.

He was answered by a chorus of "Allahu akbars" from the passengers.

Ethan had arrived at the de facto capital of the Islamic State.

The heart of the enemy.

Raqqa, Syria.

ten

From his vantage point on the bus, the first thing Ethan noticed was how deceptively normal Raqqa appeared. Traffic was heavy, with vehicles and buses sometimes moving at a crawl. Bumper stickers proclaimed "I love jihad" and "Fight The Zionists"—much later Ethan discovered that cars owners were compelled to cover existing bumper stickers with jihadist slogans.

Syria was the domain of the Korean car. Hyundai and Kia ruled the roost: on the packed streets Ethan picked out an array of compacts, SUVs, and trucks belonging to the Korean companies: Elantras, Accents, Tucsons, H100s, Cerato Fortes, Rios, Santa Fes, Bongo Frontiers. The German car manufacturer Opel deserved an honorable mention for the rusty Omegas and Vectras Ethan saw; he also spotted two Japanese pickups in the mix, a Mitsubishi L200 and a Toyota Hilux, plus a few Honda motorcycles, and the occasional groups of men riding Chinese electric bicycles and scooters.

Everything would have seemed normal were it not for the garbage littering the roadside, with black bags sometimes piled to the height of three men on certain street corners. Then there were the Kia 4000S cab overs periodically parked at the intersections. These trucks sported Soviet ZU-2 double-barreled anti-aircraft guns in back, with masked mujahadeen standing watch beside them.

Citizens walked to and fro on the sidewalks, carrying out their lives. Their paces seemed quick, and most people avoided looking at one another. The men wore ordinary t-shirts and slacks, without head-gear, though the clothing was loose, and their hair short and unstyled. They were all unarmed. Many had beards—Ethan later learned the usual style was to go about cleanshaven or with a Saddam-style mustache, but apparently the morality police were less likely to hassle those with beards, who were considered more devout.

Every girl over ten wore a black abaya and full niqab so that not even the eyes were visible. He saw a white billboard with the Islamic State banner in the upper left, depicting a fully veiled, wraithlike figure in the center. The Arabic text below read: "My niqab is my might and my glory." All the women had at least one male chaperon.

The occasional jihadis in black robes or desert digital fatigues roved the streets, moving like royalty among the citizens. They wore AK-47s or AKMs slung over their shoulders. Their beards were well trimmed, and some wore black turbans or balaclavas. Several carried scarves—probably repurposed keffiyehs—around their necks, which could be raised to shield the lower halves of their faces.

Sand-colored, boxlike buildings, two to three stories tall, crowded either side of the road. Shops dominated the lower levels, though only a few seemed open. He saw a clothing store with photos of male models dressed in business suits on the windows—the models' heads had been blotted out by big red circles. Islamic music and revolutionary anthems blared from some stores, always in male voices, and always unaccompanied by instruments. The upper levels were reserved for residents, and the balconies were invariably covered in sunblinds, partially to keep out the sun, but mostly to prevent outsiders from espying their women. Some of the rooftops had crenellations, the kind found at the tops of medieval castles. Those would make good sniper hides.

Ethan glanced down a random side street and saw a city block that was completely devastated. Rebar jutted out of gutted, bomb-ravaged buildings like bronze bones. Smashed vehicles in the street below lay buried underneath chunks of concrete. The apocalyptic vision quickly receded, replaced by ordinary life again.

Ethan checked his cellphone. No network carrier. He was able to use his offline map application to follow along with the driver, as GPS still functioned thanks to a few tweaks Aaron had applied to the phone. Ethan marked off obvious Islamic State buildings on the map as points of interest to report to Sam later.

The driver soon turned onto a traffic circle with a clock tower at its center. The base of the rectangular tower was covered in the black standards of the Islamic State: at the top of each flag white text proclaimed the first part of the Shahada in Arabic. *la ilaha illallah.* "There is no God but Allah." In a white circle below it, black text completed the Islamic creed: *Muhammadun rasul allah.* "Muhammad is the messenger of God." Cresting the clock tower were the statues of two peasants, a man and a woman both dressed in traditional robes. The man held a torch to the heavens. The heads of both statues had been ominously decapitated.

As the bus moved deeper into the city, the black flag of the Islamic State became more prevalent, showing up everywhere: on street corners, markets, electricity poles. The walls of markets were painted black, as were certain buildings guarded by jihadists. So much black. It was on their soldiers. Their women. Their flags. Buildings. Black. The color of the Islamic State. The color of fear.

The bus driver spoke into his two-way radio, apparently asking for permission to drop off the recruits. The word "full!" echoed loudly from the speaker, followed by another location to try.

The bus was waved through a security checkpoint manned by young militants, and then turned onto a traffic circle labeled *Na'eem* on the offline map. The word meant paradise. At the center of the circle was a wrought iron fence with heads mounted on its spikes. The decapitated bodies of the owners lay beneath each head.

The bus circumnavigated the circle and turned south. In moments the vehicle arrived at a gated complex, stopping in front of a Soviet-era Ural-4320 6x6 military truck. Beyond the tall stone fence, Islamic State banners waved from the top of what appeared to be repurposed government buildings.

Four mujahadeen with AK-47s stood guard at the main gate, and after a quick exchange with the driver, they opened the iron barrier. These men didn't bother to greet the passengers. When the gate shut behind the bus, Ethan had a hard time shaking the feeling he'd arrived at a prison.

The driver opened the doors at the main building, a three-story, pillared monstrosity. There were about twenty arches held up by long piers, with a colonnade supported by six more pillars above the entrance. The roof was flat, and beyond the upper railings dark-clad mujahadeen patrolled with Kalashnikovs.

A bored young jihadi greeted them at the entrance and led the twenty recruits to an office, where an older man, an administrator of some kind likely hired from the local Syrian populace, sat behind a desk with a larger model two-way radio. He wore a well-trimmed religious beard, and had no headgear of any kind.

"Salaam, brothers," the man said in formal Arabic. He sounded... resigned. "I am Akeem al'Shaam, the administrator of barrack twelve. There is no one here to receive you now. Please, have a seat and rest." He repeated the word for sit in other languages, and the recruits settled in for what would prove a long wait.

About three hours later Akeem's radio squawked to life; after a muted conversation, he spoke to the recruits again. "Please, Arabic speakers, stand on the right."

Ethan and those others who spoke Arabic moved where Akeen indicated.

"Speak English, stand here," Akeem said in broken English. Four British recruits strode to the center of the room.

"Parlez Français, tenez ici," Akeem said. Four more men moved to the left.

Two recruits remained. "Chechen?" Akeem said.

Both men nodded.

Akeem made a note on a pad of paper, then turned toward the Arabic speakers. "Are there any of you who would prefer to remain together?"

Ethan exchanged a glance with William and Aaron, but neither of the operatives raised a hand.

He remembered Sam's words. *When you're surrounded by brainwashed fanatics whose sole purpose in life is death by glorious jihad, it's good to have normal people to ground you.* Despite how she felt, he knew it would be better if they separated. The three of them were lone wolfs, and they'd simply get more done if they were apart. It seemed as if they were going to be lodging in the same barracks anyway, so they could probably communicate in the cafeteria and so forth after hours. And if not, they always had their clandestine RF devices.

Akeem repeated the question in the other languages, and the English, French, and Chechen recruits all raised their hands in turn, apparently wanting to stick together.

The administrator spoke quietly into his two-way radio and a few minutes later a man with the look of a hardened general arrived. He was dressed in green-black fatigues with a camo baseball cap, and sported a trim Abe Lincoln beard. He carried an American M16A4 assault rifle over one shoulder—the weapon used NATO 5.56x45mm cartridges, a powerful round that should be scarce in Syria, but the militants probably had a steady supply courtesy of the munitions captured in Iraq.

"I only need one recruit," the man snapped at Akeem in Arabic. Ethan knew he was an Afghan immediately by the accent.

The administrator hurriedly pointed at Ethan.

The Afghan glanced at him; those steely eyes studied him in appraisal. Then he waved curtly. "Come."

Ethan followed the man out of the office.

"I am Abdullah Hazir," the Afghan said. "Emir of *Al-Dhi'b Suriya.*" Wolf Company. "And what are you called?"

"My name is Emad," Ethan answered.

"You have made your hegira from Saudi Arabia?" Abdullah said, guessing his accent.

"Yes," Ethan said.

Abdullah flashed him a wolfish grin. "I have fought side by side with many Saudis in my time. You are savage fighters."

Ethan smiled, doing his best to appear proud of the complement.

Abdullah led him through the pristine government hallways. The floor was waxed to a polish, the walls seemed to have a fresh coat of paint, and every light fixture was in working order.

The emir took him to a processing room of sorts, where a few laptops had been placed on desks. He sat down at one of them and powered up a laptop. "Belongings on the desk. Give me your passport."

Glancing at the A4 slung over the man's shoulder, Ethan complied.

The Afghan took a picture of Ethan's face with his built-in webcam and then keyed in his passport information, just as emir Haadi had done at the border camp. That the so-called state didn't have interconnected networks to share the information came as no surprise to Ethan.

Abdullah paused to review the training scorecard Ethan had inside his passport. "An expert marksman?"

Ethan nodded.

The emir rifled through his belongings and didn't bat an eye at the USB stick or the lockpick set. He smirked when he discovered the TruPulse laser range finder, and peered through the eyepiece. "You came here well prepared. I admire the initiative." He made Ethan unlock his smartphone and proceeded to skim through the contacts, messages, and media.

Apparently satisfied with what he had seen, Abdullah allowed Ethan to repack his stuff. He sent a job to the room's network printer and signed the resultant official-looking document. It specified Ethan's barracks location and emir. Abdullah told Ethan he was to present the document at the main gate whenever he wanted to leave or return.

Abdullah brought Ethan to a supply room. Just inside, two desks joined at right angles blocked the entrance: beyond them a middle-aged man who looked like a Syrian civilian sat on duty. Several equally spaced racks divided the room into sections, and each rack overflowed with boxes of munitions and supplies.

"Ah, emir, it is good to see you!" The clean-shaven Syrian hastily stood up and extended a palm.

Abdullah made no effort to shake his hand. "Do you have any sniper rifles?" he asked brusquely.

"We should be getting a shipment of M24s from Mosul this week. And I have a couple of Dragunovs slated to arrive tomorrow or the day after. Should I add you to the waiting list?"

"Move me to the top of the list," Abdullah growled.

"You know I can't—"

Abdullah grabbed the weaselly man by the collar.

"Done!" The Syrian quickly typed a note into a laptop beside him. "Anything else?"

Abdullah released his collar and nodded toward Ethan. "He needs a weapon in the meantime. And gear."

"Of course!" the Syrian said. "The typical rookie gear?"

"What do you think?" Abdullah roared impatiently. He lifted the baseball cap to wipe the sweat from his forehead.

The supply officer retreated among the racks and returned a moment later carrying an AKM rifle and its associated cartridges, along with a sheathed combat knife and a chest harness.

"No body armor?" Abdullah said, sounding exasperated.

"We have a bunch on back order from Mosul," the Syrian said, cringing slightly as if he feared his words might invoke the wraith of the emir. "We should be getting them in a few weeks. You're at the top of the list."

Ethan examined the harness. There was a two-way radio tucked inside a pouch in the center. He opened the quick release buckle, revealing the make and model: a Hytera TC-610. A standard off-the-shelf two-way; anyone within range who flipped to the same channel could eavesdrop. He closed the pouch and donned the harness over his fatigues.

Ethan loaded a cartridge into the AKM and tested the weight, then slid the sling over his shoulder. He shoved the spare cartridges into his pockets. Next he withdrew the knife from its sheath, and recognized the make immediately: a Russian-made Kizlyar Voron-3. The black, 55-58 HRC stainless steel blade was as good as any Gerber out there. Ethan sheathed the weapon and threaded the leather holder into his belt.

The supply officer meanwhile had gone back among the racks; he returned with a black balaclava and a headband. The latter contained the full Shahada. Ethan pocketed the balaclava, and while Abdullah watched he tied the headband over his keffiyeh.

"Now you are a proper mujahid," the emir said approvingly.

Abdullah led him toward Wolf Company's quarters. Along the way he showed Ethan the cafeteria on the first floor, which was already starting to fill with militants eager for supper, and the computer room on the second, which had its own satellite Internet hotspot.

Emerging from the stairwell on the third floor, they passed a line of mujahadeen queued outside a door.

"We must share this bathroom with the entire floor," Abdullah said. "Within, there are four toilet stalls, two sinks, and one shower."

The men in line lowered their gazes deferentially as the emir passed. Though he bore no outward signs of rank, evidently they all knew who he was.

Abdullah opened a door labeled three-ten and stepped inside. "Come, meet your brothers."

eleven

Ethan followed Abdullah and found himself in what appeared to be a former presentation room. Graduated floor levels littered with sleeping bags, backpacks and other belongings led to a far wall. Metal desks and chairs had been piled one atop the other in the top left corner.

Militants were engaged in calisthenics in the main area in front of a whiteboard and projector screen. One of the participants counted out each pushup. Engrossed as they were in the exercise, no one noticed the arrival of the emir.

Weapons leaned against the wall near the entrance. There were ten Kalashnikovs: five AK-47s and five AKMs. A Dragunov sniper rifle. Two general purpose Soviet PKM light machine guns.

Abdullah led him up the graduated floor levels and pointed out a spot. "Your belongings go here."

Ethan dropped his stuff in the space Abdullah indicated.

When the militants finished the current round of pushups, Abdullah announced loudly, "Salaam, my wolves. We have another new member today. Meet Abu-Emad, who has come to us all the way from Saudi Arabia."

Ethan was met with smiles and nods of greeting. He was expecting a few skeptical scowls, or even open hostility from some of the members—the kind of looks he would receive upon first joining a unit in any normal army—but these men seemed happy, to a man, that Ethan had come. And why wouldn't they be? Another martyr had come to join them in the long march to paradise.

Ethan recognized Ibrahim and Osama Al'Jordani from the training camp; those two started forward, but Abdullah raised a hand.

"We will handle the introductions over supper," Abdullah said with his typical Afghan brusqueness. "Come, we eat!"

The men filed out the door, snatching up their weapons on the way. It seemed odd to bring a rifle to supper, but Ethan wasn't going to argue.

While waiting in the food line at the cafeteria, Ethan reacquainted himself with Ibrahim and Osama.

"It is good to see you again, Ibrahim."

"*Abu*-Ibrahim, now," the sixteen-year-old beamed. "And he is Abu-Osama."

Abu technically meant "father of." It was part of a *kunya*, or teknonym—the practice of referring to adults by the names of their eldest children as a sign of respect. Umm was the female equivalent, which meant "mother of." However, fictional kunyas were often used as *noms de guerre* among fighters, and they either chose the names themselves or bestowed them upon each other. The concept was similar to American callsigns. In this case, Abu implied "brother" more than anything else.

"Well, I guess I'm Abu-Emad," Ethan said.

Ibrahim smiled. "Yes, that's how the emir introduced you. But you know you can choose any kunya you want, right?"

Ethan found Ibrahim's grin infectious. "Then why did you choose Abu-Ibrahim?"

Ibrahim shrugged. "It's easier for me to remember. It is my name, after all."

"And that's why I'm sticking with Emad." He patted the teen on the shoulder. "Never thought I'd see you again."

"It is Allah's will," the youth said. "We were meant to be together."

With a serving spoon, Ethan filled his plate from a communal bowl of chicken and rice, then broke off a piece from a flatbread loaf the size of a manhole cover. He joined the unit at a long table capable of seating ten per side.

Abdullah proceeded to introduce Ethan to the members he didn't know.

Harb, or "war," was the youngest at thirteen years old. He was a local, a graduate of one of the Islamic State's infamous child training camps. His father had apparently died in a bazaar suicide attack blamed on a rival group.

Harb stood about three heads below Ethan's own height—about average for his age. He appeared somewhat malnourished, with deep-set eyes and hollow cheeks. Ethan would have expected a haunted look to the youth, given what had happened to his father, but he seemed content, his eyes glinting with the usual jihadist zeal.

"When my father died," Harb said. "I wanted to join him in paradise. I almost volunteered for a martyrdom operation, but after I was drafted into the youth camp I realized that was not my path. *This* is my road." He patted his Kalashnikov. "I must do my duty for Allah and stay in this world for as long as He wills it, killing as many infidels along the way as I can. I will help my brothers free Syria from the chains of the oppressor, and solidify the gains made by our righteous state."

Ethan thought back to what he himself had been doing when he was thirteen: chasing girls in the schoolyards and malls, not fighting for his life in a broken country for some war he didn't understand.

Next Abdullah introduced Fida'a and Raheel. Both of them glanced up from their meals to give the fist and forefinger salute.

"They are recent college graduates," Abdullah said. "Abu-Fida'a majored in the arts, Abu-Raheel the sciences."

"I wanted to be a journalist," Fida'a said. The man had eyebrows so thick that Ethan wondered if they impinged on his vision and bestowed a hairy ceiling to the world. "But defending my brother Muslims in Syria from the Assad regime was far more important."

Bashar Al-Assad, the official president of Syria, ruled from the southwest corner of the country in Damascus. In 2011, when the Arab Spring movement spread to Syria, with protesters demonstrating in favor of democracy and free elections, Assad squelched them with violence, causing civil war to break out. The air force bombed rebel-owned territory, often utilizing highly-inaccurate "barrel bombs" that resulted in massive collateral damage. Chemical weapons were employed. Civilians died by the truckload. The attacks rarely made the international news.

It was an overtly sectarian war. Various Sunni rebel groups including the Free Syrian Army and the Islamic Front fought openly against the Shia government forces and militias. Initially the rebels seemed to be winning, and conquered large swaths of territory. Then in 2013 the Islamic State entered the war.

At first the rebel groups cheered the arrival of the Islamic State, as they were fellow Sunnis, and they made plans to fight together. Unfortunately, suicide bombers from IS infiltrated their command structures and began assassinating their leaders. The rebels fought back, fighting a war on two fronts, but quickly lost territory, allowing the Islamic State to assume control of most of the country's oil and gas production.

Ethan looked at Fida'a with pity. He and the others truly believed they were liberating the country from the Assad regime. Fida'a couldn't see that the Islamic State was a parasite organization that had moved in to take advantage of a destabilized nation. All the Islamic State had done so far was "liberate" the locals from the very people who had fought on their behalf.

"Abu-Fida'a is Algerian," Abdullah continued. "While Abu-Raheel is Indian." The name meant fearless. "An Indian who speaks Arabic. Who would have thought? It is true our religion unites the world."

Next Abdullah introduced two men in their early twenties. Beneath their fatigues were the bulges of toned muscles.

"Abu-Jabal and Abu-Baghdadi are our heavy gunners," Abdullah said. "Both hail from Tunisia."

Ethan didn't actually consider the bulky PKMs hanging from their shoulders heavy guns, but he nodded politely.

"Greetings, fellow holy warrior." Jabal got up, shook Ethan's hand in a vise-like grip, and gave him a kiss on either cheek. His name meant mountain.

Baghdadi merely nodded from where he sat. "Welcome, brother."

Abdullah pointed out the men beside them. "Abu-Yasiri is our second youngest in the company, at fifteen. Like Abu-Harb, he's a local conscript." The indicated youth nodded. His kunya was derived from the family name of a descendant of the Prophet.

"And Abu-Sab is our resident Qatari."

"Salaam," a dark-skinned man said. He was too young to grow a beard, and wore a white keffiyeh tied with black cord. His name meant Lion.

Abdullah gestured at the big man seated across from him. "And that is Abu-Zarar, a ferocious fighter from my native Afghanistan." Zarar appeared to be in his forties, and had shrapnel scars covering the right half of his face. He towered over everyone present, even while seated. His chest was at least twice as big as that of an ordinary man.

"Abu-Zarar is one of my brothers from the days when we fought the Taliban," Abdullah said. "He is a formidable warrior. He once took three bullets in the chest and kept fighting long enough to shoot down five Taleb and carry a wounded man a mile to safety."

Zarar inclined his head. "Allah was with me that day."

"As he is everyday," Abdullah said warmly. He turned toward the last person at the table. "And finally we have Abu-Suleman. An Iraqi."

Ethan recognized the bronze-skinned man who had led the physical training session. His face was gaunt, angular, with a wide jaw and broad brow. One of his cheeks was darker than the other, as if he had suffered some sort of blunt trauma that had never fully healed.

But the feature that stood out most for Ethan were those eyes, which burned with a zeal far greater than any he had ever seen. Zeal and condescension. Those eyes seemed tortured somehow, too, as if

Suleman had witnessed unspeakable things. Or committed them.

"Abu-Suleman is our official sniper," Abdullah continued. "So with your arrival, Abu-Emad, we now have two." He gave Suleman a sly look. "He's not used to competition. He'll have to step up his game."

Jealousy momentarily flashed in Suleman's eyes, but he lowered his gaze so that Ethan could no longer read him.

"Allah-willing, no man will ever outgun me, emir," Suleman said, his voice sounding extremely subservient. "I will not fail you. I will fill ten pools with the blood of the *kaffir* before I am done." Kaffir meant infidel.

Abdullah smiled grimly. "I know you will."

Suleman glanced at Ethan. The fervent zeal shone brighter than ever in those eyes. "It is good that you have come to wage jihad, brother. We need more devout Muslims. People who understand what we are trying to build here. People who hate the kaffir as much as we do."

"We will build something great," Ethan agreed, doing his best to sound enthusiastic, though the man made his skin crawl in that moment.

"Abu-Suleman also serves as my second," Abdullah said. "I have never known a more loyal man."

Suleman smiled appreciatively, like a dog petted by its master.

Fida'a abruptly produced a smartphone and prepared to take a photo. Some of the militants retrieved balaclavas from their cargo pockets and covered their faces. Ethan thought it wise to hide his own features, so he wrapped the bottom part of his keffiyeh around his mouth and nose so that he looked like a bandit.

When they were suitably attired, they all made the fist and forefinger gesture, and Fida'a snapped his picture.

"We often take photos and videos of the brotherhood," Abdullah explained. "And post them on social media. You must do this, too."

Ethan nodded. "I'll bring my phone next time." Of course he had no plans to abet the Islamic State's recruitment efforts.

When the meal was done, Abdullah led the men from the cafeteria.

On the way out Ethan passed near William, who had just finished eating with his own unit.

"So, what do you think?" Ethan asked his friend quietly in Arabic. He didn't dare risk his cover by speaking English—even in hushed tones the language would be readily identifiable.

"I think we're in for an... interesting operation," William replied.

"The only easy day was yesterday," Ethan said, quoting a Navy SEAL motto. The slogan sounded wrong, somehow, in guttural Arabic.

twelve

The next morning after PT and breakfast Abdullah led the unit to the parking lot and told Ethan to ride with Suleman. Ethan hopped into the passenger side of a bright and shiny Mitsubishi L200 pickup. Harb jumped into the rear bed to babysit the modified ZU-23-2 anti-aircraft gun that squatted there.

"Where are we going?" Ethan asked Suleman.

"Checkpoint duty," Suleman answered, driving from the compound and pulling behind the four other vehicles of Wolf Company. Though it was early, the road traffic was already heavy.

"So, what do you think?" Suleman asked.

Ethan was slightly perturbed at hearing the exact same question he'd asked William the night before, and he wondered if Suleman had overheard. He studied the militant's profile and decided it was a coincidence.

"It's everything I dreamed of," Ethan said, resorting to the stock responses expected of him. "Finally, I feel like I'm part of something bigger than myself. Like I'm making a difference. Like I truly belong."

"You are from Saudi Arabia, yes?" Suleman said.

"I am."

"Our brothers there, they cannot make a difference in your country?"

"Not as much as they could if they came here," Ethan said.

"The brothers could plan a martyrdom operation against the embassies, and do their part to show their support for Dawlah. Urge them when you post on social media."

Ethan shook his head. "I can tell them, but the security in Saudi Arabia is extremely tight, my friend."

Suleman grunted in disappointment, as if he thought Ethan was somehow not radical enough, despite the fact he'd come all that way to wage jihad in the name of the Islamic State.

Into the conversational gap that followed, Ethan said, "I'm surprised it's so busy this early."

"Everyone rushes to get to work in the mornings, while the power is on," Suleman said. "At noon, when the electricity is cut, you won't find many shops open. At this time of year, when it is so hot, most close for siesta anyway. When the afternoon prayer is done, the roads quickly clear, so that by the time of evening prayer the city is dead. After dusk, the traffic picks up again as the night cools. Some shops reopen, using diesel generators for power, only to close again after ten so that everyone can get home by curfew."

Ethan saw a band of a niqab-wearing women who flourished Kalashnikovs. They looked like black-clad stormtroopers from Star Wars. Suleman explained they were part of the Khansa'a Brigade, a group of thirty women enforcers who earned around two hundred US dollars a month patrolling the streets and ensuring other women obeyed the rules. Basically the female version of the *Hisbah*, or morality police.

The lead pickup in the convoy lurched to an unexpected halt. Led by Abdullah, four AK-wielding militants leaped out of the bed and began setting up a checkpoint.

"Put your radio on channel two." Suleman parked the Mitsubishi L200 behind the other pickups and got out.

Ethan activated his radio and flipped to the pre-programmed channel, then joined Suleman, who had taken up a position on the sidewalk along with three others. The remaining militants handled the street traffic, conversing with each motorist individually before letting them through. A long queue of vehicles had already formed.

"What exactly are they looking for?" Ethan said.

"Weapons, mostly," Suleman said. "If a motorist has arms of any kind on board, we're going to impound the vehicle and imprison the driver and passengers, because they are most likely rebels. Also, no scandalous music must be playing on the radio."

Ethan returned his attention to the sidewalk. "And what about us?" Pedestrian traffic was just starting to ramp up.

"We perform random searches for weapons, cigarettes and cell-phones. If we find a smartphone, we check that they do not have any obscene music, or any illegal photos of the city."

"Okay," Ethan said.

"We must also watch that the men and women are properly dressed and behaved. For the women, this means full veils and abayas. For the men, proper hairstyles, and no short pants. Both sexes must wear loose clothing. The women must not talk too loudly. And so forth."

Ethan felt his brow furrow. "Sounds like we're doing the job of the Hisbah."

"There is some overlap with their jobs, yes. We must all do our part to enforce sharia while we are here." Suleman formed a fist with his free hand and raised his index finger. "We are all Hisbah, in a sense. Just because you are not officially a member of the morality police, is it not your duty, as a devout Muslim, to ensure the law is obeyed? That Allah is pleased?"

The day passed slowly. Ethan didn't see anyone improperly dressed, and those men he patted down had neither weapons nor smartphones. Suleman always looked inside the piles of flatbread people carried from a nearby bakery; apparently the craftier citizens tried to smuggle cigarettes that way.

Suleman made a point of greeting veiled women and their chaperons, mostly to ensure the women answered with a feminine voice—he explained that rebels sometimes tried to sneak past in niqabs. He and Ethan often checked the IDs of the women and their chaperons to ensure the males were properly related: they were required to be either brother, father, or husband.

"This is good," Suleman announced. "Every day fewer and fewer violate our laws. It is a sign that we are succeeding. Crime rates are almost nonexistent. We are creating a heaven on Earth here, Abu-Emad. We really are."

About ten minutes before the call to prayer, shops started to close, and the flows through the checkpoint waned to nothing. One young man came jogging past about five minutes before the call, and Suleman scolded the youth. "Hurry up, you slow-footed fool!" He fired his rifle into the air, making the youth run faster.

"Now you are showing the proper vigor!" Suleman said. "Allahu ahkbar!"

"Allahu ahkbar!" the youth answered.

The members of Wolf Company maneuvered their vehicles so that the empty road was blocked off completely, then they raced toward the nearest mosque as the call to prayer echoed through the air. By then the city had become a veritable ghost town as the last stragglers hurried into the mosque, and Ethan had the eerie sensation that the voice of the muezzin served as an air raid siren or some other herald of doom.

The main prayer hall was full, so Ethan and the others were forced to use the overflow in the balcony, which was equally packed, though men made room for them. The overflow was ordinarily reserved for women, but since the female gender was relegated to non-entity status by the Islamic State, and no longer allowed to pray in the mosques, the men were happy to use it.

When prayers were done, the group made its way down the stairs with the rest of the congregation.

"Do you notice how many come to pray?" Suleman said fervently. "I told you we were succeeding here. Creating an Earthly heaven."

Ethan's eyes drifted over the departing crowd and settled on a man dressed in a white thawb with a matching cap on his head. He wore an external harness with a pistol holstered on the side and a two-way radio secured to the front. Despite the close confines, the crowd managed to give him a respectful berth; he was like an oceangoing icebreaker—the densely packed men yielded before him like ice before the bow.

"Who's that?" Ethan said.

"One of the Hisbah." Suleman glanced at Ethan knowingly. "You envy him, don't you? Look at the respect other men show him. Greater even than they show us." His voice was filled with awe. All of a sudden he shoved Ethan forward. "Go ahead, join him in his rounds."

"But—"

"All of us should walk fully in the shoes of the Hisbah for at least one day." Suleman turned toward Abdullah, who was just behind. "Emir, may Ethan join the Hisbah for the rest of his shift?"

Abdullah regarded the receding figure of the Hisbah thoughtfully. "We have more than enough mujahadeen to man the checkpoint. By all means. It will be good for him." He turned toward Ethan. "Abu-Emad, go introduce yourself."

Ethan reluctantly made his way toward the man. He told himself it wouldn't be so bad—he never knew when a good intel opportunity might present itself, after all.

Ethan moved through the crowd and flagged down the Hisbah.

The individual in question had a well-maintained Abe Lincoln beard, with placid features and gentle eyes. He smiled calmly at Ethan. "How can I help you, brother?" He spoke perfect formal Arabic, and there was a knowing twinkle to his eye, as if he thought himself privy to knowledge hidden from other men.

"What is your name, brother?" Ethan said.

"Abu-Kaleem," the man answered.

"I am Abu-Emad. I would be honored to come with you during your shift today. If you would have me."

Kaleem's grin deepened. "Of course, brother! Let me inform my deputy." Kaleem spoke quietly into his two-way radio, and then rested a hand on Ethan's shoulder and led him from the mosque.

Together they toured the streets at a moderate pace, following what was apparently Kaleem's beat. They moved from shop to shop, inspecting the goods. Kaleem explained that it was his job to ensure everything sold was of good quality, and that the shopkeepers weren't overcharging people.

Kaleem passed a pile of garbage bags on one street corner that reached chest high, and he conscripted several passersby to remove "that eyesore" immediately. Ethan suspected the conscripts would simply dump the trash in a nearby alley or ditch.

Kaleem continued on his way, eventually stopping beside a clothing shop. He carefully scrutinized the windows before going inside.

A fully veiled saleswoman stood in one corner like a black ghost. She bowed her head immediately. A male salesman, probably the shopkeeper, nervously approached. "Salaam, blessed Hisbah."

Ethan thought the tanned, slightly overweight man was in his forties, though his full head of hair betrayed no gray—the unnatural sheen made Ethan think it was dyed. He had a lazy left eye, the half-closed lid making the other eye bulge in comparison. The absence of a beard was conspicuous.

"Salaam," Kaleem answered distractedly.

"What may I do for you today, blessed Hisbah?" the shopkeeper said. Ethan noticed he was trying very hard to use formal Arabic rather than colloquial Syrian.

Kaleem grinned widely but didn't say a word. He moved about the shop imperiously, inspecting the clothing and price tags as suited his whims. He paused beside one particular item of clothing. "This one is too expensive. You are cheating the citizens of their hard-earned money. Lower the price."

Ethan had the sense Kaleem was putting on a show for his benefit.

"Yes, blessed Hisbah," the shopkeeper said.

"Let me see your IDs," Kaleem said.

He studied the documents the man and woman produced. "You are husband and wife?"

"Yes, blessed Hisbah."

Kaleem returned the IDs and approached the sales counter from the far side. Ethan had remained near the entrance, which afforded him a clear view of the counter's opposite flank. As Kaleem neared, a young man was flushed out from behind the counter, toward Ethan. The teen stayed low, trying to keep from Kaleem's sight. He obviously hadn't realized Ethan was there, because when the youth saw him standing by the entrance, his eyes widened in fear.

Ethan glanced at the shopkeeper, who had gone very pale. The man was harboring a known rebel, apparently. Ethan returned his attention to the teen and shook his head ever so slightly.

A puzzled expression appeared on the youth's face but he seemed to understand that Ethan wasn't going to turn him in.

Kaleem spun about. "We're done here." He moved toward the door; the youth quickly dodged behind the counter and out of view.

"*Allah yusallmak!*" the shopkeeper called to their backs as they left. God protect you. The relief was obvious in his voice.

Ethan smiled inwardly. He had found his first asset. He inconspicuously noted the place on his offline map as he followed Kaleem.

The Hisbah skirted a sprawling, block-long queue to enter a bakery. Ethan remained outside, keeping a watchful eye on the crowd. He had the sense it was the only food store open in the entire neighborhood.

A man in line suddenly went ballistic and started pointing at Ethan and cursing.

"You and your Caliphate are the reason none of us have any food!" the mustached man said. "Do you see the children scrounging for scraps in the gutter? The hawkers at the street corners selling whatever junk they find in the hopes they'll have enough money to afford the exorbitant food costs? And where is the promised garbage collection? The bags pile up, but no one collects them. And you call yourself a state. Shame on you."

The two people with him, an elderly man and a fully veiled woman of undisclosed age, probably his parents, attempted to calm the individual and hold him back, but he broke free of their grasp and pointed accusingly at Ethan.

"Your Caliphate is not a paradise, but a hell! You are the same as the Assad pig. Worse! You do not follow Allah, or Muhammad. You are followers of the devil!" He began cursing the Islamic State, Allah, and Muhammad. A crime punishable by beheading.

Other people in line gave him room, not wanting to be close when the shit hit the fan.

"Shut up you fool!" Ethan told the perpetrator, glancing over his shoulder.

Kaleem was going to come out any moment, and when he did, the man was as good as dead.

thirteen

The man wouldn't stop cursing.

Ethan shook him. "I'm trying to save your life!"

The perpetrator made a grab for Ethan's AKM, which still hung from his shoulder. Ethan deftly sidestepped, maneuvering behind the individual. He wrapped his forearms around the man's neck in a sleeper hold and squeezed.

The man clawed at Ethan's arms with his nails. The mother cried out. The father wept, ripping hair from his beard. "Please!" the father shouted.

The perpetrator went limp in his arms and Ethan released him, lowering him gently to the ground. The man began to stir immediately.

"What is going on here?" Kaleem announced in an authoritative tone. He paused to take in the scene. The collapsed individual on the ground. The wailing mother. The weeping father who had pieces of his own beard in his hands.

Ethan did his best to project calmness and authority. "This man fainted. Probably from heat exhaustion."

The Hisbah glanced at the people in line, who held their tongues in complicit silence, and then he rushed inside the bakery and returned with a glass of water. He knelt, elevated the perpetrator, and held the cup to his lips. "Drink, brother. Drink."

Ethan felt his insides knot up. He expected the man to start cursing again any moment, but thankfully the blackout seemed to have brought him to his senses, so to speak, and he remained silent.

The Hisbah helped him stand, and the individual thanked him profusely. As did the mother and father. All three of them were careful not to meet Ethan's eye as they returned to their places in line.

* * *

That night found Ethan back in the cafeteria of the barracks, eating dinner with the other members of Wolf Company. Like the evening before, the overhead lamps remained powered, despite the nightly blackouts affecting the rest of the city. The militants were drawing electricity from the distribution grid at the expense of the common people, apparently.

After supper, he lingered in the cafeteria, perspiring profusely: the place felt like an oven. Eventually William and Aaron finished eating with their own respective units and joined him.

"So, what news?" Ethan said.

"Only the first day and I'm already sick of chicken and rice," William said. "That's all they eat. Chicken and rice for breakfast. Chicken and rice for supper."

"Bread for lunch," Aaron added.

"Don't even get me started on the bread." William shook his head. "Whoever said variety was the spice of life forgot to mention it to these guys."

"Any leads so far?" Ethan asked.

"Too early," William answered. "I'm just getting operational."

"You're on checkpoint duty, too?"

"Ordinarily, but today my company handled crowd control during a public 'smash and burn' of haram goods in Clock Tower Square."

"Haram goods?"

"You know, cigarettes, shisha pipes, alcohol."

"Ah." He turned toward Aaron. "And what about you?"

The other operative shook his head. "Bomber watch."

Ethan frowned. "Bomber watch?"

"Yeah," Aaron said. "My guys pile into two technicals, then take up positions in random areas of Raqqa and sit there all day on the anti-aircraft guns, waiting for Assad to send his MiGs and L-39s on low altitude bombing runs."

"You do know that the air force basically stopped using MiGs and other fighters months ago, right?" William said. "Too costly. I think Assad has lost what, half his fleet by now?"

During the initial stages of the Syrian civil war, because of the few precision-guided weapons the air force possessed, the aircrafts were forced to fly low to release their payloads, placing them dangerously close to the rebel anti-aircraft artillery. William was right—those tactics had cost the air force dearly.

"Oh I know," Aaron answered. "It's all about barrel bombs these days. But try telling that to the muj. They're all new guys. Anyway, so far it's been fairly monotonous, but let's just say as soon as I hear a passing helo, I'm ducking for cover. The other fools can martyr themselves."

Barrel bombs, essentially airborne IEDs, were dropped by Mi-8 transport helicopters above ten thousand feet, beyond the range of most MANPADs and anti-aircraft guns. Made from components costing only a couple hundred dollars, the bombs were essentially oil barrels filled with chopped rebar, explosives, and jet fuel. Though the helicopters would hover in place before the drop, it was still impossible to aim with any reasonable accuracy from that height. As such, massive collateral damage was inflicted, usually resulting in severe civilian casualties. That a government would use such a weapon against its own people was morally reprehensible, to say the least. The IEDs were so heavy that sometimes they crashed straight through the roofs of buildings before detonation, taking down the entire structures and their occupants in one blow.

"But as far as leads go," Aaron continued. "When I got back today I befriended one of the men on patrol duty outside. A fellow Yemeni."

"And what did this fellow Yemeni tell you?" Ethan asked.

Aaron rapped his fingers against the glass, as if deciding whether to divulge what he had learned or not. Finally: "The Yemeni let slip that foreign journalists are being held inside another building in the complex here. I'm not going to say which one, operational compartmentalization and all that, but man, apparently the journalists are being treated brutally by the British jihadis guarding them. They beat them multiple times a day. Waterboard them for no reason. It's like the Brits want payback for all the bigotry and contempt they faced back home or something."

"You really should tell us what building they're in," Ethan said.

Aaron shrugged, saying nothing.

Ethan looked at him crossly. "You're going to try springing them on your own, aren't you?"

Aaron shot him a Cheshire cat grin. "Nothing I like more than roughing up a few pompous bullies."

As Ethan had mentioned, all three of them were lone wolfs. But even so, there were times for teamwork. Was this one of them? He regarded Aaron uncertainly. The man was one of the best operatives in the field. If Aaron thought he could spring the journalists on his own, then he probably could.

The three exchanged small talk for a while longer. As Sam had predicted, it was good to be in the company of men who were not religious radicals for once, men who wouldn't take offense and accuse him of being a kaffir for speaking his mind. He was getting tired, however, and soon bid his friends farewell.

Ethan stopped by the computer room, intending to update Sam, but when he saw the long queue of militants waiting for a free system, he left.

Back at room three-ten, he found most of the others reading the Quran, either alone or in groups. Ibrahim and Osama were playing Call of Duty on their laptops, taking advantage of the working electricity. Harb watched. Most video games were prohibited under the Islamic State's harsh brand of sharia, but no one in Wolf Company seemed to care. Everyone knew that sharia didn't apply as strictly to the foreign fighters, a double standard they were happy to exploit. Throughout history, those with the guns made the rules—and flaunted them.

Raheel, Sab, and Jabal weren't present. When he asked Harb about the trio, the youth told him they didn't sleep there. "They are married."

"Married?"

"Yes. After dinner they return to their apartments to be with their wives, then come back in the morning."

"So everyone here right now doesn't have a wife?" Ethan regarded the remaining militants under a new light.

"Yes," Harb said. "Many left their wives behind in their home countries. Abu-Zarar and emir Abdullah, for example."

"What about the rest?" Ethan said. "I thought the Caliphate provided wives? According to the smuggler who brought me here, every foreign fighter gets one."

"Well he lied. There simply aren't enough to go around. And besides, not all of us want the burden and distraction of a wife while waging jihad."

"You can't tell me you don't want to be with a woman before you die," Ethan said.

"Why does it matter?" Harb said. "When I will have a limitless supply of women in the afterlife?"

Ethan suppressed a sigh and left Harb to the computer game.

He retrieved his charger and plugged his Android phone into a spare outlet on one of the power bars. He returned to his spot on the graduated floor and spread out his sleeping bag, intending to catch some Zs early. Though any of the other members would have readily welcomed his company, Ethan thought it best to continue maintaining his distance. On the one hand he had no desire to get too attached to anyone, and on the other he didn't want to risk saying something that might blow his cover.

Nearby, Suleman was reading the Quran softly while the emir listened. Abdullah made eye contact with Ethan and waved him over.

"Yes, emir?" Ethan said.

"Sit with us."

Ethan complied.

Abdullah nodded at Suleman to continue. He read a passage related to jihad. "Kill the infidels wherever you find them. Capture them. Besiege them. Waylay them in ambush."

That was the commonly quoted "sword verse" from the Quran used to justify violence against the infidel.

"But if they should repent," Ethan said, completing the verse. "Let them go on their way. Allah is forgiving, and merciful."

"Oh, but the West will not repent," Abdullah said. "It will not." Abdullah tapped his chin. "Life is one great jihad. We must all fight. We are all at war, if not with the kaffir, then ourselves."

Ethan nodded slowly. "I can agree with that."

Abdullah studied him. "You are not like the others. You don't have the same fire in your eyes. The same zeal."

Ethan remained silent. Was it so obvious what he was?

"I can see the conflict in you, Abu-Emad," Abdullah continued. "You are fighting a great battle with yourself. You want to be here, and yet you do not. You want to take up jihad, and yet you do not. But I tell you, be at peace with yourself, because you have done the right thing. It is your duty to defend Muslims wherever and whenever the kaffir assault them. Just as it is your duty to help establish the Caliphate. Someday, inshallah, you will come to understand that you have made the right choice."

"Thank you," Ethan said.

"But one thing I must warn you of." Abdullah's voice became stern. "If you ever let any of us down, or betray us in any way, I will kill you myself. Do you hear me, Abu-Emad?"

Beside him, Suleman's eyes burned with their fanatical fire, as if he yearned to see Ethan die by Abdullah's hand.

Ethan ignored that gaze and, mustering as much conviction into his voice as he could, he said, "I will not let you down, emir."

"Allah yusallmak," Abdullah dismissed him.

Covered in sweat, Ethan lay on top of his sleeping bag and closed his eyes, but repose did not come for many hours, even after lights out. The heat troubled him. As did Abdullah's words.

If you ever let any of us down, I will kill you myself.

He thought of Suleman's fierce gaze, and he knew that Abdullah wouldn't be the only one who'd want to kill Ethan should his identity ever become compromised.

Even so, he resolved that tomorrow he would become fully operational.

fourteen

The next morning during breakfast Ethan excused himself, claiming he had to use the washroom. He abandoned the militants and rushed upstairs, but instead of heading to the toilet he made a beeline to room three-ten.

Ethan proceeded to rummage through the various belongings and backpacks of the company members. Whenever he found a passport, he set it down and snapped a picture of the photo page. Though the identities were of limited value, he wanted to start gathering at least some intel, and that was a good start.

Sometimes he found a militant's smartphone tucked away. On the Android models, all he had to do was pop the case and look behind the batteries to expose the serial number. He'd take a snapshot and then quickly replace the battery, closing up the phone. For the iPhone 4 model he found, he used one of his lockpicks to eject the SIM and then photographed the serial number engraved on the tray.

Those numbers would prove useful to any JSOC or DIA embeds in the country, who likely had Stingrays with them—devices that imitated the signature of cellphone repeaters. Basically laptops with GSM cards, the devices could trick phones into connecting and sending their serial number and geolocation. When actual network coverage was available, the Stingray could perform a man-in-the-middle attack, allowing the device to listen in on calls, texts and Internet packets while forwarding the data on to the real tower. Of course, with the encryption technology employed by jihadis today, most of that data was worthless, especially when Voice Over IP was used to send the encoded calls and texts. Even so, the geolocation data still allowed for tracking, as long as the serial number of the target was known.

Again, not super valuable intelligence, but a good beginning.

Ethan had just put away one of the phones and was about to replace the passport of the Tunisian who called himself Baghdadi when a voice arose from behind him.

"What are you doing, Abu-Emad?"

Ethan froze. He slowly returned the passport to the backpack, then retrieved his own Android from where he'd set it on the ground. He surreptitiously stuffed the cellphone into his robe and turned around.

Thirteen-year-old Harb stood at the doorway, AK slung over one shoulder.

"Salaam, Abu-Harb," Ethan said.

"Why are you rummaging through Abu-Baghdadi's belongings?"

Ethan smiled sheepishly. "I saw him reading the Quran last night. I've misplaced my own, and I didn't think he'd mind if I checked a passage."

Harb frowned. "You don't have it on your phone?"

Ethan shook his head. "The search feature is broken."

The thirteen-year-old beckoned Ethan toward his spot in the room.

"You finished breakfast early?" Ethan said, trying to sound casual. "Or did Abdullah send you up to spy me?"

"Neither. I forgot my phone and wanted to take a group picture." Harb retrieved his cell. "What passage do you want?"

Ethan told him and Harb opened his Quran app to the designated passage, the same one Abdullah and Suleman had been studying the night before.

Harb read the first line aloud. "Kill the infidels wherever you find them." He was quiet a moment, and his eyes seemed distant. "A righteous passage. I only hope that when my time comes, I will face my death as bravely as those who have gone before me."

"But this passage has nothing to do with martyrdom," Ethan declared.

Harb regarded him curiously "Doesn't it? When killing infidels, isn't it inevitable that some of us must die at their hands?"

Though he was only thirteen, sometimes the boy seemed far older.

Ethan pretended to read the whole passage, then returned to the cafeteria with Harb. When the unit was finished breakfast, Abdullah intercepted him on the way to the parking lot. He was carrying a Soviet-made Dragunov SVD sniper rifle in one hand.

"Look what arrived for you this morning." Abdullah tossed him the Dragunov.

Two-piece wooden handguard and skeletonized wooden thumbhole stock. Detachable cheek rest. Semi free-floating, spring-loaded, chrome-lined barrel. 4x magnification PSO-1 scope. Ten-round curved box magazine containing double-stacked 7.62x54mmR rimmed cartridges, each loaded with a 9.8g projectile tipped by a sharp steel penetrator.

Ethan would have preferred something like an M24 or TAC-338, but he'd take what he could get. It was a step up, anyway.

"May Allah guide your aim," the emir said, taking Ethan's AKM in exchange.

* * *

Checkpoint duty passed swiftly that morning, and near noon Abdullah gathered the unit. "Who wants to buy lunch?"

Raheel and Ibrahim immediately volunteered.

"Let Abu-Emad go," Zarar said, grinning mischievously. "And do not give him money. The new recruit should pay for everyone as a gesture of goodwill and camaraderie. It is only right." The big Afghan playfully patted Ethan on the back. "Go on then."

"I have no money," Ethan claimed. "I haven't been paid, yet."

Zarar turned toward the others. "He has no money. What do you think of that?"

"I say we send him back to Saudi Arabia," Fida'a joked. "He comes from an oil-rich country like that, and he has no money? Who does he think he is?"

"We don't need money," Suleman said, entirely serious. "This is our town. We take what we please."

"Now now," Abdullah came over, handing Ethan some Syrian pounds. "We are good Muslims. We pay for what we take. Ibrahim, go with him."

Ethan and Ibrahim made their way down the street, searching for a bakery. Since the location of the checkpoints changed daily, Ethan had to pull out his Android and activate the offline map app to orient himself. He searched the nearby points of interest, and realized the nearest bakery was the same one Kaleem had taken him to yesterday. That afforded him an opportunity...

"I'll meet you there," Ethan told Ibrahim, who had his own mapping app running. "I have to use the washroom." He passed the money to the teen.

"Wait, where's the bakery?"

Ethan pointed it out on the map.

"What if it's not open?" Ibrahim said.

"Then we'll find another one," Ethan said over his shoulder as he detoured down a side street.

In a few minutes he reached the lingerie shop he had visited with Kaleem the day before. He doubled-back, taking a quick surveillance detection route, and when he was certain neither Ibrahim nor anyone else had followed, he entered the shop.

The owner was the only one present that morning; he regarded Ethan uncertainly, his left eye seeming even lazier than usual, the lid barely open.

"Salaam," the man said cautiously. His dyed hair gleamed in the shop light.

"What is your name?"

"Mufid."

"Where is your son today?"

Mufid dropped his gaze. "He is not my son."

"The youth I saw hiding behind the counter? Don't lie to me. He has your features."

The shopkeeper swallowed. "He's only fifteen."

"He is a rebel," Ethan stated.

Mufid shook his head emphatically. "No he's not. He just writes a blog. That's all. He's not harming anyone."

"*Blog*?"

Mufid realized he had made a mistake. "I meant something else."

"What is the web address of this blog?"

"Please, I beg you," the shopkeeper fell to his knees theatrically and clasped his hands. "Please. *Please*. Take me, not my son."

Ethan sighed. "I'm not here to take you or your son."

The shopkeeper seemed uncertain. "You're not?"

"No." He helped Mufid to his feet.

"Thank you!" the shopkeeper gave him a hug.

"But there is something else you can do for me," Ethan said.

Mufid released him warily. "There is always a price."

"There is. I want you and your son to be my eyes and ears in this city."

The shopkeeper's expression became puzzled. "What is it you want us to do?"

"For starters, tag any municipal buildings with obvious ties to the Caliphate. I'm looking for government compounds, courthouses, repurposed schools, and the like. Be subtle while you're about it. Don't take pictures unless you're certain no one is watching you. Use wikimapia to look up the GPS coordinates. I'll come by in a week or so and retrieve the data. If you can put it on a memory stick, that would be perfect. Do you have something I can write on?"

Mufid seemed dazed, but he retrieved a pad from behind the desk. Ethan wrote down the username and password to one of his gmail aliases.

"We will use the draft folder of this account to communicate,"

Ethan said. "The messages must be encrypted. Do you have The Mujahid's Security?"

"No, but my son uses this."

"Good. He can teach you how it works. We'll exchange public keys in the draft folder eventually. Be aware of keyboard loggers when using the Internet cafes. Some of the computers might have screen recorders installed, too. Even The Mujahid's Security can't protect against those, which is why I don't want you sending me anything, not even your public key, until I hook you up with some anti-malware. Until then, if you must get in touch with me, use very vague generalizations."

Mufid stared at Ethan, not saying anything for a long moment. When he finally spoke, his voice sounded incredulous: "You are a mujahid of the Caliphate. Surely you can acquire this knowledge on your own? Why do you need me and my son?"

Ethan shook his head. "I'm just a grunt to them. You and your son are in a far better position. You can talk to the residents, ferret out those who have seen Caliphate activity. I can't. If I ask questions, I draw attention to myself."

"Me and my son will draw attention to ourselves, too, if we're not careful," Mufid said. "The streets are full of locals paid to inform for the Islamic State."

"Then be careful."

Mufid crossed his arms. "What are you? MOIS? Al Mukhabarat Al A'amah?" The former was the Iranian intelligence agency, the latter Saudi Arabian.

"Let's just say I'm an interested party. And I will pay you for your help. Very, very well. In Euros, American Dollars, whatever currency you prefer."

"How much?"

"The equivalent of fifty thousand US dollars."

Mufid's eyes lit up, but he quickly hid his avarice and shook his head. "That is too low for what you ask. There is much risk involved. Now, five hundred thousand—"

"Fifty thousand," Ethan interrupted. "Take it or leave it."

"I could shut down my shop and leave town," Mufid said, the defiance thick in his tone. "You would never find me or my son again."

"You could, but you won't. You're not impressed with this so-called Caliphate. You want to see the jihadis pushed from Raqqa. As does your son. Which is why he publishes that blog you mentioned." *And you want the money.*

The shopkeeper seemed on the verge of some sharp retort but then he sighed instead. "All right. I will do this. For my son."

"Thank you."

Mufid's face hardened. "But when do I get the money?"

"When you deliver the data."

* * *

Ethan hurried to the bakery, which had a long queue of people as usual. He found Ibrahim in line near the middle.

"You don't have to wait like some commoner," Ethan scolded him. "Go to the front."

"But it doesn't feel right."

Ethan was fine with waiting, but he suspected Abdullah wouldn't share his sentiments, so he said, "Do it or we'll be here all day." Best to stay on the emir's good side.

Ibrahim obeyed, and while he went inside, Ethan lingered by the entrance.

He noticed a commotion across the street; a motorcade containing two Hyundai Tucsons and a Toyota Hilux stopped in front of an apartment building. AK-47s in hand, militants piled out of each vehicle, forming a defensive perimeter. Three of the mujahadeen went to the main door of the apartment and pressed a buzzer.

Ethan surreptitiously removed his Android phone from his cargo pocket and pointed the camera at the motorcade. He doubled-checked that the smartphone's sound was turned off and took some shots.

A moment later a Chinese man emerged from the lobby with two bodyguards, and the waiting militants enveloped them. He wore a white

T-shirt and black slacks, with a blazer overtop. No headdress.

Ethan snapped a few more quick photos, keeping the phone close to his chest as the militants escorted the Chinese national to the closest SUV. A jihadi happened to look his way the moment Ethan lowered the phone, and the man waved. Ethan returned the gesture calmly, donning his best fake smile, and pocketed the phone at the same time.

Ibrahim joined him shortly afterward, carrying a pile of flatbread.

Ethan's heart was still racing in his chest as he grabbed half the bread and began the trip back to the checkpoint. If that jihadi from the motorcade had stopped him and made him reveal the contents of his phone, Ethan would have found himself in a slight bit of trouble.

There was nothing quite like intelligence gathering in the heart of enemy territory.

He loved his job.

fifteen

Ethan sat before an old Dell system in the computer room of the barracks. The place felt ovenlike, the fans of the computers pumping hot air into the cramped environment. Every last terminal was occupied by foreign fighters eager to use the building's lone satellite Internet. The hum of the fans was punctuated by the tap of keyboards and the occasional hushed voice attempting to speak over VOIP. Young men stood in a queue outside the door, waiting their turn.

The militant immediately to his left was involved in a Skype call. Ethan heard a garbled, robotic voice come from the man's headset—audio artifacts induced by the high-latency, shared connection. Ethan wondered how anyone could communicate like that. Indeed, for the most part, the fighter typed rather than spoke.

Ethan had plugged in his special USB stick, and was waiting for the anti-malware software to complete its cleanse. After several minutes the software reported that it had temporarily quarantined thirty-four threats, including a key logger, a screen tracker, and a sound recorder.

He ran the customized versions of notepad and Google chrome installed on the USB, then browsed to wikimapia and recorded the exact latitude and longitude of all the Islamic State buildings he could remember, and those he had marked on his phone. Also, using the pictures he had taken earlier, he typed up the serial numbers of the phones he'd compromised.

He logged into a shared gmail account he used to communicate with Sam and checked the draft folder. There were no messages. He loaded up The Mujahid's Security from the stick and encrypted all the text in the notepad instance. Creating a new draft message in gmail, he pasted the encrypted text.

He connected his phone to the computer via another USB port and uploaded the best photo he'd taken of the Chinese national. He encrypted it and attached it to the message, then saved the draft and logged out of gmail.

Next he installed the Regin malware. It would spread to all the other machines on the network, allowing the Agency to spy on everything the militants did in that room, and maybe elsewhere. He didn't have to worry about the DIA monitoring his own computer access when he came, because the anti-malware software he always ran at beginning of his sessions removed any local Regin instances. Not that it mattered if they monitored him—he had nothing to hide. Currently.

He restored the previously quarantined executables, returning the system to its earlier state, then wiped all the pictures from his Android phone and left.

* * *

Ethan sat with William and Aaron in the cafeteria, which also served as a rec room of sorts outside meal hours. Other militants would come there to type on laptops or study Qurans when they wanted to get away from their units.

"Any updates?" Ethan asked his fellow operatives.

"Did you hear the alarm last night?" Aaron said.

Ethan shook his head. "Slept like a baby." That wasn't entirely true, but he hadn't heard any alarms.

"Well, the journalists are free."

"Holy shit that was quick," William said.

"When I see an opportunity, I take it," Aaron bragged. "I'm not one to dawdle. Unlike you guys."

Ethan forced a smile. "Any problems?"

"Nope. The operation went off without a hitch. I didn't even have to kill anyone." He frowned. "But fricking journalists, I tell ya... they were French, you know. Kept asking me where the *hélicoptères* were. And I was like, yeah, sure, I came rappelling in on an MH-60 Black Hawk just around the corner. Finally they got it into their thick skulls that no helos were coming, and that they'd have to go into hiding."

"What did Sam say?" Ethan asked.

Aaron shrugged. "Haven't told her yet."

"Does she even know the journalists were here?"

Aaron was silent a few seconds. "No."

"I'll bet she'll be real happy when she finds out," Ethan said sarcastically.

"Why wouldn't she be? I did my job. What I was sent to do."

"I think she would've preferred that you had involved at least one of us," Ethan said.

"Are you sure it's not *you* who would've preferred that, you who claim to be the biggest lone wolf of us all? Listen, I discovered an opportunity and acted upon it. Ask for forgiveness rather than permission, right? It's how we get things done around here. Speaking of which, what have you done since we arrived? Oh wait, you must be too busy asking for permission. I remember when I used to work for the CIA. It took forever to get shit approved. I had like ten bosses above me, and each one had to approve my op before I could get the go-ahead. All it took was one chickenshit manager above me to veto the whole thing. Eventually it got to the point where I'd had enough. I started doing the ops while I was waiting for approval. And if my bosses didn't grant their consent afterward, fuck 'em. I got a helluva lot done."

"I'm guessing you had to ask for forgiveness often while working at the CIA."

Aaron smiled wolfishly. "Let's just say there's a reason I'm not working there anymore."

Ethan glanced at William. "Any news?"

"I've managed to recruit a few locals to act as my eyes and ears,"

William said. "It's not difficult. The Caliphate isn't well-liked here. Sure, the citizens openly sing the praises of the Islamic State, but once you take off the muj fatigues and get them alone you'll hear a different tune. Amazing the intel a few packages of illicit cigarettes will buy you."

Ethan thought of the fifty thousand dollars he'd promised Mufid and felt silly. Then again, he doubted William could acquire solid intel through the promise of cigarettes alone.

"What about you," William said. "What are you working on?"

"I've lined up a few locals," Ethan said. "And sent Sam the coordinates of some government compounds I've spotted. I should have more things lined up for her shortly."

"That's code for I got jack shit," Aaron mocked.

"I've also installed Regin in the computer lab," Ethan said.

"I already did that the first night," Aaron said.

Ethan stood. "Night guys."

* * *

Every morning, Wolf Company established a checkpoint at a different location. Ethan wanted to gather more intel on the Chinese national, but he had to wait until he was stationed a little closer. He could have potentially gone on a toilet break, and then commandeered a car at gunpoint, but the heavy road traffic prevented that from being any more feasible.

Each night he checked the draft folder of the gmail account he shared with Sam, and two days later he decrypted a message that read:

Identity of national: former Chinese nuclear scientist Shi Tou Mao. May be helping Islamic State construct a nuclear weapon. Can you prove the scientist's intent, and upon positive correlation, determine the fissile supplier and terminate the scientist?

Ethan left a return message:

Will prove intent and terminate upon positive correlation. If airstrikes are available, I have potential coordinates.

He doubted any sort of airstrikes were forthcoming. The West had performed a few limited bombing runs in Iraq, but so far Syria seemed off limits. Although if Sam leaked the coordinates to the Assad regime, there would almost certainly be a strike of some kind. Hopefully not a wildly inaccurate barrel bomb. Even so, before there could be any airstrikes Ethan had to confirm that the scientist actually lived in the building.

The next day Abdullah finally set up the checkpoint within a reasonable distance of the apartment. Ethan volunteered to retrieve lunch that afternoon from the bakery across the street from his target, but Abdullah made Zarar go with him.

When he reached the bakery Ethan let the big Afghan enter by himself. Ethan waited on the pavement outside, studying the apartment. The three-story tall building spanned half the block, with a couple of decorative palm trees near the entrance. All the windows were canopied in the proper Muslim style.

About a minute passed and he wondered where the motorcade was. He checked the time on his cellphone. It was almost noon. Either he'd missed the vehicles or they weren't coming that day. Maybe the pickup had been a one-time thing.

The big Afghan emerged from the shop and he and Ethan started back toward the checkpoint. Right then three militant vehicles pulled up on the opposite side of the street. Ethan glanced over his shoulder and watched the mujahadeen form the familiar perimeter. When the Chinese national and his bodyguards emerged, the militants escorted them to one of the SUVs and sped off. The chances were high that the scientist indeed lived in the building.

That night Ethan had a reply from Sam waiting in the draft folder of the gmail account.

No approval for airstrikes from HQS forthcoming. Prove the scientist's intent, and upon positive correlation determine the fissile supplier and terminate the scientist.

Ethan wrote back two words. The seemingly random characters of encrypted text spanned half a page, but when Sam decoded it the message would read: *Will do.*

Proving the target's intent would be tricky. Just because the scientist lived in the Islamic State and had an armed motorcade escort him from his apartment around noon everyday didn't prove anything other than that he was important to the Caliphate. That may have been a reason to terminate the man in and of itself, but as mentioned in her message, Sam wanted proof of the man's intentions. Ethan did, too. Gone were the days when he blindly killed for JSOC. He had developed a conscience after going to work for Sam. Taking on deep cover operations would do that to anyone, he supposed. He understood the enemy, but more so he understood how readily the White House had added relatively benign targets to the kill list in the past. Sam did, too, and was trying to distance herself and her team from that trigger-happy mentality.

Three days later when the checkpoint was finally situated close enough to the apartment once more, Ethan volunteered to retrieve lunch again.

"No, my turn today," Sab insisted.

"I have to use the toilet anyway. I'll pay!" Ethan raced off before Abdullah could make him take Sab with him.

While jogging, Ethan retrieved his phone and oriented himself with the offline map. He paused beside a couple of street vendors to make certain none of the members of Wolf Company were following him, and when he finally reached the bakery, the motorcade was already speeding off.

Ethan hadn't brought his balaclava with him, but he did have his Saudi headdress, which he had recently started to wear around his neck like a ceremonial scarf. He raised it, covering the lower half of his face, bandit-style. It wasn't a look uncommon to the mujahadeen of Raqqa.

He hurried across the road and, with a quick glance in either direction to ensure no other militants were in the area, he approached the apartment entrance. He studied the labels beside the intercom buttons. There were no obvious Chinese names. There was, however, a name plate missing beside the apartment labeled 2B. He pressed the different buttons, starting with 2B, until someone answered.

"*Allo*?" someone shouted over the speaker. "Mahmud?"

"Yes!" Ethan lied.

The lobby door buzzed open and Ethan entered. He climbed the stairs to the second floor and approached room 2B. He knocked, taking care to stand well away from the peephole.

He heard the shuffle of feet within and then a female voice came from the other side.

"Allo?" She sounded middle-aged. So the scientist had brought a wife with him. Either that, or he'd been given a woman. Her accent was indeterminable so far.

"I have a message for the Chinaman," Ethan said. He wanted to confirm that he had the correct suite, first of all, and rather than using the scientist's name, which the man may have changed, Ethan chose a derogatory term just as one of the neighbors might have done.

"You just missed him," the woman shouted through the door. Now that he'd heard more of her, Ethan noted the distinct lack of a Chinese accent in her Arabic, lending credence to the theory that Shi had been given a local woman. Probably part of his hegira promise.

Ethan doubted she would open the door to a stranger, not while her husband was gone. As such, there was really only one other question he could ask in that moment without arousing suspicion.

"When will he return?" Ethan demanded.

"Eight o'clock tonight. Who should I say called?"

"The neighbor."

Ethan went back to the stairwell and, trying to decide upon his next course of action, lingered there on the steps.

He heard a door open in the main hallway beside him. Peering past the edge of the stairwell, he saw a fully-veiled head poke out of room 2C, the adjacent apartment. The faceless woman glanced both ways, forcing Ethan to duck from view.

The door shut softly and the pad of footfalls approached his position. It sounded like one person. She was leaving the apartment unchaperoned?

Ethan hurried up the run of stairs, moving quietly. He glanced over his shoulder twice, worried the niqab-wearing woman would spot him before he reached the intermediary platform and rounded the bend.

He waited there, halfway between the second and third floor, and listened as those footsteps quietly descended. He carefully returned to the second floor and caught a glimpse of a black abaya as the woman rounded the bend of the platform that led to the first floor. She was definitely alone.

He paused, and considered breaking into the apartment she had vacated next to his target. But he realized he was being presented with a far better intelligence gathering opportunity.

Conscious that the militants were still waiting for him at the checkpoint, Ethan followed the woman to the lobby, and watched as she hesitantly opened the front door and scanned both directions. Then she hurried outside.

Ethan moved to the glass door and was about to pursue when he realized the black ghost was headed to the bakery. She went right to the front of the line: the baker knew about her transgression, then, and was complicit in it. Ethan wondered if he could use that somehow.

"Abu-Emad, where are you?" Abdullah's voice crackled impatiently over the radio, startling him.

"You're breaking up, emir," Ethan said, turning the radio off. It was a lame excuse, but given the low quality of the radios and the interference from all the buildings, Abdullah would likely believe it.

A few moments later the woman emerged from the bakery with several loaves of bread the size of manhole covers balanced on her head, beneath a plastic container filled with milk.

She hastened across the street, almost getting struck by a Kia Rio. The driver cursed her, telling her to find a chaperon or next time he'd run her over.

Ethan retreated up the stairwell, momentarily hiding from view.

He heard the front door open and close, followed by the soft pads of her approach. She appeared at the bottom of the stairs and climbed halfway up before she noticed him.

sixteen

The black ghost froze, her body flinching. Though he couldn't see her face beneath the niqab, he could almost sense her blanch. When she spoke, Ethan heard the cold terror in her voice.

"Please, I was just buying milk and bread for my baby." Her words, a heartbreaking whimper, were slightly muffled by the niqab.

Ethan still had the lower half of his face veiled by the keffiyeh so that he looked like a mujahid bandit. "Come." He gestured up the stairs.

"Please—"

"Come!" Ethan said more firmly.

She approached. When she passed him, the milk container on her head slipped to one side, but she steadied it with shaking, black-gloved hands.

"Don't hurt me," she said as he followed her up the stairs.

Ethan purposely remained silent. He couldn't let the pity he felt interfere with his job.

At room 2C she fumbled with her keys, struggling to open the door one-handed.

Ethan, well-aware that Abdullah and the others would be wondering where he was, relieved her of her burden so that she could use both hands.

He followed her inside the apartment, stepping onto an intricately-patterned Turkish carpet that had seen better times—the edges were frayed, the colors faded. Ethan could see the living room and a side hallway from where he stood. A green polyester accent chair with flared arms squatted in front of a small glass coffee table. A similar polyester couch was positioned across from it. The synthetic material appeared somewhat worn, and Ethan guessed both were hand-me-downs. A polished counter separated the living room from the foyer.

Ethan placed the bread and milk on the counter. "Go feed your baby."

She didn't move.

"There is no baby, is there?" he said.

No answer.

"That's what I thought. Where is your husband? At work?"

"Dead."

"Look, I'm not going to hurt you." He hesitated, then lowered his veil.

When he revealed his face her body language shifted subtly. Her shoulders relaxed almost imperceptibly. She was still afraid, but she trusted him for some reason. Him, this strange mujahid who had carried a Dragunov sniper rifle into her house.

"What do you want?" she said.

"Your neighbor," Ethan said. "Tell me everything you know about him. Quickly."

Her head shifted subtly to the right, indicating she knew he was referring to the Chinese national in 2B.

"He moved in over a month ago, after the previous occupants fled. He and his wife keep to themselves, mostly. He leaves around noon every day. For work, I guess."

"You've seen the armed escort that accompanies him?"

She nodded slowly. "It is hard not to. Sometimes they come to his door, making a loud racket in the halls. Most of the time he goes down to meet them with his bodyguards."

Ethan glanced toward the door and its peephole, and then at the canopied window adjoining the family room. Confined as she was to her apartment most of the day, Ethan supposed she was well-acquainted with her only windows onto the world.

"His bodyguards?" Ethan said.

"Yes, two Chinese men. They are with him at all times. They room in the apartment."

Ethan rubbed his chin. Interesting. That meant his wife was likely confined to the bedroom when the scientist and his bodyguards were home. "He leaves at noon every day? Bringing his bodyguards with him?"

"Yes. Except Sundays."

"And he comes back with the bodyguards in the evening?"

"Yes. Around eight o'clock."

"Does he go out regularly at other times?" Ethan said. "For prayers, maybe? A nightly walk, a morning stroll?"

The voice behind that black-shrouded face became cold. "Do you believe I spend my days glued to the spyhole at my front door? I don't know."

"How well do you know the wife?"

"I don't."

Ethan rubbed his chin. "Make friends with his wife. Develop a rapport. Gain her trust."

"Why?" she said.

"Other than for the obvious reason that if you don't do as I ask, I'll hand you over to the Khansa'a brigade?" He retrieved a handful of Syrian pounds from his pocket and let them land, clinking, onto the countertop.

Her veiled head turned toward the coins. "I don't want your money."

"Take it," Ethan said. "There's more where that came from. A lot more. As long as you do what you're told."

She remained silent. He wished he could read her expression through that black veil.

"If you won't help me, perhaps I'll turn in the baker across the street. Knowingly selling goods to an unchaperoned woman is a crime."

"I'll help you," she said quickly.

"Good." Blackmail was an unfortunate part of the job, and he used it when he had to. Didn't mean he liked it. "I'll send you more instructions in a few days. You have access to the Internet?"

"There is an Internet cafe a block to the north. I go there once every few days."

"By yourself?"

Her head bobbed slightly. "Yes."

"You have no one who can act as your chaperon?"

"My brother," she said. "But he visits only once a week."

"What about a chaperon service?"

"The Caliphate does not allow them. All chaperons must be related."

Ethan chuckled softly. "That doesn't stop people from offering the service."

"It's risky," she said. "If a militant or Hisbah checks our IDs and discovers we're unrelated..."

"It's less risky than going out on your own."

She didn't have a response to that. Certainly a stubborn woman.

Ethan rubbed his forehead. "All right. Check your email by yourself, when you can. Do you have The Mujahid's Security?"

"I have this. My husband taught me how to use it."

"Good." He wrote down the username and password to one of his gmail aliases. "I'll expect a message from you in the draft folder in a few days, if not sooner, containing your public key." He handed her a memory stick he'd bought from a street vendor. "Run the program on here before you send me any messages. It will delete any malware on the machines you use." He'd given Mufid a similar stick a few days ago.

Ethan turned to go, then paused, remembering something she had said. "This brother of yours. What day does he visit?"

"Wednesdays."

That was tomorrow. "I'd like to meet him," Ethan said, never one to miss an opportunity to acquire another asset.

She took a step back. "No. We should... we should leave him out of this." The fear was thick in her voice.

Ethan was beginning to suspect her brother was a rebel of some kind. Even better.

"I insist," Ethan said. "Tomorrow, tell him you wish to be chaperoned on a date."

"And what do I say to explain how we met?"

"Tell him a mujahid knocked on the wrong door. Tell him I was enamored when I saw you."

"How do you know I'm not ugly behind this veil?" she asked, a hint of challenge in her tone.

"Maybe you are. Tell him I was enamored anyway. How often do we mujahadeen get the chance to see a woman's face these days, after all? You could look like a donkey and I'd be in love."

"But I never answer my door without the veil," she said.

"Just say you washed all your niqabs and only had a hijab handy. It's not a crime to answer your door without a veil."

"Isn't it?"

"Not if you don't let the visitor in. Tell him the mujahid insisted, and you were afraid so you opened it, just a crack, keeping your door chain latched."

She hesitated. "This is a bad idea."

"I'm the father of bad ideas. Tomorrow at eight. Al Rashid restaurant. Just in front of Swan Garden beside the Municipal Stadium."

"I know the place," she said.

Ethan grinned. "They serve amazing *fatteh.*"

"I don't like fatteh."

"Well you'll like the fatteh they serve. Eight o'clock. What was your name again?"

She hesitated. "Alzena."

He wasn't sure he believed her. Alzena was a generic name that literally meant "the woman."

Ethan smiled and said: "And I am Alrajil." The man.

* * *

At the checkpoint Abdullah and the others gave him shit for taking so long to bring the bread. "We thought you ran off to join the infidels!" Zarar joked, though his accusation wasn't so far from the truth.

That night Ethan left Mufid an encrypted message, sending the address of the target's apartment and the time the motorcade arrived. He asked if Mufid, his son or one of their associates could covertly tail the motorcade and relay the eventual destination to him. A photo of the final building would be good, too, but not required.

The next evening Ethan left the compound after prayers and jogged to the restaurant where he was to meet Alzena. By the time he arrived he was covered in sweat.

Though he'd cased the spot earlier, at night the area was a completely different beast, and at first he wasn't even sure he had the correct location, as the unpowered street lamps provided no light to read the sign, nor were there any windows on the otherwise nondescript building.

When he stepped inside, he found himself in a dining room of burnt-brick walls decorated with abstract paintings. Cylindrical light casings hung from the ceiling; lightbulbs shone dimly from within, indicating that somewhere a diesel generator was operating. Small candles inside glass bowls provided additional ambiance at each table.

The eyes of the male patrons turned toward him, and his gaze was met with either nonchalance or fear, and sometimes contempt. He wore a traditional white robe and checkered keffiyeh, but what made it obvious he was a militant was the Dragunov he sported over one shoulder. He had considered leaving the sniper rifle behind but in the end decided to bring it. The pros of being readily identifiable as a mujahid far outweighed the cons.

The two women present had raised their niqabs to eat, and while their faces were readily exposed, their hijabs still hid their hair. Both women appeared middle-aged and relatively plain, and didn't allow their eyes to stray from their chaperones, who sat across from them. Neither of them could have been Alzena, because their tables had seating for two alone.

The elderly proprietor immediately rushed forward to greet him. "Salaam, salaam. Welcome to Al Rashid!" He shook Ethan's hand enthusiastically.

"Salaam," Ethan said, smiling lightly.

"We welcome the fighters of our great Caliphate!" the proprietor said. "Welcome with open arms!"

"Wonderful," Ethan said.

The man led him to a table for four and Ethan took a seat in one of the wooden chairs. The red tablecloth had the words "Coca-Cola" on it.

The elderly proprietor hurried to the kitchen, returning a moment later with a cool towelette. Ethan used it to wipe away the sweat on his forehead and neck.

When the man had gone, Ethan watched the doorway for a minute, then glanced at the menu. Each Arabic entry had the English equivalent written beside it: *Sorcki* Salad (dry cheese with thyme, tomato, onion, parsley, olive oil), *Kibeh Niye* (raw lamb meat mixed with bulgur wheat and spices), *Makdous* (tangy eggplants stuffed with walnuts, olive oil and red peppers). The latest prices were printed on paper cutouts glued to the menu—the cost of each item had increased so many times that the cutouts formed small lumps.

Ethan's attention was drawn back to the door as a woman and man entered. The woman's niqab was still down, so he couldn't see her face. It must have been difficult for her to navigate the dark streets outside with that on, though apparently in the low light of the restaurant she could see readily enough, because she gestured toward Ethan immediately.

Upon seeing the man who accompanied her, he understood in that moment why Alzena hadn't wanted to have the meeting.

Fool, he thought.

The pair reached the table and Ethan stood.

"As salaamu alaykum," the chaperon said in a cool voice.

"Wa alaykuma salaam," Ethan returned with a calm he did not feel. He shook the man's hand.

Her brother was not a rebel at all, but rather, judging from the radio harness worn over his white thawb, and the AK-47 slung over his shoulder, he was a young, strapping member of the Hisbah.

He sat to Ethan's left, while the veiled woman took the seat across the table, also to his left so that she wouldn't reside directly across from him.

Ethan was about to initiate small talk when the black ghost lifted her veil and his breath caught in his throat.

A woman of her spectacular beauty was a rare, rare thing. She had it all. Perfectly symmetrical features. Prominent cheek bones. Strong, sharp nose. Flawless olive skin. Luscious, sensual lips. Almond-shaped eyes. He only wished he could see her hair, hidden as it was beneath the folds of her hijab.

Alzena's head was lowered, but she glanced upward for a moment and when her gaze met his, Ethan felt his heart quicken. Those eyes were like two blue, brilliant sapphires, of an azure different from anything he had ever seen. They seemed fathomless, and he felt they could swallow him up if he stared for too long. And yet for all their depth, there was a sadness about them.

The moment lasted maybe half a second before she lowered her gaze once more, her cheeks reddening slightly.

"I am Raafe," her brother announced coldly, breaking Ethan's trance. "Alzena's brother. You are Alrajil?"

Ethan glanced at Raafe. The Hisbah regarded him with open disdain.

"Yes," Ethan said.

The proprietor came over and lavished Raafe with praise. "What great works the Hisbah are doing for this city! What great changes have taken place. Allahu ahkbar!"

"Allahu ahkbar," Raafe agreed.

"Allahu ahkbar," Ethan echoed.

The proprietor gave the new arrivals cool towelettes, then took the drink requests. Water for Ethan and Alzena, a coke for Raafe. Ethan also ordered the mains: chicken fatteh, kebab *khashkhash*, and a side of flatbread.

"So you want to marry my sister?" Raafe said into the uncomfortable silence that followed the proprietor's departure.

Ethan had almost forgotten: going on a date in a strictly Muslim country was tantamount to asking for a woman's hand in marriage.

"I am considering this, yes," Ethan said. It wasn't even a lie. He couldn't resist glancing at her, though she refused to meet his gaze that time.

"It is very unusual how you met," Raafe said.

"It is," Ethan agreed, not exactly sure what Alzena had told her brother.

"The Khansa'a Brigade typically arranges weddings for foreign fighters," Raafe said. "Making chaperoned meetings such as these unnecessary."

"The women's brigade?" Ethan said. "I thought they were just sharia enforcers?"

"They are." Raafe seemed slightly insulted, as if he thought Ethan hadn't shown the proper respect due the Khansa'a by calling them *just* sharia enforcers. "But they also hunt down eligible women."

Ethan thought that was an interesting choice of words. *Hunt down.* "I didn't know."

"We need to better educate the new fighters. It would avoid uncomfortable situations such as this." Raafe tapped his chin thoughtfully. "Speaking of the Khansa'a, I will have to have a talk with them. My sister's *iddah* ended weeks ago." That was the prescribed period of mourning a woman must observe after the death of a spouse: four lunar months and ten days. "I'm sure they will find someone perfect for her." Raafe spoke as if it were a foregone conclusion she would not marry Ethan. Which she wouldn't, of course.

He studied Ethan for a moment. "There is something I would like to clarify. My sister says you knocked on her door. That you were at the wrong apartment."

"That's right," Ethan said.

"You did not go inside her apartment at any point?"

Ethan didn't bat an eye. "No, I did not."

"She did not unlatch the inner security chain?"

"No she did not."

Raafe tapped his lips skeptically. "You are one of the mujahadeen responsible for the Chinaman?"

"No."

"But you claimed to have knocked on the wrong door... or so my sister says. If you were not there to collect the Chinaman, then who were you visiting?"

"A cousin."

"Really. During the middle of the day? You *are* working for the Caliphate, aren't you?" He eyed Ethan's Dragunov.

"I was in the neighborhood with my unit. I wanted to say hello."

"In which room does this cousin of yours reside? 2D?"

"That is none of your concern."

"May I see your barrack papers?"

"Again, that is none of your concern."

Raafe smiled, though it did not reach his eyes. "Careful where you tread, Alrajil. You are balanced on a tightrope above the abyss. One misstep and you will fall. Very far."

Thankfully the proprietor arrived right then with the non-alcoholic drinks.

"So," Ethan said to Alzena when the proprietor had gone; he hoped to take control of the conversation and avoid any further uncomfortable questioning. "You are from Shaam?"

Raafe was the one who answered. "Yes. She was born in Aleppo, like me. Our family moved to Raqqa when she was six."

Ethan turned toward Alzena, trying to loop her into the discussion.

"Tell me about your dearly departed husband."

Raafe again spoke for her. "He was a mujahid from Jordan. My sister married him seven months ago. He was martyred two months later. A good man. A great one. He was the one who led me down the path of the Hisbah."

"It must be hard for her," Ethan said.

Raafe tilted his head, then glanced at Alzena. "Sister," Raafe prodded her. "Tell him what it is like to be the wife of a martyr. Go on."

She looked at Raafe, then shyly transferred her gaze to Ethan. She couldn't hold his eyes for very long. "The wives of martyrs, we are admired by the other women. Respected." Her tone was neutral, her words guarded.

Ethan waited, but she had nothing more to say.

Thankfully the food arrived.

"They are quick here," Raafe remarked.

"When a Hisbah and his mujahid friend visit," Ethan muttered. "Of course they're going to be quick."

"And what does that mean?" Raafe said.

"Nothing. Only that they honor us." By then Ethan only wanted the awkward evening to end.

He grabbed the tip of a lamb kebab and lifted the skewer from the khashkhash container; he bit off a chunk, tasting the parsley and pine nuts, though the flavor was almost overwhelmed by garlic and chili peppers.

Raafe took a kebab for himself. Alzena meanwhile stared at her hands, which were folded in her lap.

"Sister," Raafe said between bites. "Eat. Be polite."

She looked up at Raafe, her gaze distant, blank.

"Eat," her brother urged.

A fire kindled in those sapphire eyes and for a moment Ethan thought she was going to defy her brother, but then she ripped away some flatbread and nibbled at the edge. Ethan realized she had been slouching forward the entire time, avoiding any contact with the backrest of her seat.

"Which country did you say you made your hegira from again?" Raafe asked.

"Saudi Arabia," Using the provided ladle, Ethan served himself a dollop of the fatteh. He made sure to scoop up several pieces of chicken along with the yogurt and chickpea mix, though he only took a small portion of the soggy bread at the bottom of the bowl.

"And how did you originally contact the brothers in Shaam?"

"Social media."

Raafe smiled knowingly. "This is the first war that has been fought mainly over the social networks of the world. And so far, we are winning." He finished his kebab and then abruptly sat back, wiping his hands on the napkin. Ethan was expecting more grilling on his background, but instead Raafe turned toward Alzena and said, "So what do you say, sister? Will you marry him?"

Ethan had finished his serving of fatteh and was in the process of chewing a spicy khashkhash meatball, but those words made him freeze on the spot. A part of him wanted her to say yes, though he knew it was a very bad idea.

Alzena didn't look up. "I will ask Allah for guidance," she said emotionlessly. "But I believe my answer will be no."

"There you have it," Raafe said smugly. "This meeting is over."

He and his sister arose. Alzena seemed just as relieved as Ethan that the evening was finished. She lowered her veil and Raafe led her away without a word of goodbye. Ethan hadn't noticed earlier, but her walk seemed a little stiff.

Raafe paused beside the two tables where the couples sat and asked for proof of relations. When he was satisfied that no immoral meetings were taking place, he reminded the women to lower their veils before leaving. "It is far better for women to eat at home," he told the couples. "Remember that, in the future."

When Raafe was gone, Ethan stared at the uneaten food before him, not all that hungry anymore.

seventeen

Ethan stopped by an Internet cafe on the way back to the compound. The owner told him no USB sticks or other adapters were allowed, but Ethan managed to connect his device unnoticed while another customer paid.

He checked his three gmail accounts and found a message from Alzena waiting in one of the draft folders, dated earlier that day, before the ill-fated supper. He decrypted it.

I have approached Shi's wife and we have had tea. We are on good terms.

Shi's wife. Ethan hadn't told her the scientist's name. That meant she was telling the truth. *Good girl*. It also meant the scientist wasn't using an alias.

In his response, Ethan laid out what Alzena was to do next. Hopefully the incident at supper hadn't affected her willingness to help him.

Before he left the cafe, he executed the Regin payload. Nothing like installing a little self-replicating cyberespionage malware to boost one's mood.

When he met with William and Aaron in the cafeteria later that night, at nine-thirty, his fellow operatives revealed that both of their units were headed to Kobane the next day. Apparently more holy warriors were needed to wage jihad against the city, as the Kurds were responding with heavier than expected resistance.

"You have two options," Ethan said. "You can disappear, and deliver what intel you can from the shadows of Raqqa. Or—"

"Or we can go to Kobane," William said. "And strike at the enemy from the heart of their front lines."

"I like the disappear option, myself," Aaron said. "Seems to me, we're more useful alive than dead."

"I don't plan on being a martyr," William said quickly. "I think I've laid down a good foundation here in Raqqa. Intel will trickle in from the assets I've farmed over the next six months. Some of it will be actionable, some not. If I go to Kobane, I'll have an opportunity to obtain immediate actionable intel, *firsthand*. Sam has already sent word, Doug is on his way to embed with the defending Kurds. I can help him with eyes behind enemy lines."

"Sounds like you've already made up your mind."

"I have," William agreed.

Ethan glanced at Aaron. "You don't have to go."

Aaron sighed. "Shit. If William's going, guess I will, too. If only to keep his ego in check."

"But you're not even on the same unit," Ethan said.

"I know. But when Doug hears I stayed behind while William went to the front, I'll never hear the end of it. From the both of them."

William glanced at Ethan. "You think you can hold down the fort while we're away?"

"Too much work," Ethan replied in mock resignation. "I'll never manage without you guys."

"Are you planning any operations we should know about?"

"Not really," Ethan replied. Which was true. There wasn't anything the two of them could do to help him, not when they were leaving the city. Ethan was on his own.

"Don't start too many fires while we're gone," Aaron said, patting him on the back.

William and Aaron left for Kobane the next morning.

That same evening, when he checked his account in the computer room, he found a reply waiting from Alzena. She confirmed his plans, mentioning a possible date and location. He agreed to both, thanking her. He was just glad she was still a solid asset after what had happened.

A few evenings later he found himself seated in a restaurant called Al Jamal Qawiyya, literally The Camel Is Strong. He was playing a Jordanian named Samuel that night. Dressed in his thawb, he wore a white keffiyeh held in place by a black headband. He'd purchased the latter two items earlier that day specifically for the alias. In the washroom of a nearby cafe he'd changed, then snipped off a small portion of his beard and glued the extra hair to his eyebrows, thickening them. It was a poor man's disguise, but it was good enough for what he intended.

Drinking tea, Shi was already seated at the table when Ethan arrived. The scientist wore a well-fitting suit with a white dress shirt and red tie that night. The checkered keffiyeh covering his hair seemed somehow wrong when paired with those clothes. The whole getup couldn't be all that comfortable in the heat—indeed, a layer of sweat slicked the man's skin. But Ethan understood why he wore it: other than the suit he had nothing going for him. His features unremarkable. His eyes were rather unfortunately close-set, and his cheeks were pocked with acne scars. His nose looked like a steamroller had gone over it. All in all a rather unpleasant and shady-looking individual.

Ethan noticed Shi's bodyguards seated at another table a respectful distance away. They were Asian, much better looking than Shi, also dressed in suits but without the headgear. He wondered if they were supplied by the Chinese government. He wouldn't have been surprised to learn that China was using the Islamic State to fight a proxy war against the West, given the number of other countries using proxies in the region.

Ethan shook the scientist's hand—the man's palm was cold and clammy. *A little nervous, are we?*

Ethan sat down and ordered a black tea for himself. "This is a nice place." The decor was almost exactly the same as Al Rashid, replete with red Coca-Cola table cloths and abstract paintings.

"Yes, it is very nice," Shi said. He spoke Arabic with a heavy Chinese accent. The nasal, high-pitched, fast-paced rendition was uncannily similar to how a Chinese person might speak English, with the ends of many words unceremoniously chopped off.

"I am so glad to be here," Ethan said. "On this great jihad. Surrounded by brothers such as yourself." He wanted Shi to feel at ease with him, and he hoped evoking the sense of brotherhood that pervaded the mujahadeen ranks would help. He had purposely left behind his rifle for the same reason—though he did have a Makarov pistol secreted in his right boot, courtesy of the barracks supply officer.

"Yes. It is good." The scientist sounded reserved, cautious.

Ethan smiled, sipping his tea. "Thank you for agreeing to meet me."

Shi nodded quickly. "My wife says you are Jordanian."

"I am Jordanian," Ethan agreed. He wasn't overly concerned about his Saudi accent. He doubted Shi would even notice.

"And how do you know my neighbor again?"

"I don't. Not personally, anyway. I knew her husband. I sent him an email a few weeks ago letting him know I had joined the great Caliphate, and that I was currently stationed in Raqqa. His widow answered, and explained her husband had died. I expressed my condolences and we ended up in a dialog, mutually exhorting the love we felt for our lost brother. I explained the project I was involved with back in Jordan, and the widow told me her neighbor was the wife of a great scientist. She sent me your name and I looked up some of your papers online. They were in Chinese but I was able to understand parts of them with Google Translate."

"But my wife told me she met the neighbor only a few days ago," Shi said.

"Yes," Ethan agreed. "Your neighbor, the widow, only told me about you a few days ago as well."

"You worked for the Jordan University for Science and Technology?" That was part of Ethan's cover story for the meeting, which he'd research online. The wonders of open source intelligence.

"As a fitness professional," Ethan said. "I trained people at the university gym. My father, however, serves on the board of the Jordan Research and Training Reactor project, sponsored by the university. He is an influential man. He can get you on the board. We need people like you. People with experience. We're making a difference, working to develop nuclear and renewable energy in Jordan. My country imports ninety-six percent of its energy. It's time to break free of our dependence on foreign sources."

"What is the name of your father again?"

Ethan gave him the real name of one of the men involved in the reactor project. He had asked Sam to place an asset in the University's IT department in case Shi decided to email him, but she had said no such placements were forthcoming, not for a few weeks anyway. It didn't really matter—Ethan planned to glean everything he needed from the one meeting, so that by the time the scientist discovered his lie, if ever, it would be too late.

Shi pursed his lips. "Is it not strange," he said. "That the son of an obviously rich man would come to Syria to wage jihad? Most in your position would merely send money."

"My father has sent money, this is true. But I'm not the first son of a rich man to fight for his fellow Muslims. Nor will I be the last. I'm here to do my duty and wage jihad for what I believe in."

Shi frowned. "Your little father approves of this?"

Ethan felt his artificially-thickened brows draw together. *Little father.* Was the man purposely trying to insult him? "Of course not. But what can he do? Disown me?"

"Maybe he will," Shi smirked. "Imagine that. The spoiled rich boy, stuck in the Islamic State, unable to go running home to father when this is done."

"Maybe I want to stay," Ethan said.

"After what you said about your home country? I doubt it."

Ethan considered refuting him, but decided to stick with the script. "You're right. I don't plan on staying. I will do my part to fight for my Muslim brothers, but if I survive I will go home."

Shi nodded smugly. "Not a true holy warrior, then."

"Just because I don't want to burn my passport and live in the Caliphate forever doesn't make me any less a holy warrior." Ethan let anger enter his voice. "I fight for Dawlah, but I also have another fight, in my own country. Look around you, and ask yourself, with so many in the world lining up against the Islamic State, will it really last more than five years, if that? Truly ask yourself this question. And when you come to the inescapable conclusion that most likely the Caliphate will not exist, at least not in its current form, then you will realize you have no future in this country. When it falls, and the locals round up the sympathizers like you and execute them, don't blame me. The fault for staying will be your own."

"If you don't believe in them, why do you fight?"

"As I said already, Muslims are dying, and I would be remiss if I didn't come here and defend them. I will do my duty and then I will go home. True, I don't believe the Caliphate will endure in the end, but that doesn't make my effort any less sincere. Or heroic."

Shi sipped his tea for a long moment. "This board you mentioned, it pays well?"

"Extremely."

Shi pressed his lips together. "I will think about it."

Score.

Ethan finished his tea, and then, trying to keep his tone as casual and disinterested as possible, like he was merely making small talk, he said, "So what kind of work are you doing for the Caliphate?"

The man stiffened slightly. "Many things. Too complex for a rich boy with your tiny brain to understand. For a *fitness professional*."

Ethan smiled obligingly. "I know a little about nuclear science. Nuclear weapons, specifically. Take some Plutonium-239, some aircraft counterweights to use as shielding, a fishing cooler, packing foam, plastic explosives, blasting caps, firing circuits, and you have all the ingredients for a dirty bomb."

Shi wore a sour expression. "The ingredients, yes," he said with disdain. "But it takes more than ingredients to make a bomb. And for a personal trainer, you know a suspicious amount about nuclear weapons."

"Let's just say I've done my homework. If you procured some lead aprons and film badges to use as dosimeters, I could probably put together the aforementioned ingredients for you. It's really not that hard. That's what you're doing, isn't it? Building a bomb?"

Shi shook his head angrily. "You are spouting words whose meaning you know nothing about. You have read something about nuclear weapons in an Al Qaeda or Islamic State propaganda magazine, alongside recipes for making homemade ricin from castor beans, but you could not design a nuclear bomb if your life depended on it. You have no idea how firing circuits work, nor how to time blasting caps. You are a moron."

Ethan smiled politely. Perhaps it would have been better to bring his rifle after all. More intimidating that way. "You forget that my father serves on the board of a nuclear reactor project. I wonder, do you treat all of your prospective employers so poorly during the job interview?"

Shi looked away. "I'm sorry. My mouth gets the better of me sometimes."

"No, it's my fault," Ethan said. "I provoked you. I'm actually glad you're fighting for us. We need all the help we can get. You are a Muslim, aren't you?" He glanced at Shi's keffiyeh.

The scientist bowed his head in acknowledgment. "I have converted, yes."

"So you are waging jihad, too, in your own way."

Shi's eyes gleamed, like he was privy to some secret knowledge. It was a look Ethan had seen often among the mujahadeen.

"I am doing my part," Shi said. "While the foot soldiers fight in the trenches, I am at work designing something that will end this war decisively. Assad and the West are in for a very big surprise in the coming months. We're going to change history."

Ethan felt a chill travel down his spine and he knew in that moment the scientist was absolutely guilty, and must die.

Ethan lowered his voice conspiratorially and leaned across the table. "Do you need help acquiring nuclear materials? I know key personnel involved with the Jordanian reactor project. And certain smugglers..."

Shi laughed disdainfully. "I have my own contacts, but I will keep your offer in mind."

"Plutonium-239?" Ethan said.

"Uranium-235," Shi corrected with a smug smile, apparently enjoying his display of insider knowledge.

But then the grin left Shi's face as he realized he'd said too much. The scientist abruptly pushed his chair from the table. "I must go."

"Wait, aren't you going to give me your email?"

"No." Shi stood.

"How am I supposed to keep in touch with you about the reactor project?"

Shi scribbled something onto a napkin and tossed it on the table, then rejoined his bodyguards.

Ethan considered doing the deed right then with the Makarov hidden in his boot, but decided there would be too many witnesses. Plus he would probably end up in a shootout with the bodyguards.

He let Shi go, and instead glanced at the napkin. A Yahoo email address was written upon it.

When Ethan got back to the compound he sent the account ID to Sam along with a monitor request. He mentioned he had proven the target's intent, and that the scientist was looking to smuggle Uranium-235 into the country. It wasn't the fissile supplier like Sam had wanted, but it was the next best thing.

The following night he checked his email and found a courtesy message from Sam. Normally she divulged very little information regarding other operations, but on the rare occasion, probably when she felt he could use a morale boost, she told him the positive effects of intel he had sent.

Apparently Yahoo had given her team access to the scientist's account. Most of his messages were innocuous, but a few encrypted emails drew her attention. Though her team hadn't been able to decipher them, the first batch were dated from a time before the scientist had come to Syria, and were likely from Islamic State recruiters. The later batch of encrypted messages had been sent from Syria to Chinese addresses. Sam had the owners of the destination email addresses traced, and determined most of them belonged to employees of a trading company in China that was currently under investigation for illegally shipping weapons components into Pakistan. It was very likely the fissile supplier.

She signed her message with: *Well done.*

It would be up to her and the Agency to intercept the fissile material. Meanwhile Ethan would do his part in Syria: since Sam hadn't mentioned any modifications to the termination objective, the hit was still a go.

He logged out and left the compound. It was late evening, after the fifth prayer of the day, and he had some things to do before curfew.

eighteen

Ethan made his way through the busy fashion district. Power had been made available to most of the city that night as a "gift" for good behavior, and the residents were out in force. Cars and taxis jockeyed for position on the road, honking almost constantly. Pedestrians moved to and fro among the sidewalks, the neon lights of the clothing stores vying for their attention alongside the street vendors with their greasy fares of falafel and shawarma.

Ethan moved on to a quieter neighborhood near the old cemetery. The working street lamps made the area feel safer than on previous occasions. He passed two Islamic State checkpoints and reached his destination a few minutes later.

He studied the apartment building, picking out Shi's balcony on the second floor. It was covered in a canopy like the other balconies—that ruled out sniping the scientist while he was home at night. The glow from within told him the man was still awake. Probably getting in some good laptop time while he could.

Ethan's gaze drifted to the canopied balcony beside it. Alzena's. Perhaps he could use her apartment to abet the hit.

He decided against it. For her safety, it was better to minimize her involvement from that point forward. Besides, she was a distraction. He had been thinking about her much too often these past few days.

He returned his attention to Shi's balcony. Ethan could go inside and attempt to kill the man directly, but with the bodyguards present, he gauged his chances of success at around fifty percent. No, better to take the guaranteed shot. The sniper shot.

He had two options, as far as the timing of the hit went. He could perform it at noon, when Shi left the apartment. Or at eight o'clock, when the scientist returned. The entrance was poorly lit compared to the rest of the street, so that even if the power was active the night of the operation, Ethan would need a night vision scope—which he didn't have. That ruled out the evening option. But even if he performed it in the day, he needed a proper sniping location...

The closed bakery behind him was housed in the first floor of a three-story apartment building—the second and third floors were residential suites. Ethan walked to the main entrance and pressed a few of the intercom buttons. The ongoing power meant those buttons still worked.

The initial person to answer, a mean-sounding lady, refused to let him in. Ethan pretended he had a delivery but she didn't believe him. The second voice that came over the intercom belonged to a grumpy old man who promptly told Ethan to stuff his dick in a camel.

Ethan retrieved the credit-card sized leather case from his pocket. During his Afghan and Iraq deployments, lockpicking had become a hobby. There had been so much downtime between missions that he'd become a master—at one point he'd ordered almost every practice lock out there and could beat each of them in under thirty seconds.

But he'd let the skill slide. His deep cover operations made it hard to acquire the locks he needed to practice. Still, like driving or skiing, it wasn't a skill you lost entirely.

He took out the three bump keys that were supposedly designed for Syrian locks. He glanced in either direction, confirmed that no one was around, then tried all three.

The first two wouldn't even enter the lock, while the third only partially fit. He used his phone as a mallet to tap the key anyway, applying a small amount of torque in an attempt to catch the pins outside the locking mechanism. No good.

He could have made his own bump key by taking a picture of the keyhole and marking the depth of each pin with one of his picks, then sending a mockup to a 3D print service like Shapeways or KeyMe and getting the key couriered to Syria, but why bother when he had the skill to pick the lock?

Ethan replaced the bump keys and chose one of the picks, basically a thin file with a hook on the end, and set to work. After a frustrating couple of minutes, he chose another pick and tried "raking" the lock by placing the tool all the way in, right to the back, and applying torque while slowly drawing it out. That did the trick.

Inside, Ethan ignored the cramped, ancient elevator, worried that it might trap him between floors if the power went out, and he took the stairwell instead.

The rooftop door proved locked. He tried the bump keys. The first was a perfect fit. A few taps of his cellphone later and Ethan was on the open terrace.

He made his way between the blocky rooftop water tanks and television antennas. When he reached the ledge, he had a clear view of the apartment building across the street. The poorly lit main entrance was in plain view. The sun would be overhead and slightly behind him at noon. Basically the perfect spot to perform the hit.

He lined up his scope with Shi's balcony, but as expected he couldn't see through the thick canopy. He set aside the Dragunov, grabbed his TruPulse 360 and did a quick range check on the lower entrance. It was difficult in the low light, but eventually he got the finder lined up with the lobby. Thirty-three meters. An extremely easy shot with the 4x scope.

He crossed to the rear of the rooftop. There was a shared courtyard in back, hemmed in by neighboring apartment buildings. In the dim light he made out a shoulder-high cinder block fence, blocking off the far side. That courtyard would serve as a good exfil route, because he certainly wasn't going to leave by the front door after completing the hit. Too bad there was no fire escape. He returned downstairs—there was no way to get to the courtyard from the lobby, either. That complicated things, but not overly so.

Ethan visited the supply room in the barracks the next morning to inquire about rope. The Syrian on duty explained there was none left, and no inventory was forthcoming for a few weeks. Since the man also ran the black market currency service, Ethan obtained the equivalent of five hundred US dollars in Syrian pounds. He wanted to exchange more, but the Syrian didn't have enough on him.

When Ethan got back from checkpoint duty that night he left a quick encrypted message for Mufid telling the clothing store owner to secure him a static climbing rope, one centimeter in diameter, fifty meters in length, or, barring that, several vehicular tow ropes that could be strung together. He instructed the man to be at his shop at eight o'clock in the evening the next day to deliver them.

Picking up some bike gloves from a street hawker along the way, Ethan met Mufid at the designated hour. The shopkeeper had managed to procure a static climbing rope, fifty meters in length, precisely as asked. He also gave Ethan the intel he had requested previously—the GPS coordinates of various Islamic State buildings, including the destination of the scientist's motorcade—on a memory stick.

"Do I get my money now?" Mufid asked.

"I do have a small amount for you, yes." Ethan paid Mufid the Syrian pounds he had obtained from the money changer.

Mufid accepted the amount with a puzzled expression. "Where is my fifty thousand?"

Ethan wrote an IOU in Arabic for the amount of fifty thousand US dollars, signing it with an alias Sam used in the Middle East. "Bring this to a US embassy."

"But there are no US embassies in Syria!"

"Then go to Turkey or Jordan. Or wait until the US embassy reopens in Damascus." The embassy had closed down in February 2012, and probably wouldn't reopen for some time.

Mufid threw up his arms theatrically. "But that could be years from now! This is ridiculous. You promised me fifty thousand."

"And so I did. You're holding it in your hands."

Mufid fumed a moment longer, then pocketed the note. "American embassy, you say?" He stamped his foot loudly. "To hell with you and your American friends! What help have the Americans ever given us? While Assad was busy gassing us with his chemicals, the Americans watched idly, never coming to our aid. But now that the Islamic State has come, the Americans suddenly show an interest again. The West is full of two-faced, cynical, selfish liars concerned only with their own national welfare."

"I won't disagree with you," Ethan said. "But are you done your little tirade? Good. Because here's what I want you to do for me in the coming days."

He instructed the shopkeeper to buy a piece of flatbread from the bakery at eleven thirty in the morning each day, and then to wait at a nearby street corner until twelve thirty. He was to continue that daily routine until Ethan showed up to retrieve the bread.

"Why should I do this?" Mufid demanded. "You have not paid me my due! You have given me a pittance, along with a useless piece of paper."

"Do this," Ethan said. "And I'll give you the same pittance the next time we meet. And maybe another piece of paper."

Greed flashed in Mufid's eyes, though he quickly hid it. The 'pittance' Ethan offered was likely the same or more than the clothing store pulled in after a month of sales. For a chance to earn double or triple that amount with very little work, of course Mufid would jump at the opportunity—it came as no surprise when the man eventually consented to the task.

Ethan slid the coil of rope over his shoulder and hiked to the building across from his target. Once there, someone actually buzzed him inside that time. He had come earlier than the previous night, which may have had something to do with it.

At the rooftop he surveyed the steel supports holding up the water tanks. Four bars held up each tank, though they were all fairly corroded. The television antennas were little better.

Ethan looped one end of the rope around the steel support of the water tank closest to the courtyard anyway. He threaded roughly half the rope through the bar, then tossed both ends over the ledge. The dangling cords gathered into a pile on the dried grass of the courtyard below.

Ethan placed the bike gloves beside the ledge and tested the rope, grabbing both sections and leaning back to put his weight on the anchor. When he was satisfied that it would hold, he let his body dangle entirely over the edge. Seemed good.

He returned to the snipe position on the far side, dropped, and set down the Dragunov. He retrieved his Android and readied himself, taking a few deep breaths. Then he activated a timer on the cellphone and stuffed it in his pocket. He scooped up his rifle, dashed to the far side of the rooftop and yanked on the bike gloves. He grabbed the two sections of climbing rope and slid them between his legs and up across his right buttock, over his chest, about his left trapezius muscle, across his upper back, over his right deltoid muscle, along the outside of his right palm, finally looping the twin strands over his hand and gripping the ropes firmly between his fingers. The dulfersitz method.

Ethan slid the rifle strap over his neck so that the weapon hung over his chest and wouldn't interfere with his descent, then he rappelled down, his right hand functioning as the lead, his left hand behind him serving as the brake. He eased the rope through his fingers, letting it slide over his body as he dropped. He twisted his torso slightly downward to ease the friction pain on his groin, and he pushed off from the wall with his boots as he went.

When he reached the bottom of the three-story building, he extricated himself from the ropes and then pulled on one section, hand over hand, until the entire cord was free of the anchor and the far end dropped at his feet. Then he picked up the rope pile and sprinted through the dark courtyard.

He stowed the rope behind a shrub and then grabbed the wide, flat rim of the cinder block fence and hauled himself up.

The street below was quiet, the pavement clear of obstructions.

Ethan lowered himself back inside the courtyard and stopped the timer on his cellphone.

Forty-five seconds.

Exfil route, good to go.

nineteen

In the computer room of the barracks, Ethan loaded up the memory stick Mufid had given him. On it were the GPS coordinates of several government installations, including a local courthouse used to administer sharia law. He also found a photo to go along with the latitude and longitude of the building where the motorcade brought the scientist every day. It looked like a repurposed industrial complex, no doubt converted into a weapons research facility. Ethan forwarded all of the information along to Sam. She would probably leak the information to the Assad regime after he performed the hit—there would be a few barrel bombs dropped in the days after, no doubt. Whether they hit their targets or not was another story.

Sleep proved difficult that night. It felt particularly hot and stuffy in room three-ten; Ethan lay atop his sleeping bag, his loose clothes drenched in perspiration, his flushed face throbbing in time to his heartbeat. It didn't help matters that he kept mentally reviewing the planned hit. When the time came, he felt confident he could carry out the assassination without a hitch, but there were many variables that could go wrong. There always were with something like that, which was why he had tried to keep the plan simple.

He also dwelled on Alzena. When Shi was dead, the militants would almost certainly ask the scientist's wife if her husband had been in contact with any strangers lately. The wife would mention that the neighbor had arranged for Shi to meet a Jordanian only a few nights before. Members of the Khansa'a Brigade would visit Alzena. Ethan had coached her on what to say via their shared email account—she was to claim she had never personally met the Jordanian. If she was asked to reveal her email exchange with the man, she would tell the Khansa'a that it was her habit to delete messages from her inbox and sent folders, because she liked to "keep her account clean," and so she had no record of the correspondence. She had promised Ethan she would delete everything save for a select few emails from the last year, that way if the Khansa'a forced her to log in to her personal account, her story would appear true. Also, when they revealed that her Jordanian friend had assassinated the scientist, her shock would be real—Ethan had left out that small detail.

He had considered urging her to go into hiding, but somehow he doubted she would. Besides, if she kept her wits about her she should be fine.

At least, that was what he told himself. He only hoped that her brother wouldn't complicate things.

A little after midnight he eventually found sleep, only to be awakened an hour and a half before sunrise for first prayer.

Over the next couple of days the checkpoints proved too far to realistically make the hit site. Each morning as Wolf Company drove out to the latest random checkpoint, nerves always gripped Ethan, but when it became obvious that the militants were proceeding far past the necessary neighborhood, his stress quickly ceded to impatience.

By the third wasted day Ethan had become extremely antsy. If any of his fellow mujahadeen asked him a pointless question, or a civilian looked at him the wrong way at the checkpoint, he was liable to explode. When one young passerby called Ethan a pig under his breath, Ethan nearly pulled his rifle on the character.

He sensed his window of opportunity closing. The Caliphate was seeking to consolidate its hold on existing territory, and units were being vacated from the compound daily. Wolf Company might be reassigned to Kobane or another city any time. And even if he stayed, the longer he waited to complete the hit, the greater the chance of something going wrong. Someone might discover and remove the rope Ethan had left stashed on the rooftop. The scientist might relocate to another apartment, or change the hours he left for the research facility.

If William or Aaron were still in the city, he would have involved them, because the operation was hanging by a thread as far as Ethan was concerned.

Finally on the fourth day Abdullah situated the checkpoint within a workable distance of the apartment and Ethan could at last perform the hit.

That morning's duty seemed longer than usual, and he couldn't shake the tenseness that permeated his body. He distractedly checked the IDs and cellphones of passersby. The day dragged on.

Near noon, Ethan volunteered to buy bread for the unit. He hadn't asked for the privilege in more than a week, so he assumed Abdullah would allow it. And if not, Ethan would shortly excuse himself to the toilet.

But Abdullah nodded in consent.

"I go with you," Suleman announced. "You take too long, otherwise."

Ethan smiled fatalistically. "Certainly." He had never expected the operation to be easy.

About a block from the checkpoint, Ethan was about to feign intestinal cramping as a pretext for abandoning Suleman when he heard a commotion behind him.

A young boy repeatedly shouted the word "lawbreaker" at the top of his lungs. He pointed at a chaperoned woman who wore a niqab; a small portion of her veil was absent around the eye area, revealing a thin slice of skin between her nose and forehead.

Suleman turned back to deal with it. "Go!" he told Ethan over his shoulder.

Finally fate had dealt him a favorable hand.

Ethan hurried forward, feeding on the sudden adrenaline rush.

When Suleman vanished from sight behind him, he ducked into a side alley and donned his balaclava. Around it he secured the headband containing the Shahada script. When he emerged, passersby readily made way before him, that masked, menacing mujahid with the sniper rifle.

Proceeding thusly through the streets, he paused twice to make sure Suleman wasn't following, and he reached his destination about five minutes before noon. The motorcade hadn't arrived yet.

He crossed the street to the apartment containing his hide. The long queue of people at the bakery snaked past the lobby, and he shoved through. At the entrance he pressed multiple intercom buttons, and for a moment feared no one would answer. He could feel the eyes of the people in line on his back.

An old woman's voice finally came over the speaker. "Allo?" She was almost unintelligible for all the static that accompanied her voice.

"I have a delivery," Ethan growled into the microphone.

"A what?"

"A *delivery.*"

"What kind of delivery?" came the answer.

"A registered letter."

The door latch didn't open.

Ethan pressed more buttons. No one else answered. He didn't want to pick the lock, not with so many people watching. Still, he was an armed mujahid. What did it matter what the common people thought?

He was about to retrieve his lockpick set when he noticed a blazer-wearing man standing nearby, away from the lineup. He appeared hesitant; he carried several piles of flatbread balanced in one hand, and a key in the other.

Ethan pointed brusquely at the door. The man nervously stepped forward and opened it. Ethan was in.

Fate, you are fickle indeed.

At the top of the stairs, he produced his working bump key and inserted it into the lock of the rooftop door. He tapped the key with his phone and jiggled it, fumbling, wasting precious seconds. The lock ultimately opened and he burst onto the rooftop.

He ran to the ledge and crouched to observe the street. No SUVs: either the motorcade hadn't arrived or he had already missed it. He would know soon enough.

He set down his rifle and went to the opposite side of the terrace. The coil of rope and bike gloves were precisely where he'd stashed them. He threaded the rope through the water tank supports he'd picked out days before. Once the cord was properly anchored, he threw the loose ends into the rear courtyard.

He tested the setup with his weight. The ropes held.

Ethan taped a scathing note onto one of the water tanks, in full view of the doorway. The message was written in a local rhetorical style that was critical of the Islamic State, and implicated the regional Al Qaeda affiliated group, Jabhat al Nusra, in the kill. Mufid had helped craft the text.

Ethan returned to the sniping position, low-crawling to the railless ledge. Still no motorcade.

He retrieved the Dragunov, deployed the bipod, and rested it near the brink. He had considered naming the weapon—a throwback behavior from his SEAL days—but in the end decided that honor was reserved for American rifles alone.

He turned off his radio and placed his right eye against the PSO-1 scope, leaving his left open for situational awareness. He extended the cylindrical sunshade at the end of the 4x magnification scope, then adjusted the focus ring.

The PSO-1 was equipped with a stadiametric rangefinder, which he ignored—he didn't need it at that close range. Besides, he trusted the thirty-three meter measurement he had made with the TruPulse a few nights before.

It was unnecessary to compensate for bullet drop at that range, and even if he wanted to the scope's elevation knob wasn't fine-grained enough—it operated in hundred meter increments. He didn't need to adjust for windage either: not even a breeze stirred the scorching air that day. Besides, at his current range he'd need a gale force wind to blow the rimmed 54mm bullet off target.

He aimed the targeting reticle directly at the door. The three chevrons below the main crosshairs were for bullet drop compensation beyond one thousand meters, so he ignored those.

With the scope set up, Ethan settled in for the wait.

The seconds ticked past, becoming minutes. Ethan shifted impatiently. Surely it was long past noon, but he didn't dare check his smartphone: he had to keep his eye on that door. Doubts filled his mind, but he quashed them with the cold-hearted discipline of the sniper that had been dormant inside him for so long.

And then the motorcade pulled up. Ethan steeled himself.

The militants emerged and formed a perimeter around the SUVs. One of them calmly approached the entrance and pressed an intercom button.

Ethan focused all of his being on that door. Most external reference points left him. There was only the trigger beneath his finger and the door within his reticule.

The militants standing in front of the door moved away as it opened.

The scientist and his bodyguards stepped into view.

Ethan very slightly adjusted his aim and squeezed the trigger.

twenty

The recoil caused the stock of the sniper rifle to bite into his shoulder. The violent report echoed from the buildings. Bystanders ducked. Some screamed.

Shi's body dropped like a ragdoll.

Ethan rolled away from the ledge and out of sight of any militants below. He snapped the bipod closed on his rifle and scrambled to the exfil point. He heard shouts from the street behind him.

He reached the far side of the terrace and wrapped the twin ropes about his body in the dulfersitz method. He slid the rifle strap over his neck, letting the Dragunov hang over his chest.

He was about to leap backward into the courtyard when he realized he'd forgotten the bike gloves. He knelt, yanked the gloves on, then stepped off the edge.

He eased himself down in wide spurts, successively kicking off from the apartment. He descended a little fast, and slowed when the burn in his groin became too intense, well-aware that if the militants reached the rooftop before he'd vacated the courtyard, he was dead.

The rope abruptly grew slack and he fell five meters before jerking to a halt, the cord cutting into his groin. Had the mujahadeen from the motorcade already attained the rooftop? More likely the rusty steel bar he'd used for an anchor had given way and lodged somewhere else, maybe against a television antenna, saving him from the fall.

He continued the rappel, but the rope gave once again a moment later and he plunged the final two meters to the courtyard, hitting fairly hard. He rolled, expecting a water tower or antenna to barrel down, but nothing came. He tried to stand and gasped in pain—he'd sprained his left ankle.

He bit down the agony and forced himself upright. He unwrapped himself from the rope and yanked on one end, trying to take it down, but the cord had lodged against something else up there and refused to budge.

Damn it. He'd have to leave the rope where it was.

Half running and half limping, Ethan crossed the dry grass; he flinched at the jolts of pain every step inflicted. His buttocks throbbed, too, from the rope burn; he touched the fabric there with one hand but his cargo pants seemed intact, luckily.

He tripped on a small rock hidden in the grass and fell. He crawled to his feet, fully expecting a rifle report to sound from the rooftop at any moment, and with it, his world to blink out.

It seemed an eternity, but by the time Ethan reached the cinder block fence, only a minute had passed since he fired the shot. He hauled himself over the shoulder-high block and down the other side. He landed on the sidewalk beyond, ignoring the surprised looks of the passersby.

He limped onward, continuing his half run, half limp gait. He crossed the busy street, nearly getting struck by a car, and then ducked into the planned alleyway. As he neared the other side he removed his balaclava and headband and stuffed them into a pocket. Then he turned on his radio and slowed to a walk, doing his best to hide the limp when he emerged. The ankle was growing numb, fortunately, lessening the pain. It would probably be swollen later.

Ethan had done it. Still, the hit felt sloppy. He'd left behind a rope. He'd injured his leg. What else could go wrong?

A call came over his two-way radio. "Abu-Emad, where are you?" It was Abdullah.

Ethan pressed the send button and spoke into the device, which hung from his chest harness. "On my way back from the bakery. Why?"

"Hurry up!"

Ethan switched to a higher channel and listened in on the general chatter. The mujahadeen were searching for the assassin. They had no description of the perpetrator so far, other than that he might be a member of Jabhat al Nusra. They'd discovered the note, then. And probably the rope.

Ethan retrieved the pile of flatbread from Mufid, who had been waiting at the designated street corner as instructed.

"Thank you." Ethan turned away.

"Wait!" Mufid said to his back. "Am I done now, or do I have to keep coming back here with bread every day?"

"You're done!" Ethan increased his pace, biting down a flare-up of ankle pain.

"What about my money?"

"Later!" Ethan hissed.

When he reached the checkpoint a few minutes later, a convoy of seven pickups raced past, truck beds packed with mujahadeen. They were headed in the direction of the apartment.

Abdullah got off his two-way radio. "We're supposed to be on the lookout for a masked fighter," he said as Ethan distributed the bread. "A member of Al Nusra has assassinated a civilian, and may be impersonating one of our brothers. Did you see anyone?"

Ethan shook his head.

"But the crime took place at the apartment building across the street from the bakery," Abdullah persisted.

"It must have happened after I left," Ethan said.

Abdullah's eyes bored into his and for a moment Ethan thought the emir was going to arrest him. He felt each heartbeat distinctly in his throat.

Zarar broke the tension by comically tearing into a piece of bread and exaggerating the difficulty of breaking it. "What the hell did you do to this bread?" The big Afghan took a bite. "Tastes as hard as an old woman's cunt."

"Why am I not surprised you know what that tastes like?" Ethan said, doing his best to hide his nervousness.

Zarar grinned toothily; portions of chewed bread covered his enamel so that it looked like half his mouth was rotten.

Abdullah regarded Ethan a moment longer, then stepped aside to speak quietly into his two-way radio.

The others finished their bread and returned to work. Suleman lingered, giving Ethan a suspicious look before he took his place on the checkpoint.

Ethan tried hard to conceal the limp for the rest of that day. He kept expecting Abdullah to arrest him, but the emir never did.

Suleman was driving Ethan back to the compound in the Mitsubishi L200 pickup when the militant said, "What happened to your leg?"

Ethan casually thrummed his fingers on the passenger door rest. "What do you mean?"

"I saw you hiding a limp back there."

"Oh." Ethan cleared his throat, which suddenly felt dry. "I tripped on the way to the bakery. It's nothing serious."

"You weren't involved in the shooting today?"

Ethan pressed his lips together. "Of course not."

"You were gone a suspicious amount of time the last time we were in this neighborhood."

"Was I?"

Suleman muttered something underbreath. Then: "Do you swear by Allah against the forfeiture of your immortal soul and its burning in hellfire forevermore that you did not kill the civilian?"

"I swear by Allah and the Quran that I did not," Ethan said without batting an eye.

Suleman nodded. "That's good enough for me." He glanced at Ethan and affected a smile that did not touch his eyes. "I apologize for doubting you, brother."

Ethan shot him a soulless smile in kind, but Suleman had already returned his attention to the road.

* * *

A few days later, when it was apparent Ethan had gotten away scot-free with the hit, he left Sam an encrypted note. *Target terminated.*

He also placed a message in the gmail account he shared with Alzena. *Are you safe?*

He was relieved when he decrypted Alzena's single-word reply the next day. *Yes.*

He stared at that word for several moments. Then he deleted the draft and navigated to the change password screen. He entered a new password and his finger hovered over the enter key. Once he submitted that change, Alzena would never be able to communicate with him again.

Don't get involved with assets. Leave her alone.

Ethan should have stayed away. He should have changed the password. But he felt compelled to repay her for what she had done. And he wanted to do that personally, rather than by courier, because deep down he yearned to see her again, if only one more time.

He canceled the password change and left the following encrypted message instead:

I have fifty thousand pounds for you. I will drop it off this Sunday evening at nine.

Fifty thousand Syrian pounds was the equivalent of two hundred fifty US dollars. Ethan would have given more, but his stash was running low. He probably should have written her an IOU, but he didn't want to encourage her to leave Raqqa to cash it in—despite the repressive regime, it was far safer for her to remain in the city, at least for the moment.

He wasn't sure she'd allow it, but the next day when he checked the account, he found a message from her agreeing to the rendezvous.

By the time Sunday night rolled around, Ethan had cold feet. There were several reasons not to proceed with the rendezvous. She may have told the Khansa'a everything, either willingly or under duress, and visiting her could be a trap. Or perhaps she had told them nothing, but her apartment was under surveillance anyway.

Then there were the personal reasons not to go. Mainly, he liked her far too much. Or rather, *desired* her. He didn't expect anything to happen when he met her, of course. Nor did he really want anything to. He would go to her door, give her the money, thank her, and leave. When she sent him on his way, he would never see her again.

He set out at eight-thirty. His ankle had returned to normal over the past few days, so he was able to proceed at a good pace. He carried his Dragunov over one shoulder, and wore his balaclava with the Shahada headband. He ran a surveillance detection route on the way to the apartment and when he arrived he circled her block twice. None of the cars parked on the road were occupied. No one was lingering on the sidewalk. Someone may have been watching from one of the apartment windows or balconies across the street, but he'd never know because of the heavy canopies.

He decided to risk it.

Ethan proceeded to the apartment entrance. The door was slightly ajar, thanks to a doorstop someone had placed. Power was still on to most of the city that night, so he tried the intercom button corresponding to 2C anyway. No answer came. Troubling.

He entered, closing the door silently behind him. As he climbed the stairs to the second floor, all his senses were alert for the potential trap that might be sprung against him.

He skipped the second and third floor hallways, proceeding to the top of the stairwell. With his bump keys, he unlocked the rooftop door and left it open behind him as he cased the terrace. The north edge dropped to a shared courtyard, but there was no way to get down without a rope. To the left lay a neighboring rooftop, about a meter and a half away. A doable jump, but still risky. Well, if he was to properly secure his exfil route...

He took a running leap and landed on the adjacent building. He felt a small stab of pain in his ankle, but thankfully the limb held. He explored the rooftop and found a fire escape in back. That would do. He studied the courtyard below, and when he had picked out a possible exfil, he crossed back to the other building.

A few moments later he rapped warily on Alzena's door.

It opened a crack. The security chain drooped just inside, still latched, preventing the door from opening any wider. Ethan almost didn't see the figure beyond at first, because she wore a niqab, face shrouded in darkness.

"Alzena?" he said.

"Give me the money and go," she said softly.

He was relieved to hear her voice. Not a trap, then. At least not one she had set up. He was disappointed Alzena was wearing the full veil, however.

Keeping his voice down, Ethan asked, "Why didn't you answer when I buzzed?"

"I left the door open for you."

Ethan should have given her the money then and walked out of that building, like she asked. But instead he found himself saying, "Let me in."

She shook her head. "It is not decent. It is haram."

"But that's never stopped you before, has it?" Ethan said.

"What are you talking about?" She sounded astonished.

"You were leaving me messages almost every day, there. Going down to the Internet cafe alone."

Her tone became cold. "That's different."

"Is it?" Ethan said. "Haram is haram."

"Maybe I hired one of those chaperon services like you suggested."

Ethan smiled widely. "But that is haram, too." He glanced at the other doors flanking the hallway behind him. "Come on, let me in before someone sees you talking to a strange man."

She didn't comply.

He hesitated, then removed his balaclava so that she could see his face. "Alzena. Please. There are things I want to tell you, things I can't speak of out here."

Reluctantly she closed the door. He heard the click as the security chain unlatched, then she let him in, shutting the door behind him.

He stood there on the Turkish carpet. Candles lit the foyer and the living room beside it. "What's with the candles?" he said. "The power's on, you know."

"I can't afford the bill." She sounded bitter. "What is it you wish to say to me?"

He calmly walked into the family room and relaxed in the green polyester accent chair. He slid the Dragunov from his shoulder and rested it on the floor beside him.

The black ghost that was Alzena followed him into the room. She remained standing next to the counter, where three thick candles burned.

He regarded her dubiously.

"Isn't that a fire hazard?" Ethan nodded toward her veil. "Wouldn't take much to ignite the niqab. All you have to do is lean forward to grab a book or something and before you know it you're covered in flames."

"The material is fire retardant," she said flatly.

Ethan shrugged. "Doesn't mean it won't burn."

She didn't answer.

"Here." He retrieved an envelope from his pocket and tossed it onto the glass coffee table. Several crisp bills spilled out.

Alzena made no move to take the money. "You killed him, didn't you?" she said.

twenty-one

It was Ethan's turn to stay quiet, though that was exactly what he wanted to talk to her about. The question was, how to do it without implicating himself?

"I trusted you, but you betrayed that trust," she continued. "I arranged for you to meet my neighbor's husband, and you murdered him."

Still Ethan didn't answer. Perhaps it was for the best that he couldn't see her face. The disappointment in her voice was painful enough.

"Do you know why I originally agreed to help you?" she asked.

"Because you had no choice?" Ethan said, feeling a rise of anger. "Because it was either help me or be reported to the morality police?"

"I could have taken the whipping," Alzena said from behind her veil. "I could have. But I chose to help you."

"Fine. Why did you help me?"

Her voice softened. "Because I recognized you. I saw you save a man in front of the bakery the week before. Do you remember? I was watching from beyond the blinds of my apartment, as I often do, confined to this prison that is my own home. I saw you use a chokehold to knock the cussing man unconscious before the Hisbah could hear what he was saying." She took an almost imperceptible step forward. "*That's* why I helped you. I knew you were different. Or I thought you were, anyway." A sadness entered her voice. "I truly thought that you weren't like the others. That you were here to help my city. But I was wrong.

You're just a killer like the rest of them."

Ethan regarded her black form in silence. *I could have taken the whipping*. Those words reminded him of something. "Your brother beat you before we met at Al Rashid."

She lowered her head but did not reply.

"He did, didn't he?" Ethan pressed. "I saw how you sat in the restaurant, constantly trying to avoid the back of your seat. I saw how stiffly you walked."

"Yes," she said bitterly. "He whipped me when I told him, at your suggestion, that I opened my apartment door without a veil."

"A man who beats his own sister." Ethan shook his head. "Incredible."

"He is Hisbah. He can do what he wants. Like the mujahadeen."

Ethan considered his next words carefully. "I *am* here to help your city. But perhaps not in the way you might think."

"You're with the Caliphate," Alzena said flatly.

"Am I? Are you so certain?"

She paused. "You know, before the foreign fighters came, my city was one of the most liberal in all of the Middle East. We were moderate Muslims, lovers of freedom. We smoked cigarettes and shisha, and drank alcohol. The women roamed the streets freely, unchaperoned and unveiled. We stayed out as late as we wanted. We had power and water all day, everyday. And now... *this*."

"I'm here to help you," Ethan repeated. "The scientist? He was a very bad man. The world is a better place without him, believe me."

"So you did kill him," Alzena said.

Ethan still refused to incriminate himself. He didn't know how far he could trust her. She might even be wearing a wire beneath those heavy robes, though that was doubtful.

"Why did you come tonight?" Alzena said.

"To give you the money."

She raised her veil.

Ethan's breath caught. He couldn't take his eyes away from her face. Those high, chiseled cheekbones; that thin jawline, perfectly crafted nose, flawless skin. She could have been a fashion model in any other country, under better circumstances. But there, in that repressed land of no opportunity, she couldn't even show her face to strangers.

Alzena smiled, but it was a sad one. "Why did you come?" she repeated.

"I—" He couldn't break his gaze from those intoxicating features no matter how hard he tried; he found himself lost in the brilliant sapphires of her eyes.

She took off her hijab then, and let her long, flowing black hair tumble free.

"What are you doing?" Ethan finally managed, his voice rasping.

"I told you," she said huskily. "We were once the most liberal of all Muslims in the Middle East."

Don't get involved with assets, the voice of reason warned him, but it couldn't quench the unbridled fire of lust that burned inside him.

Ethan got up and closed the distance between himself and Alzena. He mashed his lips against hers. She returned the kiss just as feverishly.

He experienced a sharp pain in his mouth and pulled back in shock. He felt a wetness and touched the throbbing area; when he withdrew his fingers he found blood.

Alzena bit her lower lip playfully.

"You bitch." Ethan threw her onto the couch.

She flinched, then spun herself around so that her back was to him. "Take me," she commanded over her shoulder.

Ethan stripped off her abaya. Long, ugly welts marred the perfection of her back. He felt a moment of rage and swore he'd kill her brother if ever he crossed paths with the Hisbah again.

He tore off her panties, slid down his cargo pants, and took her from behind. Incidentally, she wasn't wearing a wire.

After he climaxed, he carried her to the bedroom, cupping her by the buttocks while she wrapped her arms and legs around his torso. His cargo pants and underwear dragged from one foot, and he nearly tripped in the darkness.

When he reached the room, he threw her onto the bed and she gasped, maybe from the pain caused by her welts, maybe in anticipation. Ethan was beyond rational thought and simply didn't care either way—he doffed the remainder of his clothing and took her again. She moaned in pleasure, raking his back with her nails, drawing blood.

Afterward they cuddled in her bed. She lay on her side, her breasts pressing into his ribcage, threatening to arouse him all over again.

She had lit a candle on the nightstand, allowing him to see her face in the dimness. Such beauty. Wasted in that country.

"How's your back?" he said.

"How's yours?" she said mischievously.

He groaned softly. The throbbing pain from her nails had almost subsided, but the scratches would probably take at least a week to heal.

"I haven't been with a man since my husband died." She regarded him uncertainly a moment. "I hope you don't get the wrong idea. I slept with you mostly to defy my brother."

"So I'm just a revenge fuck." Ethan said.

She looked at him angrily. "Don't talk like that to me."

Ethan laughed softly. "We did some pretty X-rated stuff back there, and now you're saying I can't swear?"

She glared at him one more time but it was only pretend, because soon she was snuggling against his side again.

"You surprised me," Ethan said. "Your passion. Everything about you. I never thought..."

"Just because I'm Muslim doesn't mean I am not a woman," she said, sounding slightly offended. "Maybe you didn't notice, but those who seek to impose sharia are all men."

"Oh I noticed," Ethan said.

"And you are for sharia?" she asked.

"Utterly against."

"Good."

The two rested for a time.

Alzena abruptly broke the silence. "I was forced to marry him, you know. The mujahid." She swallowed with obvious discomfort at the memory. "A member of the Khansa'a Brigade visited my apartment. She offered a large *mahr*"—that was a payment made by the groom or his family—"and despite my objections, my brother accepted. He took the mahr. He also seized the money I was sent from the Caliphate—as the wife of a mujahid I was on their payroll. But I received only what my brother and my husband deigned to give me."

"I'm sorry."

"I didn't mind so much. I needed a husband. You see, most of my family and friends fled when the Islamic State arrived. Only my brother remained. I was very much alone, and a husband made things more bearable. Though I would have preferred one of my own choosing. A better lover would have been nice, too."

Ethan looked at her in the dim light and couldn't resist joking, "When you've been with the best, the rest just can't measure up."

She slapped his shoulder gently. "Silly."

He was about to get up but Alzena, as if sensing his intention, wrapped an arm across his chest, pinning him. He supposed he could stay a little longer.

He listened to her gentle breathing, felt the rise and fall of her bosom against him, the warmth of each exhale, the smell of her hair.

He had to be very careful not to fall asleep, as he was wont to do after passionate lovemaking. He had to return to the government complex before curfew or questions would be asked.

As much as he savored that small moment of unbridled love, that tiny microcosm of passion and joy in a sea of repression and hate, he knew it would not last. It was fleeting, like all moments, good or bad. To visit her again would be far too risky for the both of them. And even if he did return, and she let him in, there would come a time when eventually he must let her go. Better to experience that moment sooner rather than later, before he became too attached.

He looked at her, knowing that he would probably never see her again, and at last shoved her arm aside. "I have to go."

"I know."

She brazenly watched him dress under the candlelight. He smiled sadly. Let her watch.

He donned the last pieces of his outfit, the balaclava and headband, and left the room. She didn't say a word. Didn't even rise from the bed. She was probably feeling the same sense of loss, of what could have been, as him.

He closed the door of her apartment behind him and it shut with a finality that made him pause.

"Goodbye, Alzena," he said softly.

He proceeded downstairs and didn't look back.

twenty-two

The days passed slowly. Ethan did his best to shut her out of his mind, with little success. He couldn't shake the memory of her and the night they had spent together no matter how hard he tried. He checked his email account daily, but there were never any messages from her.

He went for walks sometimes after checkpoint duty was over, and he got as close as her neighborhood, but he couldn't bring himself to approach the apartment. He hoped his unit was assigned outside of Raqqa soon. It would make things easier.

Four nights later he discovered a new message awaiting in the draft folder of the account he shared with her. There was no subject.

He didn't open it. Instead, his first reaction was one of anger. He had said his goodbyes. He was trying to move on. And then she had to go and contact him again.

It wasn't entirely her fault, he had to admit. He was the one who kept checking for messages. If he didn't want to hear from her, all he had to do was change the password, or never log in to that account again.

Ethan stared at the unopened message.

Don't read it. Don't read it.

He ticked the checkbox to the left of the message and moved the cursor over the "delete selected" option. His fingered hovered over the mouse button...

If he let that message go unread, he could continue his mission without guilt. He could carry on farming intelligence and eliminating high value targets as he came across them. Business as usual.

But if he opened that message, all that could change.

Don't read the message.

He deleted it and logged off.

He returned to room three-ten and tried to read the Quran on his cellphone but he couldn't concentrate. He kept thinking of the feel of Alzena's body against his. The softness of her kiss. The smell of her hair. It would be so easy to walk to her apartment and spend the next hour with her. So easy.

No. He had moved on.

He had.

Finally Abdullah announced lights out. Ethan put away his Android and slept a troubled sleep.

* * *

The next morning Ethan scooped up his Dragunov, skipped breakfast and went directly to the computer room. Curiosity was tearing him apart inside.

When a machine freed up, he logged in and moved Alzena's email from the trash to the draft folder. He stared at the unopened message for several indecisive seconds.

He clicked on the blank subject and the message body opened up. He knew something was wrong immediately, because the text wasn't encrypted. It read, in Arabic script:

I did not want to do this, but you forced my hand. Thanks to you, tomorrow I must watch my sister die under the executioner's ax.

I hope you are happy.

May Allah deny you for all eternity!

His heart felt like it was going to beat out of his chest. It was from Alzena's brother, Ethan was certain. No one else could have known about the shared account, nor possessed the audacity to write something like that.

Ethan double-checked the date on the message. The draft was saved yesterday afternoon. That meant Alzena was scheduled for execution today.

Ethan turned toward the militant who used the computer beside him.

"Brother," Ethan said. "Where do the executions take place?"

"Clock Tower Square."

"And at what time, usually?" Ethan pressed.

"In the morning. Around now."

Feeling a sudden stab in the pit of his gut, Ethan got up. "Thank you," he said stiffly.

"Go with Allah." The smile the militant gave him seemed mocking somehow, though of course it wasn't intended it as such.

Ethan grabbed his Dragunov and left the computer room, but hurried back because he'd forgotten the USB stick. When he retrieved it he went straight to the supply room.

"Abu-Emad, good to see you!" the supply officer said. "What can I do for you this morning?"

"I need free reign of the room." Ethan slapped down five hundred pounds.

The Syrian stared at the money for a moment, then he scooped up the banknotes and separated the desks that blocked off the entrance, allowing Ethan to squeeze past.

Apparently body armor had arrived from Mosul the day before; Ethan grabbed a Kevlar vest and donned it beneath his fatigues. He also took a couple of Soviet RGD-5 hand grenades, putting them in his harness. He procured a Makarov, as he had returned the previous pistol the supply officer had lent him for his meeting with the scientist. He attached a magazine preloaded with 9x18mm cartridges, chambered a bullet, engaged the safety, and tucked the Makarov into his belt. He stowed a spare magazine in his harness and filled the remainder of his pockets with Dragunov magazines. He checked if there were any US assault rifles or sniper variants in stock yet, but the supply officer told him the American weapons were always snatched up by the emirs the moment they arrived.

He thanked the man and made his way toward the parking lot. Ethan wore his camo jacket low, concealing the pistol at his belt. There was no way to hide the grenades secured to his harness, but he doubted anyone would say anything.

As he neared the exit, Ethan wondered if his cover was blown. Raafe hadn't mentioned him by name. Was it possible he didn't know who the gmail account belonged to? What *did* the man know?

Suleman intercepted him on the way out of the compound. "You! Come."

Suddenly feeling trapped, Ethan joined the militant. But Suleman merely led him to the Mitsubishi L200 pickup. Apparently his cover wasn't blown. Not yet, anyway. As usual, Harb babysat the anti-aircraft gun in the truck bed.

The Mitsubishi brought up the rear of the motorcade. As Ethan sat there in the passenger seat on the way to the day's checkpoint, wherever that might be, he strove to invent some excuse to divert the truck. He barely recognized the blur of the passing buildings, locked as he was in his own mind.

Maybe Raafe was lying? Surely her brother wouldn't send Alzena to the executioner's ax. Then again, a zealous Hisbah like him, a man who had whipped his own sister, would think nothing of ordering her death—he was drunk on power and his perceived righteousness. And perhaps Raafe truly didn't know who the gmail account belonged to; that message might have been a lure to draw out Ethan.

A lone woman wasn't worth dying for, nor giving up access to intelligence that could potentially save thousands of lives. No one else would replace Ethan—that wasn't hubris talking, but the voice of cold, harsh reason. Very few people could do what he did and do it well. Maybe a handful in the entire world. Sam believed she could eventually repurpose other units to act as her Selous Scouts, but the other case officers, paramilitaries and spec-op types lacked one essential skill or the other. They didn't have the language skills. They didn't look Arabic. They didn't have the mental fortitude.

And yet it was probably his fault Alzena was slated for execution. He was the one who had dragged her into all this. He was the one who had insisted on paying her a personal visit.

He'd disobeyed key rules of tradecraft by going to her apartment that night. Don't visit an asset who is potentially under surveillance. Don't disobey local customs if doing so puts the asset's life further at risk.

Don't get involved with assets.

He owed Alzena her life in repayment for everything she had done, and if he didn't at least *try* to save her, he'd never forgive himself.

But that was a selfish reason. It wasn't good enough, when weighed against the potential loss of intelligence. Because even if he did manage to somehow save her, what would he use as an alibi? Without one, his cover would be lost and he'd have to go into hiding.

There has to be a way to save her while preserving my cover. There has to be!

Then again, his cover might be lost already. What if Raafe knew everything and was on his way to inform Abdullah at that very moment of Ethan's involvement with Alzena and his role in the scientist's assassination?

What a mess I've put myself in.

Ethan pulled out his Android and activated the offline map. The convoy was headed southbound. Clock Tower Square was only a few blocks distant.

Alzena was there. About to be beheaded at any moment.

If I want to save her, I have to act now.

Ethan fingered the Makarov at his belt. If he had to, he could kill Suleman without any misgivings, but what would he do about Harb in the truck bed? Ethan couldn't bring himself to hurt the thirteen year old.

And then an opportunity abruptly presented itself.

The passing buildings slowed, becoming stationary as the traffic ground to a halt.

Suleman shifted impatiently in his seat. "There must be some beheadings scheduled for today." He activated his signal light and looked over his shoulder. "We should have taken the side street." He started to change lanes but slammed on the brakes as a random vehicle pulled up. More traffic arrived and in moments the Mitsubishi was hemmed in on all sides.

"Where are we setting up the checkpoint today?" Ethan asked Suleman.

"In front of the Raqqa Museum."

Ethan regarded the map one last time and then put away his cellphone. He wrapped his hands around the door handle, but didn't open it. Instead, he closed his eyes and inhaled deeply, bracing himself. One last moment of calm before the storm.

He hesitated. There was no time for any fancy planning and exfil routes. Everything would be seat-of-the-pants, and very risky. Did he really want to go through with it?

He thought of Alzena kneeling on the headblock, her beautiful face contorted in terror as the blade descended...

Ethan clenched his jaw and opened the door.

"What are you doing?" Suleman said, a hint of anger in his voice.

"I have to use the toilet badly," Ethan said.

"Wait until we reach the checkpoint."

"I can't hold it. See you at the museum!" Ethan slammed the door.

Harb looked at him in surprise from his place on the truck bed.

"What's up?" the thirteen-year-old asked.

"Diarrhea!" Ethan said over his shoulder.

He broke into a run, weaving between the stopped vehicles. His two-way radio chirped to life.

"I will wait for you by the curb," came Suleman's voice. "Hurry up!"

Ethan slid the volume knob way down, clicking the radio off. *You can wait all day.*

He dashed into an alley and pulled on his balaclava. He lowered the Dragunov from his shoulder and detached the PSO-1 via the quick-release mounting bracket, pocketing it. The 4x scope wouldn't be all that useful in the firefight to come, not at the ranges he intended. Without the PSO-1, the rifle looked similar to an AK-47, though the smaller magazine box and longer barrel would give the weapon away to the discerning eye. Still, with luck the militants would report that the attacker carried an AK, not a sniper rifle. Something less to incriminate him.

He emerged from the alley into another congested street. Ethan recognized the area—Clock Tower Square lay four blocks ahead. The problem was getting there in time through the backed up traffic. The road had been turned into a one-way today, apparently, judging from the southbound vehicles taking up both lanes. He considered jogging it, but when he arrived he would be winded—a bad way to enter a firefight. And it might be too late by then.

He crossed the street and walked up to the driver-side window of a white Kia Rio stuck in the gridlock. He pointed the Dragunov at the occupant.

"Out!"

The thirtyish Syrian immediately opened the door and Ethan yanked him the rest of the way out. Taking his place, Ethan tossed the Dragunov into the empty passenger seat, then turned the wheel to the left and accelerated onto the sidewalk. Pedestrians scrambled away. A shawarma kiosk toppled and the huge skewer of goat meat rolled over the hood of the subcompact.

Southbound, Ethan drove at thirty kilometers per hour along the sidewalk, his fingers constantly on the horn. Street vendors and pedestrians continued to scurry out of the way. He smashed through more food stands.

He had chosen the sidewalk bordering the left side of the street because if Clock Tower Square was sealed off, traffic would soon be siphoned to the right onto the only available side street; by keeping to the left, no civilian cars would block his path.

He could see the tower ahead, looming over the buildings and vehicles. The beheaded peasant statues on top ominously overlooked the city.

He reached a roadblock of four black Toyota Hilux Vigos; the vehicles were lined up front to back, blocking traffic in and out of the square. Small gaps remained at either end of the roadblock for the sidewalks, allowing pedestrians to trickle inside. Eight militants stood guard.

Ethan kept the Rio on the sidewalk, aiming for the gap between the leftmost pickup and the adjacent building. His subcompact would fit, but barely.

Four of the militants on duty rushed toward him and waved him down. One approached the driver-side door while the others blocked his path, AK-47s raised.

Ethan halted the vehicle and opened his window. "Let me through."

"Idiot, we almost shot you!" The militant spoke Arabic with a French accent. "We thought you were a suicide bomber! You didn't answer your radio."

"I said let me through!" Ethan revved the engine.

"Go back you fool."

"I have an important message for the executioner!" Ethan inched the Rio forward, threatening to mow down the fighters in front of the vehicle. They kept their weapons pointed at him.

"From who?" the militant said.

"The sheik!" That was what the Islamic State called the mayor of Raqqa.

"The sheik?" the militant said dubiously. "Well, deliver your message if you must, but leave the vehicle. This square is packed with people. You might kill someone."

Just like your executioner is about to do?

Ethan needed the vehicle for what was to come, so he reached through the window and grabbed the fighter by the collar, dragging him close. "If you don't let me through right now, *with* the vehicle, you and your French friends will be the ones losing their heads here tomorrow! I guarantee you."

He shoved the militant away, ducked behind the dashboard, and accelerated. The other mujahadeen blocking his path dove out of the way, but didn't fire. The flanks of his Kia scraped the bumper of the Hilux and the adjacent building. Pedestrians hurried from his path.

In the right rearview mirror he saw the militants regroup to aim their AKs at his subcompact; he crouched lower in the seat. His window was still open, and he heard the French mujahid shouting at them to stand down. The men must have listened because no bullets came. Lucky.

Ahead, the crowd was thick around the base of the clock tower. He didn't spot a single woman among them.

Honking, Ethan slowed to ten kilometers an hour as he plowed his way through. The gathering parted to reveal the lower half of the tower, which was draped in the black standards of the Islamic State.

He saw the chopping block next to the structure immediately. A decapitated torso lay against it, with a lifeless head at its base. A woman, dressed in black. Her head was still shrouded in its niqab.

Ethan was too late.

An overwhelming sense of defeat overcame him. He had driven all that way, prepared to do the worst to save her, and she was already gone. He felt suddenly nauseous.

He slammed on the brakes and put his head down, remembering her touch, and her smile.

Why do the most innocent among us always have to die? Why why why?

He started accelerating again, intending to turn the subcompact around, but more of the crowd cleared ahead of him and he saw that two other headblocks were arranged near the base of the tower. Another woman knelt before the middle chopping block, also wearing a niqab so that her face was concealed. Her head was lowered onto the black stone. The rear portion of her veil and hijab had been lifted to reveal her neck.

Long scimitar in hand, the dark-robed executioner stood over her. He seemed distracted by the Rio's arrival. Past him, at the final headblock, a mujahid restrained a final prisoner. Some random bearded man.

Ethan drove in front of the middle headblock, partially shielding the kneeling woman from the crowd's view, and parked. Was it her? It had to be.

It *had* to.

Leaving the driver-side window open, he grabbed the Dragunov from the passenger seat, slung it over his shoulder and, still wearing his balaclava, stepped out.

twenty-three

He made a mental note of the crowd-control militants among the throng, easily identifiable by their AKs. Four on the right side. Three on the left, including the mujahid who held the male prisoner. There was no sign of Raafe. Couldn't stand to watch the beheading of his own sister in the end, apparently.

One of the militants stepped forward, shouting, "What are you doing?" Another French accent.

Moving slowly, imperiously, like he had every right to be there, Ethan raised a halting hand toward the foreign fighter.

"Be silent, Frenchman," Ethan said in perfect Arabic. He had noticed that foreign jihadists were treated with disdain by the native-speaking emirs. He thought he'd try to play that up.

The man froze.

Good.

None of them knew who he was, not while he wore the balaclava. Perhaps he could convince them he was some high-ranking emir. Perhaps he could get through this without firing a single shot.

It was a nice thought.

The executioner regarded Ethan with a mix of curiosity and indignation. A stern-featured, middle-aged man, he was dressed in a black, flowing robe with a chador-like hood rimming his face. His long gray beard reached his sternum. He looked like a deeply religious man. Maybe an imam.

Ethan walked past him and gave the executioner a come hither gesture. He approached the clock tower; there was a metal post at each of its four corners, where guardrails once hung. Ethan stepped around the right-hand corner of the tower, out of the sightline of the three militants to his left but in full view of those on his right.

Ethan peered past the edge. The executioner hadn't moved from his spot. Ethan beckoned again, more emphatically, and finally the gray-bearded man grudgingly came forward, sword dangling from his hand.

He reached Ethan.

"How dare—" the executioner began.

Ethan decided instantly that no words would sway the man. Better to act while surprise was on his side.

He withdrew the Makarov from his belt and shot the executioner in the thigh.

Cries of fear and outrage erupted from the throng. Many people ducked.

Ethan caught the executioner and swiveled toward the four crowd-control fighters on his right, placing the headman firmly between himself and them; the clock tower at his back shielded him from the remaining men.

Though all four of the mujahadeen had raised their AKs, none of them fired for fear of harming the headman, who was obviously some important religious official.

Ethan raised his pistol and let off three shots in rapid succession, adjusting his aim slightly to the right each time. Red blooms erupted from each militant's forehead in turn, and they toppled in place like marionettes whose strings had been cut.

Before he got off the fourth shot, the last muj finally opened fire. Blood spurted from the executioner's chest as the bullets struck. Ethan felt the impacts as his Kevlar body armor deflected the reduced-energy ballistics that passed through the headman.

Ethan squeezed the trigger and the last tango went down.

The crowd was in full retreat by then.

With all four militiamen on the right side down, Ethan tossed the executioner's bullet-riddled body aside like so much refuse.

He peered past the clock tower's base. The crowd was dispersing to the far ends of the square, preventing the militants at the various roadblocks from reaching the structure.

The woman remained kneeling before the headblock, as if oblivious to her surroundings, waiting for death to come. The other man slated for execution lay on the steps, blood seeping from a fresh bullet hole to his temple. After seeing that, Ethan did a double take on the woman, worried that she too had been shot by the militants, but he couldn't discern any blood on her niqab.

There was no sign of the remaining three crowd-control fighters. Wait... on the opposite end of the structure, the barrel of a Kalashnikov abruptly protruded, along with the head and shoulders of the mujahid holding it.

Ethan ducked just as the muzzle fired. Shards of black rock broke away from the tower beside him.

Likely the other two militants were making their way around the back side to outflank him.

Ethan removed one of the RGD-5 fragmentation grenades from his harness. He squeezed the lever, pulled the pin, crossed the two meters to the rear side of the tower, and without looking he tossed the grenade beyond the edge.

He heard the loud "pop" as the fuze of the grenade ignited midflight, followed by a shout a moment later.

Ethan retreated, hugging his side of the clock tower, keeping his Makarov pointed at the edge.

One of the militants raced into view, trying to escape the grenade. Ethan shot him in the forehead.

The ground shook as the one hundred and ten gram charge of TNT in the grenade detonated around the bend. The liner could produce over three hundred fragments, lethally shredding anything within a radius of three meters, and injuring up to fifteen meters out from the site of activation. Not bad for a grenade that sold for five US dollars.

Fragments blurred the air ahead of him and Ethan instinctively looked away, though there was no chance the pieces could reach him where he stood.

Pistol raised, he leaned past the rear rim. A militant lay on the ground near the base of the tower, quivering, covered in blood.

Just then, the third militant peered past the far edge to check on his friends. Ethan adjusted his aim slightly and fired. A red dot appeared in the man's cheek and he crumpled.

Ethan lowered his aim and put the second man out of his misery. The slide on the gun locked open—he'd fired all eight rounds.

He replaced the spent magazine with the fresh one from his harness, then flicked the pistol's slide-stop lever downward with his thumb. The device returned to its forward closed position, chambering a fresh cartridge in the process.

The square was quickly emptying. Ethan sprinted toward the faceless woman, who had sat up by that point, though she remained on her knees before the headblock.

As he reached her, gunfire erupted from the northernmost section of the square. Apparently the crowd had thinned enough for the militants manning the roadblocks there to open fire.

Ethan crouched beside her, using the white subcompact car as his shield. At that range the AK bullets wouldn't penetrate the vehicle.

He hoped.

"Alzena?" he said.

That featureless black head turned toward him. "Yes?"

He recognized her voice immediately. It was definitely Alzena, though she sounded dazed. Momentary relief washed over him, but he shoved it aside. He had to remain focused. A cold, emotionless killing machine.

Keeping low, he helped Alzena to a crouch and brought her to the passenger door. He shoved the pistol into her hands.

She bobbed her head to look at it; probably didn't know the first thing about firing a 9-mil.

"Let me know if anyone comes at us from behind," Ethan said, referring to the southernmost roadblock, which was still obscured by fleeing civilians.

He swung the Dragunov down from his shoulder and aimed past the subcompact's rear bumper, toward the line of trucks that blockaded the northwest section of the square. He aligned the metal sights over the head of a militant who peered past the truck bed of one of the Hilux Vigos. The range was about thirty meters.

Ethan fired, ducking behind the Rio immediately afterward. Bullets ricocheted from the car's frame beside him in answer.

Don't hit the tires. Don't hit the tires.

"Is it really you?" Alzena said from beside him.

Ethan refused to look at her. "Couldn't let you die because of me."

"Oh Alrajil, what have you done?"

"Ethan," he said.

"What?"

"Ethan." He finally glanced at her. "My real name." It was important to him that she knew in that moment. He opened the passenger door. "Get in. Stay low."

Staying crouched, he maneuvered to the front of the Rio and aimed over the hood. He picked out the head and shoulders of another militant and let off a shot, then ducked. Behind him, the crowd on the southside of the square was thinning. The militants there would be able to join the fray shortly. Time to go.

He returned to the passenger door. Alzena had obeyed him, and sat hunched in the seat.

Ethan slung the Dragunov over his shoulder and snatched the Makarov from her. He hauled himself over her huddled form, firing through the open driver side window with the pistol as he did so. He aimed in the general direction of the northwest roadblock. It was a spray and pray tactic, with the emphasis on pray.

He slid over the center console with its stick shift, cup holder and parking brake. When he reached the driver seat he immediately ducked beneath the window. Bullets zinged past.

He put the vehicle in gear and peered over the dash to drive toward the northwest roadblock. He could've attempted one of the other barricades that sealed off the square instead, but decided it was better to deal with the devil he knew.

As the Rio neared the roadblock, he leaned out the window and aimed at the tires of the nearest pickup. He fired a couple of shots, but missed. Shooting from a moving vehicle was never his forte. The slide on the Makarov abruptly locked open. Empty magazine.

Return fire came, and Ethan ducked inside.

He steered the Rio toward the gap between the rightmost pickup and the adjacent building, the same path he'd taken on the way in. Both sides of the vehicle received fire as the militants manning the other roadblocks engaged.

"Stay down!" Ethan told Alzena, hoping the Rio would hold up to the battering.

The windshield abruptly shattered in several places, leaving big, crater-like holes. A rocket-propelled-grenade exploded near the rear bumper and the blast momentarily tilted the subcompact.

When all four wheels were on the ground again Ethan ripped past the rightmost Toyota Hilux, scraping his car against it. Bullets momentarily riddled the Rio's driver side as the militants crouching behind the Toyotas continued to fire; the shots cut out as he drove onward and the gridlocked traffic on the road obscured the subcompact.

The sidewalk swarmed with pedestrians fleeing the square, and Ethan honked constantly, alternately braking and accelerating as the foot traffic dodged out of the way. It was difficult to see through the cratered windshield, but he planned on abandoning the subcompact shortly.

In the rearview mirror he spotted a black Hilux Vigo racing down the sidewalk in pursuit. Following in the Rio's wake, the Toyota would soon overtake them since less pedestrian traffic hindered its advance.

Still honking, Ethan scanned the avenue, trying to spot an exfil route. There, an alleyway across the street, about half a block distant.

He slammed on the brakes. "Out!"

He exited the subcompact and led Alzena by the hand, weaving between the densely packed vehicles.

Gunfire erupted behind them. Ethan pulled Alzena low and continued toward the alleyway. He heard the characteristic screech of rapid braking; glancing over the hood of a nearby car, he saw that the pursuing Hilux had stopped behind the Rio.

Eight militants leaped out of the truck bed and headed after them.

twenty-four

Ethan led Alzena forward, keeping low. Bullets occasionally ricocheted from the gridlocked vehicles around them.

He reached the sidewalk and pulled her into the tight confines of the alley he'd spotted earlier. They raced beneath crowded clotheslines and over trash piles. The stench of cat urine was strong. Ahead, two street urchins were eating some bread, probably stolen; the pair scattered at Ethan's approach.

As he and Alzena exited the far end, he grabbed the last RGD-5 fragmentation grenade from his harness. He squeezed the lever, pulled the pin, and waited beside the opening.

He peered into the alleyway. The militants had only just entered.

Ethan didn't throw the grenade immediately. When the group was about five meters into the alley, he tossed the bomb and ran.

He heard the explosion and didn't look back.

He led Alena down a side street where the traffic was far less dense and he flagged down a passing Hyundai Elantra. He commandeered the white compact at gunpoint, forcing out a man in a business suit.

Once Alzena was inside, Ethan performed a mid-street U-turn and accelerated north toward the Raqqa city limits. He set the Dragunov down on the dashboard and tore off his balaclava.

Several Hilux pickups roared past on the left side of the road, packed with militants headed for Clock Tower Square.

Ethan apprehensively watched the pickups in his rearview mirror.

He saw the businessman trying to flag them down but the vehicles ignored him and sped away.

Ethan exhaled in relief. He felt a little lightheaded, which he attributed to adrenaline hangover. Of course it didn't help that he'd skipped breakfast.

"Are you okay?" he asked.

His passenger grunted some quiet reply.

"Alzena?"

"I'm fine," she said, though she sounded far from it. "Where are we going? *Where?*"

"Calm down. I don't know. Out of the city, maybe."

"What about the checkpoints?" she said, a little hysterically. "They'll ask for our IDs. I don't have mine anymore. We'll be detained."

"They'll let us pass." His eyes darted toward the Dragunov on the dashboard. "One way or another."

"They're going to kill us," Alzena said. "We're going to die."

"We're not going to die. Relax, Alzena."

Ethan spotted a checkpoint up ahead and purposely detoured to another street. He wasn't ready to deal with the Islamic State and their ilk, not yet. And Alzena certainly wasn't.

"How did you get arrested?" Ethan said, wanting to distract her. But the moment he asked the question he regretted it. He was certain the answer involved him, and he already blamed himself enough as it was.

Alzena took a moment to respond. He could hear her taking deep breaths, a relaxation technique. "Sorry, I just—" Wait, those weren't breaths: she was sobbing.

"Take your time," Ethan said.

In about a minute she had recovered enough to talk. "I... I didn't realize it at the time, but when you came to my apartment that night, the neighbor's son observed everything."

"The neighbor's son," Ethan said flatly.

"Yes. Just a boy of eleven years. His door is across from mine.

There is a spyhole."

"Great."

"When my brother visited on Wednesday, the son intercepted him and told him he had seen a strange man entering my apartment. My brother thanked him profusely and paid the child ten thousand pounds. I watched the entire transaction unfold from behind my door." She paused. "Is that how much my life is worth? Ten thousand pounds?" That was the equivalent of fifty bucks.

Ethan tightened his grip on the steering wheel. Definitely his fault. Worse, if the child had told Raafe about Ethan, then his cover had indeed been blown the moment he woke up that morning. If he had remained on duty at the checkpoint, likely he would have been arrested at some point during the day. It was a good thing he had gone ahead with the rescue attempt—if he had held back under the pretense of preserving his cover, he would have never forgiven himself.

"You don't have to come with me," Alzena said suddenly. The sorrow had left her voice, replaced by steel. A strong woman.

"I'm a wanted man now," Ethan said.

"But you wore your balaclava back there," Alzena countered.

"It doesn't matter. Your brother knows what I look like."

"Yes, but he thinks you're a different suitor," Alzena said.

Ethan felt his brows draw together. "What do you mean?"

"He doesn't know it was you who met me that night. In fact, he believes it was another man."

"What are you talking about?"

"The child didn't see your face," Alzena said. "So I told my brother a different mujahid had come that night."

"But Raafe left a message in the draft folder of the email account we shared."

"He did. I told him that was how I communicated with the man."

"So who does he think he was contacting?"

"Samuel Al Jordani, the fitness professional who knew my dearly departed husband. Not you, Alrajil... Ethan."

"You told him it was Samuel?" Ethan said in disbelief. "The alias I used to meet the scientist?"

"Yes."

"And you're certain he believed you?" Ethan pressed.

"I swore on the Quran."

"Ah." Muslim's didn't take that oath lightly. "So there's still a chance for me, then."

"But not me," Alzena added.

"You're wrong." Ethan spun the wheel and did a U-turn, heading back toward the city center.

"Where are we going?"

"You'll see," Ethan said. "By the way, if I ever bump into that treacherous brother of yours again, I'm going to—"

"You'll never meet him again," Alzena interrupted. "He volunteered for a martyrdom operation in Damascus against the Assad regime. He's already left the city. He'll be dead by the end of the week."

Good riddance.

Still, by sending that email to Ethan, maybe a small part of her brother, the part that loved his sister, hoped "Samuel" would somehow save her. That was the only explanation Ethan had for the message, since the trap theory had been disproved. Unless the email had been Raafe's twisted way of gloating.

Ethan reached the neighborhood he was looking for and parked the stolen Hyundai against the curb. He opened the door. "This way!"

Two blocks later Ethan arrived at Mufid's lingerie shop. When Ethan burst inside, the fifteen-year-old son of the owner started to duck behind the counter, but stopped himself when he realized who it was.

Mufid was conversing with a local near the entrance; when he saw Ethan, the shopkeeper promptly escorted out the other Syrian and locked the door.

"What do you want?" Mufid said curtly.

"I need you to smuggle this woman out of the city."

Mufid stared at him in disbelief, then laughed uproariously. "Incredible! Always you come here and make insane demands, expecting me to obey without question. But now you've really done it. This time, this demand..." He threw up his hands. "The camel's back is broken. I cannot do this. Taking pictures of buildings and buying bread is one thing, but smuggling people is an entirely different matter. It is too dangerous. And you know, to be honest I am tired—to the *core*—of being your dog." Mufid went to the counter and stood by his son. He placed a hand around the teenager's shoulder. "You would use my son against me? Threaten to turn him in if I disobey you? Well go ahead, I say. I won't stand for your threats anymore. In fact, I would rather turn him in myself and allow the executioner to take both our heads than continue being your lowly servant."

"I never threatened to turn him in," Ethan said in exasperation. "Look, I don't have time for this. I know you want money." He approached the counter and threw down several thousand pounds. "This is all I have. Now can we do this?"

Mufid's eyes lit up and he quickly collected the banknotes. After he pocketed the money he said, "It is not enough."

"I"ll bring more," Ethan said. "And write more IOUs, too, if that's what you want."

Mufid shook his head. "As I said, you can offer all the money in the world, but what you ask is too risky. I—"

His voice trailed off as his gaze drifted over Ethan's shoulder. Beside him, his son stared at something behind Ethan with wide, mesmerized eyes.

Ethan turned around.

Alzena had lifted her niqab.

"I know someone who can do it," the son said suddenly.

"Abdo!" Mufid said.

"My friend has done it before," Abdo said quickly, not taking his eyes from Alzena. "Trust me, he can get her out safely."

"How?" Ethan said, forestalling any response from Mufid.

"My friend has a truck," Abdo said.

"A truck," Ethan deadpanned.

"Yes. With a custom undercarriage. My friend uses it to smuggle oil into Turkey. The undercarriage can also hide a person, instead. My friend will need money to make the journey worthwhile, of course. And to pay the proper bribes."

Ethan glanced at the shopkeeper. "Mufid..."

The older Syrian shifted his gaze between Alzena and Abdo, obviously torn. Though whether it was the money he was concerned about or his son, Ethan didn't know.

"Mufid," Ethan said more firmly.

"He is my son," the shopkeeper said finally.

"Yes, but he is not the one doing the smuggling."

"But if his friend is caught, he will implicate my son," Mufid insisted.

"He won't get caught," Abdo said.

Ethan made his tone as intimidating as he could manage. "Give him the money. Or I'll take it from you."

Reluctantly, Mufid retrieved several bills from his pocket and handed them to his son.

Abdo frowned. "It's not enough, father."

Mufid glowered at Abdo, then placed several more bills into his son's open palms.

Ethan wrote IOUs for Mufid and Alzena, to be cashed in at some future date at the nearest American embassy. He folded up each note so that only the intended recipient could see the amount; for Mufid he allotted fifty thousand US dollars. For Alzena, two hundred thousand.

"I suggest your smuggler friend wait a few days before leaving the city," Ethan told Abdo. "Undercarriage or no, the mujahadeen are going to be on high alert over the next little while, and they'll probably search everything that comes through their checkpoints. Even if you have bribes."

"Why, what has happened?" Abdo said.

"I'm sure you'll be hearing about it soon enough. In the meantime, is there a place you can take her?"

"She can't stay with us," Mufid said adamantly.

Abdo rubbed his chin in a thoughtful manner. "My cousin lives nearby. He is a rebel, too, and will harbor her if I ask."

"All right, good." Ethan checked the time on his cellphone. It had been almost forty minutes since he'd abandoned Suleman. Did he dare risk returning to his unit? He had made it this far, and decided he might as well go through with the rest of his seat-of-the-pants plan. First, the alibi...

He turned toward Mufid. "Do you have a car?"

The man nodded warily. "Out back."

"Show me."

Mufid unlocked the front door and went out.

Ethan glanced at Abdo. "Move her to your cousin's residence as soon as you can."

Abdo nodded. "When father returns."

Ethan was about to follow Mufid when Alzena spoke.

"Alrajil." The urgency was obvious in her voice.

Ethan glanced at her, glad that she had used his alias instead of his real name in front of the others.

"Thank you." Her sapphire eyes shone with unshed tears.

Ethan nodded slowly. He didn't trust himself to say anything, or to even embrace her. He hated goodbyes.

Instead he turned to Abdo and said: "Take care of her." He hadn't meant his voice to catch with emotion, but it did. He felt his chin quiver.

The youth nodded. "I will."

Ethan quickly turned away, embarrassed by the display of emotion, and joined Mufid. He heard Abdo lock the door behind them.

The shopkeeper led Ethan around the block to the back of the building, where a red Toyota Yaris was parked in a stall.

"Yours?" Ethan said.

Mufid nodded.

Ethan went to the rear of the Yaris. "Show me the spare."

Mufid opened the hatchback, moved a portable inflater and gym bag, lifted the rear deck board, and pointed out the extra tire.

Ethan grabbed the tool bag and dropped his body to the pavement. With the flat edge of the wheel nut wrench, he removed the hubcap on the left rear tire, then took off two of the lug nuts and set them on the ground.

He unlocked his smartphone and handed it to Mufid. "Record a video when I say."

Ethan reattached the PSO-1 scope to his Dragunov and slung the sniper rifle over his shoulder.

"Zoom in so you can't see where the car is," Ethan said. "And can't tell there's no jack. Then start the video."

Ethan began putting on the lug nuts again. He heard the characteristic beep from the cellphone that indicated a video recording was in progress.

Wearing a big grin, Ethan glanced over his shoulder toward the camera. "This is what we do in Dawlah. We help people in need. A man's car broke down. I saw him struggling to change the tire on his own and I stopped to offer assistance." Ethan finished re-tightening the two lug nuts, then turned to fully face the cellphone. "Come to the Caliphate. Help your brother Muslims in need. It is your duty to wage jihad. Life is jihad." Aware of how ridiculous he sounded, Ethan glanced at Mufid and made a "cut it" gesture.

Ethan checked the recording after the shopkeeper returned the phone. It was impossible to tell where the Yaris was located.

"When the mujahadeen come to you and ask where this footage was taken," he told Mufid. "You will tell them Shbat street. Understood?"

"Again you put me in danger," Mufid said.

Ethan stepped forward menacingly. "What street will you tell them?"

"Shbat street!" Mufid raised his hands defensively.

Ethan nodded. "Good. I will bring you thirty thousand pounds when next we meet. Now get in the car and give me a ride."

He settled into the passenger seat, not entirely sure he would live long enough to make good on his monetary promise.

twenty-five

Ethan had Mufid drop him off two blocks from Raqqa Museum and then jogged the rest of the way. He slowed down as he approached, wiping the perspiration from his face using his scarf.

Some of the militants had begun to notice him. He could tell from the somber faces that they suspected his involvement. He had listened to the two-way radio while in the Yaris, but had caught no specific mention of his name in the chatter. The overall impression seemed to be that the incident in Clock Tower Square was the work of rebels or a competing jihadist group like Al Nusra. Then again, maybe he had simply missed his name. He'd deactivated the radio since leaving the car, after all, as he needed it off for his alibi.

Ethan steeled himself during those last few moments of his approach. He had to be ready for anything.

All the members of Wolf Company were looking at him. Their faces were wary, distrustful, even among those he considered his friends such as Harb and Ibrahim. Several in the group fingered the triggers of their AKs.

Abdullah said something inaudible into his two-way radio as Ethan closed the distance.

Suleman intercepted him. "Where were you?" The anger was obvious in his voice. "I waited, but you did not return!"

"Just filming some social media propaganda," Ethan said, doing his best to act casual. "Like you all told me to do. Here." He reached toward his pocket.

Several of the men raised their assault rifles outright.

Ethan lifted his hands, palms out. "What's going on?"

"Step back," Abdullah said.

Ethan retreated a few paces. Then it dawned on him. "You think I have a suicide bomb? Why? Whatever for?"

None of them answered.

"You all know me," Ethan entreated. "I wouldn't bomb you. You are my brothers. I'm one of you." He pointed toward his pocket. "Can I? I just want to get my phone."

Abdullah nodded.

Ethan slowly reached into his pocket and extracted the Android. He loaded up the tire-changing video and extended his hand toward the closest man—Suleman.

The militant hesitantly advanced, and snatched the phone. He watched the video, frowning, then showed it to Abdullah.

"Where did this take place?" Abdullah said.

"Shbat street." Situated on a direct path between the current checkpoint and where Ethan had abandoned Suleman earlier, Shbat was far enough away from Clock Tower Square that Ethan could easily deny culpability for the incident. "The motorist I helped owns a shop. He gave me his address, and told me to drop by if I ever needed anything. We can talk to him if you want."

Abdullah's two-way radio chirped to life. "Is he the one?"

"I am confirming his alibi," Abdullah said into the two-way radio. He checked Ethan's phone for any incriminating evidence, but there was only the one video. To Suleman, he said: "Go with Abu-Emad to this shop the motorist owns. Confirm his story."

Suleman glowered at Ethan, then walked to a nearby pickup.

Ethan was about to follow him when Abdullah raised a halting hand.

"Wait," Abdullah said. "Your weapons."

Ethan handed over the Dragunov. He had already ditched the Makarov and had no more grenades.

"The knife, too," the emir said.

Ethan gave him the Voron-3 knife and then he jumped into the passenger side of the Mitsubishi L200.

"Why didn't you answer your two-way radio?" Suleman said during the drive.

Ethan was waiting for that question. He slid the two-way radio from his belt and pretended to inspect it. He rotated the volume knob to the right, activating the radio.

"Apparently I forgot to turn it on," Ethan told him.

Suleman shook his head angrily. "Did you not find it strange that none of your brothers were speaking over the airwaves this morning?"

"I honestly didn't notice," Ethan said. "I was too busy helping the shopkeeper."

Suleman curled his lip in contempt. "You are always conveniently absent when there is an attack."

"I don't know what you're talking about," Ethan said.

"First the assassination of a very important civilian, and now this."

"What do you mean, *this?* What happened?"

"There was an incident. In Clock Tower Square. A woman escaped with a man. Many of our brothers died."

Ethan shook his head. "I swear on the Quran I was not involved."

Suleman compressed his jaw. Ethan could almost see the man's internal turmoil as he struggled to believe him. On the one hand, no devout Muslim would ever make such an oath unless it were true. On the other, an infidel would readily say something to that effect without fear of consequences.

Finally Suleman sighed, and Ethan guessed he had decided to believe him. For the moment.

A few moments later the Mitsubishi parked in front of the lingerie store. Ethan dearly hoped Mufid and Abdo had smuggled Alzena out by then. Perhaps it wasn't such a good idea to come there...

He approached the door with Suleman. The sign in the window read "closed."

Ethan shrugged. "Guess he took a break."

Suleman tried the handle anyway. Locked. "We will wait. And if he does not return, you have no alibi and will sleep in jail tonight."

A bright red Toyota Yaris abruptly pulled up behind the Mitsubishi pickup.

"There he is." Ethan wasn't sure whether to feel relieved or worried at Mufid's arrival. He was risking both their lives by bringing Suleman there. If the shopkeeper made any mistakes...

But Mufid corroborated the story perfectly, claiming Ethan had helped him on Shbat street, as instructed.

Suleman walked to the trunk of the Yaris. "Open it."

Mufid gave him a confused look. "Why?"

"Do it!" Suleman's fingers twitched toward the Dragunov that dangled from his shoulder.

Mufid went to the trunk.

So Ethan's alibi was about to fail after all. When Suleman opened the trunk he would discover that Ethan had not replaced the tire with the spare.

Ethan reviewed several jujitsu moves in his head, and selected the one he thought would best incapacitate the militant.

Mufid opened the hatchback.

Ethan was about to attack, but he held back because apparently Suleman wasn't familiar with the design of the Yaris.

"You didn't keep the old tire?" the militant asked, rummaging through the gym bag in the trunk, seemingly unaware that the spare tire was hidden underneath the rear deck board. The handle was concealed from view by a dirty rag.

"No," Mufid answered quickly. "I threw it out. Completely blown. Useless."

Suleman gave Ethan one last skeptical look, then shook his head, turning away.

Ethan frantically tilted his eyes toward the vehicle while Suleman wasn't watching, indicating that Mufid should shut the trunk as soon as possible. The shopkeeper readily complied.

Suleman clicked the send button on his two-way radio and hesitated. Finally: "His alibi is sound."

* * *

When Suleman drove Ethan back to the checkpoint, Abdullah returned his smartphone and weapons. "Never run off like that before your duty shift again."

"I won't," Ethan promised.

That afternoon the occupying army of Raqqa was mobilized, and the mujahadeen, Ethan's unit included, carried out a series of raids and arrests in the suburbs beside Clock Tower Square.

The army cordoned off the area where the fugitives were last seen on foot. The militants formed a series of roadblocks on all sides: it was assumed that someone in the neighborhood was harboring the criminals, and no vehicle or pedestrian traffic was to be allowed through in either direction, not even trucks containing produce and other foodstuffs, until the fugitives were given up. The water and electricity to the area were unceremoniously shut off.

It was the wrong neighborhood, of course, well away from where he had actually secreted Alzena. Apparently no one had discovered the stolen Hyundai Elantra, or interviewed the driver. Still, the roadblocks were a harsh reminder for Ethan that any operation he undertook, no matter how insignificant, could have serious repercussions. Operationally, he had done nothing wrong—by saving Alzena he had followed Sam's instructions to detect, deceive, disrupt, delay, and destroy—he just hoped the citizens didn't suffer overmuch for what he had done.

Unfortunately, the roadblocks lasted five days and only ended when the overall emir of Raqqa, Abu Lukman, issued a statement blaming the Al Qaeda-affiliated Al Nusra Front for the "regrettable occurrence in Clock Tower Square." A Syrian citizen, probably chosen at random, was executed for the crime.

* * *

A few days later Ethan found himself aboard one of those familiar Islamic State buses with the words Dawlah Islamiyah al Iraq wa Shaam inscribed on the side. The Islamic State of Iraq and Syria.

Yes, you want to be a state so badly, Ethan thought. *You can write it on your buses. You can put it on your compounds. But all you really are is a loosely connected group of decentralized command and control hubs manned by zealous, murdering goons who call themselves emirs.*

His unit was headed to Kobane to reinforce the fighting there. Abdullah promised it would be an easy victory. They'd go in, slaughter the Kurds, and return in a few weeks. Somehow Ethan doubted the deployment would prove so simple. But he didn't mind really. He felt he'd overstayed his tenure in Raqqa. Also, it would be good to see William and Aaron again. Assuming the operatives were still in Kobane. And alive.

The bus wasn't part of a convoy—the militants didn't dare travel in motorcades, not with Western drones potentially patrolling the skies. There were no women aboard, either. The wives and children of Wolf Company remained in Raqqa, waiting for their husbands and fathers to someday return. Making them stay behind probably served as a form of insurance, guaranteeing that none of the married fighters would ever defect or desert. That was the theory, anyway.

Beyond the window, the low-slung buildings of Raqqa receded on his left. He had so many bittersweet memories of the place. It was a city of repression, and yet the people were resilient; he knew they would bounce back once the Islamic State was expelled. He only hoped that whoever replaced the militants proved a little more moderate.

He wondered if Alzena had gotten out safely. He hadn't heard anything from her since that fateful day. He'd left messages in the accounts he shared with her and Mufid, but no reply had come from either of them. He hadn't had a chance to visit Mufid in person: when the neighborhood siege was lifted, Ethan's checkpoint duty hadn't brought him close enough to the lingerie shop during the day, and it was always closed at night. He still owed the man thirty thousand pounds, but Ethan supposed the IOUs he had written him were more than enough already.

He had to assume Alzena got out. He wouldn't allow himself to consider any other possibility. Ethan had done what he could for her; she was a strong woman and could take care of herself.

She'd have to.

Because she, like him, was all alone now.

The city faded from view, replaced by the dead, empty plain.

twenty-six

Four hours later, villages composed of boxy, one or two-story concrete homes began to encroach upon the road, like gray Lego blocks put together by the mad child of some giant. All of the buildings appeared deserted.

Ethan noted that there were fires burning on the rooftops of several houses in each village, sending plumes of smoke skyward. He wasn't sure if those fires were an aftereffect of the invasion, or set purposefully in the hopes of hiding the villages or supply lines. The thermal imaging cameras on drones and other surveillance aircraft could readily penetrate the smoke, though it did make it difficult for laser-guided ordnance to maintain a lock. GPS-guided payloads still worked fine, but that wasn't good enough for moving targets.

The small towns appeared with increasing frequency the further north the bus traveled, until the low-slung buildings flanked them at all times. The bus driver abruptly took a detour and Ethan began to see signs of activity. Soviet Ural-4320 6x6 military trucks. Weary fighters. Blast damaged buildings.

The bus parked beside a ramshackle gas station. Mujahadeen darted forward and opened the baggage hold to retrieve the munitions and food supplies the vehicle had transported from Raqqa. Someone dropped a cage and live chickens flew out, whooping madly.

"Good luck, brothers," the bus driver said, opening the doors. "I will see you all again in paradise." He gave them the fist with the raised index-finger salute.

Ethan and the others unloaded; Abdullah spoke quietly into his two-way radio and a moment later a man joined them. He looked the typical mujahid: curly Abe Lincoln beard, camouflage baseball cap, green fatigues, AK-47 slung over one shoulder. He carried a clipboard in one hand.

He and Abdullah shook hands and kissed each other on the cheeks, then Curly Beard led the unit deeper into the village. The militant conferred quietly with Abdullah the whole time.

Black standards hung from the walls of some buildings, proudly proclaiming the Shahada. Some houses displayed additional flags, these containing emblems chosen by the units assigned there. Skulls, scimitars and AKs seemed the most prevalent.

As in the outlying villages, there were large conflagrations on several rooftops, sheathing the sky in smoke; Ethan passed close to a few of them and realized tires fed the flames. The heat raised the already sweltering temperature by several degrees.

The distant echo of gunfire and mortars occasionally floated on the air; it was like listening to Fourth of July firecrackers from the suburbs. Located somewhere outside Kobane, the village was obviously the equivalent of a forward operating base, though Ethan refused to label it a FOB in his head. The Islamic State didn't deserve that honor—they lacked the proper organization and foresight required to build a proper FOB. This was just a bunch of militants crammed helter-skelter into a backwater town.

Weary-looking mujahadeen moved past with downcast eyes. Some walked with obvious limps. Others sat in doorways or on rooftops, cleaning rifles, reading Qurans, or texting. There weren't all that many—Ethan suspected most were fighting in the city proper.

Out of curiosity, Ethan checked his own cellphone, wondering if coverage from TurkCell penetrated into the border region. Nope.

But a glance at FireChat told him the offline mesh network brimmed with activity. Mostly the usual inane chatter regarding the intricacies of the Quran and its applicability to sharia, but there were also a few heated discussions regarding what should be done with civilians captured in Kobane. The participants seemed limited to the village, which made sense—the mujahadeen wouldn't string themselves out between here and Kobane just to form Bluetooth repeaters for their cellphones. Those situated on the front lines were probably having very different FireChat arguments, if they were even using the app, or their smartphones, at all.

A decrepit Soviet-era T-55 ambled past. Ethan was a little relieved to see the tank—he was worried the militants might have Abrams and Bradleys, given all the other US military equipment purloined from Iraq. Taking US-made weapons and gear was one thing, but stealing our Abrams and Bradleys, too? Well that would've been sacrilege.

Curly Beard halted beside a house, scribbled something on his clipboard, and turned to address the unit.

"Mecca is there," Curly Beard said significantly, pointing to the northeast. "Understood?"

The men nodded solemnly. Curly Beard seemed satisfied with the gravity of their response; he shook Abdullah's hand one last time and left.

The house proved unoccupied, though it was strewn with all manners of personal belongings left behind in the rush by the former occupants to flee. Clothes, photos, newspaper clippings, magazines, furniture. Abandoned memories and lost hopes.

Ethan paused beside a portrait on a desk—a young woman wearing a hijab. Oddly, she reminded him of Alzena.

Suleman rudely knocked over the picture so that it lay facedown on the table; he seemed pissed off that he had been forced to look at a strange woman's face.

Ethan moved deeper into the house and chose an inconspicuous, out of the way spot for himself in a hall outside one of the bedrooms.

Shortly thereafter the call for prayer came over the two-way radio, sung by a dulcet-voiced muezzin plucked from the jihadist ranks. The call was sorrowful: it seemed almost as if the singer wept.

Though the unit had passed a mosque on the way, Abdullah ordered everyone to pray in the house. Probably a good idea. Mosques were obvious targets for bombers.

Twenty minutes later an announcement came over the two-way radio, indicating that supper was ready for the units residing in "Section C" of the camp.

Abullah sent Yasiri to retrieve the food, and the youth returned with a canvas bag stuffed full of rice and chopped chicken.

After eating, Ethan returned to the area he'd picked out for himself and sat down. In the bedroom beside him, he saw Harb in one corner, actively engaged on his smartphone, likely using FireChat. That was probably the only place where the thirteen-year-old really felt he belonged. There he had no age, and as far as the other participants knew, he was a seasoned jihadi.

Ethan thought of the smartphone serial numbers he had sent Sam. JSOC was likely operating with the rebels in the area—before he left, William had hinted that Doug was embedded with the Kurds. And if Doug had those serial numbers, he would know precisely where the mujahadeen of Wolf Company were, courtesy of his Stingray. Though if Sam had indeed passed the serial numbers along, it would have been with the caveat that important operatives were still embedded with the owners of said phones. Doug wouldn't send those coordinates to the bombers.

At least, Ethan hoped he wouldn't. Wolf Company was probably out of range of the cellphone-intercepting Stingray anyway.

He turned to the side, shielding his own smartphone with his body, and retrieved the USB stick from his backpack. He placed his Quran on the floor nearby, open to a random page for show, then extended the RF antenna on the USB and plugged it into his phone with the adapter. He launched the DIA's encrypted messaging app.

The "members online" screen showed neither William nor Aaron's aliases. Likely they had their phones turned off to save power, though it was also possible they were out of range in Kobane. He wanted to be sure.

He stashed the Android and USB stick in his pocket, and then clambered to his feet, making his way through the house.

Abdullah sat by the front door with Fida'a and Suleman. The latter scowled at Ethan's approach.

"Where are you going?" Abdullah said.

Ethan shrugged. "I need some fresh air."

Abdullah laughed. "It is hardly fresh. But go. Return before curfew."

Ethan bowed his head and left.

twenty-seven

Ethan exchanged "salaams" with the jihadists he saw, and eventually he bumped into Curly Beard. He asked the man where he might find William's or Aaron's unit, giving the names of their respective emirs, and Curly Beard regarded his clipboard.

"Yes, both units returned just today." He gave directions to the two houses and sent Ethan on his way.

William's unit was the closer of the two, so Ethan proceeded to that location first. Inside the house he found the entire company asleep on the first floor.

The stench of FAN—feet, ass, nuts—was nearly overwhelming. Wrinkling his nose, Ethan stepped over the militants, searching the faces for his friend. The men slept so deeply that no one stirred.

He did a double take on one of the dozing fighters. Yes, it was William. Ethan barely recognized his friend. His face was steeped in grime and swollen in several places.

Ethan hesitated. William was probably dead tired and needed the sleep. Still, he might have new orders from Sam. Besides, Ethan wanted to let him know he had arrived.

Keeping his distance, Ethan prodded the operative with the butt of his Dragunov. No response. He tried again, harder.

William sat up, scrabbling madly at the rifle.

"Easy, brother," Ethan said in Arabic, conscious of the others in the room. He slid the rifle back over his shoulder.

William blinked wildly a few times, then recognition dawned in his eyes. He exhaled loudly, lying back.

"You look like a camel trod over your face," Ethan said.

"Feels about right." William agreed.

"Been in a few fistfights?"

William appeared confused. Then: "Oh. The lumps on my face. That's from the flies. They're everywhere on the front lines. They breed on the corpses."

Ethan wasn't eager to pursue that line of conversation. "Where's our comrade?"

William gave him a look that could best be described as appraising. "You just arrived?"

"I did."

With a sigh, William arose. He stumbled slightly, and Ethan braced him with one arm.

Outside, William walked stiffly through the streets, leading Ethan to a one-story house on an adjacent street.

"Our one day off and you have to disturb us like this?" Aaron complained in Arabic when Ethan roused him in a similar manner.

After the three of them had gathered in a small clearing near the house, Ethan said, "Update me."

Aaron scratched the insect welts on his face. "You're lucky you found us. Both our units just got back from four-day rotations on the front. We're only in camp for the one night."

"Four-day rotation?" William told Ethan. "Aaron had it easy. My unit was out there for *six* days. So you're doubly lucky to find the two of us in camp."

"Not my fault your unit was pinned," Aaron said.

"What's it like in the city?" Ethan asked.

"Pretty grim," William replied. "Both sides aren't afraid to commit suicide attacks. It's like fighting kamikazes, *alongside* kamikazes. There's just no sanctity for human life whatsoever. And any kaffir, excuse me, civilians, that are caught, well, the Islamic State either shoots them in the back of the head, or if the lucky prisoner happens to be a woman, they distribute her among the troops and gang rape her until she bleeds to death."

Ethan cringed. "What's the point of conquering Kobane if there's no one left for them to rule?"

"That's the thing: they don't care. They'll use the city as a garrison once they take it. Mostly they want Kobane because of its proximity to the border. That and they really hate Kurds. The religion they follow—Yazidism—well, it makes them the infidels among the infidels, apparently. And then there's the political angle. The emirs thought it would be easy for their mujahadeen to take the city. The Kurds were ill-prepared and ill-equipped, they said. When it turned out that conquering Kobane was far from easy, the emirs should have turned back. The city isn't all that important strategically. But shortly after the attack, the Obama administration began its airstrikes against Kobane. So now the Islamic State wants to make the US look bad by showing that even with air dominance, the Americans can't stop IS from conquering this small, out-of-the-way city. And even if IS loses the city in the end, they're going to draw out the battle as long as possible, again to make the West look bad."

"I tell ya," Aaron said. "This Selous Scout thing isn't all it's cracked up to be. I signed up for this job to get away from the way wars were traditionally fought, and here I am, struggling on the front lines again. I'm thinking we have to get out of here. It's ridiculously dangerous. You ask me, we should be doing what the Brit's are doing. They drop their SAS teams in eighty klicks from an Islamic State target, drive in on ATVs, execute the target, exfil on their ATVs to the extract location, then get the hell out. That last part is the key. *Get the hell out.* Classic hunter-killer style ops. Like we used to do. Remember those?" He shook his head. "I don't know why Sam ever thought this was a good idea. Place three highly trained operatives in the heart of house-to-house fighting to gather intel? It's insane."

"In Sam's defense," William said. "It was my idea to come here."

"Sam's defense?" Aaron said. "She green-lighted your damn idea. She's happy we're here. She didn't want us staying in some backwater city where the intelligence-gathering opportunities were few and far between. She wants us in the heart of the action, where the intelligence comes fast and furious, to better perform those five D's of hers: distend, distort, and disembowel, or whatever."

"We're making a difference in the fighting," William said. "You can't deny it. Though you're right: it's probably about time we absconded."

Ethan spoke up. "Listen, you guys can cross over to the Kurds whenever you want and go home. But I have to stay for at least one rotation on the front. I have to do what I came to do."

Aaron shook his head. "You'll see, my friend. You're all gung-ho now, but when you get out there you'll be wishing you'd listened to your good friend Aaron's advice."

Ethan shrugged. "We all fought in Fallujah. How bad can it be?"

Aaron laughed. "It's bad. At least in Fallujah we had guys fighting by our side we could trust. Guys who actually understood that all there was standing between them and the enemy were the men in their unit; guys who knew that fucking up could cost not just their own life, but the lives of everybody with them. Here, everyone wants to get themselves blown up. They take stupid risks. Muj are constantly volunteering to open doors they know could be booby-trapped. Rather than taking the time to disarm the door, or to find another way in, they just go right up and kick it down. Then there's the muj who step into the line of fire to lay down suppressive cover. They could stay crouched where they are, but no, they have to stand up, offering their entire body as bait as if it's the bravest thing in the world. All they're doing is reducing their numbers, making it harder for the rest of the unit to survive."

Ethan nodded slowly. "Just one rotation."

Aaron sighed. "That's how it's going to be, is it?"

"As I said, you're free to cross over to Kurdish lines whenever you want."

"Easier said than done," William interjected. "Besides, we're not leaving until you do."

"Hey, speak for yourself," Aaron said.

"You should leave," Ethan said, entirely serious. "In fact, I insist you do. The two of you have done enough. It's far too dangerous. Besides, I'm a lone wolf, remember? I can take care of myself."

William's eyes glinted like steel. "Never tell me I should leave when one of my brothers is staying behind in the line of fire."

Aaron sighed. "Shit. You and your misguided sense of duty. And I'm talking about the both of you." That was Aaron's way of saying he was staying, too.

Ethan felt he wasn't entirely grasping the gravity of the situation, but he refused to back down. He had to stay for at least one rotation. He wasn't kidding about what he'd said. He had come here to gather intel, and that was what he intended to do.

He heard the roar of a fighter jet overhead, and glanced skyward, but the thick smoke obscured the stars. He wondered why the bombers didn't simply target the fires with their thermal imagers. Then again, with so many blazes out there in the outlying villages, they would have no idea as to the actual location of the camp.

"Western jets?" Ethan said. "Or Assad's MiGs?"

"Western," William said, rubbing his eyes in an obvious struggle to stay awake. "Assad's staying out of this one."

"What about Doug, did we ever hear from him?"

"Doug's embedded with the Kurds," William said. "You'll see him online when you deploy your RF antenna in Kobane. We've been getting excellent reception from the rooftops in the city. Aaron and I have been able to communicate up to three miles away. Doug probably has a slightly more powerful transmitter and receiver, of course, so he doesn't have to get too close to the Kurdish front to stay in contact. Or maybe he's placed a few repeaters here and there."

"Knowing Doug, he's probably coming right to the front anyway,"

Ethan said. "You've been able to send him actionable intelligence, right? You said you were making a difference in the fighting."

Aaron was the one who answered. "Sometimes the bombers accept the targets we send. Sometimes they don't. Depends on the moods of the pilots, I guess."

"That means yes," William said. "We've sent a ton of actionable intelligence."

"Good. You've been transmitting your own coordinates as no-fire zones, I assume?"

"We have," William agreed. "And so far the B-1B Lancers and whatnot have actually obeyed those. But you never know with the Air Force. They've been known to confuse 'no-fire' with 'fire.'"

"I'm just surprised you haven't targeted the forward camp here, yet," Ethan said.

"Actually we did." Aaron scratched an ugly bite above his beard. "This is the *new* forward camp. The old one had the shit bombed out of it while we were on the front, thanks to our intel."

"Good job."

Aaron shrugged.

Ethan figured he'd interrogated his fellow operatives enough for the night, so he walked his friends to their respective lodgings and bid them goodnight. Then he made his way back to his own barracks and lay down. He was lulled to sleep by the distant sounds of sporadic machine gun fire and mortar explosions.

The next morning, after prayers and a breakfast of nuts and rice, Abdullah gave a short speech.

"Today we go to the front lines, my wolves," the emir said. "By following the path of jihad, inshallah, you shall all be granted a place in the garden of paradise. A place as vast as the world itself. A place with pristine blue lakes and pure emerald fields lying between mountains of musk, with golden palaces in the sky grander than anything man could ever make. A place where there is no war, and the peace of Allah rules all." He shifted his gaze from face to face. "Remain pure of heart my wolves. Fight the infidels, the enemies of Allah, without fear, because what we do here is right and just." He patted his M16A4. "With these we will remove all tyrants. With these we will erase all borders. With these we will establish a worldwide Caliphate. Die well!"

"Takbir!" Suleman shouted.

"*Allahu akbar!*" the group responded.

"Takbir!"

"*Allahu akbar!*"

"Takbir!"

"*Allahu akbar!*"

twenty-eight

Wolf Company marched through the streets toward the north side of the village. The smoke was billowing in full force from the rooftops, blotting out the sky.

The unit arrived at what could best be described as a pre-staging area. Several Kia pickup trucks idled in a row along a wide street. The members of Wolf Company hopped into the beds of two of those trucks, while other mujahadeen loaded into the remaining vehicles.

The leftmost pickup drove away, and the next vehicle in line waited half a minute before following. The succeeding pickups departed in turn after similar delays, until all of them were traveling en route to the city in a long, strung-out convoy. The vehicles had to circumnavigate several blast craters along the way. Potholes were prevalent, too, jolting the occupants almost constantly. The fires blazed on the rooftops around them.

Eventually the convoy reached what could be termed a staging area. At the edge of a village, heavy artillery in the form of long-barreled Type 59-1 Field Guns were spread in a wide row, ready to lay down covering fire. There was scant protection beyond—according to Ethan's offline map, the border of Kobane lay about a mile ahead, and no buildings resided between the village and there. He could see the city up ahead, past that gap, sprawling ominously on the plains.

The pickups lined up in pairs, grouped by unit. When the last set of vehicles arrived, the Field Guns began to fire. Their targets appeared to be near the center of Kobane, judging from the smoke and debris that spewed skyward from the city. More artillery launched into Kobane from a rocky knoll just south of the city, which the offline map labeled "Mistenur Hill."

The two pickups in front suddenly accelerated, racing across that empty region between the village and the outskirts of Kobane. The next trucks in line advanced to fill the gap, halting at the village edge. The succeeding vehicles slid forward and revved their engines impatiently.

The next pair took off about a minute later. And the subsequent group a minute after that.

Wolf Company's turn finally came. Ethan's pickup broke free of the village and raced toward Kobane, competing with its twin to be the first into the city. The militants with him appeared eager. Excited. On the road, returning trucks raced past.

He glanced uncertainly at the sky, which was open, and free of smoke. He knew a bomb could strike anytime. Indeed, he saw the criss-crossing exhaust left behind by several jets.

And then they breached the eastern perimeter of the city. Low-lying concrete buildings similar to the ones in the outlying villages hemmed the pickup on all sides. Closely packed white brick exteriors, flat rooftops, broken windows. Notable was the absence of any burning tires—the militants were probably too busy getting shot at to set up rooftop blazes. Or maybe they'd simply run out of tires.

The pickups abruptly pulled to a stop and Ethan and the others jumped out. Several militants waiting in a long queue by the side of the road immediately boarded the vacated truck beds and the vehicles turned around and accelerated back the way they had come. The exhausted-looking men who remained in the queue were probably returning from the front lines.

Ethan watched as the emir of another freshly-arrived unit moved between his troops, pumping epinephrine directly into their hearts with a US-issue autoinjector. The epinephrine basically turned them into berserker units—it would take several shots to down those men until the effects wore off. One young fighter collapsed after the injection, probably suffering a cerebral hemorrhage from the sudden spike in blood pressure.

Ethan couldn't help but smile at the hypocrisy of it. The Islamic State banned those under its rule from smoking or drinking alcohol, but injecting your heart with epinephrine was perfectly acceptable. Oh sure, some sheik had probably issued a fatwa permitting the hormone for jihad, but the irony wasn't lost on Ethan.

Abdullah led the unit down a side street. A couple of technicals—Kia 4000s cab overs with Soviet ZU-2 anti-aircraft artilleries in their beds—sped past, heading west toward the front. Wolf Company piled behind a T-55 that was slowly advancing toward the city center. Ethan and the others crouched low, letting the tank guide them in.

He spotted the odd sentinels perched on the rooftops alongside the black standards of the Islamic State, and the occasional technicals positioned at intersections, anti-aircraft guns pointed at the sky.

Kobane. A city founded in the wake of suffering. After the Ottoman Empire's Armenian Genocide of 1915, refugees started a village near a train station on the Konya-Baghdad Railway. They named their city Kobane, or "company," after the German company that had built that portion of the railway. Kobane had grown to a population of forty-five thousand by 2004, though when combined with the population of the outlying villages, its citizens had numbered in the hundreds of thousands. Those numbers began to drop with the 2011 civil war, and when the Islamic State invaded, the population levels nosedived. Most of the inhabitants fled north across the border into Turkey.

Ethan regarded the white brick buildings around him uncertainly. The damage alternated between moderate and extreme. In the moderate cases, the white-brick buildings bore machine gun marks and rocket cavities, with only the occasional collapsed structure among them. In the extreme examples, the damage was surreal. He'd be walking along a seemingly ordinary street when all of a sudden the buildings would recede, replaced by an avenue whose structures were completely torn open and gutted as far as the eye could see, the asphalt a jumble of concrete, rebar, mattresses, clothes, TVs and other personal belongings, with bodies burnt beyond recognition thrown into the mix.

The frequency of ravaged buildings and blast-damaged roadways increased the farther into Kobane the unit went, bearing witness to the relentless mortar and artillery barrage the Islamic State had inflicted upon the city. That the defenders had yielded territory before such a horrendous assault was not surprising.

The T-55 took a left, turning south, and Wolf Company abandoned it to proceed westward alone through the rubble. There were more fallen buildings than intact ones, there. The desolate landscape looked like something out of a post-apocalyptic nightmare. Blankets and tarps hung from cloth-lines looped between the few standing buildings, shielding the unit from enemy snipers. The sounds of shelling and impacts grew louder the further west the company traveled.

The group reached an open area and dashed across the street. They should have used bounding overwatch, Ethan thought, where half the platoon stayed behind and provided overwatch while the others moved forward, but Ethan wasn't about to start making strategic suggestions, not unless his life was in imminent danger. He was embedded with the enemy, after all, and he wasn't sure yet how much he actually wanted to help them.

Abdullah made Wolf Company hug the line of buildings as he headed northwest. In a reversal of the trend, most of the structures proved intact, there. Ahead, several platoons of mujahadeen were queued against the edge of an intersection. Artillery shells from the Field Guns outside of town were battering the neighborhood beyond. The rumble of exploding matter was almost deafening.

Abdullah glanced over his shoulder at his unit and smiled widely. "They are softening up the Kurds for us!" he shouted. It seemed risky as hell to be that close to the barrage, but none of the militants seemed to mind.

Upon the rooftops at either side, Ethan saw mortar men adding to the assault by repeatedly dropping 82mm shells into their Soviet M-37 mortars. He spotted DShK machine guns mounted behind sandbags on some of the buildings, and these fired randomly into the same general area.

The main artillery bombardment abruptly ceased. The mortar men and machine gunners noticed a few moments later and stopped firing in turn.

The front became eerily quiet.

Ethan could feel the tension in the air. It was almost electric.

"Go go go!" came the order over the two-way radios.

The mujahadeen queued at the edge of the intersection diffused into the ravaged neighborhood like terminates spreading over a burnt log.

The house-sweeping had begun.

Abdullah split the group into two squads and gave Suleman command of the second.

Emad was part of Abdullah's squad. The emir led them past the collapsed houses beyond the front, which he inspected only cursorily. He paused before an intact building sandwiched between two caved homes. The squad lined up on either side of the doorway, backs to the wall.

Abdullah waved Baghdadi forward.

The Tunisian slid in front of the door and kicked it open.

The next thing he knew, Ethan was sitting on the ground about five feet away with a sudden pounding headache. Fida'a lay on top of him. Ibrahim, underneath.

He shoved Fida'a off of him and helped Ibrahim stand. Everyone was accounted for save Baghdadi—the only sign of the Tunisian were the simmering boots still standing in the obliterated doorway.

"Zarar, Sab," Abdullah pointed at the charred entrance.

The two of them maneuvered inside. The big man went low, Sab high.

"Clear!" Sab said, peering out the door. That was a mistake: the moment he spoke the word he shook violently, and chunks of gore spat from his chest in multiple places.

Zarar unleashed his assault rifle at an unseen attacker inside the house as Sab collapsed.

"*Now* it is clear." Zarar dragged the lifeless body of Sab out of the way.

"Don't touch anything," Abdullah said. "Booby traps could be anywhere."

The squad split up and cleared the remaining rooms. Ethan kept back, happy to let the others martyr themselves, but they encountered no further resistance.

He heard an explosion in the next room, followed by, "I'm okay!"

Ibrahim emerged, covered in soot. He was grinning sheepishly. "Found a booby trap."

Ethan shook his head. The youth was lucky to be alive.

In the main room lay a bricked up staircase.

Fida'a rushed forward, sledgehammer in hand. In moments he'd broken through.

Zarar went first, poking his head and upper body through the trapdoor in the ceiling. "Clear!" he shouted down.

The others climbed the stairs onto the roof, where they crouched and fanned out.

The eastern rim had small crenelations filed into the stone, probably by Kurdish snipers. The western rim, which faced the town center, didn't have any.

"Sniper," Abdullah commanded.

Ethan low-crawled to the emir, who lay prostrate on the northwest corner of the roof. The man was peering past the rim. Ethan followed his gaze; he had a clear view of the street from there.

"Stay here," Abdullah told him. "Provide cover."

Ethan nodded. He was just about to suggest the same thing. And not because he wanted to cover Wolf Company.

The others absconded the roof.

Ethan settled into an overwatch position. Below, he saw mortar men and machine gunners following the house-sweeping squads. Some of the DShK gunners set up at the intersections, while the mortar men joined the squads inside the buildings and took up residence on the cleared rooftops.

Ethan was used to sniping in teams of three, taking turns with another sniper while a heavy gunner guarded the rear. While that setup worked well, Ethan was glad to be alone in that particular situation. It allowed him to perform certain clandestine duties.

twenty-nine

Ethan plugged the USB stick into his Android phone via the adapter, extended the RF antenna, and activated the DIA messaging app. Death Adder and Constrictor were online. Like Ethan, William and Aaron were the designated snipers in their platoons, and had ample time alone to set up their smartphones.

A third member was online. Black Mamba. Doug.

Hey mambo man, Ethan sent. *Ready to dance?*

Always, came the reply. *Good to see you finally joined the party, Copperhead.*

Ethan sent his GPS coordinates to Doug. *No fire zone, please.*

What's that? Fire zone? Transmitting to the Lancers now...

Funny, Ethan sent back. *Did Death Adder send the coords to the new forward camp yet?*

He did. But I'll need you to confirm your location.

Ethan did so.

The ground rumbled a few minutes later.

Forward camp is no more, Doug sent.

Ethan scanned the enemy lines through his 4x scope. Far to the west he saw a single Kurdish rebel hiding behind a concrete Jersey barrier beside the rubble of a collapsed building. Ethan had a clear shot but he didn't take it.

He moved on to the Islamic State units. Militants breaking down doors, taking fire, dying. He felt no emotion for them. None whatsoever. They had come here to die in jihad. They were achieving that dream.

He spotted a group of militants pinned down behind the rubble of a collapsed building. A Kurdish machine gunner shot at them from behind a hole hammered into the third floor of an apartment across from them. Ethan had somewhat of a shot, but again chose not to fire. He had resolved only to kill Kurds if his own life was at stake.

He swept the scope to the left. There. He spotted what he was looking for. A cluster of Islamic State militants were rushing inside a municipal building in a nearby neighborhood. Several of them began to congregate on the rooftop, and used the strategic position to shoot down at the Kurdish lines. Mortars and DShKs were erected in force.

Ethan grabbed the USB stick and was about to activate the laser pointer, but he paused first to check his flanks: a couple of mortar men lurked on the rooftops of an adjacent street, but that was it. There were probably a few Islamic State snipers that he couldn't see, though he doubted any of them were paying him any attention. Even if they did spot him, they would assume he was using some kind of laser range finder to aid with his sniping. They were used to the mishmash of foreign equipment, and certainly wouldn't be able to discern his target, not from their locations.

He pointed the USB's laser toward the municipal building. Useless. He couldn't see the laser dot at all from that distance. He retrieved the modded TruPulse 360 laser range finder instead and peered through the eyepiece. Much better. He shaded the unit with his free hand, not wanting the sun glinting off the lenses; Aaron claimed the device had an anti-reflective coating, but Ethan wasn't all that trusting of it—most coatings still reflected at least some light.

He recorded the target's position. The building was a little under six hundred meters away. Not the safest radius from an airstrike, but Ethan decided to transmit the coordinates to Doug anyway.

Got some grub for you, Ethan sent Black Mamba. *Recommend a thousand pounder.*

He wasn't familiar with the precise inventory of a B-1B Lancer, but he figured with that advice, the bomber would probably deliver something like a GBU-16, a laser-guided JDAM dropped in pairs or multiples.

Send the grub. I'm forever hungry, came the reply.

Ethan messaged William and Aaron and confirmed their positions first. Doug would perform the same location verification—it never hurt to double- or even triple-check, not when the lives of friendlies were on the line.

When he was done, Ethan set down the smartphone and returned to scanning the fray.

A few minutes later the high-pitched keen of two bombs pierced the air, followed by two near simultaneous explosions. The blastwave was deafening, and sent building fragments over his head. A piece of cement slammed into the ledge beside him about a meter from his head. Perhaps he had been located a little too close after all.

The target had vanished in a cloud of dust and smoke, along with most of the surrounding buildings. The dust cloud overcame his own position, and he covered the lower half of his face with the scarf, trying to form an impromptu air filter. Didn't work very well.

He suspected the Lancer had ignored his recommendation and dropped a couple of two-thousand pound GBU-31s instead.

Damn it.

When the smoke finally cleared about ten minutes later, he saw that the municipal building—and the militants on it—had been completely flattened, and although the surrounding buildings had suffered fragmentation and shrapnel damage the structures were relatively intact. Everything was coated in a fine layer of cement dust, including himself.

He returned his attention to the front. Most of the Islamic State squads and fire teams had advanced to the next block by then. Ethan decided to move forward. He climbed down the stairs, slunk through the streets, and chose a new house whose cratered entrance was surrounded by body parts.

"Abu-Emad, where are you?" Abdullah's voice came over the two-way after Ethan had settled in along the western edge of the new rooftop.

"Just moved to a new forward position, emir," Ethan said, then described it. Abdullah detailed his own location, and Ethan picked him out with his scope. "I see you. Got you covered."

Throughout the day Ethan sent along four more GPS coordinates. He'd learned his lesson after the first strike, and made sure the bigger targets were at least a thousand meters away. Even so, twice no bombs fell at all, once the strikes landed an hour too late, and the fourth time a couple of five-hundred pound GBUs actually dropped on cue, plinking two technicals placed conveniently close together. Other airstrikes fell in the surrounding neighborhoods, presumably guided by William and Aaron, or the Kurds.

Ethan avoided targeting any positions near Wolf Company. It was one thing to kill men he didn't know, and another entirely to eliminate those he'd worked with, even if they were on the wrong side. He doubted Doug would target them, either, even if he had their serial numbers on his Stingray, because of Ethan's proximity to the company. Besides, they seemed eager enough to kill themselves on their own. Ethan wondered how many of them would be alive when he got back.

Ethan turned off his phone between targeting opportunities to conserve battery power. When he eventually returned to the forward camp he would have to seek out a diesel generator.

A DJI Phantom 2 flew over the city at one point. One of the foreign fighters had apparently smuggled the camera-carrying consumer drone into Syria. It flew dangerously close to the front lines; the Kurds must have picked it out shortly after Ethan had, because a few seconds later the off-the-shelf quadcopter scooted skyward, ostensibly to avoid gunfire. Or maybe it was one of the infamous flyaways the model was known for. Whatever the case, the Phantom must have been struck because it lost altitude shortly thereafter and plummeted to the streets below. Ethan never saw it again.

When darkness fell he returned to his unit, which sheltered in one of the cleared homes. Without proper night vision clip-ons and infrared WeaponLights or AN/PEQ-2s they couldn't continue the house sweep until morning.

There had been two other casualties that day. Fifteen-year-old Yasiri and big Zarar. Though the latter had been the emir's oldest friend, Abdullah seemed in good spirits. As did the others. Why shouldn't they be? The fallen were enjoying the well-deserved fruits of paradise.

The men placed heavy blankets over the windows, then Abdullah activated a flashlight. He produced two pairs of AN/PVS-7 night vision goggles from his backpack. He gave one of them to Ibrahim, whom he ordered to the rooftop, and the other to Raheel, whom he dispatched to the front door.

The rest of the unit prayed. There had been no time to do so during the day—a fatwa allowed them to skip prayer during the fighting, of course.

Suleman assured them he knew the direction to Mecca. Ethan almost laughed—he was in a war zone, and praying to Allah in the proper orientation seemed the least of his concerns. Then again, God was potentially the only one protecting him from a random bullet or shrapnel fragment to the head.

After prayer they sat back and ate cold rice with pieces of chicken chopped into it, stored in a canvas bag. Fida'a had apparently retrieved the meal at dusk, along with several canteens of water, traveling back to the eastern perimeter of Kobane to grab the food from one of the delivery vehicles.

After dinner the militants found spots for themselves on the bare floor and prepared to sleep. Swatting flies, Ethan sat near Abdullah, and watched enviously as the emir produced an AN/PVS-22 Universal Clip-On Night Sight from his pack and attached it to the forward rail of his M16A4, in front of the ACOG 4x32mm fixed mag scope.

Apparently noticing his jealous gaze in the dim light, Abdullah said, "What? I have given out night vision goggles for the watch to use."

"But they can't shoot with them," Ethan complained. Not easily, anyway.

Abdullah shrugged. "If the watch spots something, they will call me."

Great plan.

* * *

Ibrahim awakened Ethan three hours later and he took his shift on the rooftop with the NV goggles. The time passed uneventfully. The streets were utterly quiet that night.

Ethan's face felt itchy, and when he scratched he felt pain. He realized he'd received his first batch of fly bites while he slept. It took all his volition to resist scratching for the duration of his watch.

When the three hours were up he went downstairs and chose Suleman as the next rooftop watchstander. Though flies buzzed around him, he fell asleep almost immediately.

Morning came and Wolf Company headed west to queue up behind other Islamic State units, waiting for the latest artillery pre-assault to end. When the barrage on the adjacent neighborhood stopped, the units quickly fanned out.

Ethan soon found himself in an overwatch position on a rooftop not all that different from his previous hides. His cheeks and forehead felt itchier than ever.

Aaron didn't check in that morning. Ethan sincerely hoped he was all right. William assuaged his fears, telling him via the encrypted messenger that Aaron probably simply hadn't had a chance to leave his unit yet. Whatever the case, Ethan and William couldn't designate any targets until Aaron contacted them, because their friend might be among any militant positions marked for bombing.

Around the middle of the day, right after Ethan had switched hides—and before he had a chance to update Doug with his position—the Islamic State lines were abruptly pushed back. Squads and fire teams fled on all sides. The Kurds were making a concerted sally forward: scores of them had been holed up within the nearby homes and apartment buildings, and swarmed onto the streets like fire ants from a disturbed nest.

Before he knew what had happened, the Kurdish front had swept right past his hide, trapping him behind their lines.

He watched Kurdish trucks roll forward, towing artillery. Mortar men set up and launched shells at the fleeing Islamic State militants. Kurdish fighters moved from building to building, performing their own house cleaning operations.

Ethan's radio squawked to life. "Abu-Emad, what is your status?" It was Abdullah.

He ducked beneath the rim of the building and turned down the volume of his two-way. "Trapped behind enemy lines. You?"

"The same." Abdullah described the position of his squad.

Ethan carefully peered past the rooftop edge and surveyed the area through his scope. He couldn't find the squad's location at first, but when the emir mentioned he was two homes away from a group of house-clearing Kurds, Ethan spotted the rundown place immediately.

"I see it."

The Kurds were quickly closing on Abdullah's location.

"Can you help us?" the emir said over the radio.

Ethan wasn't sure what to do. Should he let the Kurds assassinate his team? In theory the answer was yes. But what about Ibrahim and Harb? A sixteen-year-old and a thirteen-year-old. Just kids. Friends, even.

Intending to contact Doug, Ethan grabbed his smartphone and USB stick, but as he distractedly telescoped the antenna the Kurds formed up in front of the house where the Wolf Company squad was hidden. There was no time to reach Doug.

Ethan dropped the phone and lined up his targeting reticule over the Kurds. The men had taken places on either side of the front door, which was slightly ajar.

The Kurd nearest the door kicked it open; bullets riddled his body from within the house.

Ethan chose a Kurdish target. His finger twitched on the trigger, but he didn't fire.

"Abu-Emad, can you help us?" Abdullah asked again, more urgently.

The Kurds nearest the door unleashed covering fire into the foyer, while another Kurd dashed across the street. When he was opposite the home, the fighter lifted an M79 Osa rocket launcher.

"Yes," Ethan whispered. He terminated the Kurdish rocketeer, and in rapid succession shot two more men by the doorway. The Dragunov reports echoed loudly from the surrounding buildings.

He heard a shout from below. A Kurdish mortar man had spotted him.

Ethan ducked beneath the building's edge. A soft thud drew his attention to the terrace immediately beside him.

A grenade had landed on the rooftop.

thirty

Ethan snatched up his Android and USB stick and then rolled away from the grenade. He fell through the trapdoor and the bomb detonated as he passed inside.

He landed on the stairs and slid down several steps, jarring his back and neck. He arose unsteadily, dismissing the friction burns to his exposed hands, and descended the rest of the way to the first floor. In the kitchen, he leaped over a table—cognizant that it might be booby trapped—and dove through a shattered window to land in the alley between the home and its neighbor.

He slunk to the edge of the house and remembered to turn off his radio before he peered past. At the front of the building, two Kurds had assumed positions beside the entrance. He watched one of the rebels enter high, the other low.

Ethan doubled-timed from the alley, heading north, hugging the line of houses. He heard the sudden belt-whip of incoming bullets—shards broke away from the bricks beside him.

He dove into a nearby house, through a door hanging off its hinges. He moved away from the entrance and crouched beneath the broken front window. He lifted the barrel of his Dragunov experimentally, placing it slightly higher than the windowsill...

The reports of an AK sounded from the street outside and wood splintered from the window frame above him. He pulled the Dragunov back down.

Pinned.

He slunk deeper into the house—a rocket propelled grenade detonated in the foyer behind him. The explosion hurled him into the hallway beyond.

He hurried toward the rear of the home; the back door window revealed two Kurdish troops standing outside, about to break in. He raised his Dragunov to take them out when gunfire erupted from the fore of the house. Bullets zinged past.

He leaped to the side, into the closest available room. A lavatory. The smell of raw sewage from the backed-up toilet was nearly overwhelming. Hopefully, any attackers coming into the room would flinch at the stench, giving him a half-second advantage.

He splashed through the inch deep sewage and vaulted into the empty tub. He turned around so that he was lying on his back and then aimed his Dragunov at the entrance. The weapon was overkill at that range, but he had nothing else.

He heard movement in the hall beyond. The shadow on the wall told him a rebel lurked immediately outside the room. Judging from the shifting of that shadow, his opponent was pieing the room—moving his body in an arc to slowly scan for aggressors, a technique prescribed by many urban tacticians.

You should have just tossed a grenade, bro, Ethan thought.

A sliver of his foe became visible in the doorway and Ethan fired.

The piece of the man vanished from view and Ethan heard a wet thud. Glancing over the rim of the bathtub, he saw the dead Kurd bleeding out on the sewage-soaked carpet beside the entrance.

Someone shouted unintelligibly in Kurdish nearby. Another shadow appeared on the wall, but before the next man could present himself, gunshots came from the far side of the house. The shadow retreated.

More shouts. More gunfire. Screams of pain. Two final shots. Silence.

He heard muted footfalls, and the harsh whisper of guttural Arabic.

"Brothers?" Ethan shouted in the same tongue.

"Yes," came the response.

Ethan abandoned the tub and sloshed through the sewage. Warily, he peered past the doorway. Three Islamic State militants were spread out at different points in the hall. They wore balaclavas with the Shahada written on it. Their assault rifles were aimed at him, but they lowered the weapons almost immediately. Ethan was suddenly glad he was wearing his own Shahada headband.

Behind the militants he saw the body of another Kurdish rebel. Glancing toward the front of the house, he spotted two more fallen Kurds.

"Thank you, brothers," Ethan said. "They had me pinned."

"Come, we retake the line!" the closest man said. He had a Tunisian accent.

Ethan joined them, glad to leave that foul-smelling bathroom behind; together they cleared the home and then returned to the street.

Outside, other Islamic State squads ducked from house to house, clearing out any trapped Kurds. He saw some mujahadeen set up a DShK in the middle of the street and open fire at a Kurdish position further to the west.

He cleared another home with his new group and adopted a sniper position on the rooftop. As he scanned the road he spotted Kurdish rebels all over the place—trapped behind bullet-ridden pickups, Jersey barriers, piles of rubble, or inside doorways. Ethan resisted taking a potshot at any of them. Still, he made sure to keep a very low profile.

He radioed Abdullah and discovered, incredibly, that both Wolf Company squads had held out, and suffered no casualties. The emir thanked Ethan for the aid he had rendered.

The fighting continued all that day, proving intense at times, but as dusk approached the militants finally regained the territory lost to the Kurds.

Aaron checked-in before Ethan was about to shut down for the day. Because of a shortage of men, Aaron had been corralled into the house clearing; when the line had collapsed, he was pinned with his unit, and couldn't activate his RF antenna without drawing attention.

At that point Ethan realized William and Aaron's original assessments were correct: it was far too dangerous for operatives like themselves to function on the front lines. He decided that after his tenure on the front was done, he'd definitely get the hell out. His final gift to the Islamic State would be the bombing of their new forward camp, whose location he would discover when his unit rotated out of Kobane. He urged William and Aaron to leave sooner, but they refused to abandon him.

That evening, after he rejoined Wolf Company, Ethan sat near Harb, who read the Quran on his cellphone while he waited for Raheel to fetch supper and water.

"Salaam," Ethan said.

"Salaam," the thirteen-year-old replied. Though he smiled, Ethan could sense the weariness in the boy.

"How was your day?" Ethan said.

Harb glanced at Abdullah, who lounged across the room, and lowered his voice. "Terrible. Abdullah won't let me fight. He always makes me stay back, guarding the rear."

Ethan nodded in pretend commiseration. "How would you like to wage real jihad?"

Harb's eyes widened. "What do you mean, Abu-Emad?"

"I have been entrusted with a secret operation by the Caliph Baghdadi himself, Prince of the Faithful, and I want you to help me. Would you like that?"

The youth's eyes widened naively. "Yes! Tell me what I must do."

"First, you must swear to secrecy on the Quran. No one else can know of this."

The youth held out his phone, which had the Quran app still active on it, and placed his right palm over the screen. "I swear, by Allah and the Quran, under threat of eternal damnation, that I will tell no one of this mission."

"Good. I will let you know what to do in a few days."

Harb's brow furrowed. "Can't you tell me now?" The impatience of youth.

"No. I said in a few days."

Harb sighed. "Okay. Thank you, I guess."

Ethan had resolved to save Harb. The youth was far too young to die. Though how he would explain to the thirteen-year-old that they were going to travel among the infidels, Ethan had no idea.

He noticed Suleman's suspicious gaze. Had the man been watching him the whole time? Best not to linger beside Harb too long; he didn't need Suleman questioning the youth later.

Ethan was about to leave when Harb spoke again, his voice little more than a whisper.

"This operation was entrusted to you by the Prince of the Faithful himself?"

Ethan nodded gravely. He glanced at Suleman, but the man had returned his attention to the Quran in his lap. Good.

Harb smiled, though it seemed touched by sadness. "We're going to be martyrs, aren't we?"

Ethan hesitated, then gave the answer he thought the kid was looking for. "Yes."

Harb's eyes assumed a distant look. He lay back contentedly. "When I die, all of my virgins are going to look like Brenda Locks."

Ethan chuckled softly at the irony. "Brenda Locks? The kaffir Hollywood actress?"

Harb grinned mischievously. "Yes."

"How does a youth of your age, living here, even *know* about Brenda Locks?"

"Oh I know, believe me." He had a sly look in his eye. Ethan suspected one of the older jihadis had been showing him videos on his phone. "Some of the virgins will be blond Brenda Locks'. Some will be brunette. Some black-haired. But they will all be her. Pearl eyes, white skin, supple breasts, forever wet vaginas."

Ethan shook his head, unable to hide a smile.

"Each time I bed her," Harb continued. "No matter what version I choose, I will always find her a virgin again. And I won't have to rest, because my erection will be eternal. Yes, that is quite literally paradise."

Ethan grinned sadly, because the youth was completely serious. He ruffled Harb's hair and left him to his reading.

* * *

The third day proved slow. After two useless hides, Ethan decided to try something taller, and ended up at a mosque. He made his way through the burned-out insides, climbing the counter-clockwise spiral staircase of the minaret. When he reached the topmost balcony he found another sniper already using the location.

The man was lying prostrate on his back, rifle barrel pointed at Ethan. "Salaam."

"Salaam," Ethan answered warily.

"What brigade are you part of?" the militant asked in a Lebanese accent.

"Wolf. Under Emir Abdullah Hazir Al-Afghani."

Apparently he believed Ethan, because he lowered the rifle.

"What about you?" Ethan said.

"Emir Haadi's Swords," the man replied proudly. He shoved the barrel through a gap in the stone banister and peered through the scope. For the first time, Ethan realized the weapon was an M24A2 sniper rifle.

"I am Abu-Osama," the man added.

Of course you are, Ethan thought. "Abu-Emad."

Ethan stepped beneath the muqarnas decorating the roof-like canopy and sat down behind Osama. He didn't want to get too close to the rail in case some Kurdish sniper was milling the balcony.

"Where are you from?" Ethan said, eying the man's weapon enviously.

"*Amrika*." America.

Ethan resisted the urge to answer in English. "Your Arabic is very good."

"I was born to Lebanese immigrants in Detroit."

Ah.

"Jihad is our duty," Ethan said.

"Jihad is our duty," Osama agreed. "I made my hegira last year. Traveled to Beirut to meet my two cousins. The three of us crossed into Syria. Operatives from Jabhat Al Nusra helped us through territory controlled by the Assad pig, as well as rebel-owned lands. We joined Al Nusra, but then our commander switched sides to the Islamic State."

Ethan nodded. "Where are the two cousins who came with you?"

"Paradise," Osama said proudly. "I will join them soon, Allah willing."

Ethan debated whether to expedite the man's journey to paradise. It was his operational duty to disrupt and destroy Islamic State targets from within. That included targets from heads of state to snipers. No cog on the Islamic State terror machine was considered too small—the sniper might someday be responsible for the death of American citizens if the US ever decided to put boots on the ground. Besides, that M24 would fit nicely in Ethan's arsenal. And as an added bonus, he didn't know the man, so he wouldn't feel guilt.

He quietly pointed his Dragunov at the back of Osama's head.

"I sometimes dream of my home in Detroit," Osama said without looking at him. "The wife I left. The small child. I want to go back, but I am afraid the American government will arrest me. So I stay." He sighed. "My brothers in the Caliphate are all I have left now. Men like you. I am proud to have you at my side. Very proud. When I see you again when you are standing before the gates to paradise, I will tell Allah, that man fought beside me for what is right and good. That man fought for Islam."

Feeling like a scumbag, Ethan lowered the rifle. He didn't need to brutally execute the man, and certainly not merely to assume ownership of some rifle he coveted. The chances Osama might someday kill a US soldier were minuscule anyway.

Ethan bid the jihadi farewell and in twenty minutes he had attained another hide, a bedroom on the top floor of a three-story apartment.

Over the secure chat application he once more asked William and Aaron to leave, but his fellow operatives refused to obey. Ethan told them it didn't make sense for them to stay, and he promised to join them as soon as he got the coordinates of the new forward camp for the bombers.

Can't abandon you, bro, Aaron sent back as Constrictor. *We're staying. We're in this together.*

He's right, Death Adder added. *If something happened and you needed immediate exfil, having us on the other side makes getting to you a helluva lot more difficult.*

Half an hour before dusk, Ethan made his way back to his unit. He'd targeted just two buildings for Doug that day, and only one bomb had actually dropped.

When he rejoined Wolf Company, he noticed three missing members.

"Where's Ibrahim?" Ethan said, concerned for the sixteen-year-old.

"Shot. Raheel brought him back for medical treatment."

"What about Jabal?" Ethan asked.

"Dead."

An urgent notice came over the two-way radios. "The infidels are pushing forward near Forty-Eighth Street. All units in the area, attack! I repeat, all units in the area, attack!" The accent sounded very odd.

"Up!" Abdullah said. "Up!"

thirty-one

Wolf Company dashed into the street, following the sounds of gunfire. It wasn't completely dark yet, but Ethan would have a hell of a time targeting anything, even with the PSO-1's illuminated reticule. Broken glass crunched underfoot as the unit hastened past the burnt-out husks of several buildings.

They rounded an intersection and started to take incoming gunfire. Abdullah waved the unit back immediately.

"It's a trap!" the emir said as they huddled against the house. "There are no brothers here. We have fallen for a Kurdish trick!"

The sound of Kurdish DShKs raked air, and bricks at the edge of the house fell away in large shards.

"Back!" Abdullah said.

They fled the way they had come. Gunfire seemed to be going off all around them.

Harb tripped.

"Come on, kid!" Ethan tried to help him up, but as soon as the thirteen-year-old was on his feet again he collapsed. Ethan hauled the teen over one shoulder and carried him.

The unit retreated, finally reaching the safety of the Islamic State lines again. Mortar men and machine gunners covered their rear.

When they took shelter in a nearby abandoned house, Ethan lowered Harb to the floor. The thirteen-year-old coughed sickly.

Ethan retrieved his smartphone and set the brightness to full, illuminating the kid. His mouth was wet with crimson fluid. Ethan directed the glow downward, toward his body. Harb's shirt was blood-soaked—he hadn't worn any body armor, as none of the Kevlar jackets fit his small size.

Ethan lifted the bottom hem of the shirt and Harb moaned. Suddenly he squeezed Ethan's arm.

"I failed Abu Baghdadi," Harb gasped.

"You didn't fail." Ethan held the Android's screen over him, illuminating the multiple gunshot wounds the kid had taken. Ethan felt a sudden helplessness, and an overwhelming sense of sorrow. Why, out of all them, did Harb have to die? The youngest, most innocent of them all?

"Failed," Harb repeated. "The... mission."

"Stop saying that. You're the greatest martyr I've ever known."

Harb coughed up blood. "Really?"

"Yes. Allah has called you to his side."

"Brenda... Locks," Harb managed.

Ethan looked into Harb's face and did his best to hold it together. "That's right. Brenda Locks. She's waiting for you, brother. She's all yours."

Harb smiled wistfully and then closed his eyes. His respirations became slower with each passing moment, until all breathing finally ceased.

Ethan shut off the cellphone, welcoming the darkness. He took pride in being a big, tough man. Someone unaffected by emotion. He never cried—it was a sign of weakness.

Yet his face was wet with sorrow then.

"Why do you grieve?" It was Suleman's voice. "He is in paradise now, with our brothers. And his father. He is free now."

Ethan didn't trust himself enough to answer Suleman. Instead he lay down and closed his eyes.

* * *

The next day the surviving militants helped move Harb to the backyard. They donated the rationed water from their canteens to bath his body, then wrapped him in a linen sheet purloined from one of the bedrooms. They prayed the *Salat al-Janazah*, the Islamic funeral prayer, and buried Harb with his head pointing toward Mecca. He wasn't the first member of Wolf Company they had buried, and probably not the last, but even so, Ethan felt his loss more keenly than any of the others.

Goodbye, my brother. I hope you find the paradise you dreamed of.

During the burial Ethan noticed Abdullah had been shot the previous night as well—he had a red tourniquet wrapped tightly around his right calf, and he walked with an obvious limp.

The unit had only just finished burying Harb when heavy shelling erupted from the Kurdish lines and they were forced to hunker down in the house.

The report soon came over the two-ways and FireChat that the Kurds had attained Tall Shair Hill to the west of the city, and were using it to bomb the Islamic State positions.

At first, no one did much talking while the shells whistled in. They all knew that a bomb could easily land on the house. They were quite literally in the hands of Allah.

The more zealous among the lot seemed almost happy about the predicament. Suleman's eyes, for example, shone with a particularly bright fervor, and whenever a shell landed too close, he was always the first to laugh it off.

"This is real glory, my brothers," Suleman said. "This is what it means to fight jihad! The time of our promised martyrdom is at hand. Our whole lives have been but preparation for this moment. Bask in it, my brothers! Bask in it!"

Suleman led them in some religious song, and the group crooned until hoarse.

The shelling continued all that day and into the dark. It soon became obvious that no one would be eating supper that night.

The main battle sheik broadcast a speech over the two-way radios about an hour after sunset. He identified himself as Abu Khattab Al-

Kurdi—a Kurd. Ethan found it more than ironic that the Islamic State had chosen a Kurd to lead the extermination of his own people.

Al-Kurdi paused after each sentence so that translators could convert what he was saying into the native tongues of the foreign fighters.

"We are doing well, my brothers!" the sheik exclaimed. "And we will prevail, despite the enemy arrayed before us. We control sixty percent of Kobane. Sixty! From the hill of Mistenur, past the industrial district, to that area they call 'security square.' We are raining hell fire down upon them, and inflicting the wrath of Allah. We are conquering for Islam, my lions! Be strong now, during this time of trial, when Allah chooses to test us most. Be brave!"

The rhetoric continued like that for a few minutes, but Ethan tuned out after the first few sentences. It was hard to feel enthusiastic for bombast when shells were raining down around him.

About thirty minutes after the sheik finished his speech, the shelling abruptly ceased. Ethan and the others stayed awake the entire night, expecting the Kurdish house clearing squads to follow up the artillery bombardment.

But the squads never came.

In the morning, news came over the radios. The Islamic State had retaken Tall Shair Hill.

Wolf Company erupted in exuberant, if weary, shouts of "Allahu akbar." Similar cries broke out over the two-way radios. Ethan yelled along with the best of them.

They had served their four days. It was time to return to the forward camp.

Wolf Company marched with slumped shoulders from the front. Suleman and Fida'a helped Abdullah walk, as the emir could no longer place much weight on the leg.

Ethan was completely benumbed by that point. He considered turning around and making a run for the Kurdish lines right then.

Just one more day, he told himself. *Return to the new forward camp, record its position, then get the hell out when we come back to*

Kobane.

The group passed the mosque Ethan had visited the day before. Glancing up, he saw the minaret. Was that... yes, the black tip of a muzzle protruded very slightly from the banisters of the upper balcony, pointing toward the Kurdish lines. Something seemed off about the angle of that muzzle. Maybe he was imagining, but it seemed pointed too high.

On a whim Ethan decided to check it out. Though he was bone-weary, the potential reward was too great to ignore.

"One second!" he told the others, then swerved into the mosque and bounded up the spiral stairs.

At the balcony of the minaret he found Osama, glued to the same spot, his M24A2 jammed between the stone banisters. The skyward-angled muzzle definitely wasn't positioned for proper firing.

Keeping low, Ethan approached. The first thing he noticed was the abhorrent stench, a mixture of rot and fecal matter.

The mujahid had a large black exit wound in the back of his head, where the flies had gathered around the matted hair.

Scrunching up his nose, Ethan grabbed the M24. It seemed undamaged. As he examined the weapon, his captivated mind no longer registered the smell of the corpse. H-S Precision PST-25 fiberglass and carbon-fiber reinforced polymer foam stock with adjustable length of pull and cheek height. 416R Stainless Steel barrel with 5-R rifling. Leupold Mark 4 LR/T 10x40mm fixed magnification scope with DiamondCoat 2 ion-assist lens coating for higher light transmission and greater ruggedness. Detachable ten-round magazine. Top and side Picatinny rails for accessory mounting. Fold-down Harris bipod with RBA-3 rotapod adapter, allowing for target tracking without bipod repositioning. Maximum effective range, eight-hundred to a thousand meters.

He named the rifle Beast.

He looked into the scope, peering through one of the banisters, being careful not to get too close to the balcony's edge. Built into the lens was the standard Mil-dot reticule, with beads placed at intervals along the cross-hairs to aid in range calculation. The 10x magnification was slightly high for urban combat, but he could always resort to the Dragunov as a backup.

Beast had a "Quick Cuff" rifle sling specifically designed for the US army by Tactical Intervention Systems. It consisted of a cuff that was worn on the bicep, and a sling attached to the rifle. Most people thought of slings as merely something used to carry a rifle, but for the professional marksman, it was something far more. With the Quick Cuff sling, one could quickly assume an "unsupported" or freestanding firing position and shoot with reasonable accuracy. This was useful during ambush situations, when there wasn't time to fold down the legs of the bipod. Bipod-supported shooting was more precise, but nonetheless the Quick-Cuff improved accuracy in a bind, providing a more stable unsupported shooting platform. Some marksmen used both the bipod and Quick Cuff together.

Ethan opened up the Velcro fasteners on the Quick Cuff and removed it from the corpse, sliding the contraption onto his own left bicep and adjusting it. He slung Beast over his right shoulder and the Dragunov over his left.

He collected the spare ammunition from the corpse, securing it to his harness. A quick search of Osama's pack revealed a clip-on PVS-22 Night Vision scope. Ethan immediately pocketed it. Unfortunately, there wasn't an infrared WeaponLight or PEQ-2 illuminator to go with it.

Can't win them all.

Ethan returned downstairs and discovered the others hadn't waited for him. Ethan had to rush to catch up.

"Nice find," Raheel said, looking with obvious envy at Beast.

The survivors of Wolf Company reached the extract area, where they waited alongside those others who had completed their four-day shifts. He spotted William and Aaron standing a short distance away with their respective units; the two of them looked just as exhausted as

Ethan felt.

Pickup trucks came, offloading the mujahadeen who had come to relieve the front line fighters. In a few minutes Ethan found himself in the bed of one of those trucks with the remnants of Wolf Company. They no longer had enough members to necessitate two vehicles.

The pickup drove into the empty area between the southeast of Kobane and the nearest town. Overhead, shells screamed past, launched from the Islamic State heavy artillery in the village to the southeast.

He looked at the exhausted faces of the survivors and wondered if any of them were experiencing second thoughts about the jihad and its so-called glory. Even Suleman and Fida'a were too tired to meet his eyes, and like everyone else, stared at the floor of the truck bed.

The pickup reached the shelter of the village, where the smoke from the rooftop blazes blotted out the sun. The truck continued onward, stopping half an hour later in a town that apparently served as the new forward camp. It looked almost exactly like the old one, but there were subtle differences in the placement of the buildings. Just to be sure Ethan checked his offline map. Definitely another village.

Suleman and Fida'a carried Abdullah to the field hospital, while another mujahid arrived to show them to their quarters. It was Curly Beard. He'd survived the bombing of the old forward camp, then.

He led them to a single-story home near the center of the village. Six fighters were already lodged there.

"Meet the new members of your unit," Curly Beard said. The man revealed their names, but Ethan wasn't listening. In a daze, he proceeded to the closest corner, set down his belongings, closed his eyes and fell asleep.

Ethan awoke four hours later at the call to prayer. Afterward, the company devoured a lunch of nuts and rice, which one of the new members had apparently retrieved. As they ate, Suleman explained that Abdullah had appointed him acting emir while he recovered from his injury. As proof, Suleman showed off Abdullah's US-made M16A4 assault rifle, replete with 4x32 RCO scope and PVS-22 NV clip-on.

"You are the best group of mujahadeen I have ever served with," Suleman said. "It is truly an honor, an *honor*, to lead you in Allah's great war. I love you all." He actually seemed teary-eyed.

Ethan could only shake his head.

After eating, he wanted to check on William and Aaron, but the sudden influx of food only doubled his weariness, and it was all he could do to stumble back to his sleeping area and collapse. He understood then how William and Aaron must have felt that first day when Ethan had so rudely roused them.

It was still daylight when he awoke three hours later for the next prayer call. Wolf Company groggily went through the motions, and when prayer was done, most of them went back to sleep. The new members stayed awake, talking quietly among themselves. Suleman was conspicuously absent.

Though he wanted nothing more than to close his eyes and let the peaceful oblivion of sleep take him again, Ethan forced himself to stay awake. For one thing, he badly had to take a dump. For another, it was time to find his fellow operatives.

The toilet and bathtub of the house were already filthy from those mujahadeen who had relieved themselves before him, so he used the backyard as a latrine instead. When he was done splattering the flowerbed with diarrhea, he pulled out the USB stick and recorded the position for the B-1B Lancers. The irony wasn't lost on him. When the bombers flew overhead tomorrow, that spot would serve as ground zero for the shitstorm.

He went in search of William and Aaron. Eventually he tracked down Curly Beard and the man told him where to find their respective units.

When he reached Aaron's barracks, he discovered most of the unit asleep. There were three who were awake, however. Likely new members. They seemed excited.

"Is Abu-Aadil here?" Ethan asked, studying the sleepers. He didn't recognize his friend among the lot.

"He has been captured," one of the awake fighters said eagerly. "Along with that Saudi associate of his. They are spies!"

"What?" Ethan blinked in disbelief. "Where are they now?"

"The sharia court, I would think." That was essentially the camp prison.

"And where's that?"

The fighter shrugged. "I don't know. They are friends of yours?"

"No," Ethan lied. He thanked the man and left.

He asked around for the sharia court and finally someone pointed him in the right direction. On a whim, he stowed the modified USB stick and TruPulse range finder behind a pile of rubble along the way, making sure no one saw him do so.

Near the center of the village he came upon a large building. A wide, circular structure topped by a three-story pyramid. He thought the place might have been a Kurdish church at some point, but the bronze characters above the entrance had been chiseled away, leaving behind only a dark imprint.

Two Kalashnikov-carrying guards stood on either side of the entrance. At his approach, the left sentinel raised a halting hand.

"What do you want?" the fighter inquired.

"Is this the courthouse?" Ethan said.

"Yes. Why?"

Just then the main doors banged open and Suleman, of all people, emerged.

"There he is," Suleman said. "The final traitor. Arrest him."

thirty-two

FIVE HOURS EARLIER

Habib had feared his American masters at first. For some reason he had thought their drones and satellites could observe his every movement. And he had half believed the Americans had implanted some sort of tracker in his body when they had violated him.

But slowly, very slowly, he began to realize they really had no clue regarding his whereabouts and those he interacted with, or about anything at all, really. The Americans weren't all powerful.

They were fools.

He had fed them a constant stream of disinformation. He had lied about the number of brothers in the training camps, what the instruction involved, who the trainers were. He had lied about the electrical and power situation in Raqqa, about his whereabouts and duties therein, about the name of his emir. He had lied about everything. And they had believed it all.

The Americans had given him a Facebook account to use. He was to post encrypted text to a private group that had the nonsensical name of Al Husseini. When he had told the Americans he was headed northwest to a city without Internet, Akhtarin, they had believed that, too. He almost wished the forward camp had Internet available so that he could continue feeding them misinformation.

Habib had done well in Kobane. With Allah's help he had distinguished himself among the fighters, so that when his emir was gunned down Habib had been immediately promoted to commander of Bear Brigade. When Habib died in jihad, which of course he must, he hoped Allah might look back at his many valiant deeds and allow him to enter the bliss of paradise. It was a feeble hope, but he clung to it.

His unit had completed another rotation on the front, and he sat with the survivors in the bed of a pickup truck on its way back to the forward camp. There were only two brothers from his original brigade there with him. The others had gone to jannah, replaced by new fighters.

He was tired, like his men, but he wore a brave face. As their leader it was his job to boost morale in whatever ways he could. The airstrikes were demoralizing enough—without those, the yellow faces would have fallen long ago. In his heart he knew Allah was on their side, however, and in the end the city would cede. Even if the Islamic State had to blow every last building to hell.

The pickup arrived at the forward camp and he jumped down from the truck bed with the others.

Habib stopped dead in his tracks.

Another pickup had arrived only moments before his own, and a different unit had unloaded. Treading along nonchalantly among the brothers was the man he could never forget.

* * *

Aaron was rudely awakened by three militants he didn't know. They disarmed him and dragged him from the house while the rest of his unit watched—those who were awake, anyway.

"What's going on?" Aaron said.

"Silence!" One of the militants jabbed him in the ribs.

Another spoke into a two-way radio. "We got him."

They brought him to the former Kurdish church that served as the sharia court and camp prison. He was searched; the cellphone, range finder and USB stick on his person were confiscated. He was brought to a small, white-painted room where five men awaited. Three of them were militants like Aaron. The other two, dressed in snowy robes and skull caps, were seated before a table with a Quran and a laptop on it.

"That's him," one of the mujahadeen said.

The man seemed familiar somehow, but Aaron couldn't place him.

"He was carrying a USB stick, judge," one of the militants who had escorted Aaron said. "As well as a cellphone and a range finder. Abu-Osama is looking at them now. And we also found this among his personal belongings." He placed a fist-sized metal object on the table. "We're not sure, but we think it's some sort of communications device."

The judge pushed up his eyeglasses and picked up the device to examine it. "Do you know who I am?"

"No."

"I am Judge Mohamed Al'Sharia. Everything you say from this moment forth will be used as evidence. Do you understand?"

"What am I accused of?"

Mohamed ignored him, his attention glued to the metallic artifact. "What is this?" He unfolded the black metal panels.

It was a portable, solar-powered Internet hotspot. Military make. Aaron had acquired it after rendezvousing with a member of JSOC in Kobane a couple of days ago. He hadn't had a chance to properly hide it yet.

Aaron shrugged. "I don't know, I found it on the streets of Kobane."

The vaguely familiar mujahadeen stepped forward. "You lie, American." Such venom in his voice. Such hatred.

Then it hit Aaron.

Habib.

The foreign jihadist the contractors had raped in Turkey. Aaron still hadn't gotten over the guilt he'd felt in that moment. He should have intervened. He wished he'd had the courage to stand up to those fools.

At the time he'd been so angry at them and himself that he'd taken off his balaclava and stormed from the hotel room. Removing his mask had been an outward symbol of his defiance, almost an instinctive reaction to the repulsion he'd felt. It was a stupid thing to do, in hindsight, because although Habib had had his back to him, apparently the jihadi had seen his face somehow.

"American!" Aaron sputtered in feigned outrage, struggling to recover. He felt slightly dizzy, and had to set a hand on the table to steady himself. He blinked a few times and then, realizing all eyes were upon him, he said, loudly, "How *dare* you call me by that name!"

Habib smirked. "Do you see, judge, how he almost fainted at the accusation?"

"It's because of the sheer rage I felt," Aaron said. "It took all my will to keep myself from smashing in your face. I'm not an American kaffir!"

"Really?" Habib purred. "Then why do speak English so well?"

"I don't know what he's talking about," Aaron told Mohamed. He kept his voice calm, measured. "I've never seen this man before in my life. You must believe me. He has confused me for someone else." Aaron placed his hand over the Quran on the table. "I swear by the sacred book."

Habib slapped him in the face. "Don't touch the Quran, infidel! I have confused you for no one! I can never forget you, not after what you did!"

Aaron feigned outrage, as would be expected of one so indignantly accused, and made a grab for Habib. The other militants intercepted him, restraining Aaron.

He pretended to calm down. His mind was racing. His only hope was to poke holes in whatever fabricated story Habib might have come up with. And it *was* a fabrication—Habib would never admit to being on the receiving end of an act of sodomy. He would probably refuse to swear on the Quran. Aaron could use that.

"What is it, exactly, you think I did?" Aaron asked sharply.

Before Habib could answer, a commotion came from outside; William abruptly barged into the room. He didn't carry a weapon—it had likely been confiscated at the door.

Bad move, Will, Aaron thought. *Very bad move.*

He had hoped not to drag either of his fellow operatives into that mess.

"What's going on?" William said. "I come looking for my friend, only to discover that he has been arrested. Do you know many kaffir he has killed? Do you know—"

"Your friend has been accused of being an American infidel and a spy," Mohamed interrupted.

"Well, the accuser is wrong."

"Your 'friend' was there when the Americans tried to recruit me during my hegira," Habib spat. "The pigs attempted to rape me in my hotel room in Turkey. *Rape* me! But I fought them off before they could do so, and I tore away this man's mask before he escaped. He is a homosexual in addition to an American and a spy."

"I'll kill you for that." Aaron fought half-heartedly against the men who restrained him. At least he knew the fabricated story he was dealing with. "A homosexual, too!"

Habib grinned. "It is common knowledge that all Americans are homosexuals."

His lackeys laughed.

It was time to start poking holes in Habib's story.

"You say you resisted these Americans who broke into your hotel?" Aaron said. "How many were there?"

"Three."

"You fought off three men who caught you by surprise? Weren't they armed?"

"I do not answer to you," Habib said. "I have already explained my case to Judge Mohamed."

"If I am an infidel," Aaron persisted. "Why do I speak perfect Arabic? Why do I look and sound like I was born in Yemen? Why can I quote every passage in the Quran?"

"The crafty ways of the kaffir know no bounds," Habib said. "The

Americans are masters of deceit. Perhaps they surgically altered your face. Perhaps they made you live with a Yemeni boy so you could practice your Arabic every day—when you weren't raping him, that is."

Aaron turned toward Mohamed. "You must believe me when I tell you I wasn't there."

"The word of an emir carries more weight than the word of a common soldier," Mohamed said. "These are serious allegations, not made lightly, and we must treat them with the gravity they deserve."

"Did he swear on the Quran that his testimony was true?" Aaron said, convinced that he was about to ensnare Habib.

Mohamed bobbed his head. "He did."

How was that possible? Such an oath was sacred to Muslims.

Then Aaron had it. Habib believed he was doomed to hell for what had been done to him; if he was damned already, what did it matter if he lied while swearing on the Quran, especially if the lie allowed him to punish a perceived enemy?

Aaron struggled to find a way out of the situation but he couldn't come up with anything. One thought repeated in his mind.

Don't let them capture you.

That path led only to beheading. He didn't want his family to remember him like that: dying on video while some jihadi chopped off his head. He could already see the headline. "Purported DIA contractor Aaron Berkley beheaded by Islamic State terrorists in new Youtube video released Sunday."

A white-robed male aide entered the room, carrying Aaron's phone. "I need the PIN to unlock this."

Mohamed looked at Aaron. "What is the code?"

Aaron smiled grimly. There was a small problem with giving up access to his phone. Over the last few days, when he was in his sniper hide, he'd recorded video during the fighting, making snide comments regarding the buildings he'd targeted after they were blown to shit. "How's it feel to go to paradise, bitches?" "Enjoy your eternal erections." He'd wanted to feed his ego and show off to William and Ethan.

Probably not the best idea, in retrospect.

Also, on the offline map app he'd marked several possible locations where Sheik Abu Khattab Al-Kurdi, the battle commander, might be staying, based on bodyguards Aaron had seen around the houses. He'd also snapped surreptitious photos of the respective homes.

He hadn't had a chance to wipe any of that data before his unexpected capture.

"Your code?" Mohamed repeated.

Aaron gave them a fake PIN number.

"It's not working," the aide said.

"Give him the proper code," Mohamed said.

"I'm not really sure what it is," Aaron claimed. "I can't simply recite it from memory. It's an automatic thing. I need the phone in my hand to enter it."

The aide glanced at Mohamed, who nodded, then he offered Aaron the cellphone.

It would take too long to issue a hard reset to wipe the data: they'd realize what Aaron was doing immediately when they saw him holding down the three buttons, and then they'd pry it from his grip. Even if he succeeded, the act basically incriminated him.

There had to be a way out. There *had* to be.

Don't do anything reckless, he warned himself.

Aaron calmly entered the fake PIN code. Three times.

"It won't take my code," he lied. "I don't know why. Maybe I'm getting one of the digits wrong. I'm just too tired from my four days on the front. I need a good night's sleep, that's all."

"And we're supposed to believe you?" Habib snarled.

Aaron shrugged, then held out the cellphone to the aide, who took it back.

"The fact that you refuse to unlock your phone doesn't help your case," Mohamed said. "In fact by not doing so, you implicate yourself."

"It's not my fault," Aaron said. "I want to unlock it. I really do."

"You are to be detained until you give up your PIN," Mohamed declared. "And if you won't talk, we have men who will make you."

His greatest fear was finally coming true. Ma and pa would watch the beheading of their son online. No parents should ever have to witness such a thing. But what could he do?

Many things.

The militants who restrained him had loosened their hold slightly. So far, Aaron hadn't revealed his true strength, and he felt fairly certain he could break free with a series of sharp, explosive moves.

He glanced at the nearest muj's holster.

Don't let them capture you...

Before Aaron could act, Habib drew his pistol and fired a shot directly into his thigh.

Aaron sagged in the arms of the men who held him. The pain was unbearable. He was vaguely aware as other militants loyal to Mohamed switched to battle postures and spun their weapons toward Habib.

"What are you doing?" Mohamed said.

"Did you not see the infidel staring at the man's gun?" Habib cried. "I stopped the American pig before he could grab it. Besides, he deserves a little taste of his own medicine. How does it feel to be violated?"

"Habib," Mohamed said. "I have to arrest you for this."

"Well, in that case." Habib loosed another shot, striking Aaron in the shoulder.

Any fight he might have had left was gone with that second bullet. If the militants weren't clutching him he would have collapsed. It would have been better if they let him go, because by holding him up by the arms like that, they prolonged his torture, stretching his freshly injured shoulder joint. Torn tendons rubbed against displaced cartilage and chipped bone. Such sheer, burning excruciation...

"Habib, enough!" Aaron heard Mohamed say.

He sensed motion to his right. The next thing he knew, Habib was lying on the floor with a gunshot wound to the temple, and William was beside him, subdued by the remaining militants in the room. A handgun, probably seized from another mujahid's holster, lay on the carpet in front of William.

"What have you done?" Mohamed said.

"A lucky shot, judge," William pleaded. "He was going to kill Abu-Aadil. I only intended to wound him."

In a daze, Aaron stared at Habib. Blood pooled from the dead man's forehead onto the floor.

"Do you know what this looks like?" Mohamed said. "You have murdered a witness—an *emir*—in cold blood to save the life of a suspected spy. You are now under suspicion of being a spy yourself." He nodded toward the men who restrained William. "Arrest him and prepare him for interrogation."

"What about him?" one of the militants who gripped Aaron said.

"Bind his wounds and take him to the interrogation ward as well." He glanced at Habib's bleeding corpse. "And someone clean that up!"

"This is an outrage," William said as they hauled him away. "Abu-Aadil should be brought to the infirmary for proper treatment at the very least."

"Hold your tongue, spy," Mohamed said.

"I'm not a spy!" William shouted.

"That remains to be seen. The interrogators will extract the truth either way. And even if you are not a spy, then you will be executed for the crime of murdering an emir."

I'm sorry, William.

Aaron's vision darkened as he descended into the sweet, painless embrace of unconsciousness.

thirty-three

Ethan remained motionless.

Neither of the guards obeyed Suleman's command to arrest him, so the man did the deed himself, taking Ethan's M24, Beast, along with his Dragunov, combat knife and radio. He also confiscated the bicep cuff that was part of Beast's sling system. Suleman searched him, but didn't find anything else of concern other than his cellphone. Ethan didn't say a word the whole time—it was best to keep his peace until he knew what was going on.

Bringing one of the guards, Suleman led Ethan inside the foyer. Beyond it lay a tall, pyramidal chamber filled with rows of empty padded seats. Near a cleared central area, prisoners sat with their hands bound. Two AKM-wielding guards watched them. William and Aaron were not among the handcuffed group.

Still in the foyer, Suleman steered Ethan to the left, into a wide overflow room populated with hardback chairs. He led him into a hallway, where another mujahid with an AK stood watch.

Inside the hallway two closed doors resided on the left. He heard a shout from behind one of those doors.

"I told you I don't know anything!"

The Arabic voice belonged to Aaron.

Ethan halted. All of his being called out at him to save his friend.

Suleman shoved him onward. Ethan considered turning around and incapacitating the man and the guards right there, then breaking

William and Aaron out in a blaze of ballistic glory, but he knew the chances of a daytime escape were extremely low. The whole camp would be mobilized against them within the first few minutes.

Wait until dark, he told himself.

Suleman placed him in a third room. A windowless, furniture-less affair.

"Sit," Suleman told him.

Ethan sat on the hard floor, near the wall.

"Unlock your phone." Suleman handed him the Android he had previously confiscated.

Ethan entered his PIN and unlocked the cellphone. He knew Suleman wouldn't find anything incriminating on it. Even if the zealous militant somehow discovered the hidden app, he'd be asked to enter another PIN. Ethan would simply claim the app was some sort of malware he didn't even know he had.

Suleman retrieved the cellphone and performed a cursory check, obviously looking at the contacts, messages, and media. He probably disabled the lock mechanism.

"Watch him," Suleman told the guard who had come with them, and then he withdrew from the room, closing the door. Ethan was left alone with the other man.

He closed his eyes, doing his best to clear his mind, trying to pretend he wasn't confined to a windowless interrogation room with a militant ready to unload an AK into his chest.

The door opened some time later; a man in a white robe and skull cap entered. He wore rimless glasses with rectangular lenses. Suleman stood at his side.

The newcomer took a seat on the floor opposite Ethan, while Suleman remained standing.

"I am Judge Mohamed Al'Sharia."

Ethan nodded slowly. "It is an honor to meet you, judge. I am Abu-Emad."

"I know who you are," Mohamed said. "Do you know what crime

you are accused of?"

"If fighting for Allah and doing His will is a crime, then I am guilty," Ethan declared.

Mohamed pursed his lips. He exchanged a glance with Suleman, then returned his attention to Ethan. "You are accused of being an American spy."

Ethan feigned complete disinterest. "Fascinating. And what evidence do you have against me to support this wrongful claim?"

"We captured two spies this morning," Mohamed said. "Emir Suleman was passing the courthouse when I announced the capture later in the day, and he recognized the two captives bound before me as associates of yours."

"Associates?" Ethan said. "I have many associates in this camp. I did not know it was a crime to befriend those we fight with. May I ask the names of these associates?"

"Abu-Wafeeq and Abu-Aadil," Mohamed answered.

Ethan feigned puzzlement.

"Don't try to pretend you don't know them," Mohamed said. "Emir Suleman says you met with them in camp the first day of your arrival."

Ethan glanced at Suleman. So the man had followed him. Ethan hadn't run a surveillance detection route that day, and looking back, he wished he had.

"He says you often conferred with them in Raqqa as well," Mohamed continued.

Suleman had been spying on him for a long time, then. He had probably been trailing William and Aaron, too, which is why he 'happened' to be passing by the courthouse earlier.

Ethan let anger seep into his voice. "I convened with them, certainly, and considered them my friends at the time, but I swear to you, I thought they were foreign fighters like me, here to wage jihad for the Caliphate. I had no idea they were spies. I'm very disappointed in Abu-Wafeeq and Abu-Aadil, if what you say is true. My tongue has been too loose in their company. I trusted them. *Trusted.*" He moved his gaze between Suleman and Mohamed. "Though what really hurts, what really stabs at my warrior's spirit, is that you suspect *me* of complicity. Me! I, who have come here to lend my Dragunov, and my life, to the cause! I, who have killed in the name of the Caliphate, and Baghdadi, Prince of the Faithful! I, who have saved the life of my fellow mujahadeen!" If necessary, he could call upon Abdullah to testify for him in regards to the latter.

"Ask yourself," Ethan continued indignantly. "If I were truly a spy, would I do all of these things? Would I?"

Mohamed reverently produced a cloth-bound book. "Would you swear to your innocence on the Quran?"

Ethan pretended to hesitate, like any devout Muslim would when presented with the gravity of such an oath.

Suleman's face darkened. "If he is an infidel, then swearing on the Quran means nothing to him."

Ethan rested his palm on the sacred book. "I swear I am not an infidel."

Mohamed nodded. "Do you swear you are not a spy of the Assad regime or the Americans?"

"I swear I am neither."

Mohamed swiveled toward Suleman. "You didn't find any evidence on his person? The USB stick? Range finder?"

Ethan was suddenly relieved he'd stowed those items on the way to the sharia court.

Suleman snarled at Ethan but didn't otherwise answer.

"Emir!" Mohamed said.

Suleman reluctantly shook his head. "There was no USB stick or range finder."

"And what of his belongings in the barracks?" Mohamed said. "They have been searched?"

"Just a moment." Suleman spun around, speaking into his two-way radio. When the muffled response came he faced Mohamed once more. "His belongings have been searched. There is no evidence." He sounded extremely disappointed.

Mohamed regarded Ethan thoughtfully. "I am satisfied of his innocence."

Suleman bit his lip and for a second Ethan thought the militant was going to contest the judge, but then he looked away.

"May I go?" Ethan asked.

Mohamed nodded. "Suleman will escort you to your unit. I apologize for the inconvenience."

Ethan stood, but then paused. "May I make a request?"

"You may, but whether I grant it is another matter entirely."

"I feel that my honor has been sullied by these former friends of mine," Ethan said. "As a form of redress, when the time comes, may I be given the privilege of executing them?"

"They will likely be executed in Raqqa," Mohamed said. "So your request is unfortunately impossible." He waved a dismissive hand. "Allah yusallmak."

Ethan followed Suleman into the main camp. Before reaching the Wolf Company barracks, Suleman said over his shoulder, "The judge may have set you free, but I know in my heart that you are involved with the infidels. Though you swear on the Quran, your shifty eyes betray you. I will be watching you, Abu-Emad. And when you misstep, I will be there with my rifle to send you to hell."

When they arrived at the house, Suleman gave back the combat knife, radio, and cellphone. Ethan made a mental note to perform a thorough malware check on the Android later.

Suleman slid the Dragunov down from his shoulder and returned that too, along with the spare ammunition.

"What about the M24?" Ethan said, eying the powerful sniper rifle resting over Suleman's other arm.

"Mine now," Suleman said, turning away.

Asshole.

Almost everyone was still asleep. Ethan, feeling incredibly sapped himself, moved to his spot and lay down to catch more Z's. His belongings were shifted, he noted.

He closed his eyes, feeling guilty because William and Aaron were likely being interrogated at that very moment, but there was nothing he could do until dark.

He had difficulty falling asleep. He tried not to think about what was happening to his friends, but he couldn't quench the images. There would be some light torture performed at first, maybe some pulled nails or genital electrocutions. But when they were shipped back to Raqqa, the interrogations would begin in earnest. Broken bones. Chopped fingers. He shuddered at the thought.

Ethan wondered how long it would be before they divulged his cover, along with the identities of the assets they'd collected since arriving in Syria. Several people would disappear throughout the region over the next few weeks if Ethan failed.

No pressure or anything.

He was awakened for prayers at sunset, and afterward ate the cold chicken and rice that Raheel had fetched for supper.

There was a simmering tension to the air during the meal. Most of those he considered friends in the unit were either dead or in the infirmary. The newcomers didn't know him, and gave him wary looks while he ate. The others, firmly in Suleman's camp, regarded him with outright hostility.

When he finished eating, the recriminations began, courtesy of Suleman's toadies.

"Once the kaffir spies tell us everything they know," Fida'a announced. "They will be beheaded."

"Good," Ethan said without enthusiasm.

"They will wake up in hellfire every day," Fida'a said. "And burn with endless pain."

"Good," Ethan repeated.

"Suleman says you visited them almost every night when we were in Raqqa," Raheel interjected. "Is this true?"

Ethan glanced at Suleman. The man wore a malicious grin. His eyes shone with that particular fervor of his, along with something new: Hatred.

It was amazing how quick his fellow mujahadeen were to turn against him. Hard to believe he had once considered these men brothers.

"I didn't know they were kaffir spies at the time." Ethan said. "I'm as angry about the whole thing as you are." He turned away. "Now if you will excuse me, I want to read the Quran."

He returned to his designated spot, pulled out a flashlight, and put on a show of reading his clothbound copy of the sacred book. Surreptitiously, he prepared himself for his outing, wanting to minimize the noise he might make later: he grabbed the duct tape from his pack and slipped it into a cargo pocket. He stored his balaclava in another pocket. He placed the Dragunov within easy reach.

Eventually the call for lights out came. He turned off the flashlight and stowed it in his harness.

Ethan lay back and waited, bidding his time. His mind was too active for any sleep, especially since he had slumbered throughout most of the day.

He listened to the gentle pops of the M-37 mortars and the sluggish rat-a-tat of the DShK heavy caliber machine guns, audible despite the distance from Kobane.

He occasionally checked the time on his smartphone, careful to block the illumination with his body, and when midnight came at long last, he shut off his cellphone for good.

Clandestine time.

He was about to arise when he sensed movement behind him. He spun around.

A dark silhouette loomed above him.

"Let's go for a walk," Suleman whispered menacingly.

thirty-four

Ethan grabbed his Dragunov and stood. He was already wearing his knife and radio, and otherwise had everything else he needed, so he calmly followed Suleman into the foyer.

The man paused by the main entrance. "After you."

Ethan reluctantly moved through the doorway ahead of Suleman. He braced himself, expecting a point-black bullet to the back of the head.

But no slugs came. If Suleman had wanted to kill him, of course he wouldn't do it within sight of the unit.

The militant took the lead in the street beyond. Rooftop blazes lit the way—the stink of burnt tires was particularly strong that night.

Suleman followed a path that evaded the night patrols. As acting emir of the unit, he might have been able to explain away his defiance of the curfew. However, the fact he avoided the patrols spoke volumes as far as Ethan was concerned.

Suleman entered an abandoned house and turned on his flashlight, illuminating the insides. He relaxed on a couch in the guest room, and beckoned for Ethan to sit across from him. He set the light source between them on the coffee table, positioning the flashlight so that it shone toward the wall, indirectly illuminating their faces.

Suleman grinned widely and then, strangely, began disarming himself. He put the M24, Beast, on the floor, along with a Makarov, and a Glock hidden in his boot. He unsheathed his combat knife and set it down, too.

Ethan merely watched, dumbfounded.

"I was a soldier in the Iraqi army," Suleman began. "Stationed in a small town just to the east of Mosul. My village was invaded by Islamic State holy warriors. We were divided into two groups. Rafidites"—a derogatory term for Shia, which meant rejectors—"and Sunni. The Sunnis were spared, the Shia rejectors executed on the spot. I was with the Shia. I watched my friends die. But when my turn came, I was spared. Do you know why?"

Ethan remained silent.

"Because of Allah. He acted through Abdullah that day, and had the emir save me. Abdullah, the executioner, the savior. He brought me in when all others shunned me. He spared me when he could have easily taken my life. That day I realized everything I had believed in, everything I had followed, was a sham. *Everything.* So I threw it all aside and embraced Islam. True Islam. And I joined the Islamic State. Not just in body, but mind."

"Why are you telling me this?" Ethan said.

Suleman stared at him for a long moment, then strangely the fervent look faded from his eyes, replaced by sadness.

"I am an officer of the MI6," Suleman said softly, switching to English.

That got Ethan's attention. He sat straight up.

"Surprised?" Suleman continued, speaking with a distinct British accent. "I have been embedded almost four years. So long that I've almost forgotten my former life. What I once was is but a memory. This role, it has consumed me. I never meant to lose myself. It just happened. Moments of absolutely clarity, such as now, where I remember who I was and what I stood for, are rare. Usually I dismiss these moments. Tell myself I've moved on. That I've found Allah and the true path. But not this time. Finally I've found someone who understands me. Someone who can set me free."

Ethan shifted uncomfortably. When entering deep cover, there was always the chance of losing oneself in the role. It was why operatives underwent such extensive psychological screening. Even so, to keep up the charade for four years... Suleman was living proof of what could happen when a man was embedded for too long.

Assuming, of course, that Suleman was telling the truth.

Ethan waited for him to reveal more, but when the man remained silent, he spoke.

"Why are you telling me this?" Ethan repeated in Arabic. He refused to give up his own cover so easily.

"Isn't it obvious?" Suleman said simply, still in English.

Ethan studied the man uncertainly, then he slowly slid the Dragunov from his shoulder. He aimed it at Suleman's chest.

The supposed MI6 officer closed his eyes and began quietly reciting what sounded like a passage from the Quran.

Ethan let the aim of the weapon drift toward Suleman's head. Killing him would solve several potential problems. But if he was telling the truth, and really was an embedded operative, that made him a fellow Selous Scout...

He lowered the rifle. "I'm sorry. I can't do it."

Those eyes shot open. The fervent look had returned, and that intense hatred burned stronger than ever.

Suleman snarled. "Then you will die, kaffir." He reached down and grabbed the Makarov from the floor.

Ethan vaulted across the coffee table and smashed away the pistol with the stock of his Dragunov.

The man bolted upright, crashing into him. In moments Ethan found himself wrestling with Suleman on the floor. The flashlight shone from the rug beside him—one of them had knocked over the coffee table somewhere along the way.

Ethan managed to get on top. Suleman wrapped his hands around the Dragunov, struggling to wrench it from him. Ethan released the rifle and slammed the heel of his palm into the underside of his opponent's nose.

Suleman slumped instantly as the septal cartilage crunched against the nasal bone. Blood flowed from his nose onto his cheek, trickling onto the frayed rug in audible drips. His chest cavity raggedly heaved in and out.

Ethan snatched up the Dragunov, and then grabbed the other weapons Suleman had laid on the floor, starting with Beast. He slid the Dragunov over his left shoulder, Beast his right, stuffed the spare Makarov down the back of his cargo pants, the Glock in his boot. He stowed the extra combat knife in his other boot.

Ethan seized the man's ammo clips and tucked them into his harness. He discovered the PVS-22 Night Vision clip-on in one of Suleman's pockets, and mounted it to Beast's forward Picatinny. Finally he removed the quick cuff from Suleman's left bicep and attached it to his own, adjusting the tightness.

Suleman had remained motionless the whole time, completely debilitated.

"Kill me," Suleman finally gurgled. A small red bubble burst from his lips. Blood was evidently pouring down his throat from the mangled nose.

"No," Ethan said.

"If you let me live I'll hunt you down for the rest of your days, I swear it. I can't let you go. Not after what I told you."

"You can certainly try to hunt me." Ethan took out his cellphone and snapped a photo of Suleman's face. He'd send it to Sam if he ever got the chance. He still wasn't entirely sure he believed Suleman's story, and Sam was the only one who could set the record straight.

With the duct tape he'd stowed in a cargo pocket, Ethan bound and gagged the lethargic man, folding Suleman forward to secure his hands to his feet like a trussed pig. He left him there like that, lying on his side: if the militant worked hard, he should be able to wiggle outside by morning and someone would set him free.

Ethan hurried across the street and hid behind a small house. Tires burned on the rooftop. He donned his balaclava, hauled himself over a cinder-block fence, slunk through the backyard, and crossed into a murky alley beyond.

When he was about two blocks away from Suleman he ran a surveillance detection route, partially doubling back in case the acting emir had instructed one of the others to follow. But no one tailed him.

With that, he dismissed Suleman from his mind entirely. Whether the man was truly an MI6 operative or not was irrelevant from that point forward.

Finding a dark alleyway, he checked the offline map on his phone. He reoriented himself until he was facing the destination building, which he had marked earlier, then he memorized the route and put the Android away.

He arrived at his target and retrieved the USB stick and TruPulse range finder he had stashed in the debris earlier. He plugged the USB into his smartphone on the off chance that Doug was in range, but as expected, the operative embedded among the Kurds appeared offline. Too bad. An airstrike would have proven quite a useful distraction.

He crept onward, keeping close to the buildings. Shortly thereafter the makeshift sharia courthouse came into view.

The two AKM-wielding guards of the night shift stood on either side of the entrance. The electric lamps over the twin doors shone brightly, no doubt thanks to a dedicated diesel generator somewhere inside.

Keeping to the shadows, Ethan circumnavigated the building. There were no windows of any kind. He found another entry in the rear, though it too was well lit and watched by armed men.

Ethan maneuvered to the unguarded eastern flank of the building. He climbed a nearby palm tree and swung himself onto the three-foot ledge that bordered the wide pyramid topping the structure.

He skulked along the perimeter until he reached the front. He perched there, above and a little behind the two main guards. They stood roughly three paces apart. The perfect distance for what he planned.

He stealthily lowered himself from the ledge until he was hanging there, his back to the men, his boots two and a half feet above the ground.

Then he let go, letting his knees bend so that he landed in a crouch. He tried to touch down silently but a couple of the ammo cartridges in his harness rattled. He sensed the guards moving behind him.

Ethan twisted, withdrawing the combat knife at his belt with one hand and the spare blade from his boot with the other. He stood up, stepping forward, spreading his arms, burying each knife into the necks of both men. Composed of 55-58 HRC stainless steel that tapered to a spear point, the almost pure black, six and half inch long Voron-3 blades slid easily into the flesh, the silver-tipped cutting edges meeting little resistance.

The two militants gargled sickeningly. One fell, but the other struggled to bring about his AKM. Ethan yanked the knife forward, ripping the cartilage of the man's larynx open in a stream of gristle and gore. He collapsed.

Ethan dragged both bodies, one after the other, into the foliage that grew along the base of the building. He turned off their two-way radios and washed the blood from his hands with water from their canteens. There was nothing he could do about the crimson stains he'd left behind on the pavement, however.

Ethan opened the main doors and slipped into the foyer. Keeping close to the wall so that none of the guards in the central chamber beyond would see him, he proceeded into the overflow room with its hardback chairs. He approached the hallway on the other side of the room, knowing a mujahid awaited on watch within.

He calmly removed his balaclava and entered.

The militant on duty straightened instantly. A youth scarcely out of his teens, he sat in a chair near the closed door to the left, where Ethan had heard Aaron shouting earlier.

The militant fingered the trigger on his AK, but otherwise kept the weapon lowered.

"Salaam," Ethan said. "I am here to pick up the prisoners."

* * *

Suleman trembled in the guest room. Not from cold, as the air was warm. Nor from the pain he felt in his smashed nose. No, he trembled from sheer, unmitigated rage.

He had given himself up to Emad, believing him a true brother. Believing Emad understood him. Suleman had revealed everything to him and made his peace.

But Emad had humiliated Suleman. He had refused to grant his martyrdom request. For that, and for the knowledge of Suleman's true identity that he had obtained, Emad could not be allowed to live.

Suleman fought against his binds but it was useless.

Then he heard movement in the foyer. The silhouette of a man appeared.

Beneath Suleman's gag, he smiled.

thirty-five

Ethan stared down the young guard.

"I was not told there would be a pick up," the mujahid said.

"They are to be transferred to Raqqa immediately," Ethan said authoritatively. "Radio your emir, you will see."

"Judge Mohamed is my emir," the youth said. "He is asleep."

"Then either wake him," Ethan insisted. "Or allow me through."

The youth hesitated. "I will wake him. Come." He beckoned toward the hall, indicating that Ethan should walk in front of him.

Ethan moved casually past the militant; when he was only slightly in front, he spun to the left and gave the youth a controlled knifehand strike to the neck. He hit the carotid sinus at just the right angle, with just the right pressure, to fool his brain into thinking his blood pressure had shot through the roof.

The militant crumpled as his medulla oblongata hurried to compensate.

Ethan disarmed the man and seized his two-way radio. He tried the door. Locked. A quick search of the militant's cargo pockets yielded a key ring.

As he unlocked the door the militant stirred. Ethan grabbed the man by the wrists and dragged him inside.

Aaron lay bound and gagged in one corner of the room, but when he saw Ethan he brightened visibly. One of his eyes was swollen shut.

The right portion of his lower lip was a fat, purple mess. The big man still wore his fatigues, and likely had similar bruises over the rest of his body. He was barefooted. Gauze wrapped his left thigh and right shoulder—gunshot wounds? Smaller bandages covered his index fingers and big toes, likely where his nails had been forcibly removed.

Ethan felt sick to his stomach. They'd all undergone torture training and knew what to expect, but still... at least in training they knew it was going to end. Real life didn't afford that luxury. And the worst the instructors had ever inflicted was a good water boarding, that or leaving them tied up naked and soaking wet in subzero temperatures.

The momentarily forgotten youth was struggling in his arms. Ethan clocked him in the face, letting out his anger, and the mujahid went limp. Ethan duct-taped his mouth and then his wrists. By the time Ethan got to his feet, the youth was fighting again. Ethan sat on him and finished the job, securing his hands to his ankles just as he'd done with Suleman.

He ripped the tape from Aaron's mouth.

"Ow," Aaron complained. "You took away some of my beard, dammit."

Ethan had to smile. The resiliency of the human spirit never ceased to amaze him. Even after all he'd been through that day, Aaron still had his sense of humor.

Ethan cut away the rest of Aaron's bonds.

His friend shifted, wincing. "Damn I'm stiff."

"I know you're happy to see me, but come on."

Aaron rolled his eyes. "I said stiff, not *stiffy*."

Ethan helped him stand.

"Gah!" Aaron exclaimed. "Man, that's pain."

Ethan folded Aaron's uninjured arm over his neck. "You were shot?" He nodded toward the bandaged shoulder.

"Yeah," Aaron said. "Leg and shoulder. That could be a new shampoo. Beats dandruff better than the leading brand."

It wasn't funny. The shoulder was one of the worst body parts to take a bullet. Most of the time such a wound resulted in permanent disability, as the deltoid was simply too compact of a unit—with several highly specialized structures crowded into such a small space there was really no "safe" path for a bullet to travel. His friend would have to endure several reconstructive surgeries, and months, if not years, of rehabilitation.

Ethan tried a few tentative steps. "You're heavier than you look."

"That's what your wife always told me." Aaron's breath came in strained heaves.

Ethan peered into the hall to make sure the way was clear, then he helped Aaron through the door and locked it behind him, sealing the militant within.

Luckily, Ethan found William in the adjacent room. The other operative seemed better off than Aaron, though he had similar bruising on his face, and gauze also wrapped several of his fingertips and toes. He hadn't been shot, however, and that probably made all the difference.

After Ethan freed him, William was able to help with Aaron—he wrapped one arm around the injured operative's waist, careful to avoid his damaged shoulder.

"So what's the plan?" William said quietly, when they entered the hall.

"We make our way to Kobane, fuck up the Islamic State on the way to the front lines, then surrender to the Kurds."

"Sounds easy," William deadpanned.

Outside, Ethan led them to where he had hidden the two bodies. William and Aaron pilfered the boots and weapons of the dead men.

"Look at this." Aaron held up a harness in the dim light, revealing the five RGD-5 fragmentation grenades it contained. "I found me some Easter eggs."

Sharing Aaron between them, Ethan and William hurried onward. They kept to the shadows, avoiding the night patrols, making their way toward the outskirts of town.

The trio reached an intersection. Distant, muffled Arabic drifted to them from beyond the bend.

Staying in cover behind the nearest home, Ethan released Aaron, leaned past the edge, and raised Beast's scope to eye level. The NV clip-on presented everything in a greenish-black hue. The reticule in the Leupold Mark 4 day optic was unaffected; the beaded cross hairs appeared as a black overlay.

The dim glow provided by the rooftop blazes provided ample illumination for the NV, which auto-gated as the scope passed over brighter areas. He spotted a handful of militants two blocks to the north, guarding a checkpoint that led in and out of the village. The men lounged in front of a pair of Iraqi Army M1114 Up-Armored Humvees.

Ethan and his fellow operatives had two options. Circumvent the checkpoint and continue toward Kobane on foot, which could take all night. Or steal a Humvee.

He chose the latter option.

* * *

Suleman made his way back to the house where Wolf Company billeted. Beside him marched Fida'a. The loyal holy warrior had followed him at a distance as instructed, and kept watch on the building where Suleman had taken Emad. When the American spy had emerged alone, Fida'a had entered and cut Suleman free.

His nose throbbed. The blood loss made him weak, dizzy. It was difficult to evade the night patrol in his condition, but somehow he managed. He had refused to allow Fida'a to help him walk—he was acting emir, and must appear strong. He supposed he should visit the infirmary, but he wanted to deal with Emad first. He had already decided he would execute the kaffir in the house, in front of the unit if needbe, consequences be damned.

Assuming Emad was actually there.

At the barracks Suleman took back the M16A4 he had given Fida'a earlier. He also yanked the knife from Fida'a's belt.

His friend regarded him questioningly.

"I only need it for a little while, brother," Suleman whispered.

He went inside, the cold, black steel in hand. Suleman shone his flashlight from face to face as he roamed the house, but the kaffir was not present. No matter.

He returned the knife to Fida'a but kept the A4. He went to his belongings and retrieved the laptop secreted there. It had a GSM card and was loaded with Stingray software, allowing Suleman to track nearby active cellphones. No one knew he had that ability, not even Abdullah, who believed Suleman carried an ordinary laptop.

The offline map of the village appeared on screen. In the search field, Suleman entered the serial number he had recorded from Emad's Android phone earlier.

There.

Emad was on the north side of the village, close to the courthouse. He was moving northwest. Had he freed the other spies? It didn't matter. Suleman would terminate them, too.

He closed the laptop, leaving it turned on, then went to the kitchen. When he had brought Abdullah to the field hospital earlier, Suleman had borrowed a US-made autoinjector along with a couple of vials of epinephrine. He retrieved them from the cupboards and considered injecting himself right there, but pocketed the device instead. It wouldn't do to die from cardiac arrest before he had Emad in his sights.

Suleman started for the front door.

"Where are you going?" Fida'a said.

"I have a score to settle with our good friend Emad."

"I go with you." Fida'a retrieved his AK. The man had no love for the infidel.

Suleman considered bringing along additional members of the unit, but that would only make it more difficult to skirt the night patrol. Besides, he wanted Emad for himself. He glanced at Fida'a. His friend would be more than enough.

"Come then, brother, we go hunting."

* * *

Ethan approached the checkpoint alone.

One of the militants spotted him immediately and raised an AK. "Why are you out past curfew?" The man had a thick Roman nose.

Ethan lifted his hands in surrender. "I am a courier."

"A courier?"

"Yes. I bring a message far too sensitive to be delivered over ordinary radio."

Roman-Nose frowned. "Well let's hear it, then."

One of the Humvees started up.

"Hey!" another militant shouted.

The Humvee sped away.

Three of the fighters hurried inside the remaining Humvee and drove off in pursuit. Roman-Nose and another militant stayed behind.

Roman-Nose narrowed his eyes at Ethan. "You did this."

"I swear, I—" Ethan fell to his knees, clutching at his belly, though none of the fighters had touched him. Saliva spilled from his mouth. He collapsed, face-up, to stare unblinking into the smoke-covered sky.

Roman-Nose kicked him in the ribs; Ethan flinched but didn't otherwise move. Roman-Nose glanced uncertainly at the other mujahid... a third figure emerged from the shadows behind them and a pistol report echoed twice into the night. Blood spurted from the heads of both militants and they crumpled.

Ethan clambered to his feet, gripping his throbbing ribs.

"Nice acting," William said.

"Thanks." He glanced toward the village, worried the two shots would empty any nearby barracks or at the very least attract the night patrols, but the neighborhood remained lifeless. It helped that the firecracker-like shelling noises from Kobane were peaking at the moment.

Ethan and William quickly dragged the corpses behind the nearest building and then sprinted out of the village.

"Any trouble loading Aaron into the Humvee?" Ethan asked as he ran.

"None whatsoever."

Chatter erupted over the radio. "A Humvee has been stolen from checkpoint three. We are in pursuit. Requesting assistance!"

He exchanged a worried glance with William and dashed on.

Following the road, they soon came upon an interesting scene.

A Humvee was situated in the middle of the street, with another Humvee parked behind it. The engines of both vehicles were off. Three militants warily approached the first vehicle. One of them carried a flashlight.

Ethan and William dropped. Letting the darkness conceal him, Ethan aimed Beast at the tangos: the militants appeared as dark green smudges. He centered the crosshairs over the mujahid who carried the flashlight, and the NV clip-on auto-gated to compensate for the brightness.

He fired.

He worked the bolt, which ejected the spent shell casing and loaded another cartridge into the chamber, but before he could line up his next shot a pistol sounded twice—the muzzle flash came from the driver-side window of the farthest Humvee. Both of the remaining militants toppled.

Ethan and William approached.

Aaron abruptly sat up in the driver seat and waved a Makarov, singing, "He stuck a feather in his hat and called it macaroni."

* * *

Suleman was running. He held his laptop under one arm, trying to ignore the jolts of pain each footfall inflicted upon his smashed nose, but it was difficult. He was beginning to feel dizzy all over again.

Moments ago he had heard an ominous report issue from the road beyond the checkpoint. It had sounded like a high-powered sniper rifle going off, the kind of crack an M24 might make. Two more quick pops had followed it in rapid succession.

Emad.

He strove to increase his pace, but the dizziness was starting to get to him. Fida'a pulled ahead.

"Abu-Fida'a, slow down!" Suleman shouted, not wanting to lose his loyal holy warrior so early in the game. "Abu-Fida'a!"

But the man ignored him.

Suleman finally caught up to Fida'a. The man had stopped beside an abandoned Humvee. Three militants lay motionless in front of it, illuminated by a flashlight one of them had probably dropped.

Suleman and Fida'a cleared the Humvee with their rifles, then Fida'a checked the bodies.

"Dead," he said.

Suleman placed the laptop on the hood of the M1114 and studied the display. Emad was moving away rapidly to the north.

Suleman closed the device and plunked himself down in the Humvee's driver side while Fida'a took shotgun. He handed the portable computer across to Fida'a, who placed it on the passenger support between them. Usually the support was reserved for equipment such as SINCGARS radios and Blue Force trackers, but all of that had been gutted.

Humvees didn't have keys. The last thing you wanted to worry about during the heat of battle was picking up the starter from a fallen brother. You turned a rotary switch through two positions, and the engine activated

Suleman stared at said switch suspiciously. Was it a trap?

He returned his gaze to the road and the three dead bodies arrayed before him. He thought of Emad speeding away before him, and anger filled him.

He was in Allah's hands.

He moved the rotary switch to the RUN position. The wait-to-start lamp above it activated. He stared at it, sweating.

The lamp went out. So far, so good. He glanced at the transmission indicator lamp above the gear shift. It was lit.

Holding his breath, he turned the rotary switch to the START position.

The vehicle rumbled to life.

Slumping slightly, he released the rotary and it returned to the RUN position. Emad wasn't as good at the game as Suleman had believed—at the very least the fool should have disabled the Humvee.

He shifted uncomfortably—there was something protruding from the base of his seat beneath him. Reaching back, he discovered an un-detonated grenade. He tossed it out the window in fright, but the bomb was a dud. Allah truly was with him that night.

Emad, you keep making mistakes.

Smiling maliciously, Suleman set the topmost light switch on the lower left of the steering wheel to the Blackout Drive position, which activated the blackout lights. Then he shifted the vehicle into gear and accelerated over the three dead bodies.

thirty-six

Ethan kept checking his left and right rearview mirrors for signs of pursuit, but never spotted any other vehicles. That didn't mean they were safe. Not by a long shot.

He regretted abandoning the second Humvee. He should have told William to drive it, but he had allowed his friend to drop a grenade in the vehicle instead. Before the bomb had gone off, frantic shouting had come from the south; Ethan had feared the arrival of reinforcements, so he had ordered William into the first Humvee and driven off. He should have waited to make sure the grenade had detonated, but he had simply wanted to get the hell out of there.

I'm getting sloppy.

He was driving with the blackout lights. That, combined with the ambient illumination from the blazes in the nearby villages was more than enough to see by.

In the seat behind him, Aaron used the offline map in Ethan's Android to give directions. Ethan's only worry was that the battery would fail. The power levels were under twenty percent the last time he checked.

"Tell me how you guys got caught," he told Aaron over his shoulder.

"Someone recognized me in the forward camp."

"Someone?"

Aaron sighed. "Before you arrived in Turkey, Sam had me working with another group of DIA contractors. Apparently these guys had some of the highest success rates at turning foreign fighters."

Ethan pressed his lips together. "I think I know where this is going."

"Take a left up ahead," Aaron said. "And yeah, these guys were twisted." He hesitated. "Their methods were unorthodox, to say the least. We intercepted this one jihadi named Habib in Gaziantep who was on his way to Syria from Saudi Arabia. The contractors brutally raped him. I walked out on the thing, but I discovered later that they took pictures and threatened to show them to his family if he didn't become their asset. You know what the crime for homosexuality in Saudi Arabia is, right?"

Ethan shook his head. "Some of the contractors the DIA hires..."

"Yeah, well, I told Sam to reassign me shortly after that. Maybe I'm too squeamish. The guy was on his way to join the Islamic State, after all, a group of radicals who cut people's heads off on YouTube and rape entire villages, so maybe I shouldn't have felt so strung up about it. But there's a certain standard of human decency I follow, even against my enemy. A code. Doing stuff like that DIA team did, well, it makes me feel... vile, you know?"

"Worse shit was done in Guantanamo," William piped in.

"Yeah well, I always like to tell myself that we're better than the terrorists," Aaron continued. "That we won't descend to their base level, but you know what, we're not better. We're not." He cleared his throat before continuing. "Anyway, this agent the DIA team supposedly recruited? Well he showed up in the camp back there."

"Ah."

"Yeah. Apparently Habib had worked his way up the Islamic State ranks since the last time we met. Had me arrested. William got wind of it and tried to vouch for me, but the judge arrested him after Habib went wacko and started shooting me."

"Wait, what?" Ethan said. "The judge arrested William? Why? He should have arrested this Habib."

"Yeah, except that William snatched a pistol from one of the nearby muj and popped Habib in the head."

"Oh."

William jumped in. "What was I supposed to do, stand by and watch the guy kill him?"

"No," Ethan said. "You did the right thing."

William laughed softly. "I probably should have capped him in the knee instead, but the bastard royally pissed me off. Thought he could mess with one of my friends and get away with it, did he? And truthfully, I wanted to shut him up. I figured without his testimony, Aaron would be safe. I was wrong. After I was arrested, the judge's lackeys found the USB stick and TruPulse range finder on me and they got all excited because Aaron had them, too. When they discovered the retractable RF antennas hidden within the USBs, we were basically screwed."

"Didn't help matters when I gave up the PIN to my Android under duress," Aaron added. "And they found certain un-Islamic recordings on the phone."

"Videos of you providing commentary in English during airstrikes?" Ethan asked.

"Yup."

"I warned you about doing that."

"I know you did."

"You're supposed to be one of the best operatives in the field," Ethan scolded his friend.

"The best. Yeah. Doesn't mean I'm not human. I've paid for my mistakes, Ethan."

We've all *paid for your mistakes,* he wanted to say, but figured his friend felt guilty enough as it was. The three of them were alive and free, at least for the moment, and that was all that mattered.

The Humvee reached the final village before the wide tract to Kobane. He steered through the cement buildings, heading toward the heavy artillery at the outskirts. Under the blackout lights he spotted what he thought were a couple of militants on the guns, but none of them made any move to intercept the Humvee.

His two-way radio crackled to life. "Incoming vehicle, identify yourself."

The radio chatter from the forward camp wouldn't have reached these men, of course. Without radio towers and repeaters along the way, the distance was just too far.

"I'm a courier," Ethan said into his radio. "I have a message for the battle emir."

The militants waved him through.

Ethan drove past the heavy artillery into the empty expanse of land beyond. The southeast edge of Kobane lay about a kilometer ahead.

The sky cleared as the vehicle broke free of the tire smoke that choked the villages; the quarter moon cast its dim light down upon them. He hoped none of the passing jets or drones would mark his thermal signature for bombing.

He breathed a soft sigh of relief when he reached the city's perimeter. At the entrance checkpoint he slowed to a halt, then slid the window locking bar from its hole and lowered the Humvee's ballistic glass.

One of the fighters on duty shone a flashlight inside. Ethan was about to repeat his courier claim when a garbled voice came over the man's two-way radio. The fighter raised a hand in a "wait a moment" gesture.

"Say again?" the man spoke into the two-way.

The voice returned, but there was far too much static for it to be intelligible. Likely the speaker originated from the forward village, or a vehicle on the way to Kobane from there. Ethan did catch one ominous word: "Prisoners."

The soldier shrugged, then returned his attention to the Humvee.

"I am a courier—" Ethan began, but the fighter was already waving him through.

Ethan stepped on the accelerator.

Almost there.

* * *

Suleman crossed both checkpoints with relative ease. He simply told the lazy watchmen that he was in pursuit of escaped kaffir spies. At the second checkpoint, the soldier on duty hesitated when he spotted the bloody nose, but when the man looked into his eyes and saw the fires that burned there, he seemed to understand that Suleman was a true lion of Islam, fervently dedicated to the cause.

Suleman's nose still throbbed slightly, and he experienced bouts of dizziness. Those were the least of his problems, however: traveling by vehicle through Kobane proper proved extremely difficult. The streets were a mess, and he had been forced to backtrack several times when his way was blocked by a collapsed building or blast crater. Worse, Emad's signal no longer showed up on the Stingray.

Despite these difficulties, he had no doubt he would find Emad eventually. None whatsoever. Allah would guide him.

He switched over the two-way radio to the common frequency and spoke. "All units, be on the lookout for a roaming Humvee. Report its position, but do not attack." The last was to ensure that any militants who spotted Suleman's Humvee wouldn't launch a rocket at *him*.

"I've spotted the Humvee," a scratchy voice returned a moment later. It cut in and out with static. "It just turned off Forty-Eight Street and is heading south toward the outskirts of Kobane."

Suleman grinned wickedly. He'd recognize that voice anywhere. It was Emad. The kaffir thought Suleman would fall for that, did he? *Heading south toward the outskirts of Kobane*. Bah. It was obvious he planned on crossing over to the Kurds. Suleman swore the kaffir would die before he reached the yellow-faces. And after he killed Emad, he planned to return home to Britain, where he would be hailed a hero for his dedicated undercover work above and beyond the call of duty. At the offices of MI6, he would detonate a suicide vest as he shook the Chief's hand. His courageous act of martyrdom would serve as a beacon of hope for all Muslims everywhere, and they would rise up against the infidel oppressors worldwide.

Suleman continued making his way toward the front line, back-tracking when the streets proved impassable. He began to despair of finding Emad in time. Had Allah abandoned him so soon?

"Emir," Fida'a said.

Suleman glanced at his loyal friend. Fida'a nodded at the open laptop.

Emad's signal had returned.

* * *

"Which way, Aaron?" Ethan said.

Seven meters ahead, the way forward was blocked by a severely damaged apartment building. The entire right side had been blown away, spilling huge piles of concrete and furniture onto the roadway.

They had faced several such blockages during the flight—it was a rabbit's warren out there. Ethan had considered simply abandoning the Humvee, but with Aaron's injuries it was best to stay with the vehicle as long as possible.

"You do realize your map is slightly outdated, right?" Aaron said from behind. "It's missing some key information, namely, which god-damn buildings have collapsed!"

"Do what you can," Ethan said curtly.

His thoughts drifted to the radio chatter he had answered earlier. That man who had asked the mujahadeen to report any Humvees... Ethan couldn't be sure because of the static, but he thought the voice belonged to Suleman. He'd left the man duct-taped in the forward camp. Had he broken free already? Whatever the case, someone was pursuing them, and that someone apparently wanted Ethan for himself.

A few other radio calls had come in, questioning his intent, but he always answered in pristine Arabic, identifying himself as a courier. None of the brothers he talked to ever repeated his location over the radio for the pursuers, probably because they couldn't tell he drove a Humvee in the night.

Ethan glanced in the left and right rearview mirrors. The road still seemed clear behind them. So far. "Come on, Aaron. Pick a direction. Or I'll do it for you."

His fellow operative didn't answer.

"Aaron!"

"Go right," Aaron said.

"Finally." Ethan took his foot off the brake and started the turn. "See if you can contact Black Mamba yet. I want—"

He was cut off when something struck the front right side of the vehicle.

thirty-seven

At first Ethan thought a mortar shell had impacted, but when the vehicle veered sharply to the left of its own accord, he saw another Humvee streak past, loudly scraping the outer hull. The other vehicle tore away, halting several meters to the left.

Not trusting the ballistic glass, Ethan kept low. "You guys okay?"

"Fine," Aaron said from the backseat.

"Will?"

"I'm good," William answered. His friend was similarly crouched. "It hit the engine, not me."

The Humvee had stalled. The wait-to-start lamp was inactive, and so was the transmission indicator lamp. Staying as low as he could in his seat, Ethan tried the rotary switch regardless. The engine refused to cooperate. It was about time they left the vehicle anyway.

He peered at the second Humvee through the windshield. Lit by the quarter moon, it lay almost parallel to their own vehicle, with its tailgate facing them. The subtle, shifting darkness of smoke billowed from its engine.

Ethan opened the driver side door and stepped out, using the metal doorframe for cover. William did the same on the passenger side.

Gunfire erupted from the opposing vehicle. He instinctively ducked, recognizing the triple report of an M16. It was intermixed with the semi-automatic bursts of an AK-47. Muzzle flashes filled the night.

The other Humvee was far too close for him to practically use

Beast. And the Dragunov wouldn't suffice either, not for what he intended. He needed something capable of laying down several rounds of covering fire.

"Aaron," he shouted over his shoulder. "AK. Two RGDs."

From the backseat Aaron handed over his AK and the requested fragmentation grenades.

"William," Ethan said. "Get Aaron to those buildings." He nodded toward the intersection behind them. "Let me know when you're ready to make the dash."

Ethan returned fire sporadically with the AK. Meanwhile William made his way around the rear of the vehicle to the left side passenger door and unloaded Aaron.

"Ready!" William's voice came a few seconds later.

Ethan moved to the backside of the vehicle—an enemy grenade detonated in the spot he had just vacated. He squeezed past William and Aaron, who had taken up a position near the rightmost brake light, and then he crouched behind the open passenger side door.

He threw one of the RGD-5s. It detonated, filling the air between the two vehicles with black smoke.

"Go!" He lay down suppression with the AK. The grenade smoke obscured the line of fire from the enemy Humvee's driver side flank, so he concentrated mostly on the passenger windows.

"Clear!" William's Arabic voice carried from behind.

Ethan stopped firing. He had expended almost all of the AK's thirty round magazine. He pulled the pin and threw the second RGD-5, then retreated to the back of the Humvee. Sporadic gunfire erupted from the opposing vehicle.

He didn't need to tell William what to do.

As soon as the grenade detonated, William immediately lay down covering fire with his AK. Ethan crossed the thirty meter gap at a sprint, diving for cover behind the building at the edge of the intersection.

He returned the AK to Aaron. His friend was resting against the building, huffing, Android phone in hand.

"Someone's out of shape," Ethan taunted him.

Aaron ignored the jibe. "Black Mamba is still offline," he said between breaths, sliding the Kalashnikov over his shoulder. "I'm setting your phone to issue a notification when he comes on."

"You can do that?" Ethan said.

"Obviously." Aaron stuffed the Android and USB stick combination into Ethan's cargo pocket. "All set."

Behind him, William remained by the building's edge, occasionally firing at the other Humvee.

Ethan shrugged the sniper rifle down from his shoulder. He was about to leave his friends to find an outflanking position when two mujahadeen joined them from across the street. Perfect.

"Brothers," Ethan said. "Two yellow-faces are pinned in the farthest Humvee around the corner. Hold this position while we go around the block and outflank them."

The mujahadeen agreed.

Ethan hoisted Aaron's arm over his neck and proceeded onward. William brought up the rear.

"We're not really planning on outflanking them, are we?" Aaron said as Ethan led him through a ragged hole in a cinder block fence.

"Nope. We're getting the hell out. We'll be long by the time our pursuers realize they've been shooting at ghosts."

* * *

Suleman stared through his scope at the dead bodies of his enemies. While Fida'a had held the Humvee, Suleman had made his way to an overwatch position across the street and then mown down both attackers. Afterward, unsure if Emad or another was lying in wait to snipe him, he had ordered Fida'a to leave cover and check the bodies. The man had blindly obeyed.

"It's not them," Fida'a radioed. He sounded winded.

"Are you certain?"

"Yes."

Suleman jogged over to him. Fida'a was right. Neither of the dead men were Emad or his companions. He felt cheated.

Fida'a sat on the broken pavement, resting against the side of the building, his AK across his lap.

Suleman set his laptop down and opened it. Emad's signal was relatively close.

"Get up," he told Fida'a. "I don't want to lose him."

His companion coughed terribly, and did not rise.

"What's wrong?" Suleman went to him.

Fida'a smiled in the moonlight. His teeth were black—covered in blood. "I'm sorry, my friend," he said, wheezing. "But I must take my leave of you."

Suleman knelt beside him. Fida'a had taken an ugly gunshot wound in the chest. "Your place in jannah is guaranteed," Suleman told him.

"I know. Good luck to you, my brother. I will see you again in paradise."

His loyal friend closed his eyes and died.

Suleman slumped, filled with sadness. True, moments ago he had ordered Fida'a into the line of fire of a potential sniper, willing to sacrifice him to reveal the marksman's position. But he hadn't really expected his friend to die. Allah was with them. And when no shot came, that had served only to confirm his belief.

But he was wrong.

He felt utterly sapped. His mangled nose throbbed worse than ever.

Maybe I should just let Emad go.

No. Emad represented all that was wrong with the world—the depravity, deceit, and dishonor of the West. If he killed Emad, he would prove to himself that good could triumph over evil in the end, and that he was right in his decision to forego his infidel masters.

But he couldn't continue the hunt in his current state. He needed a little something extra.

Nose throbbing, he weakly returned to the Humvee and retrieved the autoinjector kit. The epinephrine vials had survived the crash. He loaded one and placed the injector over his heart.

He hesitated only a moment.

"Allahu akbar," Suleman declared, and injected himself directly in the heart.

He felt a stabbing pain in his chest and keeled over.

I have killed myself, he thought.

But the pain quickly subsided, replaced by an incredible surge of energy. He lived, and more importantly, he felt more alive than ever before.

Allah was with him once more.

He glanced at the laptop.

I'm coming for you Emad.

* * *

Ethan followed the noise of heavy machine guns—the sporadic din of both sides exchanging fire, the sounds growing louder with each passing moment. He and his friends were nearing the front.

Ethan and William helped Aaron in shifts. It was currently William's turn, so Ethan was leading the way, Beast in hand.

As he crossed in front of a collapsed building, a feral dog looked up and growled before running off. He was surprised no one had eaten it yet.

Ethan heard a high-pitched whistle as a Kurdish shell pierced the air. He cringed, knowing it could easily land on top of them. The keen descended in pitch, finally ending in an explosion some distance away. The Islamic State line responded with DShK fire.

As he passed an upturned Hyundai van, Ethan's Android vibrated in his pocket. He paused, directing Aaron and William behind the vehicle, where all three of them crouched. He retrieved his phone and read the notification while William watched their flank. "Black Mamba is finally online."

"Or at least in range," William said.

Ethan keyed in a message.

"What did you say?" Aaron asked.

"Basically that we're coming over," Ethan replied. "And please don't shoot."

"How did the Mamba respond?"

"He didn't. Not yet. It'll vibrate when he does, right?"

"You bet."

Ethan pocketed the smartphone and was about to rise when a figure emerged from the darkness immediately beside him. Apparently the newcomer had been hiding in the van, or behind it, because he'd escaped William's notice.

The man's assault rifle was pointed directly at Ethan's head.

thirty-eight

Ethan lifted his hands slightly, palms up. Though he couldn't see William behind him, he knew the other operative would have swiveled his own weapon toward the man by then.

"What unit do you belong to?" the newcomer said, speaking formal Arabic with a Tunisian accent.

It wasn't a voice Ethan knew. It certainly didn't belong to Suleman.

"Wolf Company," he answered tentatively.

The newcomer came closer, emerging from the shadows beside the van so that the moonlight illuminated his features. Definitely wasn't Suleman or anyone Ethan knew.

When the militant noticed the Shahada headband Ethan wore, he lowered his AK and crouched beside him. "My apologies, my brothers. I heard you speaking English, and believed for a moment you might be Americans come to help the yellow faces."

"No, brother," Ethan told the militant. "Not American. We are holy warriors who have made hegira from England."

"But your Arabic is so good," the man protested.

"Thank you."

"I was separated from my unit," the militant continued. "May I join you?"

Ethan glanced at the others uncertainly. They didn't need a mujahid with them to stir up trouble at the Kurdish lines. But he said, "Of course, brother."

The Tunisian extended a hand. "I am Abu-Ahmed."

Ethan introduced himself and his companions.

The militant noticed Aaron's condition. "Does he need to return to the infirmary?"

"No," Ethan said. "We move forward, to the front lines."

Ethan hoisted Aaron to his feet.

The instant the four of them left the cover of the van, the triple crack of an M16A4 filled the air.

* * *

Suleman swept the weapon left after the initial burst, firing again, hoping to take down at least two of his targets, but the muzzle flash momentarily blinded his night vision device—the A4 didn't have a flash suppressor.

Suleman stared through his scope at the quiet, green-black environment. The van was positioned perfectly, neatly fitting inside his field of view, but no further movement came from the vehicle. The kaffir scum knew they were pinned.

He wondered if he'd struck Emad. It was possible. Any of the four could have been him. Well, there was only one way to be sure. And that was by killing the remainder.

Suleman settled in for the long wait. He had all night.

* * *

Blood spurted in long streams from William's trapezius in time to his heartbeat as Ethan struggled to compress the wound with his hands. William remained motionless the whole time, his eyes closed, looking very pale, his forehead steeped in sweat.

"Will," Ethan said in a hushed voice. "Come on!"

William abruptly opened his eyes and groaned. "What the hell."

"You're going to be fine, Will," Ethan said. "Just a scratch."

William shifted slightly, and winced. Then he guffawed. "I think, I think I've been shot!" he said between bouts of laughter.

Ethan was laughing too. "Yeah! You have, bro! Right through your trapezius!"

"My traps!" William roared. "The mother skewered my traps!"

Aaron shook his head in the moonlight. "Goddamn SEALs."

Ethan let Aaron hold the compress, then he crawled to the fourth man. Ahmed lay lifeless on the pavement beside the van. He wasn't breathing. He had taken the brunt of the attack, with small holes punched into opposite sides of his back. That burst had sounded like it had come from an M16, and the steel-tipped, 5.56mm cartridges would have easily torn their way through the Kevlar body armor under the man's fatigues. Ethan checked Ahmed's pulse. Nothing.

Ethan returned to William. He unsheathed his combat knife and began cutting a makeshift bandage from the hem of his own pant leg. Funny how Hollywood always made impromptu bandage creation look so easy in the movies. Only after a lot of twisting and ripping was he able to wrench the fabric free.

He secured the cloth to William's trapezius muscle, wrapping it under his armpit and tightening it until the blood flow ceased.

"How's that feel?" Ethan asked.

"Heavenly," William answered.

Ethan sat back to consider their predicament. How the hell had Suleman found them again? The streets were a warren back there, and Ethan had made several random direction changes, pausing occasionally to sweep his six. Classic evasion protocol. The first encounter he had attributed to luck. But two accidental encounters in a row? Unlikely.

Ethan grabbed his Android to check for a reply from Doug. Nothing. Worse, battery power was under fifteen percent.

As he looked at the smartphone it suddenly dawned upon Ethan.

"He has a Stingray! Goddamn it." Ethan switched the cell to Airplane mode. "How could I be so stupid? He's damn MI6."

"Who's MI6?" Aaron asked in a hushed voice. "Our sniper?"

"Yeah." Ethan sighed. "Long story."

"All right, so what are we going to do about it?" Aaron pressed. "We're stuck here behind this trash heap."

"What if we bring the van with us?" William sat up. With his trapezius bandaged, his strength appeared to be returning.

"No way we're moving this piece of shit," Aaron said. "We're pinned, bros. Thoroughly."

* * *

Suleman grew impatient. He decided it was time to ask for help. It was selfish to kill the remaining infidels all by himself anyway.

Keeping his eye glued to the scope, he reached for his harness and activated the two-way radio. "My brothers, I have important news. I have trapped four kaffir spies at the corner of the industrial section. They are hidden beside the mosque there, across from a fountain on the southern side, behind an upturned van. Any mujahadeen in the area who seek glory, come to me. We will flush them out."

Smiling confidently, Suleman released the transmit button and waited for the enthusiastic replies to start pouring in.

What he heard back surprised him.

"It's a Kurdish trick!" came the voice over the common band. "They're trying to draw us away from the front lines. Everyone stay at your posts!"

It was Emad.

Suleman cursed quietly. He hadn't struck the man after all, then.

He spoke into the two-way again. "My brothers, who are you going to believe, me or the kaffir? I have already injured them. Probably killed at least one. They are wounded animals, cornered, and trapped. This is the glory you sought when you came to this land to wage jihad. Come, my brothers! Fight with me!"

"Stay at your posts!" Emad retorted. "Or the Kurdish pigs will break through!"

"Get off the line, you idiots!" a random voice barked over the radio.

Suleman couldn't believe how easily his brothers were deceived. In despair and anger, he almost cast aside the radio. Would evil win so easily?

But then he realized his mistake. He had been using the common channel.

He clicked scan and found another frequency in use by a squad nearby. The men were issuing terse instructions to one another—something about outflanking a group of yellow-faces.

"My brothers," Suleman spoke into the radio. "How would you like to become famous?"

* * *

Ethan maneuvered to the far side of the van, away from where the shots had come. He unclipped the night sight from Beast and brought it to his eye, then carefully leaned past the front of the vehicle. He utilized the night scope like a zero magnification lens to survey the immediate area. Because the device was intended for use in front of a day optic, a large, hollow black circle impinged on the view—it looked like he was observing the green-black street through a tube.

He spotted the fountain Suleman had mentioned earlier on the radio. It was three meters away, and appeared dry, with parts of its jagged rim broken away. Two meters past it lay a brick wall, roughly twice the height of a man. Ethan could see the dome of a mosque silhouetted against the night sky beyond it, maybe a football field distant.

Sweeping the scope from left to right, he noticed a blast hole in the wall, close to the fountain. It was big enough to fit a man.

"Check it out," Ethan helped Aaron to the far side of the van and handed him the night scope. "See that gap in the wall of the mosque?"

"Too far," Aaron declared.

Ethan and Aaron exchanged places with William so that he could look.

"If we make a run for it," William said as he looked through the scope. "One of us might make it."

"Not good enough." Ethan faced Aaron. "Have any RGD-5's left?"

Aaron nodded. "Two."

"We can use the fragmentation grenades to momentarily blind our sniper."

Aaron seemed doubtful. "His night vision scope is auto-gating. It'll adjust to the brightness. We'll have maybe half a second before his vision returns to normal."

"But you're forgetting the smoke plumes. They're about three meters wide, and last six seconds. That's enough time and coverage to cross from behind the van to the mosque, if we toss both grenades. We throw the first between us and the fountain. The second between the fountain and the gap in the wall."

"What if he has a thermal imager?" Aaron said.

"He doesn't. I know the man we're dealing with, and his equipment." Ethan did his best to project confidence, though he couldn't be sure that Suleman hadn't acquired a thermal imager along the way. It was a risk he was willing to take. *Goddamn MI6.*

"We'll have to toss the grenades in just the right spots," William said. "Too close to the van, or too far, and the smoke won't give us the cover we need. If we mess up the aim or timing, we'll be eating grenade fragments for lunch. Plus our sniper friend will probably fire randomly into the smoke while we cross."

"I'm open to other ideas."

There were none.

Ethan grabbed the NV clip-on from William and reattached it to Beast, then swung the rifle over his shoulder alongside the Dragunov. "Aaron, get ready to hand me those grenades." He removed the Android from his pocket, disconnected the USB adapter, and crept to the frontmost edge of the van.

The two-way radio crackled to life. "What are you doing, *Abu* Emad?" The distaste Suleman placed on the Arabic word for brother was obvious. "I can hear you down there, speaking English, plotting like the Americans spies you are!"

Ethan thought Suleman was taunting them to convince any listening mujahadeen of their identity more than anything else.

"Please be aware that the man speaking over the channel is a British MI6 spy," Ethan said into the radio. "He is not to be trusted, and should be executed on sight." He released the send button and turned toward his companions. "We move at two second intervals." That would leave enough room between them in case Suleman happened to have an RPG launcher, while still giving them enough time to cross the street before the smoke cleared. "William, you go first. Aaron, you're second. I'll go last."

"You expect me to cross alone?" Aaron said. "Ain't going to happen. Not with this bum leg."

"I'll help him," William volunteered.

"Fine. You both go first, then. I'll follow three seconds after."

"Are you looking forward to bathing in hellfire?" Suleman continued to taunt over the radio. "With pigs taking turns raping your asshole every night from now until eternity? When I plant the black flag of the Islamic State on the roof of the White House, I will take a shit in the Oval Office, so that the flies have something to eat while they breed in the corpse of the kaffir President. And I will think of you in that moment, Emad, as I am taking that shit. I will think of how you attempted to betray us. And how I stopped you."

"Ready?" Ethan asked his companions.

"Let's roll."

Ethan leaned past the van and pressed the flashlight icon on his phone; the built-in flash activated, illuminating the street. Aaron handed him the grenades one after the other and Ethan threw them. The first bounced a little farther to the right than he had intended, but it should still suffice; the second landed spot on.

"Good to go." Ethan switched off the flash.

The grenades detonated almost simultaneously.

On cue, William and Aaron emerged from their cover behind the van, trusting that the temporary smoke would shield them from view.

Ethan began counting down the seconds in his head.

One-one-thousand.

As expected, their hidden attacker unleashed random bursts into the smoke plumes.

William and Aaron reached the cover of the fountain.

Two-one-thousand.

Keeping low, William and Aaron began the crossing from the fountain to the stone wall.

Three-one-thousand.

Ethan left the van. 5.56mm bullets whipped past. He ducked behind the fountain, and then raced toward his lagging companions.

In moments it was over. He dove through the ragged gap in the wall, pulling William and Aaron inside with him.

Aaron moaned in pain as the three of them crashed to the ground. "Damn it, Ethan. A little warning would have been nice."

"Usually there isn't time to warn someone when you're saving their life," Ethan declared quietly.

The gunfire ceased beyond the wall.

"Anyone hurt?" Ethan said.

"We were fine before you piled in on top of us," Aaron complained again.

"William?"

"I'm good," his friend said, sounding slightly pissed as well.

That's gratitude for you.

Ethan surveyed the courtyard of the mosque in the moonlight. The place was a mess. The enclosure was indeed the size of a football field. The actual mosque resided on the western side and looked to be about the size of a small stadium. The blast-damaged building had partially collapsed, its white bricks overflowing onto the grounds. Several of the outbuildings had suffered, too: their smashed structures fanned out into the courtyard, leaving behind partially standing husks.

Ethan helped Aaron northward, following the wall; William brought up the rear, guarding their backs. When Ethan reached the north perimeter he turned west, again staying near the courtyard's wall and its shadow. Behind them, the eastern perimeter provided an effective shield against any outside snipers.

The trio quickly came upon an open iron gate.

While William watched the somewhat distant hole in the wall behind them, Ethan lowered Aaron, unclipped the NV scope from Beast, and scanned the street beyond the gate. He picked out an alley opposite their position, between two cinder block fences about six meters away. He handed the NV piece to William.

"There's an alley across the way," Ethan whispered.

"I see it," William said, looking through the NV.

Ethan glanced at Aaron, who sat on the ground, guarding their rear. "Want me to bring Aaron this time?"

"No," William said. "I got him."

"Wait." Ethan reattached the NV to the forward Picatinny of Beast and, clipping the sling to his Quick Cuff, he assumed a seated sniping position beside the gate. He leaned past, aiming eastward. He swept the scope from left to right, studying the green-black environment. There were a few buildings Suleman could have used as a hide, but there was no way Ethan would be able to see him in those darkened window frames.

"Anything?" William said quietly.

"No," Ethan said. "He could be anywhere out there."

"Too bad we don't have more grenades. What do you want to do?"

Ethan clenched his jaw. *Where are you?*

"We've moved about a hundred meters north of our last position," William said. "Maybe more. Do you really think our sniper has had time to relocate?"

"Depends on his initial position," Ethan said.

"Which was probably close to the van, way over to the southeast. Look, the longer we delay, the more time we give him to find a new hide."

"Let's cross," Aaron urged.

"Ethan?" William said.

"All right. Fine." Ethan didn't look from the scope. "If you're going to go, now's the time then."

"Come on, bud." William heard shuffling behind him: the sound of his friend hoisting Aaron over one shoulder. "Ready?" he asked Ethan.

"Go." Ethan scanned the eastern buildings as their footfalls receded across the street. He held his breath, counting out the moments. He thought it would take maybe three seconds for them to reach the alley-way.

One-one-thousand.

Two-one-thousand.

Before he reached three, the terrible triple report of an M16 tore through the night air.

thirty-nine

Ethan quickly altered his aim. The muzzle flash had come from beyond the scope's field of view, to the upper right, but he discerned nothing in the black squares representing the building windows there, roughly two hundred meters to the east. The rooftop appeared empty, too.

"Are you all right!" Ethan shouted. He spoke Arabic in case other militants were listening nearby.

"We made it!" Aaron called from the alleyway behind him. His voice sounded strained. "We're good."

"He's not so good," William yelled. "We made it, yes, but the sniper hit Aaron in the same wounded leg. The bullet tumbled on impact. It's not pretty."

"Damn it," Ethan said quietly. Louder: "Can he still walk with your help?"

There was a pause. William was obviously applying a makeshift tourniquet. If the bullet tumbled, Aaron would be bleeding heavily from the shredded tissue. Finally:

"Barely," William shouted back in Arabic.

"I can do it," Aaron called.

He would have to.

Ethan continued shifting his scope over the various windows and rooftops, hoping for some tell that would betray Suleman's position. There was no way Ethan could cross, not while the sniper had a bead on the gate.

"What's the plan?" William hollered.

"The two of you have to continue," Ethan said. "I'll find another way."

"We're not leaving you," William shouted.

"You have to."

"We're not!" William insisted.

"You know you can't stay. Aadil"—he was careful to use Aaron's Arabic alias—"won't make it if you do. Go. I'll catch up. Trust me. Go!"

Ethan waited for a response, but none came. His friends had gone, then. Good.

Mortars detonated just to the west and DShKs fired in answer, reminding him of how close to the Kurdish lines he was. So close and yet so far.

The eastern gap in the wall remained open to him. He could return to it and attempt a retreat that way, but with Suleman out there... he glanced at the collapsed mosque to the west instead. That was a potentially safer route. If he could scale the rubble and cross over to the building's western flank, he would be well beyond Suleman's sight line. There were several damaged outbuildings he could use for cover along the way, and plenty of deep shadows that could defeat a NV scope.

Before he could move, a sudden illumination drew his attention back to the eastern wall—multiple flashlight-carrying figures were stepping through the gap.

Suleman had managed to call reinforcements.

Ethan slunk away from the gate and hurried west inside the courtyard, staying close to the wall and the shadow it cast in the dim moonlight. He turned off his two-way radio, not wanting it to suddenly come to life and give away his position.

An attenuated beam of light abruptly swept toward him, and he dove behind a waist-high pile of bricks where one of the outbuildings had collapsed. Cement dust on the ground mingled with his sweat, caking his exposed skin.

He remained motionless, watching, listening.

The light seemed to be coming closer. Judging from the footsteps, the militants were still about thirty or forty meters away.

He considered fighting back, but he couldn't be sure how many tangos there were. And without a flash suppressor, he'd reveal his position after the first shot.

He rolled onto his back into the rubble, grimacing as the sharp pieces of debris dug into his spine. He swept a hand over the loose bricks, letting them pour over his legs. A particularly loud machine gun exchange was taking place somewhere to the southwest, masking the soft clinks. One brick hit his right knee a bit hard and he felt the patella crunch. Nothing he could do but grin and bear it. When his legs were covered, he moved on to individually positioning the bricks over the rest of his body; he moved as quickly as possible, cringing whenever he thought he placed a piece too loudly.

By the time the search team reached him, he had blanketed himself and his equipment almost completely in debris. Only his left arm was exposed—the arm he had used to position the final bricks. Hopefully the camo sleeve, combined with the cement dust coating the hand, would serve to mask the limb.

The nearby machine gun fire ceased and he became conscious of his own rattled breathing. He held it, remaining motionless, feeling the weight of the bricks pressing down into his body. His right knee throbbed.

Two pairs of boots crunched over the rubble beside him. The ambient light brightened momentarily as a flashlight passed over his position; the illumination filtered through the crack he'd left for his eyes, blinding him. Then the light, and the footfalls, moved on.

Ethan exhaled softly.

The searchers had split up, judging from the occasional shouts from the different parts of the courtyard. Unlike the rest of the city, the acoustics there were surprisingly good, with minimal echo and distortion, allowing him to pinpoint sound sources with relative accuracy, and he knew two separate groups were moving westward toward the mosque; muted voices, meanwhile, came from the northeast and southeast, telling him that militants had stayed behind to guard the iron gate and the wall rupture, respectively.

A louder exchange abruptly drifted to him from the gate. It sounded like the militants on watch were greeting someone.

The conversation ceased and someone new approached. Alone.

The two other groups were returning from their search of the mosque at that time, and converged on the newcomer close to Ethan's position.

"Salaam," the newcomer said. It was Suleman.

"There is no one here, brother," another militant said in Arabic.

"He has to be here," Suleman said. "We had men watching both exits. I know this place very well—I was pinned here a few days ago, and there is no other way out. Did you check all the outbuildings? The mosque?"

"We did. Most of the buildings have collapsed. As for the mosque, much of it is gone, and what's left is mostly open space, with a few closets and side rooms. We searched them all. I tell you, he is not here."

"*He is here!*" Suleman hissed.

The two-way radios crackled to life. "We need reinforcements in the industrial area, north of the mosque! The yellow-faces are attempting a sortie. Hurry!"

Ethan recognized William's voice and mentally thanked his friend.

"My brother, I am sorry," the militant said. "We are needed elsewhere. He is just one man."

"He is *not* just one man," Suleman said. "It is what he represents. If we let him go, we send a clear message to the American pigs that it is all right for them to infiltrate our ranks with their dirty spies. That it is all right to kill us in the dark and sabotage our equipment and assassinate our emirs."

But the others were already retreating, judging from the footfalls.

Suleman cursed them, something about a pig raping their kaffir arses while they burned for all eternity. The usual.

Ethan listened as Suleman's footfalls receded—his boots crunched morosely over the rock, dirt and glass. A distant clink sounded whenever the man experimentally poked his rifle into a rubble pile.

The footsteps slowly shifted toward the northern wall and faded as Suleman traversed the gate. Gunfire came from somewhere outside the courtyard, masking his retreat, and when it ended, Ethan no longer heard the man.

He badly wanted to vacate the courtyard, but there had seemed something off about Suleman's exit. His footfalls had seemed too loud. Too dramatic. Like Suleman merely wanted him to *think* he was leaving. It was a tactic Ethan would have used himself. He remembered the certainty he had heard in Suleman's voice, the *conviction*, when he had told the other militants that Ethan was still in the courtyard.

And so he remained still, hidden beneath those bricks. The wind picked up, and the entire courtyard descended into darkness. Likely the breeze had brought with it the black smoke from the southern villages, occluding the stars and moon.

The nearby shelling stopped entirely, so that he existed in an eerie microcosm of sensory deprivation. The smallest sound might betray his position, but it worked both ways—Ethan kept his ears open, listening intently.

The silent, dark minutes passed.

The sporadic shelling and machine gun fire started up again, though the detonations and muzzle flashes were obscured by the mosque and surrounding walls so that no light reached the courtyard. Sound however did penetrate, of course, and the ground shook as a mortar detonated nearby.

Ethan told himself he was overthinking everything. Suleman had gone.

But he waited another ten minutes anyway.

Just when he was about to begin extricating himself, he heard a subtle shifting noise, like the sound a brick might make when disturbed on a rubble pile. It came from the eastern side of the courtyard.

It was possible the loose brick was displaced naturally by reverberations from the shelling.

Somehow Ethan doubted it.

Suleman was out there, stalking him.

The game was afoot.

Ethan waited for a mortar to strike nearby, then lifted his free arm and removed a brick from his face, letting the shudder of the explosion mask the sound of his movements. He continued to wait for impacts and machine gun bursts, and in that way he slowly extricated himself from the pile.

He positioned himself on the dirt beside the rubble, and winced—his right knee was still tender from the brick he'd dropped on it earlier.

The drifting smoke had cleared somewhat overhead, allowing the starlight to filter down. The moon however remained shrouded. Because of the starlight, he was able to discern the outline of the rubble beside him, which blocked half the courtyard from view.

Lying flat, he slid Beast from his shoulder and tentatively peered through the 10x scope. The magnification was workable for the football field dimensions of the courtyard. In those sections of the grounds not obscured by the rubble pile beside him, he saw a green-black world of collapsed outbuildings, broken cobblestone and twisted shrubs, hemmed in by impenetrable regions of black wall.

Suleman could be lying in wait anywhere among that mess, indiscernible from any other mound of debris. And in the starlight, Ethan would appear the same to Suleman.

He discerned the slight illumination marking the northern gate, but couldn't see the rent in the eastern wall from his current position. If Ethan wanted to trap someone in the courtyard, he would have chosen a hide with both exits in sight. Given the separation between the two, he probably would've picked a spot near one of the exits themselves, in case someone tried to sneak past him.

Where are you?

Ethan considered retreating toward the mosque and reverting to his original plan of using the debris to scale the western wall, but it would take him forever to crawl that way without making a sound, and there was no guarantee he wouldn't slip up somewhere along the line.

He decided to move slightly away from the debris beside him for a better view of the courtyard. He very carefully low-crawled forward, literally at a snail's pace, taking three minutes to cover the five feet. When he was in place, he folded down the Harris bipod, set the legs on the ground, and then brought his eye to Beast's scope.

He swept the field of view along the battered landscape; the sniper rifle swiveled on its bipod courtesy of the rotapod adapter. He was able to discern the entire eastern half of the courtyard, though that only meant more caved buildings and broken shrubs. He did, however, pick out the rent in the eastern wall, but he couldn't discern a thing on either side of it. He continued scanning the area, but there were simply too many areas the starlight didn't reach. A base level of brightness was required for night vision to work, and those shadows just weren't cutting it.

Where's a damn PEQ-2 when you need one? Then again, an infrared illuminator would've only given him away in the current predicament.

He listened to the nearby rumble of DShKs and mortars, and his mind wandered. Perhaps the sliding brick had indeed been a natural displacement. Surely Suleman would have made another noise by then?

Ethan shook his head. He refused to underestimate the man a second time. Suleman was there.

He steeled himself for the long wait. Patience. That was the key to any sniper duel: the hunter with the most patience won.

Ethan moved his field of view between the two exits, knowing that Suleman could be anywhere in that darkness, even right beside him. He tried to memorize the location of every shrub, rubble pile, and outbuilding. His hope was to spot an anomaly: some bush that shifted ever so slightly between glances; some cobblestone pile that moved a foot a minute.

Unfortunately, Suleman would very likely stay put. That was what Ethan was doing, after all.

Time was running out. Ethan had to find a way to draw the man out. He couldn't afford to remain there all night. When news spread of the bloody escape of the kaffir spies from the forward camp, more militants would be willing to listen to Suleman. The man could be texting for reinforcements on FireChat at that very moment, with the light from his cellphone shielded by very careful arrangement of his clothing.

His cellphone...

Ethan had an idea.

forty

A mortar shell struck unnervingly close, scarcely beyond the walls of the mosque so that the ground shuddered violently. Ethan's lungs rattled in his ribcage.

He crept behind the debris beside him, letting the piled bricks shield his body from most of the courtyard. He removed his Android from his pocket. The screen was black, and would remain so until he attempted to unlock it. He unwound the scarf from his neck, then carefully removed the jacket portion of his fatigues, exposing the Kevlar vest underneath. He placed the smartphone beside his face and layered the scarf and jacket over his head, tucking in the edges of the fabrics.

He hesitated, then unlocked the cellphone. The brightness was set to the dimmest value from his earlier usage. He would know if any of the light seeped from his cover soon enough, however—when the bullet came.

He loaded up a timer app and started a countdown. Soundlessly, he adjusted the volume and brightness levels to maximum, and then quickly locked the Android. The screen blackened.

He doffed the jacket and scarf to retrieve the duct tape from his pocket; very slowly, he quietly unraveled a small piece. When it was of suitable size, he carefully tore it away. Then he turned on his radio, leaving the volume too low to produce anything audible, and depressed the send button; he wrapped the tape around it so that the radio remained in "transmit" mode. Probing in the dark, he secured the two-way radio to the smartphone with another piece of tape, being careful not to obscure the Android's screen, nor to press some button that would light it.

Satisfied, he snaked forward until he was slightly past the edge of the rubble pile again. He placed the rifle on the ground via the bipod, and with his 10x scope, located a clearing near the center of the courtyard; in the middle grew a particular arrangement of shrubs that could easily be confused with a prostrate human body under the night vision. He panned to the left and right to ensure a relatively clear corridor, and then, keeping his body aligned to the chosen spot, he extricated himself from Beast and threw the phone-radio combination.

The jury-rigged contraption clattered loudly on the broken cobblestone of the clearing, landing roughly twenty meters away. He could almost imagine Suleman swinging the barrel of his M16A4 toward the noise.

Ethan scanned the eastern portion of the grounds through Beast. His heart was beating rapidly in anticipation. He wondered how close to the foliage the phone had landed. Would it be near enough?

Come on. Come on.

His Android seared to life in the center of the courtyard. The screen cast a bright green bloom about the smartphone, which the night vision quickly auto-gated. The cell had landed right beside the humanlike shrubs: the foliage looked even more convincing under the illumination, at least from Ethan's position, appearing as a man lying face down with a backpack beside him.

The triple-report of an A4 sounded from the far side of the foyer as his opponent fired on extinct. The muzzle flash of the unsuppressed rifle had been situated beyond the field of view of Ethan's scope, but he'd caught it with his other eye and immediately swiveled his aim in the general direction.

Your first mistake, bro.

Suleman had missed the phone, and the bright screen continued to provide ambiance, enough for Ethan to pick out additional minute details from the surrounding ruins. Suleman would be able to do the same, of course, except that without knowing Ethan's general location, he had a far greater zone to cover.

Focusing on the area that had given rise to the muzzle flash, Ethan spotted the partial outline of a newly visible black-green form that may or may not have belonged to a sniper, located close to the eastern gap in the wall. Suleman? Or another humanlike shrub?

In the background, an annoying chime sounded from the Android, repeating incessantly into the radio. If Suleman tried to call for help over the main channel, his transmission would be drowned out by the noise, that or blocked entirely, thanks to the "busy channel lockout" feature of the radios, which prevented outgoing transmissions while the line was active. He'd have to use one of the less-trafficked squad channels, if he dared.

Ethan waited for the sniper to fire at the phone again and confirm his position, or for the target in his sights to move, but his opponent did neither. Suleman obviously realized the trap he had fallen into.

Ethan kept his aim on the indistinct figure. He could shoot anyway and hope he was right. But if he was wrong, then his own unsuppressed muzzle would betray him.

And then Ethan noticed the black-green form beneath his reticule seemed to shift slightly. He stared at it very carefully. No, it wasn't moving after all. He must have imagined it.

Wait a moment...

There *was* motion there. Very slow, very gradual, almost undetectable motion—what appeared to be a limb was sliding backward.

Suleman was attempting to relocate deeper into the shadows.

"Gotcha," Ethan whispered.

He aimed for the center of the object and squeezed the trigger. The muzzle flash momentarily flooded his scope with green. Ethan worked the bolt, chambering a fresh cartridge, and repositioned his reticule over the indistinct outline. It no longer moved.

After several moments he folded closed Beast's bipod and stood.

He approached warily, keeping his rifle aimed at the tango, pausing every ten steps or so to recenter the scope, but his quarry never moved.

Ethan kept the muzzle pointed at the lifeless silhouette as he closed. He couldn't discern the features in the dim light, but he had little doubt as to the identity of the dead man: only Suleman had wanted to kill him badly enough to stalk him in the dark for the past hour.

He placed his index and middle fingers over the radial vein. The man's wrist felt clammy. No pulse. Ethan experienced a moment of pity.

You wanted me to kill you, Suleman. You got your wish.

Sliding Beast over his shoulder, Ethan snatched the M16A4 from the corpse and searched the vest for a spare magazine. He found one and pocketed it. In the man's backpack he also discovered a laptop, Stingray-capable no doubt. He tried to turn it on, but the battery seemed dead so he unleashed a burst from the A4 into the machine's aluminum shell. The man carried no other weapons.

Ethan raced back to the phone-radio contraption he'd juryrigged. Right when he reached it the Android's power failed—the screen darkened and the alarm ended. He scooped up the bound devices and ripped away the tape that locked the radio in transmit mode. He accidentally brushed the volume switch in the process and an angry militant barked over the channel in Arabic:

"Thank you for turning that pig shit off!"

Ethan turned the volume low so that he could listen to any relevant updates, then he slunk to the northern gate and carefully scanned the outlying street with the A4. The 4x magnification of the RCO scope was much better suited to an urban environment than the 10x on Beast.

When he was convinced the way was clear, he dashed to the safety of the alleyway across the road. He emerged and headed west, keeping close to the buildings, wondering if William and Aaron had taken the same route.

The sky between the buildings ignited as a mortar ominously struck nearby.

He reached an intersection. The second-story window of a house to the south lit up with the muzzle flashes of DShK fire. On a rooftop a block away to the west, the shimmer of another heavy machine gun answered it. He aimed the scope of his A4 toward that rooftop, and in the green-black environment illuminated by the starlight he saw what appeared to be eastern-facing sandbags. If he was right, that was a Kurdish defensive position.

Almost there.

Ethan darted across the street; as he closed with the defensive position, machine gun fire abruptly whipped past just beside him. He dropped, low-crawling behind a broken fence.

He rose to a crouch, keeping his flank pressed to the cinder block fence. He thought it was the Kurds who were firing at him, so he shouted in English, "I'm American! I surrender! I want to cross to the Kurdish lines! I am friends with Black Mamba!"

The two-way radio squawked to life with the Arabic voice of an Islamic State militant. "I've found another deserter trying to defect to the yellow-faces!"

Whoops.

Stone chips flew into his face as mujahadeen fired from somewhere to the east. Those bullets traced a path along the wall toward his head...

He spun away, diving into an open door; inside, he got up and hurried through the foyer at a crouch, worried that he might trigger a booby trap—the moment that thought entered his mind, he banged his hip against an unseen counter in the dark. Not a booby trap, but certainly painful.

He heard shouts outside. "He's in there! Use the rockets!"

Ethan sprinted to the far side of the home and leaped out the shattered rear window, landing in the small courtyard beyond. He felt a shockwave rip past as the room he'd vacated only moments before exploded.

He sprinted through the yard, pulling himself over a chest-high cinder block fence.

Gunfire whizzed past from his right.

Ethan dove behind some rubble situated in the middle of the road. No, not rubble. It was an upturned Jersey barrier, barely high enough to shield him. The Dragunov dug into his arm below him. He turned onto his back, flattening himself, and slid the rifle down. He let off a few random shots at his opponents without looking over the barricade, then discarded the Dragunov when the magazine emptied.

More shots came in. Bullets ricocheted from the barrier above him, sprinkling his temple with slivers of concrete. He was pinned worse than ever. The tiny barricade might protect him from gunfire—at least until the militants outflanked him—but it certainly wouldn't save him from a rocket or grenade attack.

He was done.

forty-one

I'm with you, my brothers," Ethan shouted in Arabic. "I fight the yellow-faces!"

But the militants kept firing.

As he lay there on his back beside the barricade, he found his gaze drawn inexplicably to the stars. The quarter moon had broken free by then. So beautiful.

More cement broke away as bullets pounded the Jersey barrier. It would be so easy to give up. To let them outflank him and fire their rockets while he just lay there, doing nothing, staring at the moon one last time before he died.

A voice growled at the back of his mind in protest. It spoke a quote from Winston Churchill that had helped Ethan endure SEAL training, a quote he'd always kept close to heart.

Never give in—never, never, never, never. If you're going through hell, keep going.

Well, if ever he was in hell, it was then.

Keep going.

Staying low, he surveyed his surroundings in the quarter moon-light. There was a single-story shop to his left. Five meters away. The front door was invitingly open.

He could make it.

He *would.*

The incoming gunfire momentarily ceased. He heard the militants calling out instructions to one another from opposite sides of the street. It sounded like they were preparing to outflank him.

He switched the A4 fire selector to burst mode, then pivoted so that he lay face down behind the Jersey barrier. He brought his knees forward as far as he could without exposing the rest of his body, took two deep breaths, then lifted the muzzle of the A4 over the barricade and unleashed two separate bursts without aiming.

He pressed the assault rifle into the barrier and, using it as leverage, clambered to his feet. He sprinted toward the shop, firing off two more bursts, spray-and-pray style, to his left.

Return gunfire echoed in the night and bullets whipped past. He felt a rude poke in his left bicep and knew he'd been shot. He dove into the ruined shop, landing prostrate on the floor.

By then his left bicep was pulsing with an excruciating, burning pain. He had hoped the distraction of battle would lessen the agony, but no such luck: it felt like a steaming hot carving knife had been driven into the muscle, and some cruel torturer was twisting it, cutting into the tendons, fascia, and bone. It was an illusion, of course. The pain was the aftereffect of the round passing clean through the head of the muscle, and his subsequent attempts to move the arm. It was fortunate the bullet hadn't deflected into his torso, as the protection from the Kevlar vest was dubious at best.

Hot blood drizzled down his forearm from the entry and exit wounds. The lesions were located conveniently below the Quick Cuff. Ducking behind a table, he dropped the A4 and opened the cuff's velcro attachment, quickly retightening it to stanch the bleeding.

He scooped up the A4, stumbled to his feet, and made for the rear of the building. He spotted the silhouettes of several men beyond the windows there. Surrounded. He steered toward the open trapdoor in the ceiling instead, where the moon beckoned invitingly. The roof would prove a more defensible position.

Left arm dangling uselessly, Ethan started up the stairs but tripped halfway. Instinctively he tried to extend his injured limb to cushion the fall, sending a jolt of pain through the muscle; he smashed into the stairs, only worsening the excruciation. Beast, hanging from his left shoulder, dug into the tissue.

With his right arm, he braced his other rifle—the A4—against the steps, and forced himself up. He heard shouts outside.

"He's on the roof!" came the Arabic words.

He heard the characteristic tumble of a fragmentation grenade on the rooftop above.

Ethan was far enough from the trapdoor to consider himself safe, so he chose to stay on the stairs. He swiveled to face the foyer, lay back against the steps, and balanced the A4 on his chest while he set the fire selector to semi-automatic. Then he raised the rifle awkwardly with his good hand, pointing the muzzle toward the main door across from him.

An explosion rocked the ceiling as the grenade detonated, sending a blast of displaced air down through the trapdoor.

Ethan scarcely batted an eye. He kept his rifle arm extended, leaving a slight crook in the elbow. He tried hard to maintain a pistol grip of sorts on the A4, with a straight wrist so the force of the recoil would transfer into his arm rather than the joint. The unbalanced weight was difficult to sustain, however, and he found himself using his right leg to help support the barrel.

The silhouette of a crouching man appeared in the doorway.

Ethan centered the muzzle on the muj's torso and fired one-handed. The trigger guard banged against his fingers and he felt the recoil energy transmit into his elbow, but he hit the target.

The man dropped like a fly.

A grenade bounced inside. Ethan hauled himself to his feet and raced through the hole in the ceiling. The bomb detonated, sending a fireball through the trapdoor behind him.

He low-crawled westward, toward the side street, and peered over. Militants milled below. Ethan immediately ducked.

He heard movement in the room below.

Staying prostrate, he spun around and aimed the A4 toward the trapdoor.

So this is the end, he thought. *Surrounded by mujahadeen, going down in a blaze of glory.*

There were worse fates. He was doing what he was born to do. Fighting on the side of good against radicals who sought to destroy the world. This was the good fight.

The best fight.

The sound of artillery fire ripped through the air. Bright threads of light drew his attention to the side street. In the distance, from the Kurdish lines, a pickup truck roared over the potholes. A ZU-23-2 anti-aircraft gun was mounted in its bed, and it fired directly into the militants who had him surrounded.

Another technical advanced from a parallel road, also from the Kurdish positions. It too unleashed havoc with a ZU. Ethan flattened himself, knowing how notoriously inaccurate the weapon could be when fired from a moving vehicle.

The gurgled screams of mujahadeen filled the air as the 23mm shells tore through them at a firing rate of over four hundred rounds per minute. The rooftop shook as some of the rounds collided with the side of the building.

The first pickup surged past and Ethan heard the screech of braking tires, followed by a loud crash. He thought the vehicle had plowed into the upended Jersey barrier.

The second technical pulled up behind it, judging from the sound.

Their anti-aircraft guns continued firing sporadically.

Ethan heard the burst of an AK-47 downstairs, followed by a single rifle report from the street. Another AK salvo. Another rifle crack. He kept his A4 aimed at the hole in the rooftop.

The exchange continued for about half a minute, with the rifle reports sounding successively closer. Then the stairs creaked below.

Ethan held his A4 steady on the trapdoor...

A head appeared; before he fired, a familiar voice bellowed: "Death Adder coming up!"

Ethan slumped. "Damn it, Wil, I almost popped your head off."

William climbed onto the rooftop. "I've been trying to message you."

"Phone's dead. How the hell did you find me?"

William ignored the question. "Can you walk?"

"Yeah. It's the arm that's busted."

William helped him to his feet, though he accidentally wrapped a hand around Ethan's injured bicep in the process and he nearly blacked out. "Sorry."

William led him downstairs. "As to how we found you, we've been listening in on the radio chatter, but we also had one of the Predators zoom in on the neighborhood. Wasn't hard to pinpoint your location—we just looked for the biggest firefight in the area."

Ethan emerged from the shop, feeling like he was walking in some sort of dream. He was vaguely aware that the pickup, a battered and muddy Kia 4000S, had turned around. In the truck bed a Kurd manned the anti-aircraft gun, guarding their rear, releasing 23mm bursts down the street every few seconds.

William led Ethan around the front and opened the passenger side. Ethan lethargically hauled himself into the seat with one hand. William squeezed in beside him and shut the door.

Ethan wasn't sure in the dim light, but he thought the driver was Doug.

"How's it hanging?" Definitely Doug. He floored the accelerator, sending the Kia leaping forward.

Ethan was too stunned, and too battle-weary, to speak. The adrenaline hangover and the throbbing pain in his bicep didn't help matters. Only moments ago he had come to terms with his own death. But he was going to live. He was actually going to live.

"We would have come sooner," William said. "But the damn Kurds made Aaron and I undress when we reached the front lines. They thought we carried suicide bombs, even though Doug told them we were on their side. Aaron couldn't fully undress because of the leg wound, and when the Kurds realized how badly he was injured they finally let us through."

"The bastards can be a little hard-headed at times," Doug admitted, swerving around a blast crater. "But they're fierce fighters."

The pickup jolted savagely over a series of potholes. The Kurd in the truck bed continued to fire the ZU in controlled, likely inaccurate, bursts.

"How's Aaron?" Ethan asked finally.

"Safe," William replied. "He's got a Kurdish surgeon attending him. One of the best, apparently. He's going to be fine. Like you, Ethan." William wrapped a brotherly arm around his neck. "You made it. We all did."

* * *

Doug and William brought Ethan across Kurdish lines, eventually dropping him off at a courtyard set among a ring of mostly intact apartment buildings. The area apparently served as some kind of command and control center.

Ethan sat on a Jersey barrier by a campfire as a Kurdish corpsman cleaned the wounds on his bicep. The corpsman didn't suture either puncture, instead leaving them open to drain—after he was done cleaning, he applied a field dressing and removed the Quick Cuff.

Ethan drank the water the man provided him, and sipped soup from a cup. He rested for a moment, and listened to the distant sounds of battle that periodically disturbed the night. He was feeling better, thanks to the analgesic the corpsman had given him, but also incredibly drowsy. He drank a red bull someone offered, and that helped perk him up.

On the Jersey barriers around him sat other Kurdish fighters, their faces subdued. They looked identical, feature-wise, to their Islamic State equivalents, though their skin was slightly more olive than other Arabs, and none of them wore beards. Also, the fervent, knowing look common to the mujahadeen was not present among any of them, though a few possessed haunted expressions. One fighter was a woman.

Some of the men spoke quietly among themselves, obviously about

Ethan, judging from their sidelong glances. Unfortunately he didn't understand Kurdish, so he had no idea what they were saying.

One of the Kurds raised his voice, gazing right at Ethan as he spoke.

The corpsman translated in broken English: "He says you look strange for an American."

Ethan studied the Kurd. He was an older man, gaunt and bent. Crow's nests lined his eyes, sharp ridges climbed his forehead. He looked like a street vendor. Probably had been, before the war.

"For missions like this," Ethan said. "They *want* Americans who look strange. That way we fit right in."

The older man spoke again and the corpsman translated. "The battle emir says if he met you in the field, he would mistake you for Islamic State scum and shoot you down."

Ethan bared his teeth in a smile. "Tell your battle emir he could certainly try."

The corpsman translated, and the battle emir erupted in a hearty guffaw.

Ethan was about to stand, as he was eager to check on Aaron, when Doug arrived.

"I have someone here who would like to meet you," Doug said.

The operative stepped aside and Ethan felt his heart quicken.

It was her. He'd recognize those penetrating blue eyes and that breathtaking face anywhere.

Alzena wore a hijab without the veil, but instead of an abaya, she had on desert digital combat fatigues. She also carried an assault rifle slung over one shoulder. An M16A4 in fact.

"You're a soldier now?" Ethan said in disbelief, reverting to Arabic.

She shrugged, taking her place on the Jersey barrier beside him. "You thought I would flee my country without a fight?"

Ethan considered her words, then grinned. "Yeah."

She frowned. "You don't know me."

Ethan became serious, and nodded slowly. "No, I don't."

The other woman at the campfire asked Alzena something in Kurdish; Alzena looked abashed for a moment, then answered in the language. The other woman grinned mischievously.

Ethan felt one of his eyebrows rise in disbelief. "You're Kurdish?"

"Half Kurdish," Alzena corrected him. "On my mother's side."

"Interesting."

"Like I said, you don't know me."

Ethan stared at the campfire.

"So, here we are," he said into the uncomfortable silence that followed.

"Here we are," she agreed.

Out of the corner of his eye he saw her raise a hesitant hand, lifting it toward him, but then she pulled it back. She tried again a moment later, this time seeming surer of herself, and rested a palm over his knuckles.

Ethan gazed into the pools of her deep, sapphire eyes; he wasn't entirely sure if the flickers he saw there were reflections from the flames, or her own fiery spirit.

"Fight for us," Alzena said.

Ethan looked away, exhaling deeply. "I already have." He slid his hand out from under hers and wrapped it around the stock of the M24 beside him. The feel of the fiberglass and carbon-fiber reinforced polymer foam comforted him.

"Fight for us," she repeated.

Ethan felt the ground rumble as a stray mortar landed beyond the ring of apartments. "I fight where I'm needed."

"You are needed here," she said firmly.

He pressed his lips together. "Here."

He glanced at the others around the campfire. Kurdish refugees turned soldiers. Muddy faces. Dirty fatigues. Haunted eyes.

They stood against ruthless oppressors who wished to thrust a radical interpretation of a peaceful religion upon them. They needed training. They needed guidance.

They needed hope.

Ethan's fingers involuntarily tightened around Beast, and then he released the weapon entirely.

He met Alzena's gaze.

"I'm only staying for the baklavas," he said.

She grinned. "What about the fatteh?"

"And the fatteh," Ethan agreed. "Can't forget the fatteh."

She launched herself at him. Her hug seemed stronger than any embrace he had ever felt before.

Staring into the flames, Ethan held her with equal fervor. Another shell exploded in the distance.

I am needed here.

This is the end.
Thank you for reading Clandestine!

www.isaachooke.com

CPSIA information can be obtained at www.ICGtesting.com
Printed in the USA
LVOW10*1513300415
436755LV00002B/21/P